Much Ado About Muffin

VICTORIA HAMILTON

BERKLEY PRIME CRIME, NEW YORK

BERKLEY
PRIME
CRIME

An imprint of Penguin Random House LLC
375 Hudson Street, New York, New York 10014

MUCH ADO ABOUT MUFFIN

A Berkley Prime Crime Book / published by arrangement with the author

BERKLEY® PRIME CRIME and the PRIME CRIME design are trademarks
of Penguin Random House LLC.
For more information, visit penguin.com.

ISBN: 9780425282588

PUBLISHING HISTORY
Berkley Prime Crime mass-market edition / August 2016

PRINTED IN THE UNITED STATES OF AMERICA

10 9 8 7 6 5 4 3 2 1

Cover art by Ben Perini.
Cover design by Colleen Reinhart.
Interior text design by Kristin del Rosario.

This is a work of fiction. Names, characters, places, and incidents either are the product of
the author's imagination or are used fictitiously, and any resemblance to actual persons,
living or dead, business establishments, events, or locales is entirely coincidental.

PUBLISHER'S NOTE: The recipes contained in this book are to be followed exactly as
written. The publisher is not responsible for your specific health or allergy needs that may
require medical supervision. The publisher is not responsible for any adverse reactions
to the recipes contained in this book.

Penguin
Random
House

To all the English teachers out there; I know your job is difficult. I know some days you feel like you're not making a difference. Trust me, you are. Somewhere in your class is a shy girl, the introvert who never puts up her hand and who stammers through presentations. But she will "get" your enthusiasm for books; that spark will catch fire, and if you tell her just once that she has done a good job on a book report, or that she is "insightful," she will remember it for the rest of her life. Thank you. And know this; you may just have created an author.

Prologue

❋ ❋ ❋

HOME. . . . WHY AM I not home?

I woke up with that thought and crawled out of bed, padding barefoot over to the window that looked out on straight rows of olive trees in the grove on the hillside in the distance, and the cork forest even more distant. Closer to the villa was the vineyard, long, cultivated rows of grapes that would become sweet white wine once harvested. The Paradiso family—my late husband's older brother, along with his grown-up daughter and son, were now all that was left—was diversifying under the wise guidance of Antonio, whom I call Tony, my late husband Miguel's older brother.

But in my mind and heart was another landscape, one from which I was separated by thousands of miles of ocean and land: Wynter Castle, my own property, near the tiny town of Autumn Vale, in upstate New York.

I had been gone from it for so long, well over two months now, lost in the magical, wealthy, and cultivated world of the Paradiso family. I was called to Málaga, a part of Andalusia,

Spain, by an urgent request from Tony. My former mother-in-law was dying, and he begged me to come and make peace with the woman who had disliked me intensely for the few years I knew her and was married to her favorite son. Tony hoped I would forgive her for her interference in my marriage to Miguel and let her die in harmony with the heavenly Father to whom she was devoted.

I went, we made our peace and talked long hours. I held her hand as she writhed in pain, refusing sedatives or painkillers, following the example of her hero, Pope John Paul II. Peace came with death while I was there. I found a solace in her passing that had evaded me with all the other deaths I had suffered through: my beloved grandmother and mother when I was just twenty-one, and then my husband, Miguel, eight years ago.

But Maria Paradiso had been gone over three weeks already. I had helped Tony through the funeral and various relatives visiting. Maria had a large extended family, most of whom descended upon us for a week. Tony's supercilious daughter and playboy son, on the other hand, fled as soon as they could after the funeral, leaving me with Tony, who mourned his mother with a depth of feeling I respected, even if I didn't share it.

But . . . it had been weeks. I had friends at home waiting. Why was I still ensconced in my luxurious room in the palatial Villa Paradiso?

More than one reason, but a biggie was that I had been asked a question, one I had not yet answered. Tony asked me to marry him. He's a good and generous man, smart, sophisticated, classically trained on the piano, very much like his younger brother, Miguel, but missing some of my late husband's fire and passion. He would be an ideal husband in so many ways. I wouldn't need to worry for the rest of my life. But I didn't love him and never would.

So I awoke longing for home. I had dreamed of strong

arms holding me, but in that dream when I opened my eyes it wasn't Tony's face I saw, nor even Miguel's, but that of Virgil Grace, sheriff of the county law enforcement unit.

I missed him. And I missed my friends, Pish in particular. I missed my daily routine, baking muffins for the villagers, talking to Shilo and Jack, visiting with Gogi and Hannah and Lizzie. I missed *home*, Wynter Castle and Autumn Vale. I had missed the whole summer, which I had not yet experienced in my inherited castle, hurried away by that urgent phone call the very day after Virgil and I had a romantic, delicious interlude in the long grass near the forest.

As suddenly as I had flown to Spain, I made the decision to leave. Of *course* I would not marry Tony. Why hadn't I answered immediately? I had closure with Miguel's fierce and irascible mother. She confessed that she had resented me taking Miguel away, even as she knew it wasn't me but his ambition as a fashion photographer that kept him in New York. I, in turn, admitted that I had resented her when Miguel left for six weeks to care for her while Tony was away. It was over, both sides forgiven.

I had been gone so long, but with time and distance comes perspective. I could see how I had struggled and worried about Wynter Castle, my inheritance, for ten long months, wondering whether I could ever make it pay more than a miserly sum. It had taxed me, as had continued battles with some of the folks in Autumn Vale and the bad luck that saw three deaths on my property.

Life at Villa Paradiso was so easy, carefree, pleasant. Tony's persistent good nature had shown me how trouble-free my life could be. Servants took care of everything, even cooking fabulous meals accompanied by equally fabulous wines. I spent evenings listening to Tony on the piano, or we took short jaunts to the coast to lie on the beach, then dance in a Euro-cool bar. I had been sucked into a vortex of ease.

Then, like a pailful of icy water, came the shock of a life not my own anymore: Tony started making assumptions, plans, arrangements. The day jaunts extended without my knowledge into a few days away here, a couple there. He made plans and then told me what we were doing. And with whom. Miguel had done the same, which wasn't so bad because I loved him with all my heart and I was young, eager for experience. He made it so much fun.

It was different with Tony, a kind of benevolent control, an assumption of his right to guide my life. It had become irritating, and yet every time I tried to talk to Tony, he changed the subject. So when I awoke thinking of Wynter Castle and Autumn Vale, I knew it was long past time to go home. I hated how lazy I'd become, how accustomed to having everything done for me. Tony laughed when I whined about it one day, and said I was very American to worry about my indolence.

But worst of all, I had, by tiny degrees, drifted away from my friends. During the first couple of weeks in Málaga I had made plans for when I returned, gotten involved even from afar, and missed home like crazy. That changed as Maria lingered halfway between Earth and heaven. Phone calls became shorter and less frequent.

As I stood staring out over the Paradiso olive groves and vineyard, I realized that I hadn't spoken to Pish for two weeks, and Virgil, not for three. Shilo, my best girlfriend in the world, a sweet, fragile gypsy child, wouldn't come to the phone last time I called her at her and her husband Jack's house in town. My cell phone had died a few weeks back, I couldn't replace it until I got home, and so no one called me at the villa because the serving staff couldn't—or wouldn't—speak English and so never took messages.

I whirled around from the window, threw on some clothes, and called a travel agent that minute, booking the first flight back to New York, and a commuter flight from

JFK to Rochester. Then I told Tony, expecting a big fight or a guilt trip. I got neither. I think he was relieved, and wondered if he'd proposed because he hadn't known what else to do with me, and had thought we may as well marry if I was going to stay. Tony is a very practical man, and I had been a malleable and content partner.

He kissed me good-bye—on the cheek, all very chaste, as had been all of our interactions—and had his driver take me to Costa del Sol Airport. I got the flight to New York, then caught the commuter flight to the Greater Rochester International Airport, arriving at about ten AM. Pish was to meet me at the baggage claim.

Except he didn't. When I retrieved my one bag I turned and there, standing with his fists clenched on his hips, arms akimbo, legs astride, was Virgil Grace, a scowl on his face. "Are you ready? Let's get out of here."

Chapter One

HOO BOY, I had forgotten how good-looking Virgil Grace is: six feet something of dark-haired, dark-eyed, steel-jawed man. Two-plus months without my muffins—and I don't mean that as a euphemism; the man loves my baking—had worked off the slight thickening at his waist, and his jawline was now as chiseled as granite, his cheekbones razor sharp, his dark eyes shadowed.

"I'm ready," I said, hefting my carry-on over my shoulder and grabbing the handle of my one suitcase on wheels.

"Is that *all* your luggage?" He glared skeptically at it.

"Yes, this is *all* my luggage!" I didn't mention that Tony was sending the rest after me. I had beat a hasty retreat from Villa Paradiso, but while in Spain I had done a *lot* of shopping. Gucci and Bulgari shops litter the Costa del Sol like Dollar Tree stores in Buffalo, and both Tony and Maria insisted on funding me in my extravagance. Where would I wear Euro fashion in upstate New York? I hadn't a clue.

Truth was, I had relapsed into old spendthrift ways, shopping out of habit and boredom.

"*I'll* take it," he said, and jerked the suitcase handle out of my hand. He grabbed my carry-on for good measure—all I was left with was my sizable Balenciaga handbag—and strode off toward the sliding glass doors.

I trotted after him, my face flushing with heat. "What happened to Pish?" I called after him, trying to keep up with his lengthy strides. I was wearing heels, darn it. "He was supposed to be picking me up."

"Your houseguest needed him," he growled over his shoulder.

"My *houseguest*?"

"You'll find out soon enough."

That sounded ominous, but then I was back in the nutty world of Autumn Vale, where odd people descend on Wynter Castle like falling leaves in the vale in autumn.

He led me to his official sheriff's department vehicle, which he had parked wherever he damned well pleased, as cops do around the world. He expertly got us onto the 490, then the 90, driving all that way in virtual silence, other than the conversational feints I thrust, which he parried with grunts and then more silence. Finally, I twisted around in the seat, the belt straining at my shoulder, and said, "Virgil, I think we need to pull off somewhere and have a chat. You're clearly angry."

He slowly swiveled his jutting jaw and stared at me before returning his attention to the highway. "Why would I be angry?"

"Because, well, it would be understandable. I mean, we . . ." I trailed off, shook my head, and turned back in my seat to stare straight out the front window at the countryside as we headed down the 90 for a short jaunt before we would thread through Batavia to catch the 98. It was a boring stretch along the 90—or the Governor Thomas E. Dewey

Thruway—ditch to the left of us, beyond which was the other lane, and ditch to the right of us, with a view of fields, broken only by an occasional line of scrubby, dry-looking trees, soared over by hawks hunting for mice. We drove on in even deeper silence, other than squawks and shrieks from the police radio, until we threaded through Batavia and turned onto 98. He reduced his speed accordingly as we drove through the green landscape, rural patches broken by small towns along the way.

"Virgil, I care about you a great deal," I said, carefully tiptoeing around the edges of his angry silence. "I love my life in Autumn Vale; that's what's bringing me back."

He was silent. When I stole a glace, I saw his dark, thick brows knit in a frown over his chocolaty eyes. His grip on the steering wheel, at ten and two, was white-knuckled. Finally, he growled, "So this isn't just a pit stop to pick up your stuff so you can move to Málaga, or wherever the hell that Tony character lives?"

I got it, *finally*, the reason behind his mysterious fury. I recalled our last phone conversation, when I had talked about Tony, how good he was to me, how sophisticated, how learned. His fluency in four languages, his kindness to his mother, his love of the arts. Virgil Grace was *jealous*! And jealous, in this case, was good; when a relationship is new and fragile, it's natural to feel jealousy, and really, I had given him plenty to feel jealous and insecure about. My stomach jittered. How could I reassure him? I half turned in the seat again and watched his profile. "Virgil, it's not a pit stop. I'm coming *home*."

His stern look relaxed a smidge.

"I missed you all like crazy," I continued, my tone soft. "I missed Autumn Vale. I missed Becket; I've never had a cat before, and didn't realize how much a part of my life he is! And I missed Gogi, and Pish, and Shilo . . . and . . . Virgil, I missed *you*."

He looked like he wanted to say something, but he focused back on the road. He shook his head, stared out the window, and brooded for a while. "Did you honestly miss . . . us?"

I wasn't going to go into the various emotional stages I experienced, missing them all like crazy for weeks, and then the gradual Novocain numbness as I let Tony take over my life. I didn't want to talk about that just then, though I needed to, at some point, to let him know how I now had a different perspective on my marriage to Miguel after having been in his family home for two months.

"I figured a lot of stuff out while I was gone," I said. "Maybe we can talk about it, but not right now. I did miss you all in so many different ways. Autumn Vale and you all fill in the holes in my life." I sighed and played with the strap of my purse. "This is going to sound sappy. Gogi is the mom I miss so much, the mom I never really had. Binny is the sarcastic little sister. Janice is the kooky aunt. And you . . ." I looked over at him. I couldn't go on; I wasn't sure where we stood. But I reached out and rested my hand on his arm, where the dark hairs lay across his forearm like silk, his shirtsleeves rolled up. His muscles flexed under my fingers. "*You* most of all."

The drive wasn't long enough to get it all sorted out, and just forty minutes or so after leaving the airport we turned onto the winding lane and drove up to Wynter Castle.

Wynter Castle. It was almost noon, and the slanting sunlight of late September gave a golden hue to the beautiful old stone of my early nineteenth–century real American castle. It is so lovely to me now, but when I first arrived it seemed desolate; the ivy creeping up the stone walls, the huge Gothic diamond-paned windows that line it, and the arched double oak doors seeming giant-size after the compact apartments of Manhattan.

Virgil pulled to a stop on the gravel drive, right by the flagged terrace, hopped out, and grabbed my bags out of the trunk. His radio crackled to life again, as it had intermittently on the drive, this time with a dispatcher's voice squawking something about a disturbance at the Vale Variety and Lunch.

"I gotta go," he said, rounding the car and slamming into the driver's seat.

"Wait, Virgil, when can we talk?"

"Gotta take this call. I'll call you. Later," he said, waving out the driver's-side window as he backed around, skidding off down the drive with a spray of gravel.

"Well, hello to you, too!" I stood for a moment, and breathed deeply, letting the quiet of the country, the smell of warm grass, the sound of the slight breeze tossing the treetops, calm me. I was home.

I toted my bags up to the fieldstone terrace and pulled open the oak door, hit by a wave of sound. Pish's expensive audio system, which he had installed as a gift to me—or to the castle—blared some opera singer belting "*O Mio Babbino Caro,*" a glorious Puccini aria with soaring high notes, one of the few opera pieces that most folks recognize. I had heard the singer before; the trembling top notes sounded familiar.

I let the door close behind me as I stood in the cavernous great hall, turning slowly and taking in the tapestries that covered some of the stone walls, the grand staircase that swooped up, splitting in two, and the galleries above that let onto multiple rooms, and the glorious rose window above the stairs. I felt tremulous and emotional, ready to burst into tears.

Until the opera singer did it for me. Just then the opera CD took an odd turn, the singer breaking into a storm of weeping. As I set my carry-on bag on the big round table in the center of the great hall she spoke.

"Pish, darling, I can't do it, I *can't*!"

Huh?

The storm of weeping again, then Pish's soothing murmur. Not a recording, then, but what was going on? I stood silent. The speaking voice was even more familiar than the singing. I located the source of the sound despite the amplified version piped through the sound system, turned, and headed into the dining room, a long room with the arched diamond-paned windows that looked over the drive and lane, and off of that, the library, one of the turret rooms. I went to the door and looked in.

Tears welled in my eyes. There was my darling Pish, my sixty-something, lean, brown-haired, best friend and kind-of father figure. And he was with another woman! She was an auburn-haired beauty, lush figure (not quite as voluptuous as my own), medium height, with lovely hands that fluttered as she wept on Pish's shoulder. A microphone hooked up to a bank of audio equipment on an ugly modern stand took up the center of my library.

"I'll never get the high notes again, I swear it, Pishie! Much *less* perform in front of *people*!"

I cleared my throat, and you would have thought I'd caught them in *flagrante delicto*, the way they leaped guiltily apart, and how Pish stared, his blue eyes wide. She, her fluttering hands pressed to her bosom, well exposed in a low-cut tank top, stared at me with gorgeous false-lashed contact-fake green eyes.

Roma Toscano. Oh, yes, I remembered her all too well. She had tried to steal my husband, Miguel.

"Merry, *darling*!" Pish yelped after a moment. He skipped across the room, taking me into a hug, his slender frame pressed to my more ample body.

After a babble of welcome and our teary reunion, he reintroduced me to Roma Toscano, though I reminded him that we had met. She was a minor-league opera singer, a friend of Pish's. We had met about ten years before at one of Pish's opera galas in support of the Lexington Opera

Company. Roma had virtually ignored me while she flirted outrageously with Miguel. I learned later that she had stalked him, to some degree, showing up at one of his shoots in St. Barths and retaining his talent agency as her own.

All—supposedly—a coincidence. Miguel laughed it off, but I knew the truth. She had tried to encroach on my territory, and I didn't appreciate it. Still, that was ten years ago.

We repaired to the kitchen and sat at the long trestle table that centered the work area, which I affectionately examined, having been absent from it for so long. The kitchen was designed and modernized, astonishingly, by my late great-uncle, who had thought to make a professional kitchen for an inn, into which he had at some point considered making the castle. The work area is long, with stainless steel surfaces, a deep professional sink, a six-burner stove, and a huge stainless steel fridge. At the other end of the long space is a more homey seating area, with big wing chairs in front of a fireplace. It is my favorite room in the castle.

I wanted nothing more than to catch up with my dearest friend, to ask after all our mutual acquaintances, hear every little detail of the last two months. But instead I had to listen to Roma as Pish coaxed her into telling me her story and how she had ended up at Wynter Castle.

"This darling, *darling* man came to me in my hour of greatest need!" she explained, clutching his arm and laying her head on his shoulder, which in the past had been available for only my head.

Pish explained that in late July he took Lush, his aunt who had been staying at the castle, back to the city. She missed her friends terribly. That was when he connected with some of his old friends in the arts community. "Roma is the principal soprano of the Lexington Opera Company in the city."

So she had worked her way up. When I knew her she was one of the minor singers and a stand-in.

"Or at least she *was* principal soprano until she had a little problem."

She chuckled, a warm, throaty sound, and patted Pish's upper arm, flirtatious as usual. I surmised that she was one of those women who flirt with everyone: male, female, gay, straight.

"He's being far too kind, as usual," Roma said, fluttering her fake eyelashes. She hugged him harder, making her cleavage bloom over the low-cut tank top until it was as if two mounds of pale bread dough were struggling to escape a loaf pan. "I had a breakdown of epic—I might say, *operatic*—proportions." She threaded her fingers through his longish hair and mussed it. "I had an incident of stage fright, my voice locked up, and I ruined an LOC performance of *Linda di Chamounix*." She looked across the table at me. "That's a Donizetti piece; you wouldn't know it. Anyway . . . I was let go."

"*Most* unfairly!" Pish said, patting her hand and gazing at her with fondness. "Poor dear had been working too hard."

"Not fair," I agreed. "Maybe if you went back to them and—"

"Ah, but you haven't heard all of it," she said, wagging her finger at me and giving a trilling laugh that lightly tripped on a descending scale. "As a soprano I'm high-strung. That was *not* the end of it." Wryly, she explained that she ended up threatening the LOC conductor with graphic violence, though she made it seem like a comic scene in an operetta, merely a charming flight of fancy on her part. The conductor unexpectedly (in her telling) took it personally, especially when she added some insulting language toward his wife and ugly children. She was about to be charged but fled and ended up on the GWB (the George Washington Bridge) threatening to jump.

"I wasn't *really* going to jump," she said. "I just needed to think."

"Poor darling," Pish said. "I talked to the LOC conductor, got the police to drop any thought of charges, and after a little bit, brought her back here. This is the best place for her to recover. And now we are working on her voice, *and* her confidence."

I got up to make a pot of tea, not wanting Pish to read my mind. I turned on the jet under the kettle and stared out the window, which looked off toward the forest, just beginning to get that tinge of rusty brown and gold that is a precursor to full-on upstate autumn. I was being totally unfair—and after he had been so good as to watch over the castle while I was away—but I had been looking forward to having the place just to us. I knew he was taking Lush back to the city, but he hadn't, in all the times we spoke, told me about bringing Roma to Wynter Castle. I felt blindsided and slightly resentful, especially given my own personal history with her, which he may have forgotten. I struggled to push those feelings back. I'd acknowledge and deal with them later.

When I came back, full teapot in hand, I was composed. "I'm sorry I wasn't here to welcome you to Wynter Castle, Roma, but I hope you're enjoying your stay."

"I am, though it's taking longer than I thought to . . . to regain my confidence." She fluttered her lashes and cast down her gaze, the first real sign I had seen of her lack of self-assurance.

Pish put his hand over hers on the table. "And *that* is why I have decided that the Autumn Vale Community Players' next work will be a little opera piece, something obscure, nothing anyone has heard before. Our mistake last time was in trying something too big, too well-known." He spoke of them tackling *Die Zauberflöte*, Mozart's incredibly challenging opera.

That was not their *only* mistake, or even their most grievous; the biggest mistake had been giving "Der Hölle Rache," one of the most supremely difficult soprano arias of all time, to a dear friend, Janice Grover, who couldn't hit high C with any tone. "Too well-known? Pish, no one in Autumn Vale has heard *any* opera before—except Janice, of course." She was our local bank president's wife and the owner of Crazy Lady Antiques and Collectibles; her slaughter of the Queen of the Night aria in their last production had been an epic fail, though it had generated enough talk and laughter to keep everyone smiling for weeks at her expense. "And Gogi, and maybe Doc."

"Ah yes, but we're going to tackle an opera version of *Much Ado About Nothing*. It has some *lovely* bits, and we've started working on it."

Shakespeare's romantic comedy as an opera? Who knew? "So why were you working on 'O Mio Babbino Caro'?"

"That was Pish's idea," Roma said, with an affectionate glance at her new impresario. "He thinks that if I record a few pieces and he puts them on the Internet, he can make me a sensation!"

"I've got Zeke working on making a video to back her singing, and we're going to take some footage or photographs of her in costume, out in the woods, and set it to the video and put it online."

"And how is your writing going, Pish?" He had been working on a follow-up book to his *NYT* bestseller, *Cons, Scams, and Flimflams*, using as inspiration the banking scandal that had plagued the Autumn Vale Community Bank.

He shrugged. "I'm stalled right now, but it'll come."

Stalled because he was putting all his creative energy into a diva? I eyed Roma with distaste. Maybe I wasn't being fair, but she is one of those women who suck up every little bit of attention and still crave more. Was there more to his writers' block? Pish had been hurt by his last romantic fling and subsequent breakup with a senior federal agent,

Stoddart Harkner, so perhaps this distraction was what he needed.

I spent the rest of the day unpacking, doing laundry, and napping after the long flight. I ordered a new cell phone, which would arrive by courier the very next day. I went out briefly to look for Becket, my uncle's orange tabby, who Pish said had spent most of the summer outdoors. I called and called, and thought I saw him on the edge of the Wynter Woods, but he didn't come home. It was just us for dinner, and after, Pish and Roma retreated to the library to attempt the song again. I felt oddly lonely.

I went to bed early, determined to make an apology round of visits the next day. I had been out of touch and totally self-focused for weeks; it was time to expend some energy outward. Not that I had been wrong to stay away so long. I felt more at peace in my heart. I now had a handle on what many thought was excessive grief and mourning for my husband and understood why it had gone on so long, and what I now was ready for.

I had plans.

THE NEXT MORNING I TRIED TO CALL SHILO; I WANTED to get together with my best female friend, have tea, and visit, but there was no answer at her home. All I got on Jack's real estate line was a recorded message. I'd try again later. My cell phone arrived by courier, and I set it up immediately, relieved to be back in contact with my world.

The Merry Wynter Apology Tour would have to start in Autumn Vale. I took a brief walk toward the woods, calling Becket, but the grass and weeds had gotten too long, and though I tried my best, I couldn't see anything near the woods but a brief flash of orange. I was heartsick; poor Becket must have thought I'd abandoned him. After my uncle died, Becket spent most of the year in the woods, and he'd gone back to those habits after I left. I thought I wasn't important to him, that I was someone handy who made sure he had fresh food and water, but it seemed that my "abandonment" had affected him more deeply than I could have expected.

Maybe some of my humans—like Shilo—felt the same?

My gorgeous old boat of a car, a Cadillac Fleetwood left to me by my great-uncle Melvyn Wynter, started up with a cough and a hesitation, like an old person getting up in the morning. As I drove along the road toward Autumn Vale I remembered the morning, more than a year ago, when I had first approached the village to ask directions to my castle. I had met Doc English (an old friend of my great-uncle's) in the village, though then I just knew him as an odd, scuttling, weirdly dressed elderly gentleman. I also encountered Sheriff Virgil Grace, who had ogled my cleavage then led me out to Wynter Castle, where I met Jack McGill, the real estate agent who had been trying to sell it for me. From there, I encountered the dozens of wonderful, odd, happily strange people who had become friends and, in some cases, enemies.

It took me a while to get used to the castle and village but now, driving along Abenaki, the main street in Autumn Vale, which still had some boarded-up shops, along with the various businesses that fed, clothed, and entertained the townies, I felt that I had come home. I pulled into a street parking spot outside of Crazy Lady Antiques and Collectibles and, since I was right there, I opened the door to the antique shop and edged in past the fire hazards—also known as her stock—Janice Grover has piled in the way. As I crab-walked in, I heard a shriek and a crash.

I hurriedly threaded my way through the junk toward the noise and saw a huge, framed antique mirror on the floor, cracked from side to side, with Janice, in a colorful floor-length dashiki, standing over it, staring. Her face was ghostly white, and she said, "Seven years of bad luck! Oh Lord, as if I haven't had enough of that."

"Janice, it's okay," I said. "You don't believe that superstitious nonsense, do you?"

She looked toward me through the dust-specked gloom. "Oh, Merry, you're back. About *bloody* time. I was beginning to think you'd gone for good. Poof, a disappearing act!" she said, waving her hands.

"I never intended to stay that long, but things happened." I started helping her clear up the big shards of mirror.

"Hmph. So now that you're home, what are you going to do about that *awful* woman Pishie's taken up with?" she said, her voice fading in and out as she disappeared to get a broom and came back. "Kick her out of the castle?"

Not a fan of Roma Toscano, apparently. "I know her from years ago. I'll tell you how if you come to the Vale for a coffee," I said, giving the short local name of the Vale Variety and Lunch, which was, as it sounded, a variety store and luncheonette.

She sighed and nodded. As we cleaned up the glass I listened to her complaints about Roma, who she said was pushy and snobbish, then we walked down to the Vale. I felt like dancing my way down, I was so happy to be back. But I had to wonder, had my time away changed perceptions of me? I hadn't been in Autumn Vale long enough to be considered a fixture, and folks could view my two-and-a-half-month runner as a symbol of how uncommitted to the place I was. I'd have to work my way back into their good graces.

We wove through the variety store aisles, mounted the two steps to the coffee shop in back, and nabbed a table, the same funky fifties diner–style ones that had been there since the fifties, when they were new. I eyed the domed glass dessert containers on the lunch counter and noticed muffins, not mine. So *someone* was baking muffins, but who?

Mabel Thorpe, the manageress, a tiger lady with a

redoubtable beehive of stiffly sprayed curls (often gray, but at that moment radiantly orange and yellow, like autumn leaves), came over to the table and threw down the gauntlet in the shape of the specials of the day sheet. "We have muffins; really, *really* good muffins," she said, glaring at me. "You want one? On the house."

Good Lord, I hadn't thought *she* would be angry at me. "I'm happy you have someone baking them for you. Did Binny finally break down and start baking normal stuff?" Binny Turner, who owned the only bakeshop in town, was rigid in her insistence on making European-style treats to suit international palates. Of which there were few in Autumn Vale. Or none.

"Nope. Pattycakes has taken over where you left off."

"Pattycakes, huh?" The daughter of a former tenant of mine, "Pattycakes" was Patricia Schwartz, a fifty-three-year-old woman who had a deft hand with cakes and cupcakes.

"Come on, Mabel, her muffins aren't as good as Merry's." Janice was a staunch friend and defender. "No one's are. So what was going on in here yesterday? I heard you had quite the commotion. Virgil even showed up, siren blaring."

Mabel's frostiness thawed, and she sat down with us and signaled her waitress to bring coffee and some of the muffins. Once I tasted one I was happy to note it was *not* as good as mine.

"It's Minnie again," she griped, naming Minnie Urquhart, the local manager of the postal station. "Isadore was doing her job—"

"Her job?" I squawked.

Just then I saw Isadore Openshaw, Autumn Vale hermit and bad-tempered library helper, hairnet in place, slump out from behind the lunch counter with a bus tub. She cleared the tables near the back wall of breakfast dishes and coffee cups, then turned and saw me. Her eyes widened, but she made no other signal that she noticed. She retreated past swinging doors behind the counter into the kitchen.

"Her *job*," Mable said firmly. "She's the best dishwasher I've ever had. She doesn't socialize, doesn't smoke, and I can practically *feed* her her wages. She takes home whatever is left at the end of the day."

I was happy for Isadore. She was a perpetual outsider, mostly because of her personality disorder, which I can only call Hates-the-World-itis. But I *did* hope she was getting paid at least minimum wage. One never knew with Mabel, who was tight-fisted, if rigidly upright: had the skinflint side won out, or the rigid code of ethics?

"*Anyway*?" Janice prompted, glaring over at me, then returning her gaze to Mabel.

"Isadore was doing her job when Minnie Urquhart came barging in and bumped into her," Mabel said, her gruff voice tinged with annoyance. "She knocked poor Isadore flying, then stormed over to Crystal's table and began yelling at her about something Crystal was getting Brianna to do."

I was mystified. Crystal, Brianna? But Janice seemed to know who these people all were. I had been gone only two and a half months, but felt like I had fallen back out of the rabbit hole and now did not know who was who in Wonderland.

Chapter Two

❉ ❉ ❉

"OH, COME ON, Merry," Janice said, when I complained of being out of the loop. "Crystal Rouse is the crazy dame who runs Consciousness Calling, that new age mumbo jumbo crap that Emerald is involved in."

I felt a tingle of uneasiness. "But Em is doing so well with them! She's straightened out her life, gotten Lizzie settled down, and . . ." I caught a glance between Janice and Mabel and the tingle buzzed up the scale into wholesale anxiety. "What's going on?"

"You'll figure it out soon enough," Mabel said, with a throaty chuckle. "I need a cigarette. You fill her in on the rest of that crew, Janice." The manageress disappeared through the swinging doors into the kitchen.

"'Rest of that crew'? What does that mean? Is Emerald okay? There's some trouble between Minnie and . . . what was the name? . . . Crystal?"

"Shush, let me drink some coffee." Janice cleared her throat, took a long slurp. "Okay, so last time, on *How the Stomach Turns*—"

I chuckled and eyed her affectionately as she took another slurp of coffee, appreciating her humorous asides. Janice is two hundred fifty dashiki-covered pounds of forthright laughter. She and Simon, her banker husband, are big people, and Janice favors a Bohemian-on-crack appearance: colorful muumuus, big earrings, hair done up in an extravagantly curled bun that gradually comes loose through the day until it resembles a bird's nest once the chicks have learned to fly. She once told me she was never going to disappear in a crowd, so she may as well stand out. "Be serious for a few minutes. You're the only one who will tell me all the gossip in Autumn Vale. Doc will tell me exaggerated stories and Gogi will tell me what she thinks I ought to hear. Pish has been too taken up with Roma, and Shilo . . . well, she's not speaking to me, I think."

"She's always been such a ray of sunshine, but lately she's a ghost of herself," Janice said, with a frown. "Jack is worried, I know that."

"I'll look into it. So what *is* going on with Minnie and this Crystal person?"

"I know you don't like Minnie. She can be a proper pain in the posterior. But she's got her good points. She rents rooms out, you know."

"Is that the limit of her good points?"

"Seriously, she *does* have good points," Janice insisted, her chins wobbling in sincerity. "She rents rooms out for reasonable rates to folks who couldn't afford anything else. She makes meals for her 'kids,' as she calls her boarders. It's her own dysfunctional family."

I was silent for a moment, not sure how to respond. Minnie had made it her mission in life to make me miserable, as had other members of her *real* dysfunctional family.

"Aha, those are two of the current boarders right now," Janice said, lowering her voice as two young fellows slouched in and took seats across from each other at a table along the wall. "Karl Mencken and Logan Katsaros; I don't know which is which. Cripes, boys are such pains at that age. My own boys looked like that: greasy, unkempt, like they didn't have a home or family."

I eyed the two guys. Both were medium height and skinny, but that's where their looks diverged. One had blue eyes, light brown hair, and acne, with the beginnings of a weedy beard or goatee on his chin and multiple piercings, both lobes stretched with so-called flesh tunnels. The other guy had stooped shoulders, greasy black wavy hair, brown eyes, olive complexion, and no visible piercings, though he did have a neck tattoo of a peace dove on his right side.

They seemed shifty to me. If this were a bank and they were acting as they were, talking in whispers and looking around at each individual, I'd have hugged my purse and gotten out of there quickly. But all they did was get coffee and drink it, while still muttering to each other.

"Lovely pair."

"I know. There's one more, a girl, Brianna something or other."

"Does Minnie have any kids of her own?"

"I don't know. She *could*, for all I know. She's lived here for a long time, since getting the job taking care of the post office, but originally she's from Ridley Ridge, like all the Urquharts."

"That doesn't surprise me." I call Ridley Ridge, a town slightly larger than Autumn Vale that is up the ridge and down the highway a few miles, the Town That Hope Fled, or The Saddest Place on Earth.

Janice gobbled down the muffin, then mumbled, "It's not bad, I guess, but your muffins are better. *Any*way, as I said,

Minnie's current boarders are those two jokers and Brianna something or other."

"They look shifty. What do you know about them?"

"Not much. Both from out of town."

I don't get "vibes," as some people call it, but there seemed something off about those two.

"Anyway, back to Crystal Rouse," Janice said. "With Emerald's help she has gathered quite the bunch of dummies who go to her meetings, which are supposed to be all about motivation and self-fulfillment. You know the shtick: if you put your desires out into the universe, you will receive what you need. Load of crap. Sure, *some* of what you get from life is from what you put out there, but *no* one deserves cancer, or divorce, or a crippling accident."

"It's a scam made to make people who aren't successful or healthy feel guilty," I agreed. "So that's what Consciousness Calling is all about? Have you been to a meeting?"

"I did go out of curiosity," Janice admitted. "But the relentless *cheeriness* got me down!"

I smiled and chuckled. "Couldn't the world use a little more cheerfulness?"

"Not the idiotic variety that spouts platitudes like it's philosophy!" A few people around us had heard our conversation, and one nodded, her eyes wide.

"You got it, Janice!" the woman said, leaning across her table toward us. "I went and asked Crystal what to do about my lousy cheating almost-ex. She said I clearly had let myself go, and that's probably why he cheated!"

I eyed her and saw a middle-aged woman who was pretty normal: some spreading across the middle and the bottom, graying hair, and a few crow's-feet tracking around her sparkling eyes. "Any guy I've known who cheated did it for their own reasons, something lacking inside themselves."

She nodded. "I'm not taking the blame for getting old when

he's the one who looks like a pregnant sumo. I didn't complain about *his* sorry butt, and he thinks *I've* let myself go?"

"Anyway . . . Crystal Rouse?" I said to Janice as the other woman got up to pay and leave. "I'm concerned Emerald has been roped into a scam."

"She's a big girl; she can figure it out on her own," Janice said. "I like Emerald, but if she's going to keep spouting this crap I'll avoid her until she's recovered."

"I guess I'm more worried about Lizzie," I said. "I'd better get going. I have a few more people to see today, now that I'm back." I paused. "You know, Janice, I am sorry I didn't come back for so long." I told her about Maria's passing. "Time there helped me figure things out. As much as I loved Miguel, he was used to me doing whatever he wanted. I think he and I would have had to renegotiate our marriage as we got older."

"There is not a marriage around that doesn't require renegotiation as the years go by, honey," she said, and patted my hand.

Reminded about Roma by my mention of Miguel, I told her in brief how I knew the woman, and Janice rolled her eyes. Mabel came back and crouched down near our table, the smell of tobacco smoke on her breath. It's not an odor I find offensive, oddly enough. Lots of models smoke, and sometimes they did so while I was styling them, a profession I picked up after my brief plus-size modeling career.

"I s'pose Janice has brought you up to speed. Anyway, Minnie came in yesterday afternoon, sent poor Isadore flying, then stomped over to Crystal and Em's table—whole damn luncheonette shook; you know Minnie—and shrieked at her that Crystal was trying to turn Brianna over to the devil, that she was brainwashing a kid who didn't know any better, and she'd better be careful, or there'd be hell to pay."

"What did Crystal say?" Janice asked.

"It was Emerald who jumped up and told Minnie to keep

her fat trap shut, and that she'd better not threaten Crystal, or she'd get what she had coming to her," Mabel said.

"I thought this Consciousness Calling stuff was making Em calmer," I said.

"Hah!" Mabel brushed some ash from her sweater sleeve, poked an errant sunset curl back into place on her forehead, and continued. "Anyway, Crystal gave Emerald this look— chilled *me* to the bone—and the girl quieted down right away. It was like hypnotism or something. Crystal stood and faced Minnie. You haven't met her yet, right, Crystal Rouse?"

"Not yet," I replied.

"She's one of those people who always has a self-satisfied smirk on their faces, the kind you want to smack off. She told Minnie that she was clearly a deeply unhappy woman. She said if she'd just give Consciousness Calling a chance, it might help with her *weight* problem, she said, and her *anger* issues. I tell you, if Crystal says *one word* to me about smoking I'll dump an ashtray on her head." Mabel growled in the back of her throat. Her employees call the lunch counter manageress "the dragon lady," mostly for how smoke so often curls out of her mouth after a deep drag, but also because of that growl. "Anyway, Crystal said Brianna showed a lot of promise and was on her way to finding peace and happiness."

Standard self-help group fare. "Peace and happiness are good, right?"

Mabel's mouth twisted in a sour look. "Minnie gave Crystal a shove, and that's when someone called the cops, giving them a play-by-play. Emerald jumped up and bopped Minnie on the nose, made it bleed."

I rolled my eyes skyward.

"All the while, Crystal was chanting, *this too shall pass, it is what it is, we must agree to disagree*, and *let's put a pin in this and talk later*! I tell you, I felt like bopping *her* in the nose after a few minutes of that mindless drivel."

Janice snickered and so did a couple of others. Some

clapped. "*Way to go, Mabel!*" one called out, while a few patrons called her *Bruiser* and *Mabel Dempsey*, asking when the fight was scheduled. The two young fellows exchanged looks and got up, shambling out of the café.

Mabel watched them go, then said, "Virgil came, but it was all over by then except for the blood on the floor. No one is pressing charges. But then this morning Brianna came waltzing in asking people for money for that Consciousness Calling crap! Trying to gather *followers*, for the *cause*!" Mabel stood, towering over our table as she eased the kinks out of her knees. "I won't have that. Told her to can it unless she was collecting for veterans, and then she said, maybe I valued dogs and cats over humans but I shouldn't."

I bit my lip. "Did you clarify veterans versus veterinarians?"

"Nope. Told her to hustle her butt out of here and that's it. *And* I told her to tell Crystal not to send her lackeys in to collect dough from my customers."

"Are you sure the money was for Consciousness Calling?" Janice said. "Could have been a handy excuse to make some pocket change."

"Maybe," the manageress said. "Anyway, as much as I'm not fond of Minnie, that Crystal character gets on my last shaky nerve and shreds it like a cat on terry cloth. I'm choosing sides in this one, and I stand with Minnie. Rouse is not welcome here, and neither are her followers."

Janice and I left soon after. She had her shop to run, and I had a lot I wanted to accomplish. It felt good to get back in the swing of Autumn Vale happenings. The Villa Paradiso torpor was drifting away like mist on the wind, and I felt alive again.

We stood outside the variety store and luncheonette for a moment, then walked toward her store. Zeke and Gordy slouched out of the door that led to their apartment over Binny's bakery. It warmed my heart that both fellows' eyes lit up when they saw me. They eagerly told me what was going on in their lives. Gordy was headed out to his uncle's farm, where he was working fairly steadily.

"Gordy's giving me a ride to work," Zeke said. "I got a job in Ridley Ridge in the sheriff's department, doing custodial."

Getting a steady job in a depressed area was a big deal. I congratulated him sincerely. Gordy pointed out his "new" car parked at the curb. His uncle had given it to him so he could get to work and back. It was a real beater, with damage on the front end and lots of Bondo and duct tape holding it together, but if it got him from A to B, then he was better off than he had been.

As they chugged away from the curb, I asked Janice to wait for a moment while I skipped into the bakery. Binny's Bakery was the first place I entered in Autumn Vale, and as such it holds a special place in my heart. The walls are lined with shelves of teapots, and the place always smells wonderfully of Binny's fabulous baked goods: focaccia, Portuguese rolls, cream puffs, Napoleons, and lots of other goodies. I stepped up and in, the little bells chiming over the door. This time it wasn't dour Binny at the counter, but a smiling Pattycakes.

"Merry!" she cried, raising the pass-through and sidling through the opening. She hugged me tightly; it was like being hugged by a fragrant pillow, soft and squishy. "I heard you were back. Roma called me last night. She was afraid she'd made a bad impression on you, but I reassured her you were probably just worn-out from your flight."

I felt the subtle criticism. "You and Roma are friends?"

A voice from the bakery intoned, "More like freaking mother and daughter if you ask me!"

"Binny!" I cried. "Come on out here. I came in to see you."

Binny Turner strode out from behind, her tunic covered in flour, her dark hair tucked up into a hairnet. She regarded me seriously, then looked over at Pattycakes, or Patricia, as she was properly called. I sensed some tension.

"It's good to see you, Binny. How is your dad doing?"

She gave me a rare smile. Her father, Rusty, had been

missing for a long time, almost a year. When she got him back a year ago, after tragically losing her brother, she had worried about his health for a while, as well as his legal bills, given the tangle he was in from his involvement with a con artist's web of deceit. "He's doing a lot better. In fact, he's got Turner Construction up and running again. There's lots of work. They're going to be moving a house off a lot near the sheriff's department, which has bought some land to expand. Dad's not doing much himself, yet, but he hired a few guys to work, plus Junior Bradley to manage the construction office and job sites."

"Really? That's great, Binny." Junior was an underqualified zoning commissioner who had messed up often during his tenure and who was facing some legal woes of his own. It was a bit of a surprise that he'd gotten work in the construction business, but he had been Binny's brother Tom Turner's best friend, almost like another son to Rusty, and he did need a job.

Patricia smiled and wriggled her eyebrows. "He's hired some out-of-towners, good-looking guys," she said. "Hubba hubba."

"I'm surprised you've had time to notice, with Roma calling you with her latest tale of woe every time you turn around," Binny said, her tone dark.

My gaze volleyed between the two women. The sense of trouble brewing between them was clearly on point.

"She's an uneasy soul," Patricia said mildly. "You need to cut her some slack."

Binny turned and headed back to the work area. "I'll give her enough slack to hang herself," she tossed over her shoulder. "Nice to have you back, Merry. Maybe you can start baking muffins again. Patricia is too *busy* for muffins most of the time."

Patricia shrugged her ample shoulders. She's a big woman, like Janice, but favors comfortable yet kind of fashionable Alia plus-size wear, today a pair of tan capris and a madras blouse in pastels, her long hair wound up into a bun on the top of her head. She glanced back, then leaned toward me. "Binny doesn't like Roma, as you can tell."

"They're really different women," I murmured. If Patricia was a fan, then I wasn't going to spoil Roma's friendship by giving my own opinion of the diva.

A customer entered to order a birthday cake, so I returned to Janice, who stood waiting outside. As we walked on to the antique store, I told her what had gone down.

"I don't blame Binny a bit." Janice sniffed. "That Roma is a pain. Got Pish wrapped around her pinkie, and Patricia, too? That's too much. I was promised—*promised!*—that the next piece our group did would *not* be an opera. We were supposed to do an operetta or a musical, like my favorite, *The King and I*!" She waltzed down the sidewalk and sang a snatch of "*Getting to Know You*."

I was pleasantly surprised. She had a lovely, light soprano voice perfectly fit for operettas. You wouldn't have known that from her last performance, as Queen of the Night from *Die Zauberflöte*.

She stopped and turned. "Instead, thanks to Roma, we're doing an awful rendition of *Much Ado About Nothing*, with her royal highny in the lead part. Pish wants me to be Dogberry. *Dogberry!*"

I gave her a look of astonishment, since that was clearly what was called for.

She stared at me for a minute. "You don't have a clue who Dogberry is, do you?"

"Not a single clue," I admitted as we got to her shop.

"Dogberry is the foolish constable, *and* he's a he, *and* a tenor!" She went in and slammed the door, then poked her head back out and said, "Say hello to Hannah and Gogi for me, will you?"

Chapter Three

HOPING TO SEE both Gogi and Doc, I retrieved the Caddy and drove to the Golden Acres retirement home. The seniors' residence started life over a hundred years ago as a gracious home on a quiet, shady street a few blocks from downtown. Gogi had expanded it with a modest two-floor addition that stretched behind the house, giving room for a couple of dozen folks of varying abilities.

The front of the residence had been kept much as it was as a private home. I pulled up to the curb and parked, gazing up the sloping lawn to a grove of maples along a smooth pathway. The day had warmed up swiftly; upstate was suffering a hot and dry September. Several of the residents were sitting on benches in the shade, chatting. My favorite, Doc English, was not among them, I was disappointed to note. I was looking forward to seeing him.

I strolled up the walk, nodding to folks as they watched my progress, pausing in their conversations to do so. I entered through the double doors, passed the reception desk, and headed for one of the common areas, a living room furnished with comfortable but supportive sofas and chairs.

Bookshelves lined the walls, except for a table that held urns of tea and coffee. In the corner on a sofa sat Doc, my favorite old-timer, with a book held up to a strong light. He was reading *Democratic Vistas* by Walt Whitman, a work I knew was political rather than poetical. Doc truly *was* a medical doctor, who had earned his degree partly with the help of the GI Bill. But in his retirement he had taken up poetry and prose reading with a vengeance, and at ninety-plus could hold an abstruse conversation with anyone, including Pish, one of his favorite people. Pish had been a financial wizard before his semiretirement, but he shared with Doc an appreciation of American poetry.

I watched for a moment, love for the old dude welling up in me. He is the closest I will ever get to knowing my great-uncle Melvyn Wynter, who left me Wynter Castle. Doc and my uncle were childhood friends and enlisted in the army after Pearl Harbor, served with honor, and came back from WWII together. He felt like the grandfather I'd never had.

Something must have caught his attention, because he turned slightly, his thick glasses sliding down his nose, and saw me. His expression gladdened; there is no better way to say it. He grinned, gappy teeth exposed. I knew why I had come back, and why Autumn Vale had wormed its way into my reluctant heart: it was love, pure and simple. Love for the people, for my family history, which I was just learning about, and for individuals like Doc English.

He tossed the book aside and struggled to his feet, holding his arms open; even as I walked toward him I noticed with concern a bandage around his foot.

"Merry, honey, I thought you were gone for good," he said in my ear as we hugged. "And so did Pish, lemme tell ya. He visited me two, three times a week, faithful as a beagle, and told me he was afraid you'd sell up and marry that Spanish creep." His hearing wasn't that good, so he talked loudly. Some of the others in the living room eyed us with curiosity.

"I thought about it, Doc," I joked, even as I felt a pang in my heart that Pish had hidden that fear from me. "Easy life; I didn't have to move a muscle. I was in danger of turning into one giant plate of paella!"

He patted my hips. "You look good. Feel good, too." He paused and eyed me, his smudgy glasses askew on his beaky nose. "Or maybe you're back just to collect your things."

I smiled. The men in my life seemed worried about my intentions. "I'm back for good, Doc." I put my arms around him and squeezed again, then released. "For *good*, for good."

He stared at me. "You mean you've finally decided you ain't going to sell the castle?"

"I'll find some way to keep it. I'm staying." It was a momentous proclamation, but somehow, some way, I would keep Wynter Castle.

We sat and talked for a while. He had a sore on his foot that, because of his type 2 diabetes, wasn't healing. But he was doing fine, otherwise. He told me more unvarnished truth in a half hour than anyone else would in two days.

Emerald had moved into a house with Crystal Rouse. Doc called Consciousness Calling "that pack of mumbo jumbo crap." I expressed my concern for Lizzie in the midst of it all. Lizzie, he told me, was still volunteering at Golden Acres, which she had begun doing as community service after a run-in with the law, and kept doing because it suited her.

"What do you think of Roma Toscano, the diva Pish invited to stay?"

He chuckled. "Pish brought her to meet me. I kinda like her. She adds a little color to the neighborhood, a little vivacity. She flirts with me. *And* every other man in sight. But I kinda feel sorry for Pish; he creeps around visiting folks Roma's upset so he can placate 'em. Puttin' out fires she's started with her tongue. I told him, stop worrying about it so much. People get too cranked over stupid stuff, then that's their problem, not his."

Hmm . . . so everything wasn't so shiny happy in Pish's world. I stored that info to use on him later, when I tried to persuade him to send Roma back to the city. I told Doc I knew Roma from days gone by, but I had other concerns I wanted to discuss. "I'm worried about Shilo, more than anyone. She won't answer when I call her on the phone. I'm going to have to track her down and get her to talk to me."

Doc frowned and wiped his glasses on the corner of his plaid shirt, managing to make them more smudgy than they had been. I took them from him and got a tissue.

"I seen her in the park one day talking to someone," he said, blinking blindly. "Not Jack."

"That doesn't surprise me. She's a friendly girl," I replied, polishing his glasses and handing them back to him.

He put them on and squinted, grunting. "Better. Thanks, honey. No, this was something else. She looked scared, don't know why."

"What did the guy look like?"

"Skinny, dark, dressed in city clothes, you know . . . blue jeans, a leather jacket—even on a hot day—and fancy boots."

"Did you talk to her?"

"I was going to, but she saw me and hurried off; don't know if you've noticed, but I ain't so fast. Bet she didn't think I recognized her from a distance."

"How long ago was this?"

"Oh, 'bout a month ago or so."

"About the time she stopped coming to the phone to talk to me." I pondered it a moment. "I'll go see her later today. She's not going to weasel out of it. Can I tell her what you saw if I need to?"

"Sure can."

"Doc, my friend, I've been here over a year, haven't I?"

"Yup."

"I'm thinking of throwing a party to celebrate. What do you think?"

"I'll be there with silvery tinkling bells on."

I left my friend behind with his book and unsmudgy glasses and found Gogi in her small office off the reception area. She was glaring at a book of figures, her cheaters down low on her nose as she kept glancing from the book to the computer screen and back. It looked like she was trying to reconcile what was in the book with what was on her monitor.

"Merry!" she cried when she saw me. She leaped up and circled the desk, hugging me closely. "Glad you're back. *Some* folks thought you were gone for good, but I knew you'd come home."

Home. I was home. One of the folks who thought I was gone for good may have been her son, Virgil. "I was speaking with Doc. Is his foot going to be okay?"

"We hope so. It'll take some time. It was funny to listen to him and the doctor consulting over it."

I sat down opposite Gogi and thought for a moment, watching as her eyes strayed back to her screen. "Gogi, before I left, Virgil and I had a talk. I know about his ex-wife." Virgil's ex, Kelly, was the daughter of Sheriff Ben Baxter, head of the sheriff's department for Ridley Ridge and its surrounding county, which abutted ours. Their marriage had been hasty, entered into for all the wrong reasons by them both. When she left Virgil, her father was angry; to him, marriage was for life. In a moment of weakness she told him that Virgil had been cruel to her, and had even struck her.

Virgil had spoken to her since, and she regretted it deeply—I had read the letter she wrote to him acknowledging her wrongdoing—but she was too afraid of losing her father's love and, more important to her, his respect, and hadn't gotten up the nerve yet to tell her father the truth. I hashed this out with Gogi. "It's unfortunate that the very next day after we . . . uh, talked, I got the call that Maria was dying and headed to Spain."

"And even more unfortunate that in two-plus months you couldn't make it back here, even for a visit."

Her eyes were cold, her expression neutral, but I could tell she was hurt, mostly for her son. She was right; I *could* have come back to Autumn Vale, even if it was just a brief visit. "I care about Virgil, Gogi, but I'll admit I was confused, and I got caught up in my late husband's family. I don't know if I can explain it, but it was like going back to the security and comfort I felt while married to Miguel. This last year has been tough, and being with the Paradiso family . . . it was like shedding all that responsibility for a brief reprieve. Like returning to a cocoon."

"It wasn't just you leaving, or even you staying away," she insisted. "But you sounded so *different* when you called people. *I* noticed it. *Pish* noticed it. I'm sure Shilo and Virgil did, too."

"You're right." I paused for a moment and looked down at my hands, wanting to get the words right. "At first, all I could think about was coming back to Autumn Vale and . . . and Virgil. But after a while I began to feel numb, like that life, that *lifestyle*, had anesthetized me. I know now that it was partly the security and comfort that made Miguel so attractive to me. I had been through so much, and here was this wonderful, gorgeous, wealthy man who wanted me and *only* me. I loved him deeply, so the lifestyle was a bonus." I paused, but then forged on. "But I don't love Tony. He asked me to marry him, Gogi, and that woke me up. I think his proposal, offhand and kindly meant as it was, shook me out of my fog."

Gogi sighed and nodded, then reached across the desk and took my hand. "I'd like to stay angry at you, but I can't. As a woman who has struggled in her life, I get it." She had lost two husbands and been through a serious bout with breast cancer. "You need to tell Virgil this. He thought . . ." She shrugged and shook her head. "That's between you two. You sort it out."

It dawned on me in that moment that Virgil may have interpreted my extended absence and increasing withdrawal as a reluctance to get involved with him in the face of his complicated ex–marital status. "I appreciate your insight. I don't regret being gone that long. I *can't* regret it, because I finally got the perspective on my marriage that I needed. I've idealized Miguel, completely forgetting that he was a mortal man. But I do regret how I've hurt you all. Even if I needed to figure things out, I could have expressed that. I'm sorry."

I paused, emotion overtaking me, and stared out the small window that overlooked the lane to the back parking lot. Gogi was silent, but I could feel her watching me, her hand still holding mine. A hot wind tossed the trees in the distance. "Miguel and I fought once because he went back to Spain to care for his mother for six weeks when she had the flu and Tony was out of the country. But until now I had forgotten the *real* reason we fought: He wouldn't take me with him. He said it would upset Maria. Upset his mother to have her *daughter-in-law* around! I was right to be angry about that; he should have put me first in that case. It would have given Maria and me a chance to make friends. He wasn't perfect, but in eight years of mourning I had forgotten that."

She smiled and squeezed my hand. "Now tell *Virgil* all that. I'm rooting for you two."

I didn't tell her *everything* I had learned, of course, how I had figured out that my romantic interlude with Virgil had scared me. Retreating to Spain right then had cemented my fear that if I moved on and left my love for Miguel behind I would risk losing someone all over again. Virgil is in a sometimes dangerous business. He carries a gun, for heaven's sake. If I came to care for him as much as I thought I might, it would be a risk for so many reasons.

I took a deep breath and let go of her hand. "Hey, to change the subject, I heard about problems between Minnie Urquhart and Crystal Rouse. What the heck is going on with all of that?"

She looked more troubled than I thought she would be. "I don't like Minnie; you know that. *Everyone* knows that. But I'm almost on Minnie's side in this. I don't trust Crystal. I've tried to give her the benefit of the doubt, but her simplistic magical positivity message is at the very least a nonanswer for those with real problems in their lives, and at worst a kind of blame-the-victim philosophy."

"I'm concerned about Emerald; she's been sucked into the woman's little group. But Em's a lot more sensible than people give her credit for. She'll figure it out for herself soon enough."

"I hope you're right."

Now that we had the problems of everyone in town sorted out, I went over my plans for the party celebrating one year at Wynter Castle, and she was enthusiastic. "Will people come, do you think?" I asked.

"Give them free food and they'll come. You could always feature arias by the world-famous soprano Roma Toscano."

We ended our conversation on a laugh and walked back to the kitchen, where she showed me a couple of improvements she'd made. I saw a young girl working at the Hobart commercial dishwasher, her hair up in a hairnet, her face shiny with steam.

"That's my new hire, Brianna," Gogi murmured, to the shushing of the hot water.

Ah, Minnie's other boarder. "How's she working out?"

Gogi shrugged. "All right, I guess. She shows up most of the time and does what she's told. It's only part-time. Dishwashers are hard to come by, even in Autumn Vale."

I laughed and told her I'd seen Isadore at the café, washing dishes for Mabel.

"I wish I'd thought of hiring her here," Gogi said. "She's sullen, but probably not as much as Brianna."

I said good-bye to Gogi, who retreated the way we had come, but I stopped to use the staff washroom before leaving. As I exited through the back door, I noticed Brianna off to one side of the parking lot with a guy; it wasn't one of Minnie's other boarders. He passed her something, a package. When she saw me watching, she hastily shoved it in her pants pocket, then hustled past me through the door into the kitchen. The guy slipped away, through a line of trees that bordered the back of the parking lot.

I was left with an uneasy feeling, but shrugged it off and drove back through town. On the off chance it was open, I stopped by the library. Sometimes when Hannah has free time she opens up the library just because: because she adores books, and because she wants people to have access to books, and because it's what she loves to do. The door was unlocked. I entered and found that Isadore was at one of the tables, reading while eating an apple. I put my finger to my mouth in a shushing gesture, and softly approached the desk, behind which Hannah sat in her mobility wheelchair, thumbing through a picture book.

"Do you have any books on the power of friendship and forgiveness?" I asked.

She looked up and grinned broadly. "Merry! I heard you were back, *finally*."

I circled the desk and bent over, hugging her small, frail body, which held so much courage, compassion, and radiant life. There was a chair next to her, as always, and I sat, glancing at the book she was reading. It was a manga version of *Much Ado About Nothing*. "Aha! Has Pish roped you in for the opera?"

"He wants me to play Beatrice," she admitted, a pink tinge coming to her cheeks. "I don't know if I can."

Hannah had a lilting soprano voice, but it was fine and soft, like silk thread, perfect for her part in the inaugural Autumn

Vale Community Players opera in the spring, when she was one of the three children in *Die Zauberflöte* along with Lizzie and Lizzie's bestie, Alcina. "Pish is hard to resist once he has his mind set on something," I said, with sympathy. "Poor Janice is beside herself. She wanted to do *The King and I*."

"Me, too! I would have loved to play one of the parts. My mom was ready to sew me the most gorgeous kimono."

"You could have played Lady Thiang," I said. "She's the chief wife of the king. So have you met Roma Toscano?"

Isadore snorted, like a dragon in her lair. Hannah giggled, her slim hand, tiny rings on her bony fingers, over her mouth.

"Isadore doesn't like her much, but I think she's interesting!" Hannah said. "I've never met anyone like her."

"Probably not." I, on the other hand, had met many divas in the modeling world, and they generally had two things in common: absolute self-absorption coupled with crippling insecurity. I suspected Roma was the same. I stared at Hannah, her big gray eyes luminous in the dim and dusty library, her tiny body adorned with a long dress that covered her withered legs. "I've missed you *so* much," I said, and teared up. How could I have stayed away so long? These people, this place, grounded me.

"We *all* missed you," Hannah said, placing her hand on my arm, her cool, light touch like a fairy breath. "You know, you only miss people if you love them."

Isadore looked up from her book, stopping midmunch, and nodded, her odd green eyes aglow. "Missed you, too," she whispered.

Chapter Four

BEFORE I LEFT town I girded my loins and entered the post office, one of the buildings squashed together across Abenaki from Binny's Bakery. There was an alleyway to the left of it, and a vacant storefront on the right. It all looked ready to tumble down around Minnie's ears. I entered, the buzzer sounding. Minnie was on the phone, whispering and looking flustered, her puffy cheeks ruddy. She muttered something hastily, and hung up.

The post office was long and narrow, with a wall of post office boxes on the right ranging from small at the top to larger ones along the bottom. Along the left wall were supplies to purchase: envelopes, brown paper for wrapping, bubble wrap, and tape. About halfway down was Minnie's counter, and behind her a door to what I assumed was a mail-sorting room.

Minnie stared at me. She's a woman in her sixties, broad-beamed and not tall, with messy gray curls. She wore a postal uniform, a pale blue golf shirt and navy pants, stretched across her heavy form. First I collected my mail from our post office box, and then I approached the counter.

As far as I knew no one actually *liked* Minnie. We all put up with her because what else could we do? I had long ago switched everything I could to email and paid most bills online. But . . . there are some things you can't avoid using the post office for.

"How are you today, Minnie?"

She nodded, picking moodily at an old scab on her hand. "Heard you were back."

"I am. And some of my luggage is being sent back to me by post. It should come soon, within the next few days, I hope: a suitcase and a box."

"Okay. Fancy schmancy, from Italy?"

"Actually, I was in Spain," I said.

"Same difference."

I gritted my teeth. "Minnie, I heard you had a run-in with Crystal Rouse. What's the deal with her?" I was anxious to know what was going on, since Emerald, and therefore Lizzie, were involved. Lizzie and Em had lived with me for a while, and I had become attached.

"That witch had better watch out. She's got my Brianna reeled in and full of some crap about wishing for something and getting it. What a load!"

For once we kind of agreed on something, though I wouldn't put it so baldly. "I'm going to look into it. I feel responsible for Lizzie, since she and her mother lived at the castle for a while."

"The castle," Minnie said darkly. "You open up your place to all kinds of weirdos, don't you?"

"What do you mean?"

"Nothing," she said as the phone rang. "Just . . . nothing. I gotta take this."

I left mystified and concerned.

*   *   *

OVER THE NEXT COUPLE OF DAYS I SLOWLY GOT BACK
in the swing of things, even though Roma Toscano, who
seemed to take up every waking minute of Pish's time, filled
my castle with chaos. I'm not sure how that was possible,
but her stuff was everywhere, and *she* was everywhere,
every time I turned around. Plucking at my sleeve, asking
questions to which I had no answers, asking me where Pish
was, what there was to eat, if I had any wine left, and where,
by the way, the key to the wine cellar was. I kept that hidden
because the woman could drink us all under the table, and
did, the second evening I was home, when I saw Pish sloshed
for the first time in years.

The only safe spot was my own bedroom, the beautiful
turret room I had taken back after our spring visitors left.
Even with Roma ensconced, it was good to be home. I slept
in late the first couple of days, spoke to my estate lawyer,
Andrew Silvio, on the phone—we were close to tying up
the inheritance, finally—and got reorganized. My schedule
got back to normal, somewhat, though I felt like something
was missing.

For one thing, Becket had not come back, and I was worried. Also, Virgil was being evasive. His schedule seemed
to be completely full, and Gogi told me, when I called her,
that he had taken on numerous volunteer coaching jobs after
I left. She implied it was to fill his time so he wouldn't feel
lonely, but I thought maybe he was avoiding me.

And for another, though I had seen almost everyone, I had
not connected with my best and oldest friend. I had stopped
by Jack and Shilo's home on my way out of town, the day I
started my apology tour, but no one was there. The place
looked abandoned, the grass unkempt and the flowers wilted.

I called and called but got no answer. Not to be defeated,
three days after getting home I finally tracked down Jack

and found out that he and Shilo had recently bought another house in an older section of town. Pish had been so taken up with Roma that I guess he didn't know, and no one else had told me. They probably thought given how close I was to Shilo, I'd already know.

The midcentury ranch he owned when they wed wasn't her, Jack explained. Shilo is fey and creative, wildly imaginative and special in so many ways; a tract home was too staid. Sniffing an opportunity, he had put in an offer on an empty home in the old section of town and bought it at a ridiculously low price. They had partially moved in so they could renovate while living in it, with the revitalized Turner Construction doing some of the heavy work. The ranch home had been rented out to tenants who hadn't moved to town yet.

He gave me the new address. Unwilling to beat around the bush with something so important to me, I asked him, was Shilo angry at me, as others were, for staying away so long and being so distant?

He was silent for a few moments. "I don't think so." He sighed heavily. "Something is bugging her, but she won't tell me what. I'm out of town today, but she's at the new house. Go see her, Merry. You're her oldest friend. Help me figure it out."

I hung up, feeling a cold chill race through me. When I first met Shilo she was a skinny, scared teenaged model living in a modeling agency apartment with several other skinny, scared teenage models. She didn't talk much about her family, and I didn't push her, because I observed that when you pushed Shilo about her past, she pulled away or cut you off. Over the years we had become best friends, but I still didn't know much about her past except that she was estranged from her family. I thought she came from the South; her accent had been fairly strong when I met her, though she eventually lost it.

Sometimes I wondered if I should have tried harder once we got close, but she was as fragile as a dandelion; one puff and she'd shatter, I always worried. Fragile, and yet so incredibly strong in other ways. She must be strong, I often thought, because there was clearly something in her life that had wounded her, and yet she kept going. If Jack thought something was wrong, maybe now was the time for me to push. I remembered what Doc had told me, that he saw her talking to a strange man, but she hurried away when she saw Doc walking toward her. It made me uneasy.

Minutes after hanging up, I was in the big Caddy, heading to the address Jack gave me. I drove into Autumn Vale, wound through the streets, and turned down the avenue that had a little parkette on the corner. I had discovered the tiny pocket park the previous fall; it was entered through a wrought iron gate over which the words *Come and Partake of Nature* were written in iron scrollwork. This was most definitely an old section of town. There was an elaborate Italianate house, a Colonial, and then there was the house Jack had described, with a Turner Construction truck parked outside.

I pulled up to the curb. When I got out I noticed two men were using a jack to support the roof of the rickety veranda of the Queen Anne–style mansion; the men must be Rusty Turner's new hires, I supposed. One was a stocky, balding African-American man whose fringe of hair had some gray in it, and the other was a biker-looking fellow probably in his late forties, with gray threaded through his long ponytail.

The black guy had noticed me as I got out of the car, and smiled as he cranked the jack and locked it into place. "Nice-lookin' old Caddy you got there," he called out.

"It is a sweet ride," I replied.

The other guy turned, eyed me with indifference, and returned to his job, checking to be sure the hydraulic jack was firmly in place. Around the side of the house parked on a weedy, cracked paved drive I spied Jezebel, Shilo's rickety old car, so I hoped I'd caught her at home.

I ambled toward the house. It was a fixer-upper, that was for sure. If Jack hadn't told me that the foundation was in perfect shape, I'd worry that it would tumble down around their ears. The house was a big clapboard Queen Anne, with a wraparound porch that extended on one corner to a round jutting section. The porch was in rough shape, with rotting boards and spindles, the railing split and falling off. But as I examined the home overall, I could see that the clapboard siding seemed in good repair, though it needed a paint job, and the windows were newer, double-hung, and installed sometime in the last twenty years or so.

I strolled through the old wrought iron gate and toward the house. "My name is Merry Wynter," I said. "You two must be Rusty Turner's new guys. Are you new in town?"

"I am," the balding guy said. "Dewayne Lester at your service. Just got to town two weeks ago. I'd shake your hand, but I'm kinda busy." He lifted a four-by-four into place on a second jack, under the beam, his maroon T-shirt stained with a V of sweat down the front and back, as his workmate silently pushed the jack into place and cranked.

The other guy didn't say a word.

Dewayne eyed him with an expression of distaste. "This here is Pete, and he's all business, no time to be polite."

"Rusty don't pay us to talk," Pete grunted, working the jack until it pushed the four-by-four right up against the veranda roof beam. He was stringy, ropy muscles winding around sinewy arms, exposed by a plain white tank top shoved into tight paint-stained jeans, while Dewayne was stocky, with the build of a prizefighter gone soft, broad of shoulder, though he had a potbelly hanging over the waist of his string-tied sweatpants.

"Rusty is a friend of mine," I said. "I'm sure he's lucky

to have you both, and I'm glad his business is starting up again. Is Shilo home? I see her car."

"Yup, she's there," Dewayne said, straightening from his work and pulling a cloth out of his pocket. He wiped beads of sweat off his forehead. "She's stripping wallpaper today."

I laughed. "I know something about that."

"Merry Wynter. I've heard your name around town. You're the lady who inherited the castle!" Dewayne said, jabbing the cloth in my direction.

"I am."

"Shilo talks about you sometimes."

"I've been away for a couple of months." I climbed the steps and peered anxiously up at the roof. "Is it safe to come through the front?"

"Sure is," Dewayne said. He hopped over and opened the door with a toothy grin.

I slipped through, then turned and thanked him. He seemed like a nice guy. I then stepped into the foyer. As my vision adjusted to the gloom, I saw what had attracted Shilo. The foyer was bright, though dusty, and the floors were all hardwood. The moldings and baseboards were original wood, too, and the staircase that climbed in stages from the foyer to a landing, 180-degree turn, then the rest of the way up, was all the same gorgeous dark-stained wood. A beautiful pendant light hung in the middle of the big, open space.

A movement startled me, but it was just Magic. "How are you, sweetie?" I cried, picking up Shilo's bunny and cuddling him against me. "Shilo!" I called out as I began to explore.

"Hello?" came back a ghostly echoing call.

I followed the sound, walking through a parlor to a dining room, and found Shilo, dressed in overalls and a tie-dye T-shirt, her long dark hair in braids. She was up on a tall ladder stripping hideous stained wallpaper. She turned and saw me, and a welcoming smile broadened, then faltered.

"Merry!" she gasped, and unsteadily climbed down the

ladder, spray bottle and putty knife in her hands. She dropped them and crossed the floor, gently took Magic out my hand, set him aside, then hugged me hard. "I've missed you so much," she said, her voice muffled against my shoulder.

I held her for a minute, rocking back and forth. Shilo and Pish were the friends who were there for me when Miguel was killed in a horrible accident on the highway to Vermont. They were there through his funeral, when his mother berated me, telling me it was all my fault that her son wanted to stay in New York, and so ended up dead on an American highway. And they were there when Maria demanded I give back his name; I was to no longer call myself Mrs. Paradiso.

And they were both there through my long years of mourning, the only two people who never told me to get a grip and get over it. Sure, I was there for them, too, through trauma and trial, but I think I leaned on them a lot more than they leaned on me. Whatever was wrong in Shilo's life, I needed to figure it out and help her.

She led me around the place with excitement, and I was so happy for what seemed to be a new phase of her life. Where once she had been a vagabond, a self-described gypsy girl, she was settled, with a wonderful husband—Jack McGill had fallen completely in love with Shilo almost immediately, and they had married within months of meeting each other—and now had a project to work on. So far I hadn't noticed the sadness people reported.

We finished in the kitchen, which was basically gutted. Shilo had a table and chairs set up, and a long, scarred table that held a microwave, coffeemaker, and hot plate. She made a pot of herbal tea and sat cross-legged on the fifties dinette chair, while Magic snuffled around the room, hopping from place to place, leaving dark pellets behind. I reminded myself to never walk barefoot in her home.

I apologized for having been gone so long and seeming so distant on the phone. "Shilo, you deserved better. You *all* deserved better. I was selfish, caught up in my own needs; I'm so sorry."

She hugged me again and patted my shoulder, her eyes shining with tears. "I know, Merry, I know. We—Pish and I—did understand, but it hurt."

"Am I forgiven?"

She nodded. Shilo and Pish both knew my past, and understood that when I left to go to Maria's deathbed, I hadn't much hope of a true reconciliation. "But Maria had changed a lot over the years," I said. "She regretted how she had ostracized me. I now get that part of that was Miguel's responsibility. He should have been willing to stand up to his mother for my sake; it would have made a difference. I felt guilty about feeling that way, but it was a legitimate response that I had been too afraid of losing Miguel to express."

"So what about Virgil?" she asked.

I sighed. "I need to apologize properly to him, and then I think we have some talking to do." I left it at that. "How about you and Jack? You doing okay?" I was looking for a way to open up a conversation about the people who were worried about her. So far she had been nothing but cheerful, but it did feel like there was something just under the surface.

And there it was: something *was* wrong. She didn't meet my eyes, as she tried to smile. Examining her face even as she looked away, I noticed that she was pale and seemed even thinner than usual. "Are you okay, Shilo? Is anything wrong?"

She shook her head. "No way. Jack adores me, Magic is alive, and I'm fine! What could be wrong?"

Despite her jaunty attitude, my bull-crap alarm was going off. She was agitated, though, and I didn't want to make our first get-together in months into an uncomfortable inquisition. I let it go for the moment. "So Rusty has his business going again! I'm so happy. And you and Jack hired them to do some of the work?"

"We've only been in here for a couple of weeks, and Rusty's guys only started working yesterday." She jumped up to move Magic away from an extension cord, then unplugged it and wound it up. "They're going to have the veranda restructured by next week, then they're going to paint the whole house for us. I can do a lot of the interior stuff, and Jack is handy, but there's so much to do we need help."

"The one guy, Dewayne, seems like a nice dude."

Her eyes sparkled, and she plunked down in the chair across from me. "You'll never guess who he is."

"Tell me!"

"He's Minnie Urquhart's new boyfriend! They met on a dating website, and he moved here to be closer to her!"

"Holy crap, really?"

"Jack and I came out to the castle to talk to Pish, but he wasn't there. When we told Roma about Dewayne and Pete helping us on the house, she said she'd seen Dewayne around. I guess he was at the post office talking to Minnie, and she figured out their relationship. As normal as he looked, Roma said, there must be something seriously wrong with him to go out with Minnie." Her smile faltered. "And then she said some rude things about Minnie's size and her name and her age. It was kind of awful."

"And Pish wasn't there to hear it. That's how she operates. She knows Pish doesn't like cattiness, so she never says stuff when he might hear and see her for what she really is."

"He may be catching on to her ways, though," she said with a sly smile. "I take it Pish hasn't told you about some of Roma's exploits around town? She's got half of Autumn Vale up in arms at her."

I felt the cold hand of dread clutch at my stomach. I've been trying desperately to get the folks of Autumn Vale on my side. Another rude guest at the castle was not going to help. "I've heard some stuff from Mabel Thorpe and Janice Grover—and Doc, too—but not from Pish. He's been too busy trying to make us bestest friends to tell me about her failings. What's gone on?"

"You've gotta hear this one. It involved Roma and *Minnie*, of all people."

"Battle royale, I'm assuming, given both of their characters."

Shilo had witnessed this incident firsthand. Pish had kept up my tea parties, trying to make nice with the natives, he called it, meaning the Autumn Vale townies, who were still split on whether I was a blessing or a blister on their fair town. A week or two ago Pish had one to which he invited Minnie, in the mistaken belief that it would endear her to me and my tenure at Wynter Castle.

"So Minnie was at the same table as Roma. Roma had just performed something in Italian or Spanish I didn't recognize, and returned to her table," Shilo said. "I was there to help serve, and I was close enough that I heard what Minnie said; she told Roma she had strangled cats that sounded prettier than her. Roma got all red in the face and said Minnie probably *sat* on the cat and killed it, rather than strangling it. Pish somehow managed to calm them both down, but as everyone was leaving, Minnie was in the great hall, bent over, huffing and puffing, tying her shoes, when Roma came down the big staircase with what everyone thought was a dagger raised above her head."

"Oh no! What happened?"

"Roma let out a high-C screech, said she'd slash her throat for insulting her singing, and fell on Minnie. It wasn't a knife, though, or a real dagger, just an antique letter opener; she has a whole collection of them, I guess."

"Was Minnie hurt?"

She shrugged. "Not that I saw. Roma slashed at her, but in a kind of wild way. I don't think she actually intended to do any damage, she was just going through the emotions."

I smiled at her verbal slip, but felt like it described Roma appropriately, always "going through the emotions."

Shilo frowned and thought for a moment. "I kind of feel like Roma has spent her whole career trying to behave like people expect from an opera diva, you know?"

"I would have kicked her out, if I'd been there. I've worked too hard on the people of Autumn Vale to have Roma destroy it all. I know Minnie doesn't like me, but the last thing I need is for her to have more fuel for gossip about me and mine."

"Don't blame Pish," Shilo said softly. "He's trying to help."

Bringing Roma to Wynter Castle was in no way helpful to *me*, but I couldn't say that. I owed Pish so much in my life that he could ask anything of me, and I'd do it. I took a deep breath. I would try again to get along with Roma. I'd try very, *very* hard, for Pish's sake. "Let's talk about *you*," I said to my best girlfriend. I searched her dark eyes and saw a misty cloud of some unexpressed pain. How to press her without upsetting her? "You tell me you're happy, and I can see how you love this house, but what about everything else?" I wondered if I ought to mention what Doc had seen, but it was our first visit, and I didn't want to rock the boat. I'd wait to see if she brought up the stranger she was talking to.

She took my hand and said, "Merry, please . . . everything is good. There is not a thing any of you could possibly do to make me happier."

I wasn't entirely satisfied with that answer, but an hour later, after talking over all her plans for the house, I left, with a promise to talk in a couple of days.

Chapter Five

❈ ❈ ❈

I WAS SEETHING about the whole Roma/Minnie thing by the time I got home, but fortunately Pish was closeted in the library with Roma trying to get something on tape, so I had time to calm down. During dinner I edged the conversation toward the confrontation between Roma and Minnie. Pish gave me a look, so I stopped. As much as I was going to try to get along with her, we would have to have a serious chat about his protégé.

Tony texted me that afternoon in response to my question about my luggage, that he had shipped it with a tracking number, as he'd said he would. On his end the tracking showed that it was in Autumn Vale. It was quite possible that Minnie was messing with me; it wouldn't be the first time. It was Tuesday; the post office closed early Monday, Tuesday, and Wednesday. I glanced at the clock, but I still had time, so just before closing I called and asked Minnie if my luggage had arrived.

"No," she said abruptly.

"My brother-in-law said that the tracking app shows that it *has* arrived in Autumn Vale."

"Well, it hasn't. You saying I'm lying? Wanna make something of it?"

I was taken aback; I had not been rude, just forthright. I heard a murmur in the background. Who was she talking to in the post office? "Minnie, it has to be there. Who should I believe, you or the U.S. postal service app?"

"Hey, don't you threaten me!" she yelled.

"Threaten? I didn't—"

"That's enough outta you, Merry Wynter; I don't have to listen to your bull. Come in tomorrow and see for yourself!" She hung up.

I stomped around and pushed a vacuum cleaner upstairs for a while, then went out and called Becket, to no avail. Later I called Gogi to vent. She had her own campaign going against Minnie, and was sympathetic. I cheered up when we made plans to go shopping in Rochester the next day. I wanted to go to Lane Bryant, so we decided on the Mall at Greece Ridge in Greece, a suburb of Rochester, because they also have a Charlotte Russe, which has gorgeous plus-size clothes, and an Ashley Stewart, a plus-size store. My sweet Shilo calls me "plush-size"; leave it to her to find some cute way to put it. Gogi wanted to hit Christopher & Banks, which was having a BOGO sale. She was looking for work-appropriate dresses, but she doesn't do fuddy-duddy sixty-plus women's wear. Of course, we'd also stop at Barnes & Noble—I planned to buy new bestsellers for the library—and Sears.

THE NEXT MORNING I DRANK MY COFFEE WHILE SEND-ing texts to some New York friends to fill them in on my return from Spain, then got myself going. It was Wednesday . . . Hump Day for the five-day-a-week workers of the world. I grabbed my purse and headed through the dark great hall toward the big double oak doors, but one creaked open as I approached. Roma entered, swiftly and quietly, turning and stealthily closing it. Odd. Roma was a sleep-in-late kind of woman.

"What are you doing up and about at such an early hour?" I asked.

She jumped and whirled, leaning back against the door. "Uh, I was out walking," she said, nerves fraying her voice. "Trying to . . . to expand my lungs, you know, to get more air in them. We're doing another session this morning."

"Okay."

She seemed alarmed and was breathing fast, almost panting.

"Were you jogging? You seem out of breath."

"I was just walking fast around the field, by the woods. Gathering solace from nature!" She brushed past me and clattered up the stairs, disappearing along the gloomy gallery to her room, her high-heeled boots making clomping sounds.

I left the castle, shaking my head in perplexity, but paused by my car and listened to the quietude: crickets, a couple of crows cawing, and not much else. Except for an odd *tick-tick-tick* sound. I glanced around. Some new insect? Weird.

It was humid, so there was a heavy mist over everything, fog clinging in drifting layers to the wood's edge. I contemplated my property, thinking back to when I first arrived. I often saw a flash of orange, but didn't know for a time that it was probably my late uncle's cat, Becket, who had disappeared after Melvyn died. Was he doing the same now, creeping close and watching the castle? I strolled to the edge of the parking area and peered through the mist toward the woods. Was that a hint of orange in the distance? "Becket!" I called, but if it *was* him, he disappeared. It hurt to think he felt I'd abandoned him. I would take some treats into the woods and find him.

Gogi awaited me at the front door of Golden Acres. I watched her buckle the seat belt, then looked at my watch as I pulled away from the curb. "If you don't mind, I'd like to stop at the post office and see if my luggage has arrived yet," I said. "That episode on the phone with Minnie has left me uneasy. I don't know why. *Despite* her being a jerk, I'd still like to apologize for Roma's behavior."

"Right, the operatic scene at the tea party," Gogi said, glancing over at me. "I wasn't there but heard all about it."

I eased around the corner onto Abenaki as I told her my theory about Roma trying desperately to live up to the legendary divas of opera and their infamously touchy temperaments. "It's like she goes out of her way to stage scenes."

"On the other hand, she could just be spoiled rotten."

I parked across from the post office. As I got out of the car I waved to Binny, who was in her bakery window changing out the display. She waved and went back to work, trading back-to-school décor for fallish fake autumn leaves and gourds. Down the street, a couple of townies entered the Vale Variety and Lunch; morning coffee there is a tradition for many folks and more reliable than the newspaper for local gossip.

I crossed the quiet street. Just one car was parked in front of mine, and there was no traffic but a tractor that slowly chugged through town. A male jogger in black bike shorts and a T-shirt disappeared around a corner. As I approached the tiny post office, I was puzzled; Minnie was never late to work, and yet the post office was dark. I rattled the door. Locked. I cupped my hands and peered in. Nothing. There was a faint glimmer of light through the darkness—a room in back?

Gogi joined me. "Minnie hasn't opened yet? That's unusual."

"But it looks like she's there. Look . . . you can see a light at the back. Maybe something delayed her from opening."

"Let's go around and talk to her. You can at least ask about your luggage."

"Okay," I said reluctantly. I didn't want to disturb Minnie in the middle of work, but I did want to make my apology while I still felt apologetic.

Gogi led the way down the alley between the post office and another vacant, boarded-up storefront, and around to the back, which was plain brick with an unpainted steel door and no windows. There was a parking lane that ran behind the row of shops, just as there was for the shops across the street.

"There's her car," she said, pointing to a run-down gold-hued Buick LeSabre with a peeling vinyl roof. The lone vehicle parked there, it was low to the ground, like the suspension had been beaten up and had no will to live, or lift.

I approached the door and knocked. "Minnie, you there?"

The near silence was deafening; even the crickets had stopped. I ignored a tingle of uneasiness as I tried the handle of the door and pushed. It opened; the lights were on in the room beyond the door, so I stepped through to a smallish space lined with pigeonholes and metal shelves loaded with packages and envelopes. Several mailbags were on the floor, newly arrived, I assumed.

"Is she there?" Gogi asked.

I didn't answer as I tiptoed in, with her close behind me. Something was off; my scalp prickled. There was a terrible odor in the air, the smell tangible even to my tastebuds, as if I were holding a hairpin in my mouth. Gogi gagged and made a retching sound. I turned and saw what she saw.

Minnie Urquhart's large body was partially stuffed in a big canvas postal sack, blood dripping from a dagger stuck right through her blue golf shirt. I moaned, covering my mouth, my stomach twisting, but in those few seconds, stunned and revolted and afraid as I was, I still recognized the weapon. *Not* a dagger; it was a decorative letter opener that had been jammed into her side.

Gogi cried out and I swore, both at the same time—a delayed response of horror warring with disbelief. Gogi, though, with more presence of mind than I, pushed past me and pulled the canvas sack aside until she found Minnie's neck. She touched her carotid artery, feeling for a pulse, while I stifled the urge to vomit or run.

Gogi turned and looked at me, shaking her head. "She's dead."

"Are you sure?"

She moved out of the way and I saw Minnie's eyes, wide and staring, pupils dilated. Her double chins were flaccid and sagging, her mouth gaping open, some kind of white powder coating the sprouting hairs on her chin. Blood was everywhere; she was soaked in it. There was no expression on her familiar face. Tears welled in my eyes, but Gogi grabbed my forearms and backed me out.

"Merry, she's been murdered," she said, her voice guttural and trembling. "We need to get out of here, in case the murderer is still inside, and call Virgil!"

She pushed me out and we stood in the back alley, shivering even on a warm, humid September day. "Go get your phone and call Virgil." I took a deep breath. "I'll stay here and make sure no one goes in . . . or out."

She paused, shook her head. "No, Merry, what if—"

"No one would stick around after . . . after doing that," I said, my voice getting steadier now that I couldn't see poor Minnie.

"You're right. I'm going to get my cell phone, but I am going to call *while* I'm walking back to you."

Gogi walked swiftly along the back of the post office and disappeared around the side. I had become less squeamish in the last year, but still, my stomach churned as I stepped back through the door. I had to look, I just had to! Poor Minnie. Poor, *poor* woman. I may not have liked her, but she was an Autumn Vale citizen and cared about our town.

I took a deep trembling breath and examined the scene. On closer look, Minnie wasn't actually stuffed in the mailbag; that would have been impossible. She was slumped on the floor, and now that I was looking for them, I saw spatters of blood across the floor and on the other canvas mail sacks that were lined up for processing. She was in a heap, one arm was in a mailbag, and there was another empty mailbag partially pulled over her. Her uniform was a pale bluish golf shirt that blended with the stained dull gray of the canvas postal bag. *Everything* had blood on it; she must have been stabbed more than once, judging by the multiple bloody spots on her body. Her hands, too . . . There were cuts and bruises on the one palm that I could see. I held back the violent urge to throw up, my stomach roiling at the smell and the blood. Poor woman, to have suffered such horror in her last minutes on Earth. Who would do such an awful thing? Tears wet my eyes.

There was blood soaking through the canvas bag that Minnie was partially in, her right arm and shoulder concealed. The letter opener was jammed into her right side, under her breast and through her uniform shirt, with a big patch of blood soaking the shirt around it. It had looked like a dagger at first because it had a brass hilt and steel blade, like a tiny version of a Musketeer sword from the movies, with a miniaturized knuckle guard that protected the hand when the sword was held, and a small silk tassel, now soaked in blood.

I heard the distant wail of a siren and took one last long look, then stepped out the back door, standing in front of it, swaying in revulsion and fear, trying to assemble my face in some kind of stoic expression. My mind raced. Roma. Did she? Didn't she? *Could* she have?

Impossible. Wynter Castle was a long way from the scene.

Roma didn't own a car and perhaps didn't even drive; many New Yorkers don't. Minnie hadn't been dead that long, I didn't think, judging by the smell, the sight and her habits. By my estimate it could have been a half hour, maybe more, given what I knew about her arrival, usually about ten minutes before she was to open, and the fact that she hadn't turned on the lights or opened the actual post office.

She must have been killed shortly after she arrived, but before she started opening up for the day's business. The killer must have been someone who knew her schedule, though that pretty much covered the whole town. For all her many faults, she was as regular as clockwork when it came to opening and closing. I hadn't thought to see if I could tell if the day's fresh mail had been delivered by truck yet. Maybe the delivery guy had seen her and could provide a time frame.

The siren was closer; did I have time for one more look inside to see if I could tell if there was fresh mail? Gogi, her face pale as bleached linen, came around the corner, cell phone in hand, as a sheriff's department car, driven by Virgil, screamed down the back lane by the post office. He jumped out, drew his gun, and ran to his mother first. "You okay?" he asked, hand on her shoulder. She nodded. He looked over at me, his expression unreadable. "Merry?"

I nodded. Another car approached, and he directed Deputy Urquhart to go around the front and make sure no one exited the building that way. I was impressed; from Gogi's phone call he must already know Minnie, Deputy Urquhart's aunt, was dead, and didn't especially want the nephew to be one of the investigators on the scene. Nothing got past Virgil, and everything he did had a reason. He then told the other deputy, a young woman, to back him up, and they went in together to establish that she was indeed dead. They came out two minutes later; he was grim-faced, but confirmed that there was no one else in the building.

He radioed in, then guided us away from the action as the late summer heat began building, shimmering in the air. He left for a moment, directing his deputies on a search of the business district, such as it is, of Autumn Vale. They were to look for anyone who was not where they should be, and any stranger or unknown vehicle.

He came back to us, his gaze softening as he saw his mother's white, frightened face. Gogi, as owner and operator of a senior's home that also provided hospice care, had seen more than her fair share of death. But this was murder, and it was different. He gave her a brief side hug and touched my shoulder, while I drank in the comfort of a strong and capable man. I'm no shrinking violet; I can take care of myself. But Virgil is as solid as they come—big, square-jawed, muscular, and tough without surrendering his humanity—and in an emergency it was nice to have him near.

"I have to make a call," he said. "This murder happened in a post office, so I have to call the United States Postal Inspection Service."

"Who are they?" I asked.

"You could say they are the police arm of the post office. I can't do anything more than secure the scene."

Frustrating for him. Virgil is a doer, not a waiter.

"Why don't you two go over to Binny's, or somewhere else close? But don't discuss this with anyone!"

"Can we go to the Vale for coffee?" I asked.

He shook his head. "The morning crowd has already gathered. You won't survive unscathed with that pack of gossip hounds."

He was right, of course. We could sit in my car, but folks passing by would be sure to stop and try to get us to talk about what was going on.

"What should we say to Binny and Patricia?" I asked. "It's obvious *something* has happened."

"Just say . . ." He pondered that for a second, his brown

eyes thoughtful. "You found Minnie dead, but that you can't say anything else because it's post office business now, and you have to talk to them first."

Gogi nodded and I agreed. Of all people, Binny was safest to sit with. She is relatively incurious when it comes to anything other than food and money.

We did exactly as he said. The bakery was a safe haven, and I never got tired of examining her collection of teapots, begun when her mother was still in town, Binny once told me. They line the walls of the front of the shop, impeccably clean, as is everything in her bakeshop. The front of the store is relatively small, with curved old-style glass cases filled with treats, and stacks of Binny's Bakery white pastry boxes behind the counter ready to be filled with her excellent bakery goodies.

Binny was alone. She brought us out a couple of folding chairs, and we sat along the wall under one shelf of teapots while she made a pot of herbal tea.

I remembered something I noticed, though it hadn't made an impact until this moment. "Was Minnie in here this morning before she went to work?" Gogi sent me a look, but we were all thinking of Minnie, and we couldn't *not* talk about her.

"She stops in *every* morning at about ten to eight," Binny said. "Or . . . *stopped*, I guess, not *stops*. Jeez, that's so sad. She'd buy a dozen assorted pastries, '*to share,*' she always said, but I don't think she actually shared them."

I nodded. I had noticed one of Binny's bakery boxes on the counter by one of the shelves. It was spattered with blood, like everything else. "What time does the mail truck get there?"

"He's always there by eight twenty or so. Sometimes he goes to the Vale and picks up a coffee to go, but this morning he was a little late; I noticed because he drove out of town fairly quickly without stopping."

Hmm . . . interesting. The police would look into that, I was sure. "Did Minnie say anything? How did she seem?"

Binny looked up from her task; she was building more bakery boxes, standing at the pass-through to talk as we sipped our tea. "She was pretty normal, I guess," she said. "She complained about the heat, and said her feet were aching already. Did she have a heart attack or something?"

I shook my head and exchanged a glance with Gogi. "I don't want to speculate."

"It's weird; I can't believe she's gone. She was always my third customer of the day."

"Third?" I said.

She nodded. "Isadore comes in first thing. I save her day-old stuff, and she buys what she likes. Lately, now that she's making a little money at the Vale, she's been buying everything. She's so skinny! I don't know what she does with it all. The second is Helen Johnson, *most* mornings. She's always got some church group meeting that she's buying treats for. I don't think she knows Isadore comes in before her and buys all the day-olds."

"They're kind of friends, aren't they?" I asked.

"I'm not sure. I think they were, but not lately. Helen is pushy, and Isadore is kind of a recluse."

Kind of was an understatement.

"Bad mixture," Gogi said.

"Pish keeps trying to befriend Isadore, but he's going about it all wrong," I said. "I think she's probably closer to Hannah than anyone, but Hannah doesn't push, she . . . *pulls* with her kindness."

Zeke and Gordy charged into the bakery all agog, wanting to know what the cops were doing at the post office. I followed the rules Virgil had set out, and simply said Minnie had died.

Gordy looked alarmed. "Did they . . . did *they* get her?"

Gogi gently said, "Who are 'they,' Gordy?"

He glanced around and bent closer, his shoulders hunching, and whispered, "NWO forces!"

Zeke sighed and looked impatient, rolling his eyes.

"What is NWO?" Gogi asked, head to one side, her gaze intent.

"The New World Order! She's a government worker. Maybe it's beginning." He shuddered slightly, then poked his head back out the door, looking up at the sky. "Have you seen any government troops?" he asked, looking back to us. "Was there a helicopter, a black one, and guys wearing helmets?"

"No, not at all," Gogi said.

This was a part of Gordy's descent into conspiracy theory belief. For the most part he went about his life like any small-town fellow. However, get him on the topic of his all-encompassing theory that the world was being taken over by some strange amalgam of government forces, illuminati, black ops, and aliens, and he becomes ever so slightly unhinged. Zeke was silent. Gordy's beliefs seem to be the only source of tension between the two friends.

"There were no government troops and no helicopters, Gordy. There *is* no conspiracy. What are you boys up to today?" I asked, to deflect the conversation away from Minnie's demise.

"Gordy's driving me to work in Ridley Ridge," Zeke said.

"Then I'm going to work at my uncle's."

I had hired them to look after the grass and landscaping when I first arrived, before they were both gainfully employed. "Would you two have time to come out and look after the grass at Wynter Castle?"

Zeke brightened. "Sure would, as long as we can do it on our days off! Gordy, you up for it?"

Gordy, his expression clear now that he had been deflected away from his fretful bugaboo, agreed that he could borrow his uncle's farm equipment.

"Say, Binny, we've got a problem," Zeke said, turning to

the baker. He shuffled and sighed, his Adam's apple moving up and down his throat. "We got this guy staying with us. He, uh, came to our door last night and we don't know what to do."

"Yeah, we don't know what to do," Gordy echoed, swiping his wispy hair off his forehead.

"About what?" Binny asked. "Who is he?"

The two exchanged glances. "His name is Karl. We have to be gone all day, but he's not out of the place yet, and we don't . . ." Zeke sighed and shifted on his feet, rolling his shoulders. He seemed excessively twitchy. "We don't want to give him a key to the apartment to lock up when he leaves."

Karl . . . I had heard that name lately. Where? When?

"Why is he staying with you? Who is this guy?"

"He's actually, well . . ." Zeke's Adam's apple goggled. "He's one of Minnie's boarders. He came over last night and asked if he could crash on our couch."

Bingo. *That's* where I had heard the name before! Janice had filled me in on Minnie's boarders.

"We said okay," Gordy added unnecessarily.

I filed that info, since that put one of her boarders pretty close to the scene of the action. "Why did he want to stay at your place if he's boarding with Minnie?"

Zeke's gaze shifted to me. "He had a humongous fight with her last night and took off."

Chapter Six

✖ ✖ ✖

"WHAT DID THEY fight about?" I blurted out.

Gogi gave me a quelling look, but I had to ask.

"Gordy knows Karl from meeting him a couple of weeks ago at the pool hall in Ridley Ridge. They played a few games, then Gordy gave him a lift back to Autumn Vale. I guess they hung out at our place playing video games." Zeke didn't look happy about that, and cast his friend a censorious look. "So he knew where we lived. We were watching a *Dr. Who* marathon and he banged on our door. I guess him and Minnie fought, but he didn't say what over. He said the other two didn't help much; I don't know what that means. When he stormed out he came to our door. What were we gonna do?"

Tell him to take a hike, I thought. But then I have done much the same thing in the past—caved in to an unwanted visitor—so who was I to judge?

"Did Miss Urquhart have a heart attack or something?" Gordy asked.

Binny caught my panicked look. "Don't worry about it, guys. I agree: don't give him a key."

We hadn't told Binny it was murder, but she's a smart cookie when she's paying attention.

"So what should we do, Binny?" Gordy asked plaintively. "About Karl, I mean?"

Binny's father owned the building the bakery was in. They rent out the two two-bedroom apartments upstairs, tenanted by Zeke and Gordy in one, and Patricia and Juniper—a strange and silent girl who had landed in Autumn Vale after a series of odd events—in the other. Though Binny had originally designed the ladies' apartment for herself, she had moved back into her dad's home after his rough patch. "I'll take care of it," Binny said. "Tell him to come see me when he's leaving, and I'll lock up."

"You don't seem to trust him, fellas," I said. "What's up?"

The two shrugged. I found that revealing, and was itching to tell Virgil about their guest who had had a beef with Minnie just last night. Maybe this would be one murder that would solve itself.

"If you don't want him there, tell the guy that your landlady told you it was against your rental agreement to have long-term guests," Binny said. "In fact, I'm telling you now: he can stay one more night, but then has to find someplace else, okay?"

Gordy looked relieved, but Zeke, though he nodded, still seemed worried about something. Binny gave them a bag full of bakery goodies, then they left, first back upstairs to tell Karl what to do, and then off to work.

Though Binny and Gogi kept talking, I had trouble paying attention. My mind was at the castle. Despite the potential for an easy solution, the fact remained: Roma had attacked Minnie at the castle with one of her decorative letter openers. If the weapon was a part of that collection, it was hard to imagine how some boarder of Minnie's had gotten it out of the castle and used it on her.

I took Gogi aside, and we whispered about Karl. She agreed that it was important information. She stepped outside and called Virgil. Shortly after that, Virgil's female deputy approached the building and went up the stairs through the door to the right of the bakery to question both Karl and, presumably, Patricia. Juniper had left hours ago, Binny said, before dawn, since she had clients for her Jumpin' Juniper Superclean service.

Binny disappeared into the work area of the bakery for a while, and came back with coffee made in a French press and a plate of madeleines. Several people had come into the bakery meanwhile, and I popped up to serve them. Having worked on and off in Binny's shop I knew where everything was and how to work her computerized cash system. People were curious about the scene. Apparently there was a crowd gathering nearby, and by now everyone in town knew that Minnie was dead. We steadfastly refused to answer questions, saying it was a police matter. Folks eyed Gogi when I said that—as mother of the sheriff and a prominent businesswoman, she was known to everyone—but for the most part didn't press. I had no doubt they would find out all about it at the Vale Variety and Lunch.

There was a lull; Binny came out and we had our breakfast. I wasn't sure if I could eat, after what I had seen. But Gogi and Binny are good company, and the madeleines were delightful: gorgeous, golden brown, perfect shell imprint and lemony, with just the right buttery texture, like tiny sponge cakes. Dipped in French press coffee . . . *délices sacrés*. I could imagine I was in a patisserie on the Rue Bonaparte in Paris. I often told Binny that her considerable talents were wasted on the people of Autumn Vale, who mostly wanted a good bran muffin and a dozen chocolate chip cookies, (not that there's anything wrong with that— both favorites of mine, too) but she labored on, presumably converting unbelievers to French, Viennese, and Italian pastries one palate at a time.

During one of the lulls, while Binny went to the back and starting cleaning up from her morning baking, Gogi asked me, "So what are you going to do about Roma?"

Maybe turn her into the feds, I thought but did not say. I still wasn't sure how to handle the information I had: that the weapon used to kill Minnie was very likely a decorative letter opener from my guest's collection. "Helping Roma is important to Pish. I feel like I should ride this out, let him do what he needs to do for her."

Patricia came through from the back, tying a white apron on over her chambray shirtdress. Her expression was sober as she approached the pass-through. "What a shock!" she said, leaning on it and watching out the front window. "The police were at my door; that's why I'm late. Minnie Urquhart is dead? How? Why?"

"We can't talk about it," Gogi said, with a glance to me.

She nodded. "The deputy told me that they were bringing in the feds. I guess whatever happened, happened in the post office?" She eyed us both.

I nodded. "Yes, it did, and that's all we can say. We found her."

"Oh, honey, I'm so sorry!" she said. "Poor kid . . . to come back to *this*."

"How is it going, living upstairs with Juniper?" I asked.

She chuckled, a warm comfortable sound. "That girl is a scamp!"

Juniper? A scamp? I was taken aback. As much as I truly did like her, the sullen and silent Juniper I knew was not so much mischievous as malevolent. "I'm glad you're getting along."

"I'm teaching her how to bake and cook. The child knows *nothing*. Last evening she made us homemade pizza; it was so good! We gave some to the boys, had a little pizza party. I think Gordy's got a thing for Juniper, but she's not interested in him. Poor fella. He's so caught up in his own little world that he's missing so much."

That was one way of looking at Gordy's kooky conspiracy theory obsession. From dealing with him I had come to the conclusion that if all conspiracy theory nuts were like him, they combined suspicion of unnamed otherworld and international "powers" with a dreadful naïveté when it came to people in their own lives. I was more than a little worried about Karl, but Binny had said he had to leave, so I hoped he would. Or be arrested.

"I guess they've got a visitor who stayed overnight?"

"Yeah," Patricia said, with a slight frown. She started collecting dribs and drabs to one tray using long tongs, and took empty trays to the back. She returned to the counter. "I heard a commotion last evening and peeked out; it was one of those kids who board at Minnie's place. I guess, from what I heard, he had a fight with Minnie and stormed out."

"Did he say what it was over?" I asked, ignoring Gogi's side glance.

Patricia was opening her mouth to speak again, but we were all stopped by the sight out the window; it was like a parade down main street. There was a procession of large black cars, and trailing them at the end was a cube van. Along the side was emblazoned *Federal Bureau of Investigation—Mobile Command Center.*

SHORTLY AFTER THAT, VIRGIL APPROACHED THE BAK-ery with a shorter man who wore a dark suit and a serious demeanor. Virgil beckoned us to come out. The day was turning hot, but while I felt beads of perspiration, the dark-suited, sunglass-wearing man seemed completely impervious to heat.

"Gogi Grace, Merry Wynter, this is Agent Esposito,"

Virgil said, his voice tight with tension. "He'll be the lead on this investigation."

"We're setting up a space a few doors down, ladies, if you don't mind joining us and telling us what you found this morning," he said, with no inflection. He turned back to Virgil. "That's all for now, Sheriff. If we need you, we'll let you know."

And that was how the guy dismissed local law enforcement? Esposito likely thought he had gleaned all he could from the sheriff. I could tell by the set of Virgil's shoulders as he walked away that he was crazy angry at being treated like a gofer, but I also knew it would not affect his professionalism one iota.

Agent Esposito led us three doors down, stopping at one of the vacant office spaces that dotted the streetfront. Gogi pointed out Emerald's new shop, Emerald Illusions, just two doors away. The mobile command unit was presumably parked somewhere behind the post office, which was completely cordoned off from the street, I noticed as I glanced over my shoulder. I also saw blue-shirted strangers knocking on doors and searching garbage cans all along Abenaki. This would surely send the local gossipmongers into a frenzy.

Esposito led us inside. They had commandeered three tables from somewhere, and several fellows in navy golf shirts emblazoned across the back with *FBI* in yellow letters were working on the wiring and phone lines, and installing other electronic equipment. A young woman was setting up a printer on a table along the back wall. It was an empty storefront, but because the big windows were covered in brown paper, there was a yellowish glow to the light. He guided us to a couple of chairs by a desk that was halfway back.

"Sorry about the spartan conditions, ladies. We're getting set up. The mobile command unit doesn't have room to conduct interviews."

"That's perfectly all right," Gogi said graciously. She set

her purse down on the floor and took a seat across the table from Esposito, as composed as she always was. I sat in the rickety chair next to her, praying it would hold up.

"I'm surprised at the level of setup you're going through," I said, glancing around at the bustle of activity. "This may very well be a simple domestic case."

"You mean because of the information Sheriff Grace's mother supplied to him?"

"Sure. Just because Minnie was murdered in the post office doesn't automatically make it an FBI matter, does it?"

"Regardless, it *is* still a U.S. Postal Service matter, and they've called us in to investigate. Now let's get down to it so you ladies can go about your day."

I eyed him with surprise. Did he think we were going to trot off shopping after finding an acquaintance brutally slain? Attend a tea party? Have a manicure?

What followed was standard questioning for the most part. Each of us were separately interviewed, Gogi first, while it was taped and video recorded using equipment the golf-shirted crew had set up. Esposito sent her away with a caution to not talk about the crime, and I was taken through my whole day from the moment I left home, which entailed a lot of explaining. Agent Esposito was highly entertained by my castle and tortured family history.

I confirmed, along the way, what we had learned of Karl the boarder and his fight with Minnie the night before. But then came the sticky question I had been hoping to avoid.

"Did you notice the weapon used to kill Urquhart?"

"At first I thought it was a dagger."

"But then?"

I shifted in the uncomfortable chair and sighed. There was no way to avoid this. "Then I realized that it was more likely a decorative letter opener, or something like that."

Esposito nodded. "Did you recognize it specifically? Had you seen it before?"

"Not at all. I've never seen it before in my life."

"You have a houseguest currently staying at the castle?"

I nodded. "Roma Toscano. She's an opera singer who my friend Pish invited to stay."

"She had a run-in with Minnie Urquhart two weeks ago."

He was well-informed, I had to give him that. The chair creaked as I shifted. "I heard about it, but I wasn't here. I was visiting family in Spain. If you want information you'll have to ask those present."

He nodded, a thoughtful look in his gray-green eyes. "She was apparently brandishing a letter opener, one of her collection, just like the one in Ms. Urquhart's body right now."

"*Just like it?* How do you know that?" I burst out, then shut my mouth.

"*Is* the letter opener part of that collection?"

It was a fishing expedition and nothing more, cobbled together from some vague hints of the attack and Roma's collection. But from whom? "You'll have to ask Roma, because I have no idea."

"We have an agent on his way out there this minute, and I'll follow momentarily."

Darn. I wished I had thought of phoning Pish, but I hadn't.

"Now, what about you, Ms. Wynter? You interest me. You seem to have discovered a lot of bodies since moving to Autumn Vale . . ." He checked a paper at his elbow. ". . . just over a year ago."

"That's not pertinent to this," I said sharply.

"You and Ms. Urquhart had an acrimonious relationship."

"It wasn't personal. I didn't know a thing about her private life, but she took a disliking to me right away, for some reason—I'm not the only one in town she was like that with, mind you—and insisted on gossiping about me."

"But you had a fight with her on the phone yesterday, before the post office closed."

"How do you . . . ? Never mind." I recalled my sense that there was someone in the post office that she was playing it up for. Was that his source? I told him about that. "She never stopped trying to turn people against me."

"Must have been annoying."

"It was nothing to kill anyone over."

"What do you know about Mrs. Grace's campaign to run Ms. Urquhart out of town?"

"Good grief, it's nothing like that." I eyed him with distaste. "You have a Machiavellian idea of small-town relationships. There were some questions about Minnie's competency and, quite frankly, her honesty and work ethic. She may always have been to work on time, but some of us thought she might be sneaking a peek into people's mail or even appropriating some of it. That's a federal crime."

After a couple more questions he let me go and I joined Gogi, who was at the Vale. One thing this town needed, I thought, was another café, or tearoom, or *something*. An alternative to the Vale Variety and Lunch, where a two-course meal was a grilled cheese sandwich and tomato soup. Not that there's anything wrong with that; sometimes you just *want* a grilled cheese sandwich and tomato soup. But sometimes you want a cappuccino and biscotti, or a cup of Earl Grey and a cucumber sandwich.

It was packed, and I knew several of the patrons. Bad combo when you've just found the murdered body of a local hero/villain, depending on where your sympathies lay. Though I had yet to meet anyone who considered her a hero.

"Did you *really* find the body?" Helen Johnson, two tables over, asked, whispering it loudly across the table between us, which was occupied by a farmer I didn't recognize.

"Yes, we did," I said, including Gogi, across the table from me, in my gaze.

Isadore, who was clearing tables, thumped her bus pan down on an empty table and cast a look around. Helen eyed her nervously and shut up. I confess I did wonder what had happened between the former friends.

"Why don't we get out of here?" Gogi whispered, leaning across the table. "I should get back to Golden Acres, make sure my folks aren't upset by the news. We'll plan our shopping trip for another day, next week maybe."

Out on the sidewalk I heaved a sigh of relief, even as I eyed the post office with trepidation. "I wonder if Hannah knows yet," I said.

"Maybe. Probably not, though, unless someone went in to the library and told her."

I made a sudden decision. "I'm going to go tell her myself, or if she's already heard, make sure she's okay."

"Hannah is tougher than you seem to think. That girl has had dozens of operations, hundreds of treatments and medications. She's resilient."

"But tenderhearted," I said. "I won't rest unless I do this."

Gogi touched my shoulder, then pulled me into a hug. "You're a good woman, Merry Wynter."

"Do you want a ride?"

Gogi shook her head. "I think I'll walk. I need some peace before I enter the fray."

We walked together as far as the library, then she walked on alone. I entered the library, the cool, calm oasis that Hannah had created in the weird little burg that was Autumn Vale.

"Merry, my good friend!" she called out, looking up from a catalog on her desk. "I'm so sorry. I heard what happened, and that you found her."

And in that moment I knew that I had come to the library not for Hannah's comfort, but for my own, and my eyes watered. I needed to see her sweet face and know there was so much goodness in the world that countered the evil that men do. "Hannah, it was so awful," I said, circling the desk, hugging her frail little body to me, and sitting in the visitor's chair next to her wheelchair. "It was terrible. I think it's worse because I didn't like her, and now I feel guilty about that."

"You need a good cup of tea," she said, and set about her task, the wheelchair moving smoothly and quietly to the table behind, where she plugged in the kettle and got down the teapot. She set out a tray and some cups. "I tried my hand at *montecados*, a kind of Spanish cookie," she said over her shoulder. "While you were gone I tried to do a few Spanish things, so I'd feel close to you. I made these and they turned out, so I made some more last night, hoping you'd be in."

My breath caught in my throat, and I was happy that she was still turned away, reaching for a plastic container of treats, so she didn't see my grimace. All the time I had been gone, though I thought of her, I didn't consider that she was missing me, that I was important to her. I'd *never* make that mistake again.

I carried the laden tray to one of the library tables that marched down the center of the long cement block room. Isadore, with the instincts of someone always hungry, entered, and Hannah silently poured us all some tea—I noticed she'd already had three cups on the tray—and set the little cookies, pale circles with an almond pressed into the center of each one, on a pretty antique plate.

After a moment of imbibing, I tried one of the cookies. They were good: tender, not too sweet, with a faint licorice flavor. Isadore didn't seem too fond of them and drew out a bag of peanut butter cookies, took her tea, got a book from a shelf, and began reading.

"I don't often talk about Minnie because I know she was difficult, and I know you two didn't get along," Hannah said. "Minnie didn't get along with many people. But she came in here sometimes, and we talked on occasion."

"She was a reader?" I said.

Hannah nodded, her gray eyes thoughtful. "She liked— this is going to sound strange now, but she read a lot of true crime books. Especially Ann Rule; I always saved new Ann Rules for her when we got any in."

"Minnie seemed so gossipy and judgmental." I shared how Minnie had told me, before she decided I was the devil, that Gogi Grace had murdered her two husbands for the inheritance and insurance.

Hannah smiled sadly. "I told her that was nonsense, but she was stubborn once she got something in her head. I always had a sense that Minnie craved drama, and never got it. She moved here from Ridley Ridge, but that was as far as she ever went in life. I think . . ." She hesitated and watched me. "I *think* that's why she didn't like you. She saw how . . . how interesting you are, and how worldly. You represented everything she craved, but couldn't have."

I felt my cheeks flush.

"That's not your fault," Hannah said, reaching out and touching my hand. "But you've been places and seen things. You were married to a fashion photographer, and inherited the castle. You've had a dramatic life."

I frowned down into my teacup. I've always considered myself the most prosaic of women. I've *met* dramatic people, folks like Roma, and my friend Zee, also known by the name she chose for herself, Zimbabwe Lesotho, an internationally acclaimed artist. Even Shilo is more mysterious than I. "I'm just a woman things happen to," I said, and Isadore, over in the corner, snorted.

"I felt sorry for her," Hannah said softly. "She took in boarders not just to make money, but also because she was lonely, and I think she liked to help young people."

"What do you know about her current boarders?" I asked.

She eyed me, but then looked thoughtful. "Well, there's Karl Mencken."

Isadore growled. "Jerk," she muttered.

"He's not a nice boy," Hannah said. "He teases Isadore when he sees her."

"What does he say?" I asked the woman.

She reddened and shook her head, but then said, in her creaky, seldom-used voice, "Calls me the weird old cat lady and holds his nose, like I smell."

"Wow. That's dumb." Isadore always smells pleasantly of talcum powder and Jergens. So that was the little crud who was couch surfing at Zeke and Gordy's. I was glad, now, that Binny was helping them get rid of him.

"Brianna's a nice enough girl," Hannah said. "She's twenty-three and moved here from Houghton, a small town about fifty miles away. She comes in once in a while looking for romance novels and fashion magazines, and we talk about celebrities." My young friend pinkened and her nose went up, as if daring me to criticize her occasionally plebeian tastes.

But, hey, I'm not much of a reader, and I *love* a good romance story. Gossip about celebrities used to be my stock in trade, so no criticism from me. People seem to think that because I hang out with Pish I'm hoity-toity. Most of what I know about opera, classical music, and art I learned from him. "She works part-time at the retirement home. I saw her there," I said, but didn't mention the drug deal I suspected I'd witnessed. "And there's one more."

"Logan Katsaros. But he only comes into the library looking for Brianna, so I don't know much about him. I think Brianna is going out with him."

Isadore went back to work, and some library patrons came in, so I hugged Hannah good-bye and left, walking back toward my car. It was one of those September days that feel dusty and yet damp at the same time, the yellowing grass and dying plants a reminder that autumn couldn't arrive fast enough for many of us. Autumn Vale is in a valley, so the breeze is limited and the heat lingers, radiating off brick and shimmering off of asphalt in mirages that look like puddles but aren't. I prepare ahead on days I know are going to be like that, so my long hair was up in a chignon, off my neck, but still . . . the back of my neck was moist and there was a trickle of sweat down the middle of my back.

But I was alive, and poor Minnie wasn't. That knowledge clouded the day, closing in over me like waves over the drowning. And somewhere among the townies, likely, was a killer who was hugging to themselves the knowledge of what he or she did, congratulating themselves on getting away with murder.

As I walked toward my car, I saw Emerald outside her shop sweeping the stoop. "Em," I called out. "Emerald, it's so good to see you!"

She turned and smiled, but it was a frosty smile that didn't reach her eyes. I felt a chill, even in the heat. "Hello, Merry. How was your trip?"

I approached cautiously, like you might an unknown cat you weren't sure you should reach your hand out to. "It had a purpose, and it went well. I made peace with my late mother-in-law before she passed away."

She nodded and turned away.

"I'm excited for you and your new endeavor. Emerald Illusions . . . nice name. It's a massage therapy shop, right?"

"Not really."

I followed her in. "Emerald, is anything wrong?"

She turned and eyed me. "No, of course not. What could be wrong?"

It certainly looked like a space for massage therapy; there was what appeared to be a massage table in the center, and peaceful harp music played over the sound system. The place had been scrubbed clean: blond hardwood floors, pine shelving along the walls with books, flowers, shells, and giant geode crystals. Everywhere on the walls above the shelves were signs: *Ask What You Want of the Universe*, *Stop What's Blocking You*, *Give Yourself Freedom*, *Align with the Divine*, and other vague sayings.

There was a beach glass bead curtain across the door that
led to the back. It was pushed aside by a middle-aged woman,
who came to the front of the shop and joined Emerald. "Who
do we have here," she asked, her voice light and breezy,
"Emerald?"

"This is Merry Wynter," my friend said with heavy em-
phasis. She and the woman exchanged meaningful (to
them—I had no clue of the meaning) glances. "Merry, this
is Crystal Rouse."

Aha! I examined her frankly while she examined me.
She was in her forties or fifties, with sun-spotted skin and
clear blue eyes. Her hair was frizzy and blonde, with some
dark graying roots showing. Her clothes were pretty normal;
no shamanistic robes or anything, just shorts and a T-shirt
that said *Ask Me About CC!* which I assumed meant Consciousness Calling. She reminded me of the typical weight-
loss coaches of the nineties, the ones who wore T-shirts
screaming, *Ask me how I lost fifty pounds!*

"So I hear you found another dead body," Emerald said.

I was taken aback by her tone. "Along with Gogi, yes."

She exchanged another of those knowing looks with
Crystal. The bells over the door chimed, and Lizzie stomped
in, head down, frizzy hair wildly tangled, and threw down
her purse.

"Lizzie!" I cried with relief.

She looked up, blinked once, and surged forward, throwing her arms around me. As we babbled our hellos, she
dragged me outside and hugged me again. We exchanged
our "missed yous," etc., and then I looked down into her
eyes. "Why are you home from school so early?"

She shook her head in disgust, cast a look into the shop,
where her mother was watching us, and turned away. "Why
were you gone so long, Merry? That bitch has her tentacles
wrapped around Mom so hard I can't even break through."

I was taken aback by her vehemence. "You mean Crystal

Rouse? Lizzie, your mom is an adult; she can do what she wants. What's important is she's still your mom and she loves you."

She grabbed my arm and marched me around the corner, then burst into tears. I grabbed her into a hug and we stood like that for a few minutes.

"Lizzie, I'm so sorry I was gone so long. What's going on?"

"I hate that woman . . . *hate* her!" she wailed, swiping at her wild hair. "She's got Mom hypnotized or something. Crystal can do no wrong. Do you know Mom invited her to move in with us? And Mom is paying the whole shot, *everything*? Crystal pays *nothing* . . . I know 'cause I asked. Mom's trying to make a go of the shop, but she's gone back to her old job to pay for it all, so she works all day at the shop and then she works at the bar in the evening. I never see her except with that . . . that . . ." She sputtered to silence.

An FBI car turned the corner, obvious with its tinted windows. "What's going on, anyway?" Lizzie asked, straightening and watching the car roll past. "There were weird rumors going around at school about something happening in Autumn Vale. I had a problem in class, so I went to my counselor and she let me go home early."

I told her what had happened, and how Gogi and I discovered Minnie dead. Lizzie is tough as nails about a lot of things, and death and dying is one of those things. Being a teenager, she probably thought that Minnie, in her sixties, was pretty much done with the fun part of life anyway.

Not at all perturbed, she shrugged. But then her expression darkened. "Maybe Crystal did it. They *hated* each other!"

Chapter Seven

❊ ❊ ❊

EMERALD POKED HER head around the corner. "What's going on? Lizzie, I got a call from your principal. He said your counselor sent you home for personal reasons. What does that mean?"

She shrugged. "I was feeling cruddy. I'm better now. You working tonight?"

Emerald looked wary. "Yes." She waited.

"Can I go to Golden Acres? It's my afternoon to serve tea. Merry can take me."

"I don't want you imposing on Merry," she said, scowling.

When Emerald scowls I can occasionally see a bit of Lizzie in her, though most of the time I see Lizzie's aunt Binny in those scowls. "It's not an imposition," I said, hoping to defuse the tension.

"Still, she can walk," Emerald said, crossing her arms over her chest.

"Wait here," I said to Lizzie. She rolled her eyes at me. I strolled up to Emerald and took her arm, tugging her back around the brick building corner toward her shop. "Em, is anything wrong? Did I do anything to upset you?"

"Why do you say that?" she asked.

"You're acting different." I searched her face. "We're friends, but you'd never know it by how you're behaving."

She looked over her shoulder. Crystal had come out of the shop and was futzing around, edging closer, trying to listen, it looked like. "I don't know what you're talking about."

Okay. I'd have to try a different tack. "So, I don't understand a lot about this Consciousness Calling stuff. What's up with that?"

She focused back on me and her stance relaxed, arms uncrossed. "There's no way I can explain it all to you. You need to talk to Crystal. She's the most *amazing* person!"

Her face glowed with new energy, and she smiled; I was happy to see that at least. Emerald is a pretty woman: slim, dark-haired, lively. But not so long ago she had a lot of problems in her life, among them a rebellious teenager, a broken relationship with her mother, and a deep fracture between herself and Lizzie's father. Just when she and Tom were working things out, he was murdered. We'd all seen her through some healing with her mother and Lizzie, and now it seemed that she was finding personal happiness. I only wanted the best for her after all that.

"Do you do meetings, or what?"

"We have classes," she said. "It's so inspiring. You *have* to visit one!" Then her face fell. "But I won't be at the next few. I have to work."

"I heard you were back at the bar in Ridley Ridge. I thought you were getting into massage therapy so you wouldn't have to work there anymore."

She stiffened. Maybe it sounded judgmental, even harsh; I hadn't meant it to, but I was becoming aware of how close to us Crystal had gotten, edging down the sidewalk, and I became irritated. Couldn't I talk to my friend without her hovering?

She drifted over, put her arm over Em's shoulder, and said, "Emerald and I are building something here, and only *some* people, those rare folks with the inner light, will understand." Her voice was melodic, her tone patronizing. "You may not be ready for the message."

"The message?" I looked from Crystal to Emerald and back.

"We're all working toward the peaceful and prosperous life we deserve. Emerald deserves that more than anyone I know, and *I'm* going to help her get it."

The clear implication was, the rest of us didn't care enough to see her happy. I burned inside; I'd given Emerald a job and a place to live, helping her leave her job at that ratty bar. There's nothing wrong with tending bar or serving cocktails, but the place in Ridley Ridge was a hole, worse than most dive bars, and the job didn't go well with a troubled rebellious teenager who needed her mom on evenings and weekends.

However, Emerald glowed, her smile radiant, and she hugged Crystal. "See? You *should* come to a meeting, Merry! She's the *best*."

"I'll make it a priority," I said, but I don't think she got my sarcasm. "I'll take Lizzie over to Golden Acres." I returned to my teen friend, who had been sneaking peaks at us all talking from around the corner. "C'mon, kiddo. I'll give you a lift."

"You don't like her, do you?" she said, trotting alongside of me and looking up, scanning my expression. "*Finally*, someone who hates Crystal as much as I do!" she hooted, fist pumping the air. "The big phony."

"Lizzie, I don't even know the woman." She quieted after that and we found my car. Once inside, I glanced over at

Lizzie, who fastened the three-point seat belt—I had them installed by my mechanic when he revived the Caddy from its long slumber in the converted carriage house garage, replacing the lap belts it came with—and hugged her bag to her chest, her expression morose. "How is Alcina?" I asked, of Lizzie's best friend, a free-spirited homeschooled girl a year or two younger than Lizzie. She was given to wearing old wedding dresses and constructing little gnome homes in my woods, which Lizzie then photographed.

She shrugged. "I haven't seen her lately. Mom is so busy she can't give me a lift out to Alcina's place, and anyway, Crystal has her convinced that Alcina's parents are Wiccan antiestablishment weirdos."

I pulled away from the curb. "Wow, judgmental. First, what's wrong with Wiccans? I've known a few, and like them a lot better than those who are scared of them. And second . . . I don't think Alcina's folks *are* Wiccan, are they? And third, I'd think that someone like Crystal would be careful about judging other people harshly. I mean, this whole CC stuff feels kind of woo-woo to me. I'd think she'd be more open and accepting."

Lizzie squished around, tugging at her shoulder belt. "I know, right?" she said, her pale face earnest. She swept back her mop of frizzy hair, exposing a blooming pimple on her forehead. "It feels like Mom doesn't make her own decisions anymore, and I'm . . ." She fell silent, took a long, shaky breath, and said, "Merry, I'm scared."

"Why are you scared?"

"I don't wanna go back to living with Grandma. I mean, I *love* Grandma, and she's okay, but I'd rather live with Mom. But we've been fighting a lot lately. She's being weird about stuff."

Weird about stuff—what did that mean? It was too much to address all at once, but I'd help her through it. I remembered all too well how it felt to have conflict with your mother, like your whole world was unstable, untrustworthy. But right now, I had another question. I slowed and pulled up to the curb by Golden Acres, unbuckled, and turned to my young friend. "Lizzie, what did you mean that maybe Crystal is the one who killed Minnie? And that she hates her?"

"Haven't you heard about how Ms. Urquhart stormed a CC meeting one night?"

"I heard something about it. Were you there?"

"I was; Mom was working. But me, I have to make coffee and clean up afterward. It's such *crap*." She *harrumph*ed and hugged her bag. "Crystal calls me a junior Consciousness Calling officer, as if I ever asked to freakin' join her cult. It's kid labor, that's what it is."

I kept my patience and got back to the issue at hand. "So tell me more about all this . . . Where did Crystal Rouse come from?"

It was like I had opened the floodgates on stuff Lizzie had been holding back for months. When Emerald first got involved with Crystal, the woman was living with a CC follower she had met at a franchise meeting in San Diego, Aimee someone or other. A franchise meeting—that gave me pause. So CC was right there with Burger King and Dunkin' Donuts? She apparently had a falling-out with Aimee about the time that Emerald got seriously into CC.

I digested what I'd learned. "I thought your mom was taking a massage therapy course. We *all* did. Gogi and I talked about it, that if she set up a massage spa she'd have lots of customers locally. So what is the massage table for?"

Lizzie cast me a look. "You have *got* to come to a meeting. First they chant the contexts, then they do something called 'calling inner consciousness.' You have to lie down on the table and let people stand around you and poke at you while asking you to call up your deepest memories."

"Sounds horrendous. What is that supposed to do?"

"Help you erase all your negative programming from when

you were a kid—you know, let go of all the crap people put on you through your life. You're supposed to be freed from it all and go forth without being weighed down by guilt."

"That doesn't sound so bad. We could all use some help to get rid of that stuff."

She glanced at me darkly. "Yeah, but the crud people *say*! It's embarrassing. Crystal's always in charge, and it's like hypnotism, or something. She's started doing private sessions for people who don't want to do it in a meeting."

"I can understand that. People may be embarrassed by what they say, right?"

"Yeah, but why let some ding-dong like Crystal into all your intimate secrets? She laughs about it with Mom."

"That doesn't sound like Emerald."

"Mom goes along with it because *Crystal* says it's okay. *Crystal* says they're just friends blowing off steam." She snorted and rolled her eyes.

The one thing I had always appreciated about Lizzie was her stubborn independence, her lack of need for approval. It caused her endless trouble, but would save her in the long run. "So what happened between Crystal and Minnie?"

She gnawed her fingernail, talking between bites. "Brianna is one of Minnie's boarders, right?"

"I've heard about her and the others. Hannah told me."

"Brianna has been coming to CC meetings, and Minnie didn't like it. She came to one herself, and sat in the back muttering and staring. When Crystal started doing a calling on Brianna, Minnie got all red in the face and tried to haul Brianna off the table. A big fight erupted. Everyone there ganged up on Minnie, and she left in a huff."

"Brianna stayed?"

"Yeah. She was crying and Crystal took her into another room and made her sit and talked to her about it for a half hour while everyone else sat around looking at each other. Dopes didn't even talk. Didn't want to upset Crystal."

"When did this happen?"

"Week ago or so. Maybe two weeks. Since then Brianna has started to look for somewhere else to live, I guess. Crystal wanted her to move in with us, but for once Mom put her foot down because Brianna would have had to share a room with one of us, and guess who *that* would've been? Mom said no and Crystal backed down."

I was silent for a long minute, staring out the window. I was sure the FBI would hear all about Crystal and Minnie's confrontation and wondered what they'd make of it. I fretted, too, remembering what Mabel had told me about Em's confrontation with Minnie—"bopping her on the nose"—and what Esposito would make about that. Silly, I know; Emerald did not kill Minnie, I was sure. "Look, Lizzie, if the FBI wants to talk to you, tell them everything you've told me."

Her eyes widened. "Do you think they will?" she asked. "That would be so *seriously* cool. I could tell all those jerks at school that I was wanted for murder and they'd leave me alone."

"Couple more years, kiddo, and then you can go to college for photography." We got out of the car and headed up the drive toward Golden Acres.

"CC wouldn't be so bad if they didn't insist on making everything so stupid, like you could solve anything with a calling and a smile and spouting some dumbass saying. *You can do anything you want, just want anything. Make the world better by putting on a smile.*" Lizzie made a rude noise. "Life isn't like that. You can't wish your problems away, or Crystal would disappear."

I found Doc in the living area, so I stayed for tea. We chatted, and naturally spent some time talking about my morning experience. He took my hand and we sat like that for a while, his long, bony fingers interwoven with mine. "I've known Minnie ever since she moved here from Ridley Ridge," he said. "At first she worked part-time at the post office, but when the old fart who ran it died, she stepped into the job full-time."

I glanced over at him, sensing some sadness. "You know, she gave me a hard time almost from the beginning, and she's always bad-mouthing Gogi."

"Don't mind me; seems a shame, a kid like that getting murdered,"

Only a ninety-something would consider sixty-something Minnie a "kid."

"Some people are born like that. She was a funny sort, liked to collect trophies from her conflicts, kinda like war trophies." He snorted, chuckling as he continued, "One time she and Hubert went at it when he told her he'd been abducted by UFOs, and she said he was full of it. Course, we all *know* Hubert is full of it, but Minnie didn't seem to get that he was joshin' her. Anyway, a while later I went into the post office for something, and there was Hubert's toupee, hangin' from a clothes peg . . . looked like a scalp. Gave me a start, lemme tell ya."

Lizzie served us tea, and then played checkers with Hubert Dread over in the corner. Dread is a funny guy, and most of what he says is tongue-in-cheek. Unfortunately, Gordy is his nephew and believes the old guy's tales word for word. I blame Hubert for being the genesis of Gordy's conspiracy theory nonsense.

We chatted about Spain. Doc had been there once in the fifties and never forgot it. He had even gone to a bullfight, though he said it left him sick and changed his mind about blood sports in general. We were silent for a minute. I was thinking about leaving—I needed to get home and figure out what to do about Roma—but Doc had something else to say.

"Ya know, I noticed something while you were gone," Doc said.

"Mhm?" I said, sipping my almost-cold tea.

"Got a theory: I think some folks are catalysts. Like in

chemistry, the active ingredient, you know, that speeds up reactions. You're a human catalyst."

I looked over at him, squinting in puzzlement. "What do you mean?" Doc's conversation occasionally wanders into the abstruse, for lack of a better word, and often borders on the metaphysical.

"When you came to Autumn Vale you sped up the pace of things; things that mighta happened anyway happened faster. Now, I get why you went to Spain, and why you stayed so long, even if others don't." He glanced over at me, his eyes large and blurred behind his smudgy glasses. "But when you left, there was a void, a vacuum. Nature don't like a vacuum, you know. Other folks stepped in to become the catalysts. Only you were a *good* catalyst, helping folks, like me, and Hannah and Lizzie over there. That girl sure missed you something awful."

This was why he confined most of his conversations about life to Pish, who understood him. "What *do* you mean? Who exactly became the catalyst while I was gone?"

"I'd say that Crystal woman and her horse manure. Look at who she's affected: Emerald, Lizzie, Minnie, that kid Brianna. The only ones in your circle unaffected are Gogi and Hannah. And me."

"Well, and Shilo."

"Nope. Not even Shilo was free of the crap. Used to be Shilo and Em palled around, but now with that Crystal woman takin' over, Em don't have time no more for Shilo or anyone else."

Even her own daughter. Lizzie was missing spending time with Emerald now that her mom had gone back to bartending at night. "It's a good theory, Doc, but I can't believe I'm a catalyst, good or bad." I stood, bent over, and planted a kiss on his balding head. I grabbed his glasses, cleaned them on the edge of my shirt, and planted them back on his beaky, spotted nose. He blinked once and nodded. "I have to get back to the castle," I said. "I desperately need some normal. I think I'll bake some muffins."

I drove home trying not to think about what I had experienced. With others around I had been able to put out of my mind the blood, the terror, and the sight of Minnie's open, dead eyes, but alone the horror came back. I had only ever seen one facet of the postal employee's personality, the unreasoning harridan who disliked me almost from the day I arrived. But there had been more to her, and maybe if I'd tried a little harder . . .

That was an unprofitable line of thought. I pulled up the lane and sat for a moment, staring at my castle. The midday heat shimmered in the air as I got out. The castle always looks a bit lonely to me, like it's lacking context. The open area around it is fairly flat, though there are anomalies I didn't notice at first when I was overwhelmed by my inheritance, outbuildings and groves of trees dotting the landscape. But something else was needed.

Somehow, some way, I had to keep my castle. It was mine, and had burrowed its way into my heart, the closest thing I had had to a home since Miguel died. But *how* to keep it? And how to transform it from a lonely outpost into a part of its surroundings? If two hundred years of owners hadn't managed to accomplish that, I wasn't sure I could do any better. My uncle had been planning to build a community around it, but his desperate plan to construct and sell modern condos and homes left me cold. Wynter Castle deserved much more.

I listened to the high whine of a cicada in a tree. There was so much I needed to do. Life tumbled in on me, all the stuff that Minnie would never be *able* to experience. I vowed not to waste another year of my life mourning what I lost, avoiding what I was afraid to do. When asking myself what I really wanted, I knew. Long-term, I wanted to live in Wynter Castle and be with my friends in Autumn Vale for the rest of my life. But in the short term I wanted to find out what was bothering Shilo, help her find the peace that seemed to be eluding her, and see if Virgil Grace was still as interested in me as I knew he was before I left.

And I wanted to find my cat. I scanned the edge of the woods; no orange flash. No Becket.

I grabbed my purse, crossed the drive, and entered the coolness of the castle with a sense of relief. Except there seemed to have been a tornado in the great hall. Sheet music drifted over every surface like early snow, and down the stairs was a tumble of clothes, as if they had been thrown from the gallery. A pink lace bra drooped from my stunning chandelier like some trophy from a frat party. I heard someone screaming and started to shake all over.

I dropped my purse and raced up the stairs. "Pish! Pish? Where are you? Are you okay?"

Pish dashed from Roma's room as a pair of silk pajama pants sailed out and landed on his head. He tossed them aside and looked at me, blinking. "Merry, thank God you're home. Are you all right?"

"You've heard about the murder," I said flatly, listening to Roma's shrieking voice, no words, just screams.

"The FBI have been out here in the person of Agent Esposito, asking some uncomfortable questions, according to Roma. You've heard, I'm sure, about the clash between Roma and Minnie."

I nodded. Roma was still screaming at the top of her lungs, but Pish studiously ignored that, backing up, grabbing the doorknob, and closing the door on her ranting. I only caught one in five words, but what I heard consisted of complaints about the castle, Pish, Autumn Vale . . . and me.

We stood staring at each other, and all I could think about was the razor-sharp decorative letter opener stuck in Minnie as she bled her life out on the post office floor. "Didn't the agent ask to search Roma's room?"

"They did, and she refused. She is, uh, surprisingly knowledgeable about her constitutional rights to refuse, after her little trouble in New York, and they didn't have a warrant." He took a long, shaky breath. "Yet."

Yet. The word chilled me. "We need to talk," I said. "My room, Pish, right now."

He glanced over his shoulder. "I should go and calm poor Roma—"

"*No.* This is important. My room. Or . . ." I listened to her screaming. I needed several feet of stone between us. "The kitchen instead. And put on some Schubert."

I marched downstairs, weaving through bras, panties, and gowns that draped artistically over the graceful wood railing and slid down the steps. Balefully eyeing the mess when I got to the bottom, I thought maybe I'd inflict on Roma the rule my grandmother had for me: no food until the mess was cleaned up. Or, in Roma's case, no wine until she had cleaned up. If she was going to behave like a spoiled teenager, I'd treat her like one. I had lived with Lizzie in the castle for months and never had this kind of drama.

I stomped to my peaceful kitchen, which Roma only entered for meals and wine. A Schubert sonata came through the wired-in sound system. It was a lilting, tripping, bold piano rendition, and I took in a deep breath. It was blessedly cool in the kitchen, a benefit, in summer, of thick stone walls. I made a pot of tea and put together a tray, carrying it over to the fireplace, which currently held only a vase of dried flowers.

Soon autumn would come, and then winter. A fire would blaze cheerily in the hearth; my castle would be as cozy as a castle can be. I wanted Roma gone before that. I wanted my winter alone with Pish. And hopefully Virgil. It did occur to me that I was jealous of the attention Roma was getting from Pish, but it was more than that; she was one of those dramatic, self-destructive types who bring chaos to every situation. Heaven knows in my life I had dealt with enough actresses and models with huge dramatic personalities. I didn't need to live with one now.

The next movement of the sonata was calmer, quieter, softer. I took a deep breath and sat in one of the wing chairs, where Pish and I had spent many an evening hour. He entered the kitchen, softly padding over to me. He took my hands, bent over, and kissed my cheek.

"I'm sorry, my dear. I know what you've been through today, and then to come home to this . . ."

I was silent as he took the other chair, and poured the tea, wondering how to broach the topic of what I had seen. "Let's be quiet for a moment, Pish," I said. "Have some tea with me."

He did what I asked, but finally, watching me, he said, "Tell me what happened. Is Gogi okay?"

"Everyone we love is fine," I said, with a watery smile. I could feel tears welling up, and maybe that wasn't surprising. I was home; I could relax and let the tears flow. The piano music trilled and burbled, like a brook running through our conversation. "Oh, Pish, it was awful," I finally said, my voice clogged with unexpected sobs. He knew what had happened, but I didn't think he knew everything. "Gogi and I found Minnie at the post office, dead, stabbed with . . . stabbed with one of Roma's letter openers!"

Chapter Eight

❈ ❈ ❈

H E WAS ABSOLUTELY still for minutes, just sitting there staring at me, holding his cup. It turned more and more sideways until he spilled tea on his tan slacks. He jumped up and took his cup to the sink, then ran some water, dabbing at his slacks with a dampened cloth. He returned and sat, a wet blotch on his pristine pants.

"I must have heard you incorrectly, my dear. Did you say you found Minnie stabbed with . . . Pardon, but did you say one of Roma's letter openers?"

I nodded, one tear finally spilling over and running down my cheek. I wiped at it with the back of my hand. "At least I think it's one of hers. Where else would it come from?" I took a tissue from the box on the table and blew my nose. "Gogi and I went by the post office to pick up my luggage from Tony, but it wasn't open, so we went to the back, and the door was open and . . ." I shook my head and wept for a few minutes, finally sniffling my tears back. The tissue was now sodden, so Pish handed me another, his expression unreadable. I blew my nose again and tossed the tissues at the trash can, missing. I leaped up, disposed of them properly, then returned to my chair.

The music had switched to a Beethoven sonata. Not the Moonlight Sonata; that is not, contrary to what I once thought, the only sonata Beethoven composed. This one is often called The Tempest, or No. 17 in D Minor.

In a flat tone I described the scene. "The letter opener looked like a little saber, with a silk tassel and everything." I retched slightly as I recalled it, soaked in her blood. I swallowed some tea, trying to keep myself under control. It was only now, hours later, that I was shaking, crying, and retching. Weird.

"Merry, that doesn't mean it's one of Roma's."

"Don't you think that's too much of a coincidence, that she was killed with a letter opener?" I stared at him, but he remained blank, pensive almost. "Pish, I've heard about the run-in those two had. Roma threatened Minnie." I leaned toward him. "With a *letter opener*!"

"What are you saying, Merry?"

His tone warned me to tread carefully. But I am his friend; *she* was just a cause. I know I was being harsh, but that's how I felt. "I'm saying, it is probably hers, and the FBI will figure that out sooner or later. They'll be back with a warrant."

"It doesn't matter anyway," he said. "Roma was here all morning, so she couldn't have killed Minnie."

"Not necessarily true. When I left this morning, she was coming in from a walk."

He smiled. "My darling, she is *not* a woman to walk. And walking from Autumn Vale would take her . . . oh, an hour or two at least! She'd never make it."

That was true. *And* she was in high-heeled boots. However . . . "Pish, where do you keep your car keys?"

"On the ebony dresser valet in my room. Why?"

Pish wears a sleeping mask and earplugs most nights,

and he doesn't lock his bedroom door; neither do I. In fact, I've put things in his room while he was sleeping and he didn't awaken. I recalled the noises as I left in the morning: the crickets, the crows . . . and the *tick-tick-tick*.

I got it, in that moment, why the sound was familiar: *that* was the sound of a car engine cooling after it had been driven a fair distance. I knew then beyond a shadow of a doubt that Roma Toscano had been somewhere that morning, easily as far away as Autumn Vale. But was it to murder Minnie?

I bolted up and raced for the stairs, gathering some of her clothes and shoes as I went. Pish followed. As I whirled around the top to the gallery and stomped down to her bedroom door I hesitated only a moment, wondering if I ought to knock. But this was my home, and she hadn't respected that. Why should I respect *her* privacy?

I flung the door open and found her lying on the bed, snoring. I tossed the clothes to the floor, took two giant steps, grabbed her shoulder, and shook her as Pish entered the room behind me, pleading with me to be gentle. I was in no mood for gentle, and in fact I was lathered up into a fury I have rarely felt. *This* was the woman who tried to steal my husband. *This* was the woman who was making my home a wreck. *This* was the woman who was trying to steal my best friend from me.

"Wake up!" I shouted as I shook.

She scrambled up in the bed, her long auburn hair streaming over her shoulder, wearing a peignoir—honest to God, half-naked in a filmy peignoir in the middle of the day, like some François Boucher painting—and shrieked, "What's wrong? What's going on?"

I stood back and glared down at her, my hands balling into fists. Was she a killer? I couldn't imagine it, but I'd been surprised before. I no longer thought in "types" when I considered who could commit murder. "Where were you coming from this morning, when you snuck in as I was leaving?"

"I told you, I went for a walk in the woods," she said sulkily, drawing the covers up over her. She cast a beseeching look toward Pish.

"No, you didn't say that. You said you walked around the edge of the field."

"I didn't say that. Exactly."

"Did, didn't—that's beside the point. Where were you?" She shook her head.

"I happen to know that you slipped into Pish's room, got his car keys, and took his car. You were coming home from *some*where as I left."

"Pishie, darling, what is *wrong* with her?" Roma's beautiful eyes filled with tears as she looked past me.

"Did you take my car, Roma?" Pish asked, his tone gentle. "You can tell me. I won't be angry."

She nodded and murmured, "*Yes.*"

"Where did you go?"

"Just . . . for a drive. Please, Pishie, don't let her bully me anymore. I've had a dreadful day."

A dreadful day? Was that because she had killed Minnie? I turned and left the room, giving Pish a look.

Agent Esposito arrived minutes later, but he still did not have a warrant. They take time to get, apparently. I sent Esposito to the breakfast room, since the library was taken up with recording equipment, and summoned Roma using the intercom. Let her tell them whatever she wanted, lies or the truth; as for me, I would tell them what I knew.

I retreated to the kitchen and started rummaging through my pantry. I was out of a lot of stuff, which would mean a shopping trip, likely out of town. Autumn Vale didn't have much in the way of groceries, just the variety store. Ridley Ridge did have a sad, dim grocery store, but their produce looked like it had come out of a compost bin, and the meat like it had been ravaged by wolves. The people there seemed not to know or care about that, and shopped there more often than not. I'd rather forage in the Dumpster behind a Whole Foods.

But I had cereal, and so made bran date muffins.

Esposito found me in the kitchen. He looked around and nodded. "This is quite the place. So you inherited the castle from a relative you didn't even know existed?"

"Not exactly," I said, taking the finished muffins out and setting the double pan on a cooling rack. I briefly explained about having met Uncle Melvyn when I was a kid, before the estrangement between him and my mother. "Now I have to figure out how I can afford to keep it."

"I've heard about your various enterprises," he said dryly. "Sheriff Grace has filled me in."

I glanced over at him, but he wasn't taking a shot at me, I decided; he was surprised at what I'd been through in the last year. I turned and leaned back against the counter. "So what do you want? Or need?"

"We need to search Ms. Roma Toscano's room. I'm expecting the warrant any minute. All she's doing is delaying the inevitable by not cooperating. Does she rent that room from you?"

"No, she's visiting. My friend is recording her."

"Then you can give us permission to search her room."

I eyed him warily, and thought about it. "Until you have the warrant I won't give you permission to search a guest's room." *No matter how much I dislike her,* I thought.

"That's disappointing. Do you often shelter suspected killers?"

I had been unsure at first, but now I was starting to actively dislike Agent Esposito. "On occasion. For kicks I leave my door unlocked at night and a loaded AK-47 on the hall table."

I'd love to say he went away then, but he didn't. I gave them permission to search the rest of the castle, and let them go about their business. Pish called his ex Stoddart Harkner, but I don't know if it was for advice or help. Esposito and the others stuck around for hours, then finally left. Something was holding up the warrant.

Roma was subdued when I next saw her. She ate her dinner in silence, and then retreated to her room. To sharpen the rest of her letter openers, maybe? I didn't know what to think.

Pish thanked me for standing up to the FBI. I told him the truth; I did what I'd want someone else to do for me. He took my hand, kissed my cheek, and then went up to check on Roma.

I was cleaning up the kitchen when I heard a tap on the window. It was Virgil. I pointed to the butler's pantry door, which was on the long hallway off the kitchen, and met him there. I invited him in. He asked what went down, and I told him all we'd been through that day. As a police officer he was concerned that I was supporting Roma's right against search, but he understood. He wouldn't slam Esposito, though his granite jaw tightened when I spoke about the man.

I made some coffee and invited him to sit by the empty fireplace with me, but he said, "Why don't we go outside instead?"

I agreed and followed him out to sit on the flagstone terrace by the front door, where I had a white wrought iron table-and-chairs set. It was almost sunset, and the sky was golden, the air clearer and cooling. We set our cups on the table and took chairs across from each other. It wasn't where I wanted to be, but I was feeling my way through our relationship, now that I was back from being gone so long.

"You know if I could, I'd make Esposito leave you alone, right?" he said, glancing over at me as he cradled his coffee in his hands, his forearms on his knees.

"I know." We sat in silence for a while again. In the

distance I heard a howl. Coyotes. I felt a shiver down my back and sent up a silent prayer that Becket would come home. I *knew* the orange blur I saw on the edge of the woods was him. I would look for him again the very next morning.

I glanced over at Virgil, deep in thought. How could I raise the subject of the time we spent together in the long grass near the woods, the day before I headed to Spain? We talked and experienced much that sunny afternoon; I could still feel his lips against mine, his hands, his weight against me in the tall grass. But absence had shattered the sense of closeness.

"Merry, I wanted to talk to you about something."

I sighed with relief. Maybe he'd bring up the topic himself. "What's up?"

"It's something that's been on my mind for a while. I've talked to my mother about it."

His *mother*? I'm close friends with Gogi, but I wouldn't share the details of my love life with her, especially not when it concerned her son. "Okay."

He stared off toward the woods. "The sheriff's election is coming up, and I'm running unopposed right now. There is another officer who would like to run," Virgil said. "He'd do a good job for this county. I'm thinking of withdrawing from the ballot."

"This doesn't have to do with Kelly, does it?" I asked.

He shook his head. "Truth is, I'm thirty-six in a week. I have a year left of eligibility if . . ." He glanced over at me. "*If* I want to try out again to join the FBI."

I was stunned. Years ago, Virgil was to go for training to the FBI academy, Quantico. But his mom was diagnosed with a serious form of breast cancer, and he, the youngest, was the only of her children still in Autumn Vale. He gave up his dream so he could nurse his mom through the mastectomy, the chemo, and the rest of it, while joining the local sheriff's department as a deputy. She had an especially bad bout and was bedridden, she told me. But he never complained. Once she recovered, he ran for sheriff and won. He'd been sheriff ever since.

"If I'm chosen, it would mean going to Quantico, and after that I could be transferred anywhere."

I didn't want him to go away, but this was his lifelong dream. And then something else hit me: he'd come to *me* to talk about it. That told me so much about where his head and heart were. He's a man of few words, but actions speak louder anyway, right? I watched him. He had drained and set his coffee cup aside, and squinted off into the distance, sitting still with his elbows on his knees, his hands clasped together.

He'd come to *me*.

I went to him and knelt on the hard flagstone between his knees. I looked up at him and took his face in my hands. His eyes are a delicious chocolate brown, but were somewhat shadowed by his thick dark brows as the sun set, glowing golden against my lovely castle. He searched my gaze, his expression intense, unreadable.

I chose my words carefully. "I don't know another man in the world who more deserves to do exactly what he wants than you, Virgil. I know you'll make it." I let my fingers thread through his dark, mussed hair, and stared up into his dark eyes. Something changed in his gaze, softened. I was about to kiss him when the big oak door opened and Roma joined us. We leaped apart like guilty teenagers, me stumbling backward to my feet.

"Why, it's the *sheriff*," Roma said, eyes wide, as Virgil stood. She sashayed over and touched his arm. "I wish *you* were in charge of this awful murder investigation." She rubbed her hand up and down his bicep, which, I have to admit, is one of my favorite things to do.

He cast me a beseeching look, but I shrugged. She was

not *my* pet project. I watched and waited; Miguel and I had a huge fight when Roma did this same act, almost exactly ten years ago. Miguel played along, flirted back, and told me after that she had annoyed him. I said he didn't *look* annoyed, and we got into an argument. I was childish, yes, but he had been dismissive of my concerns.

Virgil shrugged away from her hand, irritation marring his handsome face. She stopped and looked puzzled.

"I have to go, Merry," he said, circling her to get to me. He took my hands, looked deep into my eyes, and said, "It means a lot to me to have your support. On the other thing . . . I'll try to keep you in the loop of what's happening if Esposito will tell me anything."

We shared a too-brief kiss, and he strode to his sheriff's department vehicle, got in, and skidded off down the lane. I turned to talk to Roma, but the door closed behind her.

ESPOSITO CAME BACK THE NEXT MORNING WITH THE warrant, and Roma was forced to allow them into her room. Before retiring the prior night, Pish had confided to me that Roma had told him that the letter opener was likely hers. There was one missing, one piece of an antique pair that rested on a decorative stand with a matching magnifying glass. She didn't know how it had gone missing, or when. I kept my own counsel; it still seemed entirely possible that she had executed Minnie in hot blood, but I didn't feel enough fear to kick her out. I did, however, lock my room overnight.

Roma consulted with a lawyer but decided, against his advice, to give the FBI the rest of the set, since she didn't want it in her room. Knowing what someone had done with the letter opener gave her the creeps, she said.

Esposito took me aside in the kitchen. "Where do you keep your car keys, Ms. Wynter?"

I saw what he was getting at. Soon I would have to decide to whom I owed loyalty. "In my purse beside my bed."

"Is there any way Ms. Toscano could have accessed them and used your car yesterday morning?"

"No."

"What about Mr. Lincoln's car?"

"You'll have to ask him."

He nodded. "Okay."

"Agent Esposito, as much as I don't like Roma, I also don't believe that she crept into Autumn Vale and murdered Minnie with no one noticing."

Esposito watched my eyes. "Reason?"

I paused for a moment as I wiped the counter and hung the damp cloth on the towel holder. "That woman has never done anything in her life without an audience. When she threatened the LOC director, it was in front of the orchestra and chorus." I wasn't giving away any secrets; he knew all about her legal troubles in New York. "When she threatened Minnie, the scene was timed for *precisely* the moment when folks were gathered in the great hall. She *must* have an audience, and every indication I've had is that her threats, as graphic as they sound, aren't serious."

He was thoughtful, and my perception of him began to shift subtly, as he didn't speak immediately. Finally, he said, "Sounds like a classic case of narcissistic personality disorder, but that doesn't preclude violence."

"However, I still believe that her need to act her life out on a stage of some sort would mean she'd want a witness."

"I'll take your expert psychological assessment into consideration," he said. "In my opinion, other needs could supersede her desire for an audience."

I had been considering telling Esposito about Pish's car *tick-tick-tick*ing as it cooled, but held off. He appeared willing to pin the crime on Roma, and though I couldn't blame him for coming to that conclusion, my real reticence had to do with Pish. It was his car, after all.

"Was Pish Lincoln absent from the castle during the early morning hours, to your knowledge?"

"No, of course not. Why would he be?"

He watched me for a moment, then said, "Deputy Urquhart of the local sheriff's department—the decedent's nephew—has given us a list of those who had recent run-ins with Minnie Urquhart. Your friend was one of them. He apparently stormed into the post office and had a shouting match with her over what he suspected were anomalies with his mail. He accused her of stealing magazines."

"You actually think Pish would kill someone over missing magazines?"

"Ms. Wynter, I've known of people shot to death over a cold cup of coffee."

Chapter Nine

OVERNIGHT A SHIFT had occurred in the weather pattern, as often happens in upstate New York. The heat and mugginess of the previous day had fled. The air felt crisper, a welcome breeze tossing the tops of the trees in my forest. Wearing pants tucked into walking boots—you don't risk ticks in the long grass and brush, not with the danger of Lyme disease—I was determined to search the woods looking for Becket. He was coming home. I had a pocketful of treats, and I wasn't afraid to use them.

I had dreamed of Virgil, and thoughts of him lingered—his touch, his kiss, the closeness I craved and didn't know how to initiate. I'm not a shy woman, but he is a different man from any I've ever been with, somewhat insular, guarded, quiet, calm, strong. He's not exactly open, but neither is he entirely closed off.

What would happen between us if he made it into the FBI? Would we miss our chance? I couldn't let myself think about that.

As I walked toward the woods, I thought instead about the crime, and how the death of someone I didn't like at all and barely knew could still shift my world in the small-town interdynamics of Autumn Vale. Minnie Urquhart was a part of that world, and I guess I had never stopped to wonder why she was as she was, or what else was going on in her life. We're all like passengers in little pods; sometimes it's hard to put ourselves in *other* people's pods. All we experience is how they impact us, not the other way around. Doc's theory of me as a catalyst was troubling and too philosophical a point to me.

Looking at it from another way, I could frame it differently. Autumn Vale had been stable for years before I arrived. Deaths left holes in the personality array of the community, yes, but they were expected from time to time. I, however, was an unknown quantity and had thrust myself into so many people's lives so quickly I had made waves, the ripples of which were felt through the community. If that was being a catalyst, I guessed I had to cop to that.

The woods were before me. An uneasy rustle tossed the treetops, and some dark clouds crept across the sky with a rumble of thunder. A year ago these woods had seemed foreign to a gal more used to the urban jungle. Now I knew that the trees in these woods had been planted many decades ago by my grandfather and great-uncle as an arboretum. I could even name some of them.

I approached the first, the big tree that stood out from the edge of the forest like a marker to the path, a bur oak. Touching the bark, vertical ridges like rivers running up the tree, I stared into the darkness and took a deep breath, inhaling the nutty scent of leaves and needles. Then I forged into the forest.

"Becket, where are you buddy? Come home; I miss you. Be-cket!" I called, stretching out the syllables into two notes.

I rattled his treat container, an old humbug candy tin of my
great-uncle's that I had found in his desk. It was what he'd
used for the cat; I knew that because of the crumbled rem-
nants of kitty treats in it.

I had a weird déjà vu moment. A year before I had seen
the orange cat on the edge of the woods and gone looking
when people told me it might be Becket, my late uncle's cat,
who disappeared soon after Melvyn died. So much had happened in a year that I felt like a different person, and yet
here I was, looking for Becket and contemplating a murder
that I had discovered.

I was losing track of the possible killers, there were so
many, at least in the police's eyes, no doubt. Esposito didn't
know what a lovely, nonviolent person I was. He *had* to be
considering me as a suspect, as well as Gogi, or maybe both
of us together. The person who discovers the body is often
the murderer, I have heard, though that hasn't been my experience. So far.

But there were others. I mentally ticked them off on a
list as I walked and called to Becket.

Roma Toscano, though I had argued against her to
Esposito. She had motive; Minnie had injured her ego and
humiliated her in front of others. Despite my speech to
Esposito, that *did* make her a suspect. She had the means,
with Pish's car, and the opportunity, since she wouldn't tell
us where she had actually gone that morning.

Crystal Rouse—I couldn't let my personal dislike of her
lead me astray, though I found her behavior toward Emerald
unsettling, drenched with such a proprietary air. She and
Minnie had clashed at one of the meetings, so Crystal was
another suspect. I was going to have to attend a CC meeting,
perhaps pretending more curiosity and open-mindedness
than I felt.

Emerald. I didn't believe for a moment she would kill

anyone, but I was sure the agent would be looking at her
seriously, since she was Crystal's acolyte and would seem,
from an outsider's perspective (and maybe in truth, judging
from what I had seen), to be pretty firmly under the woman's
thumb. *And* she had punched Minnie on the nose.

"Be-cket!" I trudged farther into the woods, getting close
to where poor Rusty had had his almost-lethal run-in with
a killer in the autumn of last year.

Karl Mencken: he was a serious contender. He had an
argument with Minnie that apparently got heated enough
that he stomped out. I paused and thought. He'd said that to
Gordy and Zeke, anyway. Was there another side, silenced
now that Minnie was dead? I made a mental note to find out
more. They were *all* suspects, not just Karl. Living with
Minnie, given her personality, may not have been easy. I
knew zero about their arrangement, aside from the fact that
she had three boarders and their names. Hannah knew more;
I'd talk to her.

And then there was the supposed new love life she had
embarked on via online dating. Shilo had shared that Rusty's
new employee was going out with Minnie and had moved
to Autumn Vale for that purpose. Was he the only one she
was involved with online? Who would know? I needed to
find out if she was especially close to anyone in her extended
Urquhart family, someone she may have talked to.

And here I was going over suspects as if I was investigating, a habit I had fallen into after the events of the last year.
But once again, I felt I had a personal stake in this. If Roma
was guilty, if she had used Pish's car . . . I shivered with
dread. I couldn't bear for him to be in danger.

I stopped dead on the spot, listening to a blue jay in the
tree above me. It had followed me from my first entry into
the forest, flitting from tree to tree, squawking the whole way.
I put my hand up to my mouth and called, "Be-cket!" There

was a rustle in the undergrowth near an open spot. Was it him? "Becket! C'mon, sweetie, come home. I *miss* you!"

I used to be one of those people who thought women who talked to cats as if they were human were idiots. And yet here I was, in the woods, treat can in hand, wanting with all my heart to find my own animal familiar, the independent ginger tabby who had become my companion. I stared at the thick undergrowth. "Becket, *please* come home. I miss cuddling," I confessed. "I miss taking walks with you, buddy. Come *home*."

I heard a querulous, demanding yowl of unhappiness. "Becket! Where are you? Come on out."

I saw some brush rustle, dry leaves dropping as a bush shuddered, and there he was, tentative, distrustful, emerging from the shadowy underbrush and standing, watching me. I sank down onto the forest floor cross-legged and rattled the tin. "Come on, sweet boy," I crooned, rattling the treats again. I didn't care that I had become the kind of person I used to make fun of. So I was a cat lady now. So what? "I won't be doing that again, going away for months at a time. Ever. *Never*."

He stretched casually and ambled along the edge of the brushy area, sliding side glances my way. He looked awful, weed seeds and burrs matting his fur, skinny again like he was when I found him.

"C'mon, Becket; I have treats." I rattled the tin. Pish had told me that Becket had seemed okay at first, but over the weeks he'd stayed away longer on his trips into the forest. Finally, he just hadn't come home. Pish had called him, but my friend isn't much of an animal person and Becket had never warmed up to him. Pish's trip back to New York to take Lush home had lasted a couple of weeks, and though my friend had arranged for someone to leave food out for Becket, the cat must have decided he had truly been abandoned.

I kept talking softly and Becket got closer until finally he approached, gulped down some treats from my palm, climbed into my lap, circled once, and promptly fell asleep purring. I hugged him close and cried, letting go of all the angst and fear I had experienced since yesterday.

We sat like that for a long time as I thought about the seasons of my life. For a while after my mother and grandmother died within months of each other, I was a wild child. I tried a lot of things: acting, modeling, drinking to excess, even a little pot to ease my sorrow and emptiness. I wasn't overly successful at anything, and none of it made me happy. Jobs were increasingly scarce—there were never a whole lot of jobs for plus-size fashion models, and the ones there were went to harder-working, more disciplined girls than I—so I turned to styling other models and actresses, finding a talent and love of the job.

Finally I had found something where my opinions on what suited people mattered. Around then I met my sweet friend Shilo. I was on a styling team at a fashion shoot and met Miguel, and through Miguel, Pish. I was on to the next season of my life as wife to a wealthy, cultured, loving man.

A little more than two years passed. When Miguel was killed in a car crash, I leaned on my friends heavily. I holed up in my apartment, wrapped in a heavy cloak of devastation, but eventually I got strong enough to work and live, though not happily, not for a long time. That was a season of sadness.

I found a way to move on as much as I was able, but love didn't interest me. You're only given one great love in life, I thought, and mine was gone. That long season was calm, serene at times, even, but there were things churning in my body and heart, things I wasn't even aware of at times. It all seemed too much to bear, the day-to-day work of booking jobs and keeping going.

For a brief time I thought being assistant to a testy,

troubled model was the answer to my melancholy stasis; I knew how to handle her most of the time, and she seemed to need me. I was looking for that sense of being needed, though I didn't realize it at the time. It was a disaster, and I ended up accused (unjustly) of stealing a valuable necklace that I suspect she either lost or pawned.

Maybe it took that to shake me awake. I had inherited but had not yet come to see Wynter Castle. I arrived in Autumn Vale, met Gogi, Doc, Hannah, and the rest, Pish and Shilo joined me, and life changed. And then there was Virgil: handsome, passionate, sexy, strong. Going away for so long had given me a fresh perspective, how alive this place made me feel, and how dull life was, even amid luxury, while away. Here I awoke every day with purpose. Maybe purpose is the secret to a happy life. It *could* become my season of contentment and joy.

I carried Becket back to the castle and up to my room, setting up his bowls filled with food and water, his litter box, and a comfy nest made of my bathrobe on the bed, where I set him, sleeping still, purring throatily. I had lots to do and had to go out, but when I got home he was getting attention to his matted fur and burrs, whether he liked it or not.

I had lunch with Pish—Roma was a no-show, despite an invitation—and talked nonstop about Becket, and what I had been thinking while I hunted him down. My friend chatted, but seemed troubled and distant. As I collected our plates and glasses, moving them to the big sink and squirting dish detergent over them, I looked over my shoulder.

The lines on Pish's tanned, lean face were more pronounced. This business was getting him down, but didn't he know he could confide in me? I had left him in the lurch when I headed to Spain. He had just broken up with Stoddart, and even though their affair was brief, Pish doesn't go into anything halfway. When he loves, he loves wholeheartedly. But *our* love was long-standing, and he had to know he could tell me anything. He had an old and bad habit of keeping anything sad or troubling from me, though, thinking I couldn't handle it.

I turned from the deep sink, my hands dripping with soapy suds. "Pish, tell me what's going on."

He got up and dried as I washed. "Roma's still not telling me what she was doing the morning Minnie was killed. I've hired a lawyer, a guy from Ridley Ridge that my attorney in New York recommends."

"A criminal lawyer?"

He nodded.

"For yourself, or for Roma?"

"Both. Esposito is not kidding around, and I know it looks bad. Especially after what Roma did in New York, the threats against the LOC musical director. That episode involving Minnie looks bad, too, but Minnie, in her own way, was every bit as much a drama queen as Roma is."

I smiled at his acknowledgment; he recognized Roma's shortcomings but loved her anyway. As he did me. I wiped my soapy hands and hugged him. "Pish, we'll figure out who did this. I don't think it was Roma, but keep working on her; she's hiding something."

He hugged me back, hard. "I'm so glad you're back," he said, his voice muffled against my shoulder.

"I'm never leaving again."

"Truly?" he asked, holding me away from him and gazing at me.

"Truly. Hey, I promised Becket. You don't promise things to a cat unless you're serious."

We finished up and I drove to town, determined to get to the bottom of a lot of things. I visited Gogi first, and sat in her office chatting over a cup of cappuccino made in the new coffeemaker that Virgil had given her as a birthday gift. It reminded me that Virgil's birthday was in a week. What to get him? Myself, perhaps, gift wrapped? I would enjoy the unwrapping.

"Agent Esposito has had his time with me," Gogi said, frowning down into her cup. "That man! He made me feel like I had done it. I'm sympathetic now to folks who tell little lies, or who get nervous under questioning by the police. I always thought if you were innocent, there was no reason to worry."

"That's because you have Virgil as a son." I watched Gogi across the desk. She is a neat, tidy, sixty-plus woman with a cap of glossy professionally dyed blonde hair and impeccable fashion sense. It wasn't quite autumn yet, so she still wore a lightweight safari-style cotton skirt suit and Cole Haan slingbacks. "Why was Esposito questioning *you*? I can't believe he'd think you killed the woman."

"I had a bit of a run-in with Minnie in early July. She knew I was working to get her replaced and confronted me one day when I was walking. She drove right up on the curb, hustled out of her car, and berated me in the nastiest language. I was worried and called the police. It was Deputy Urquhart who responded—imagine my luck—and he was neutral to the point of being ridiculous. Minnie was smart enough to tone it down in front of her nephew, and I had no witnesses to the altercation."

I thought for a moment. "Urquhart told Agent Esposito about that run-in, and that's why the agent is targeting you?"

She shrugged. "It's the only thing I can think of."

The Urquhart family was the one blight on my life in Autumn Vale. "Does she have any family who would know what was going on in her private life?"

"I don't think so; she's alienated most of her family in Ridley Ridge. I know because I've tried to find someone to talk some sense into her. Why do you ask?"

"I've heard that Minnie was doing online dating.

Apparently one of the guys that Rusty has hired was going out with her. They met online and he moved here to be close to her. What do you know about that?"

She shook her head and blinked, but didn't answer. "This murder seems too personal for someone who just met her; the way she was killed, I mean. That guy would have no access to the weapon."

"Roma's letter opener," I said, with a grimace. "I'd like to know how the killer got it."

"The one thing I do feel guilty about, and maybe this is why I was so uncomfortable talking to Agent Esposito, is that this clears the way for what I want to do about the post office."

The idea was to move a variety of services to a vacant building on a side street, one that had been built for offices back in the Victorian heyday of Autumn Vale. With elections coming up she had gotten local council members who were running for reelection on her side. If she had her way the township offices, as well as other departments, would share a compartmentalized but wheelchair accessible space with the post office.

"How were you getting information on her?" I asked, thinking of that campaign to get Minnie fired.

"*I haf my vays,*" she said in a vamped-up accent, and winked.

We talked a little more. I told her Virgil had discussed his FBI plans with me.

"I'm glad he told you," she said, putting her hand over mine, where it rested on her desk. "I know we'll miss him if he makes it and heads off to Quantico, but—"

"But it's time he did something for himself," I said. "He has my support, Gogi, whatever he wants." My feelings were a lot more complicated than that, but I was not going to tell either of them how much I wished he wouldn't go. I got up and tugged at my walking shorts and jacket. "I'd better get going. I want to figure out who did this. I don't believe Roma did, but she's making it hard not to suspect her."

I headed over to Jack and Shilo's new home. Dewayne Lester was working alone, using a plane on a new handrail, wood chips forming curls and falling to the beaten-down grass under the sawhorse. It appeared that they had stabilized the porch and supported it structurally, as the jacks were gone. Dewayne looked up and smiled as he saw me.

"Is Shilo home?"

He nodded. "So is Jack. He's changing his clothes and is going to help me, since my partner is out of commission today."

"Pete? What, too much beer at the bar in Ridley Ridge?"

"No, his allergies are acting up. The guy has eyes so red you'd swear he was a zombie. He says he's always like this in fall—ragweed or something."

"I'm sorry. Shouldn't make assumptions." I paused and watched his dark eyes as he regarded me calmly. "I heard you and Minnie were going out."

He nodded. "I've only known her a few weeks. She was getting back into dating, I guess, after some time."

"I'm the one who found her dead. I'm so sorry."

He nodded. "It's an awful thing. She had her flaws, but she just wanted to be loved."

"Don't we all?"

"You, I hear, have a thing with the sheriff. *If* we're talking love lives, I mean."

I smiled in acknowledgement of his jest. "*If* we're talking love lives. You took quite the chance, moving here to be with Minnie, though you only met online."

He eyed me warily. "Where'd you hear all that?"

"Around."

"She had another fellow, too, who she was talking to. I don't know that she was all that thrilled when I told her I was coming to stay in Autumn Vale for a while." He straightened and put a hand to his back, stretching. "I'm not much for staying in one place. Here sounded as good as anywhere, and there was a job available with Rusty. So I moved." He shrugged as if moving to a new town was no big deal.

Something was odd about Dewayne Lester, but I couldn't put my finger on it. He was not out of the running as a murder suspect, in my book. "Did she ever say anything about the kids who boarded with her?"

He bent back to his work. "She was worried about one of 'em."

"Which one?"

"I don't know. She didn't tell me his name."

His. "But it was definitely one of the *guys* she was concerned about? In what way? Worried *for* him, or *about* him?"

He paused again and looked up. "You sure do ask a lot of questions."

Shilo erupted from the house, stomping across the porch and trotting down the stairs, gypsy skirts fluttering with movement, but she stopped abruptly when she saw me.

Jack came flying out after her. "Shilo, wait, honey, I'm sorry, I—" He, too, stopped as soon as he saw me.

"I came by to talk. Is it a bad time?" I looked between Shilo and Jack.

She gave me a quick hug and mumbled something about an appointment. She jumped into Jezebel and roared away. I stood staring after her as Jack joined me.

"We were in the middle of an argument," he said glumly.

"What was the argument about?"

"I don't even know. She got a letter, and I asked who it was from. She wouldn't tell me. It was just idle curiosity on my part; no one gets actual letters in the mail anymore. I guess I thought it might be from her family." His homely, bony face was drawn down in a hangdog expression, and he shoved his hands in his pants pockets. "She threw it in her purse and said she had to go out. I grabbed her arm to get her to stop for a minute, and she got mad, said I was being snoopy and she didn't want that."

I was worried, and so was Jack. He didn't know what was wrong. Shilo had been moody for a few weeks, and had started avoiding him, he told me. "I'll get to the bottom of it, I promise, Jack. I'll track her down and *make* her tell me what's going on."

"Not right now, Merry, please," he said, touching my arm. "I never want her to feel like I'm trying to cage her, you know?"

The worry in his eyes made me tear up. He loved her so much. I couldn't swear he had nothing to worry about, couldn't reassure him that she'd stay with him forever. I just didn't know.

Jack got me an Adirondack chair from the shed and plunked it down while he and Dewayne got to work. As Dewayne sanded and planed, Jack applied a wood sealant, prepping the railings and spindles for white paint. When Dewayne left to go get some more supplies from the Turner Construction site, I took the opportunity to ask Jack what he knew about the guy.

Jack sat down on the grass and frowned, shaking his head. "Not much. He seems like a good guy, but he's kind of sketchy about his past, you know? I guess he's ex-military—I noticed a faded old Desert Storm tattoo on his shoulder one day—but other than that . . ." He shook his head and stared up at the sky.

"Have you known Minnie for long, Jack?"

"Sure, but we didn't have the same friends or anything. Something was going on in her life, that's one thing I'm sure of. A few weeks ago she called me to come evaluate her house."

"Evaluate her house? Why would she do that? Was she going to sell?"

"She said no."

"Why else?"

"Lots of possible reasons: she may have been thinking of new insurance coverage, making out her will, taking out a loan using it as collateral, any number of other things."

I watched him. "But you have an idea, don't you?"

"I'm not sure, Merry. But I do know one thing that troubles me. Minnie has recently been spending a lot of time talking to a drug dealer I know of in Ridley Ridge."

Chapter Ten

"A *DRUG* DEALER?" I blurted out.

Jack nodded.

I laid my head back and thought about it, but then sat up straight. "Whatever else she was, Minnie was *not* a druggie. Really, the idea's ridiculous, and you know that better than I do. So why would she be talking to a drug dealer? Maybe he's another one of her nephews and she was trying to straighten him out."

"He's not related, I know that. I'll ask around."

Dewayne screeched his battered pickup truck to a halt along the curb. As he returned to his work I regarded him thoughtfully. "I imagine the police have spoken to you about your relationship with Minnie. Probably asked you where you were that morning."

"I *have* spoken to the police about my relationship with Minnie." He straightened from cleaning a spindle with mineral spirits, the smell tangy on the dank, listless air that had rolled in after the brief promise of cooler weather this morning. "Are *you* asking where I was?"

He seemed a little defensive, but after all, I was a stranger and he owed me no information. "It's none of my business, is it?" I smiled, even though I did wonder, where *was* he that morning? Perhaps there were ways to figure it out. I got up and shouldered my purse. "Jack, walk me to my car?" As he got to his feet I turned to Dewayne. "I didn't mean anything by asking questions, I promise you. Snooping is getting to be a bad habit with me."

"So I've heard," he said, and bent back to his task.

Jack took my arm and we moved toward my car.

"Where is Dewayne staying, Jack? Was he staying with Minnie?"

"Nope. As far as I know he's staying in the trailer on the Turner Construction site, kind of acting as a night watchman."

I remembered that before I left in the spring Binny had said something about kids breaking into the Turner Construction storage shed and stealing tools. They must have done a background check on Dewayne if they trusted him so much.

"I'm going to try to talk to Shilo, Jack," I said as we approached my car. "There's something I'm concerned about." I told him what Doc had seen, and how Shilo had behaved. He had a right to know. We all only wanted what was best for her, but she had a hard time trusting that. The letter she had received but not shared with Jack worried me. He nodded, but didn't say anything.

I changed the subject, and filled him in on the little I'd heard about Karl Mencken's run-in with Minnie the night before she died. As I got in my car, I asked, "What's the address of Minnie's house?"

He gave it to me, I pulled away and drove there, a seedy backstreet minutes away. There were still many parts of

Autumn Vale that I hadn't explored, and this area was one of them; the whole neighborhood looked run-down, like folks had stopped caring a long time ago. As I slowly cruised, I noticed a couple of houses for sale, and a few that looked abandoned.

I found the correct address and saw that Minnie's house was a century bungalow in desperately poor condition with two huge trees out front. One, an old, leaning poplar with dead branches, was far too close to the stone foundation, which was cracked and mossy, with crumbling mortar. There was an overgrown forsythia bush in front, so big the branches trailed down to the ground. The clapboard siding was probably once a brilliant white, but now it was mostly bare gray boards, stripped of paint by time and weather. What little remained was peeling and bubbled. The whole thing had an atmosphere of desolation and decrepitude. Even the concrete block porch in front, with two columns supporting a porch roof, looked dizzy, leaning drunkenly to the right.

Two of Minnie's boarders, Brianna and the dark-haired boy—probably Logan Katsaros—exited, talking intently. They must still be living there, but I was sure the FBI had searched the house from top to bottom. It wasn't as if she had died there, but they still would have searched for clues to anyone who may have wanted her dead.

Janice had told me that Minnie made virtual offspring out of her young boarders, Karl, Brianna, and Logan. Who knew what tensions and turmoil went on within the walls of that moldy, decrepit-looking house? One or all of them could have their own reasons to kill Minnie, who must not have been the most congenial of landladies despite trying to mother them.

My curiosity, once stirred, would not be put to rest. I had to find out, I thought, watching them descend from the crumbling porch onto the walk, where they paused as she rummaged in her shoulder bag for something. With not much thought and even less planning, I got out of my car and headed toward them. Had they conspired to kill Minnie so they could . . . what? At best they'd be out of a home, and at worst, they'd be the subject of a police investigation as well as being out of a home.

Unless there was something *else* going on. Had Minnie caught them at something illegal? Was that why she was visiting a drug dealer in Ridley Ridge? I could not forget seeing Brianna with that suspicious package in the parking lot behind Golden Acres.

I approached with what I hoped was a friendly smile. "Hi! Are you the owners of this house?" I asked.

The boy eyed me with interest. "Why?"

Brianna dug him in the ribs with her elbow, but he shrugged and moved out of her reach.

"I've been told there are some houses along this street for sale. Is this one of them?"

"It will be," he said.

"I'm looking for cheap properties to buy up and re-develop." To them I must have looked businesslike in my dressy shorts and jacket.

"I've seen you before," Brianna said, her voice laden with suspicion. "Coming out of Golden Acres."

"Sure. I visit an old fellow there, Doc English. Now, about the house . . . Who can I talk to about it?"

"Us," the fellow said.

I thrust out my hand and took his in a shake. "I'm Merry Wynter. I own Wynter Castle, that big place out of town? But I'm looking for investment opportunities in Autumn Vale. And you are?"

"Logan Katsaros."

"Pleased to meet you. And you are?"

"Brianna," she said, without elaborating, and without offering her hand.

"So you think I could obtain this house, and maybe some of the others along here, for redevelopment? I don't think you mentioned who owns the house?"

"That's up in the air right now," he said. "But we could maybe arrange for you to get first dibs for, like, a commission?"

Brianna grabbed his T-shirt sleeve and jerked it. "We can't *do* that." She turned to me. "This was Minnie Urquhart's place, and she's dead."

"I'm so sorry!" I said. "You rented it from her?"

"We rent rooms," Logan said, with an appropriately sad expression, given that he was trying to help facilitate a sale of the property just seconds before.

"So who owns it now? I mean, who is the inheritor?"

"We don't know," Brianna said. "You'll have to talk to the lawyer, Mr. Silvio, about it." She grabbed Logan's wrist. "We have to go. I'm late for work."

"I guess the police have been here already?"

Logan turned back to me, even as he was being dragged away. "Yeah. They've had a good look around, but she wasn't killed here, you know. So it's not haunted or anything."

"Okay. Thanks for the information." I smiled and waved, and he waved back, winking, before striding off with his arm slung over Brianna's shoulders. She shrugged it off.

I got back in my car, retrieved my cell phone, and called Janice. Simon, her husband, was the local bank manager; after a scare when he thought he might lose his job and face prosecution for some funky goings-on at the bank, he had pulled up his socks, relearning his trade and making all of us proud. Janice was the only one I knew who would be able to get bank information from him, so I told her what I needed to know and she said she'd call me back.

Logan had mentioned Andrew Silvio, the lawyer. He was pretty much the only lawyer in town, and had been my uncle's probate attorney. As such, we had gotten to know each other pretty well. But he was a stickler for the rules, and would not likely offer me private information about Minnie Urquhart's affairs. However . . . as in the case of Simon, his wife was much more likely to be able to wangle info from the man than I would be. I called Gogi, who was in a book club group with Sonora Silvio and knew her much better than I. She might be able to find out what I needed to know.

I sat for long minutes staring into space, thinking. When I was young I was always moving, hopping from place to place, restless, fretful. The older I get, the more apt I am to stare out windows for long periods of time without moving. Stillness allows the brain to access the furthest recesses of the mind. That's my story, anyway.

At length I rustled around in my purse once more as I sat and stared at the dilapidated home that was Minnie's castle, and fished out a notebook. I had too many things to consider, find out, and confirm, and too little brainpower. So I made a list.

Where did Roma go the morning Minnie was killed?
Why was Minnie having her home evaluated?
Who was Minnie's next of kin, and who inherited
    whatever she left?
Why was Minnie seen talking to a drug dealer on
    more than one occasion?
How did the killer get the letter opener, presuming the
    killer and Roma weren't the same person?
Was there a reason Minnie was killed at the post
    office? Was anything stolen?

My phone chimed. It was Janice.

"Simon was pretty cagey," she said, her voice full of satisfaction. "But I got your answer. Want to trade?"

"Trade?"

"Quid pro quo, Merry. You do something for me, I give you information."

"What do you want?" I asked. With Janice, you never knew, and I couldn't promise without knowing. She might want something ridiculous or devious.

"I want you to talk Pish into scrapping *Much Ado About Nothing* and get him to do *The King and I* instead."

"I can't do that!"

"Why not? Pish will do anything you tell him."

"No, he *won't*." If I made a big deal out of it, he probably would, but that's the thing: I would *never* make a big deal out of it to get him to do something for my benefit. "We don't have that kind of relationship."

"Okay, fine, you don't want the info enough, then."

I sighed and rolled my eyes. "I'll talk to him, but I can't *promise* I can talk him out of *Much Ado About Nothing*."

"You have to try, Merry. I mean really *try*!"

"Okay, I will really *try*. Hannah would prefer *The King and I*, too. She'd like to play Lady Thiang. Now, what do you know?"

"Minnie did come into the bank and ask for a loan. But she didn't want to tell Simon what it was for. He told her that he couldn't give her a loan for some unspecified purpose. And anyway, if she was going to use her house as collateral she needed to get an evaluation done first. I guess she called Jack to do an evaluation. You know Jack; he's a straight shooter. He apparently told her that her dump would get her enough for a loan for a pack of gum and a coffee. Maybe."

I smiled but felt some sadness. Minnie seemed like one of those folks who struggle to understand life, while lashing out blindly at those who could be her friends if she let them. I never wanted to make an enemy of her, but neither did I try too hard to be friends, not after the way she spoke about Gogi to me. "Did she ever go back?"

"Yeah, just last week. She went in to talk to Simon about getting a loan to fix her house up. She said if she ever wanted to pass it on, she had to smarten up and make it worth something. It was all she had, her legacy."

"I wonder what that meant?"

"I have no idea. Minnie and I weren't on the best terms."

Maybe Minnie was getting older and thinking of family; maybe she had a nephew or niece she was especially close to. It didn't appear to have anything to do with her murder, but it was a part of the riddle, like that piece of sky in a jigsaw puzzle that doesn't look quite right until it clicks into place. Maybe this would make sense once seen within the context of more information.

My phone rang. It was Gogi, and she told me that Sonora had discovered a lot from her husband. "Minnie had been in to see Andrew about estate planning."

"Estate planning?" I opened my car window and stared at the dispirited, sagging house that was crying out for a wrecker to do his job.

"He'd done her will years ago, but she wanted to change it. She wanted to know if there was some way to tie up her estate so that her inheritor would have to abide by certain rules to get his or her bequest."

"Did Sonora use that wording, *his or her*?"

"Yes."

"So no clue as to whether the inheritor would be a man or woman, or even if she had a specific inheritor in mind?"

"Sonora wouldn't know that. But I'd say if Minnie was rewriting her will, she had someone in mind. I believe she'd already done it, from how Sonora put it, but that's third-person information, of course."

"And Minnie wanted to place some strictures on her inheritor. What kind, I wonder?"

"Sonora didn't know, but her husband said people try to do that all the time."

I was left with more questions than answers; I hate when that happens. "If you hear anything, let me know."

There was silence for a moment, and then Gogi said, "Why are you looking into this, Merry?"

I explained about Roma, and how I feared her outburst would impact the FBI investigation.

"You have to give the agent some credit, Merry. Aren't you taking this rather personally, anyway? This is Roma's problem if her actions have gotten her in hot water. Maybe she'll learn from it."

"You're right in a lot of ways, Gogi, but maybe I don't have as much faith in the power of human growth as you do. Roma is Pish's friend and protégé, and I don't want him troubled."

Gogi chuckled. "You don't need my advice. Just go on and do what you do; it's worked out so far."

After we hung up I revved the Caddy and pulled away from the curb. I wondered if investigating Minnie's death was a way for me to try to assuage my guilt . . . or not guilt, but sorrow at the way things had been between Minnie and me. I'd never been able to mend our rift, but I could, perhaps, help find who'd killed her.

Even though that wasn't my job. I had other things that should be a priority. Like finding out what was bothering my dear friend Shilo so I could help Jack make it better, or helping Lizzie and Emerald. I was most certainly going to attend a CC meeting, which I understood was scheduled for this very evening. But first I was going to enlist my very own super sleuth, Robin to my Batman, Watson to my Sherlock, Hastings to my Poirot.

There need to be more female crime-fighting duos.

I parked by the library hoping Hannah would be in, and she was. She pretends the library is only open three days a week, when in reality it's open most days for those who know to try the door.

We had tea, and I talked over what all I was trying to

find out. Hannah is consistently my best sounding board because she has a deep maturity based on reading, studying, and a humanity that had taken suffering—she had been through innumerable operations and medical treatments in her less than thirty years—and transformed it by some alchemy into an uncynical yet practical knowledge of people. She also has a wickedly subversive sense of humor not everyone gets to see.

"Minnie must have had an heir in mind, if she was asking about enforcing some kind of behavior by her will," I said. "Do you know any of her nieces and nephews? Maybe it's Deputy Urquhart."

"I wouldn't assume the heir is biological family," Hannah said.

"You're right. Minnie had created a kind of surrogate family with her boarders. Maybe it was one or all of them who were going to be, or had become, her heirs?"

"That's possible. And if that's the case, even a thousand dollars seems like a lot of money if you don't have any."

Especially if you were an addict, I thought. That might tie in with her conversations with a drug dealer in Ridley Ridge. Was she trying to straighten out one or all of her boarders? Was the will an attempt to enforce better behavior, and had it backfired, with the heir (or heirs) deciding to kill her for the money rather than straightening up? Much would depend on whether she had actually gotten around to creating the will that would apply strictures on her heir's behavior.

"So, I came here for another reason," I said, setting aside my teacup. "Have you ever attended one of these CC meetings?"

"Emerald's shop isn't wheelchair accessible," she said. Much of Autumn Vale was not wheelchair friendly. "Why do you ask?"

"I'm concerned about the effects Consciousness Calling and Crystal Rouse are having on Emerald, and more particularly on Emerald and Lizzie's relationship."

Hannah nodded gravely. "Lizzie was crying on my shoulder before you came back from Spain. She didn't like Crystal moving in with them. She says now with Emerald working so much, Crystal is constantly monitoring what she does. You know how independent she's always been; it's driving her bananas. Crystal has got Em believing that too much freedom has made Lizzie rebellious toward her mother."

That was pretty much what Lizzie had said to me. My young friend is smart. But the more you try to control her, the more rebellious she becomes. It was only with a liberal amount of freedom that she and Emerald had started to patch up their fractured relationship. Lizzie is independent, but uses her time wisely. She isn't taking drugs or stealing cars; she takes pictures. Her photos are artful, her intentions pure. Alcina, from whom she was being kept because of Crystal, is a good friend to her in so many ways. Like Lizzie, she's creative and independent. Even if she hadn't been, forbidding the friendship was the way to make a rebellious teen more likely to head off the rails rather than toe the line.

"I got an uneasy feeling about Crystal when I met her. I'm going to the CC enrollment meeting tonight for that reason, but also because I've heard from Mabel, Janice, and Lizzie that Minnie's boarder Brianna is involved. Could you do a little research for me? I've also heard that Crystal came here to stay with another Consciousness Calling follower; I think the name was Aimee? Who is she and what is her current relationship to Crystal? And I want to know about this whole CC thing."

Hannah jotted some notes. Shyly, she eyed me then looked away. "If you're going to be home tomorrow, maybe Mom and Dad could bring me out to the castle? I haven't been out for a long time."

"You're on. Come out tomorrow morning and bring me news!"

She tapped away on her computer keyboard and watched her monitor, biting her lip and frowning. She looks like a fragile china doll, the old-fashioned kind with the two tiny china teeth showing. But far from fragile, Hannah was tough as nails, and I loved her like a combination little sister and daughter. Her parents were two of the sweetest people I'd ever met.

"Ah!" she blurted out. "I've got it!" She turned to me, her big gray eyes shining in the dimly lit library. "I've got a name. I knew I had seen it on social media—a friend of a friend, you know? The woman Crystal stayed with when she first got to town was Aimee Jollenbeck. *And* she's heavily into Consciousness Calling, from what I can see. She's probably your best source of info on Crystal and CC."

"Yes! Now I have Aimee's last name." I hugged her and headed out of town, making a brief stop at the variety store for several tins of red salmon. Only the best for Becket. I drove back to the castle, bracing myself for whatever I may find, aware that I had promised Janice I'd raise the topic of *The King and I* with Pish.

Chapter Eleven

�֍ ✖ ✖

THE CASTLE WAS quiet . . . *too* quiet. A peremptory sign on the library door simply said *Recording*. I listened for a long few minutes; Roma hit the high note in "*O Mio Babbino Caro*" over and over, her voice cracking each time in the same spot. "Make her sing '*Il Dolce Suono*,'" I muttered, heading for the stairs with one of the tins of salmon and a dish. That was rather mean-spirited of me, since at the end of that aria, Lucia di Lammermoor expires.

I cooed and fawned over Becket for a while until he was eying me with the disdain cats save for those who are loopy over them. I watched him gobble up his salmon and then bathe himself all over in the slow thorough way that meant he knew he now had all the time in the world. He looked awful, with his orange-and-buff fur matted into clumps, his bones sticking out on his haunches where he had lost too much weight.

"You, mister, are not going out for a few days," I said, though I knew I'd let him go out when he wanted. That was the arrangement we had: I fawned all over him and cuddled him whenever he allowed it. He, in turn, wandered when he felt like it, came home if he cared, and let me take care of him, petting him and spoiling him rotten. It was my first boyfriend all over again.

I headed down to the kitchen to bake muffins. As I peeled and chopped apples, I thought of my list of questions. I had answered one, at least.

Minnie was having her home evaluated because she wanted a loan to fix it up, and she wanted to fix it up so it would be worth something when she passed it on to her heir. But who was the heir? I still didn't know. I wondered if the heir was aware of the bequest coming their way when Minnie died, and whether they were sufficiently cold-blooded to hasten her passing.

I put together an oatmeal streusel and played with the ingredients, finally coming up with what I'd call Apple Crisp Muffins. I popped them in the oven, setting the timer, then stared into the freezer for a few minutes. It would be quiche for dinner, since I had frozen pie shells and lots of eggs, cheese, and frozen spinach.

The phone rang while I was sautéing onions and garlic. It was Virgil, and we chatted, but he seemed distracted and admitted it was driving him nuts not to be in on the investigation into Minnie's murder, especially since she was one of *his* people, a Valeite.

"I'd love to crack the case and rub the FBI's faces in it. To *hell* with Esposito," he growled.

Interesting attitude for a man considering joining the FBI, but having dealt with the agent, I wasn't shocked. He treated Virgil like a gofer and messenger boy. Hesitantly, I told him what I'd discovered about Minnie's attempts to make her home worth more to leave to an heir. "So she was thinking of her own mortality, but I'm not sure it's connected. She was getting older and decided to do something, I guess."

I could practically hear him think.

"That doesn't sound like Minnie. She was difficult, and I know you two didn't get along, but—"

"Virgil, she made my life hell! And I'm not the only one; your mother had her problems with her, too. About the second day I was in Autumn Vale Minnie told me Gogi was a double murderer . . . that she had killed both her husbands."

"But she wasn't proactive. Minnie waited until something happened to her."

I bit my lip. Virgil did have a way of ignoring my outbursts. Was that most endearing or annoying? "Maybe something *had* happened. Did she have any health issues? Something that might worry her enough to make a change?" It was something to look into, but not for me.

We talked awhile longer, and I told him about Shilo acting odd, and what Doc had said about seeing her talking to a man. I fussed a little about Crystal Rouse, Emerald, and Lizzie. After a few minutes I could tell he was stifling either laughter or a yawn, and I wasn't sure which I preferred. "What is up with you?" I asked as I scooped the sautéed onions into the crust and crossed to the big professional fridge for eggs and cream. "Are you bored or laughing or what?"

"It sure didn't take you long to get back into the swing of Autumn Vale, and making everything your business."

I had a decision to make; I could either be offended or go along, and I did see the humor. I laughed. "Jerk. So what are *you* up to tonight?"

"I'm coaching the junior hockey team. We have our first formal practice tonight."

"You'll miss that when you go to Quantico," I said.

"*If* I go to Quantico; I haven't been accepted yet. Heck,

I just printed off the application today. They may not want an aging small-town sheriff."

"Virgil, you're in better shape than most twenty-five-year-olds, and you're smarter than any cop I've ever met. You'll make it."

He then asked if he could take me to dinner out of town one evening. I felt a flutter of nerves, and said, "Sure, but you can come out here for dinner anytime, you know."

He growled, a throaty murmur. "I am not going to be subjected to Pish's pet opera singer's pawing. I'd rather take you away from the castle."

I smiled. He was not saying that for me; Roma's relentless flirting made him uncomfortable. I ate dinner alone with a book in front of the empty fireplace. Well, not *totally* alone; Becket came down and had a bit of quiche with me. He expressed no desire to go out, and followed me back upstairs when I took a plate of dinner to Pish.

He was in his sitting room working at his desk. Maybe writing? But no, he was doing sketches for the *Much Ado About Nothing* staging. He is a Renaissance man, capable of most things he puts his mind to, and anything he puts his heart into.

"There's lots of quiche, if Roma wants some. I wrapped it and put it in the fridge."

"I'll tell her when she comes back. She went for a drive."

A drive? Where? I wondered. "Pish, has she told you yet where she was the morning Minnie was killed? You have to know that she could have been anywhere, even Autumn Vale."

He just shook his head and leafed through his sketches. "What do you think of this?" he said, pushing a sketch across his desk.

So, we weren't to speak of his pet's potential as a murderess. He started eating while I glanced over it.

"I thought of making it a roving performance, creating

several different sets in the castle and having the audience follow. You see this is the gallery," he said, pointing to a sketch with the end of his fork. "And this," he said, pushing another sketch toward me, "is by the big windows in the dining room. We would break between scenes and have the audience move."

"It could work. Would the voices resonate in each place?"

He got technical then, but the simple answer was yes.

When he was done, I broached the subject dear to Janice's heart. "Have you given thought to doing *The King and I*, as you promised?"

"I didn't promise, Merry, I said I'd think about it. I'm the program director and make the final decisions."

"Okay, you're the boss. I promised Janice I'd talk to you about it."

His gaze kept straying back to the drawings, and his attention, too. "Right now I'm concentrating on *Much Ado* for Roma's sake. She needs this, Merry."

I took the empty plate and touched his hand. He didn't need to explain to me. "I'm going out for a few hours," I told him.

"See you later, then," he said absently.

"I may commit a murder or two while I'm out," I said, watching as he bent over the sketches again, his attention wholly focused.

"Okay, love. I'll be here. Tell me how it goes."

I didn't know what to expect at a Consciousness Calling class. Would we be holding hands and singing "Kumbaya"? Taking a weird communal massage and dishing all our dirtiest laundry, as Lizzie had said? I drove into town and parked on a side street as the last rays of sunshine gleamed in the windows along the streetscape. It was still hot, so I'd decided on tan walking shorts and a pale blue silky tank top.

This evening's Consciousness Calling event was supposed to be an introductory session. I had seen the flyers all over town, stapled or taped to every telephone pole saying there would be a session Thursday evening, seven pm, and promising refreshments. I grabbed my purse and strolled the street. They practically roll up the sidewalks in Autumn Vale after five PM, except on Friday evenings, so everything was closed.

Emerald's shop, however, was ablaze with light, which glowed from the window and lit the dimming sidewalk outside it. I followed a youngish harried-looking couple in, wondering if this was their version of date night. There isn't a lot to do in Autumn Vale. The nearest movie theater is a drive-in on the other side of Ridley Ridge, and there are no bars in town. For that, too, you had to go to "sin city"—aka Ridley Ridge—where there was the run-down divey cocktail lounge where Emerald worked.

As the door started to close behind me, someone else rushed in. I turned to find Helen Johnson, a woman I knew to be a staunch supporter of the local church. I smiled at her and she looked uncertain, crossing the room and standing on the edge of the bank of fold-up chairs in the center, as if waiting until I sat so she could choose her seat. I was surprised she was there; this kind of new age stuff would be, I thought, anathema to her. But I had to imagine that many folks would check it out for gossip's sake.

Two more singles, a middle-aged man and an older woman, entered, and—surprise, surprise—Dewayne Lester, dressed in a clean T-shirt and jeans. He smiled and nodded. Interesting. There were seven of us newbies. Logan Katsaros was present, leaning against the wall, staring down at his cell phone. Beyond the curtain that sectioned the space from a back room I heard voices, whispering that rose to sharp words, and then Crystal herself emerged, her expression flashing from one of annoyance to a deliberately serene look of inner peace.

The curtains slashed open with a rattle of the beach glass

beads, and Lizzie stomped out to stand at the back. She was fuming inwardly so hard that she didn't even see me. Brianna followed. The girl caught sight of me, and her eyes widened. She sidled over and nudged Logan, who looked up, caught sight of me, and shrugged, murmuring something to Brianna. She smiled timidly at me, and I smiled back.

Well, this was working out. I was here to check things out, mostly for Emerald and Lizzie's sake, but if I could answer some questions about Minnie's relationship to her boarders I was all for multitasking. I cleared my throat and caught Lizzie's eye, gratified to see a smile replace the sullen look of fury. She rolled her eyes, then cast a significant look at Crystal, who was greeting the young couple at that moment, and rolled her eyes again. I nodded, then took a seat a row away from Dewayne, settling my purse on my lap. Helen abruptly plopped down on one on the far edge.

Music filled the room, one of those babbling-brook-overlaid-by-bird-noises-and-harp-music CDs meant to induce calm or irritation, depending on the person. I prefer my music as music and my bird noises in the woods. I snuck a glance over at Helen. She looked tense, her fingers white-knuckled where they clutched her pocketbook. Dewayne looked relaxed as he scanned the group, then sat back, the chair creaking with his weight.

Crystal finally noticed me, and her expression soured, though she regained her serenity in a flash. But she had stiffened, and her body language changed. I was not welcome, but she couldn't exactly throw me out in front of the others.

Brianna, like a proper acolyte, had moved to the front and stood to one side of Crystal watching her intently. Logan, who had taken a chair on the fringe of the group, looked bored, chewing gum, crossing his legs, then uncrossing them and fidgeting. The couple were whispering, bending toward each other in what looked like some kind of spat that ended in frigid silence.

Crystal gathered us all with a sweeping glance, then clapped her hands together in a prayerful attitude. This evening she looked more the part, wearing a white calf-length gown belted at the waist; it appeared to me to be an intentional echo of religious garb. Helen, wide-eyed, fidgeted in her seat, tucking her blue knee-length skirt under her thighs on the plastic folding chair.

"Welcome, all you *dear* people," Crystal said, holding out her hands palms down as if it were a benediction on us all. Her voice was different than when she normally spoke in conversation. "Welcome to our introductory session of Consciousness Calling, a system of living that will *free* you of guilt, worry, and fear, and bring to the surface your hidden reservoirs of strength, positive energy, and *healing*." She paused and looked around. "Healing," she repeated. "Think about that: whatever is ailing you, whether it is body, mind or spirit, you have the ability to fix it yourself. No therapy. No psychologist. Just *you*, and the power of positivity."

She spoke in the same vein for several minutes. Was this all there was, endless psychobabble positivity chatter that I could hear in any self-help group?

But when we had been lulled into receptiveness, I supposed, she got down to brass tacks. "As babies we know instinctively how to get what we want without being bogged down by the expectations and desires of others. But through our life we become burdened by guilt, overwhelmed by the neediness of others, depleted by the negative emotions surrounding us and the confusion of everyday life."

Everyone nodded. She had struck a nerve.

"With Consciousness Calling, you can learn to *rid* yourself of all that toxic negative energy. Abandon worry, escape guilt. You can become *truly* free to receive from the universe exactly what you *need*," she said, pointing and letting her finger rove over the audience. "What do you *need*? Whatever it is, you can have it."

She had them, I could see it. The young couple were rapt, leaning forward, as were the two singles. Even Helen was transfixed. Who didn't want to escape guilt and worry? The only holdout was Dewayne, who sat back with a neutral expression.

"It's simple, and *anyone* can do it. You need to open your heart, and let your body become one with your mind. You must stop trying to *control* the people around you, as you don't wish them to control you," she said, flashing a glance in my direction.

I heard Lizzie snort in the background and saw the severe look Crystal threw her way. From then on I started listening with more vigilance.

"Control is an illusion," she said, her voice becoming even more fluid, with almost a singsong quality. "Give up control. *Allow* yourself to be happy. Give yourself *permission* to become prosperous. Release those in your lives who only want to tie you down, make you bend to their will, destroy your confidence and peace. The universe wants to *reward* you, but you've been blocking it from giving you peace, love, happiness . . . and *prosperity*." She approached the crowd and met their gazes—except for me, who she skimmed over—and lowered her voice further, the sensation intimate. "You *deserve* money. You *deserve* happiness. You *deserve* all the nice things in life. Others have it; why not you?" She looked at the young couple. "Why not *you*?"

They nodded and both murmured what sounded like "Why not me?"

"Do you have people in your life who are tearing you down? Those are downward-trending people, DTPs. They want you to fail so *they* can feel better about themselves. They're *losers* on a downward spiral, and you are *winners* willing to do whatever it takes to become wealthy, influential, and happy. Once you become your true self, they may get angry," she said, pointing. "They may say you've changed.

Well, you will have; you will no longer be the *sucker* who makes them feel better about their *pathetic* lives. They'll try everything to make you come back into their loser fold and behave like the wretched, hopeless, joyless *losers* they are."

Helen sat back, an expression of distaste on her face. She shifted in her seat, sitting up straighter, clutching her purse tighter.

"But you're *better* than that," Crystal continued. "*You've* made the decision to make something of yourself, of your life. Do you wish you could find the strength to confront that boss who only wants to put you down? Or your mother-in-law who is always so snide?"

Nods, again, among the crowd, especially the young couple. But Crystal had lost Helen. The churchwoman's mouth primmed with a moue of distaste. Dewayne simply watched, a thoughtful look on his face, his beefy arms folded over his chest.

"I can help you eliminate the sources of turmoil in your life. But you need to *trust* me. Can you do that? Can you *trust* me?"

It was the siren song of the guru; *I can teach you to be happy, you just need to abandon all caring for those in your life who offer more complications than a bean sprout.*

There were murmurs of assent.

"We're going to do a focus exercise, Chanting the Contexts," Crystal said. She began, and those inclined followed.

"I deserve love. I deserve happiness. I deserve wealth. I am whole, I am complete, I am perfect as I am."

She went through that again and again, gathering people into her chant as she repeated it. I slipped into a meditative state, and caught myself saying, "I deserve love," with the rest of them.

There was a moment of silence, and I looked up to find Crystal staring at me with an odd, vibrant intensity. I was taken aback, my breath caught in my throat. She broke it off, and at a hand signal, Brianna sprang into action and wheeled out the massage table I had noticed along one wall. She centered it in front of Crystal.

Crystal put her hands on the table and smiled. "This is the cleansing table, where with just *one* Calling Inner Consciousness session I can help you remove from your life every *single* obstacle to happiness, wealth, freedom of mind and body. Do you want to be *rich*? I can help you. Do you want to find your perfect lover? Freedom from worry? Let me help you! Do you wish for better health? I can help you rid your body of those nagging problems that are keeping you from living and walking in perfect health."

Brianna appeared at her elbow with a clipboard.

"We do group Callings, but I'm only booking *private* Calling sessions for this week. They're far more effective for those seeking the maximum benefit, a quick fix to all your life's troubles and turmoil. It's *very* intense, and I can only do two every day. Maybe three. Four at the most. Let me help you receive the light and make your life *exactly* what you want it to be."

Logan had disappeared at some point during the session. I hadn't even noticed, and I realized that it was Crystal's quality of voice and the way she emphasized certain words that had made me so rapt I had missed some stuff during the chanting. Interesting. As strong as I thought myself, she had managed to snag me. She had the combined mesmeric quality of a county fair huckster and an evangelical preacher—a dangerous combination.

Lizzie and Brianna set up a little table with a kettle and jar of instant coffee and some bakery boxes of goodies I recognized as Binny's. Helen fixed a cup of coffee in a Styrofoam cup, snagged a cream puff, clutched her purse to her chest, and hustled out of the place as if she had accidentally strayed into a black mass ceremony, scattering white powered creamer as she beetled out.

The young man and woman were already signing up on the clipboard. After a brief, intense conversation, he got his wallet out of his pocket and pulled out a card.

"And there's the payoff." Lizzie was at my elbow, arms crossed over her chest.

"What do you mean?"

"He's got his credit card out," she muttered. "It's either that or cash to book a session. She's a freakin' genius."

Crystal made them sign something, then wrote down his credit card number. The other two unknowns in the class were lined up waiting, and I examined them. I had seen them around before, but I didn't know their names. Both looked uncertain, but when you want a better life it's tempting to believe someone who tells you they know all the answers. Crystal was convincing.

"Maybe she *can* help people," I murmured.

Lizzie looked up at me with a snort of disbelief. "What is it with adults? You're all so . . . so brainwashable."

Lizzie was young and despite her difficult life so far, she still had the faith that if adults left her alone, she'd manage just fine. When you get older, life crowds in on you; there are so many demands, all competing. Sometimes to fulfill all of other people's needs and expectations you sacrifice your own. Crystal had tapped into a desperate desire for release.

"I know that's Brianna, Minnie's boarder," I said, motioning toward the girl. "What's she like?"

Lizzie shrugged. "She's okay. Messed up in the head, but okay otherwise."

"Messed up in the head?"

"When she was kicked out of the foster care system at eighteen, she didn't know what to do. She was practically homeless. But then she moved here and found a job and lived at Minnie's."

"A pseudo-family." With Minnie as pseudo-mom. "I

talked to her once, but I'd like to speak to her again. Can you get her out of here?"

"Sure." She went to Brianna, motioned toward me, and the girl nodded.

Lizzie and Brianna followed me out the door, watched by Dewayne. Crystal noticed, but she was tied up with the couple, and trying to keep the attention of the two singles, who were getting impatient and starting to eye the exit themselves.

The evening was cooling off. I turned as the two girls followed me out and down the walk a few steps.

"Bri, this is Merry Wynter," Lizzie said. "She wanted to talk to you about stuff."

I gave my young friend a look. That was not what I had in mind, her being warned that I wanted to talk to her. She'd be on her guard and probably report back to Crystal. "We've met," I said pleasantly to Brianna. "I'm sorry about Minnie." I hadn't thought it through, and my lack of planning was going to make for an awkward moment. "Actually, I know I didn't say it when we met before, but I'm the one who found her. Dead. It's . . . it's terrible, and when I saw you here I wanted to say, I'm sorry."

Brianna's face was blank of expression and she didn't reply. I examined her for a moment, the petulant lips stained with bluish lipstick, her dyed hair pulled back in a messy ponytail. How could I find out what I wanted to know? "I understand Minnie came here to the Consciousness Calling a couple of times. There was some kind of confrontation with her."

Brianna shrugged. "It wasn't her thing."

"That must have been awkward for you. Is anyone pressuring you to leave the house, with Minnie gone?"

The girl, her eyes rimmed in dark makeup and her lashes thickly coated in mascara, stared at me with suspicion.

"Why did you talk to me and Logan earlier? And why didn't you say who you were? Minnie *hated* you. She told, like, everyone. Maybe *you're* the one who killed her."

"Merry would never hurt anyone!" my young friend bellowed, hands balled into fists. "You watch what you're saying or I'll—"

"Lizzie, enough!" I held up a hand and gave her a look, then returned my gaze to Brianna. I hadn't figured that Minnie would have openly talked about me to her boarders. But what else did she have besides work and her various interpersonal wars? "I didn't kill Minnie. I felt sorry for her, in a way."

Brianna snorted and looked away.

"How did you learn about what happened to Minnie that morning?"

She shrugged. "Cops came hammering on the door. I was in the shower getting ready for work, so Logan answered."

"That's right, there were just the two of you. Your roommate Karl had a big fight with Minnie the night before and stormed out."

She sharply turned and stared at me. "Who told you that?"

"The guys he's crashing with."

"He didn't *walk* out," Brianna bluntly stated. "Minnie *threw* his ass out . . . kicked him to the curb."

Chapter Twelve

I **OPENED MY** mouth to ask why, and what their argument was about, whether it had become physical, but Emerald strode down the sidewalk toward us.

"Merry, what are *you* doing here?"

Taken aback by both her arrival and her abruptness, I waited a moment so I wouldn't snap back, then said, "I took your suggestion and came to the introductory CC session."

"What are you doing home from work so early, Mom?" Lizzie asked, hope in her voice.

"I hated leaving Crystal to manage this all on her own," she said, her gaze slewing uncertainly from me to Lizzie to Brianna and then into the shop, where Crystal was still dealing with potential clients. "I knew *you* wouldn't be much help," she said to her daughter. "What are you doing out here gabbing?"

Lizzie whirled and headed off down the street. "I'm going home!" she yelled over her shoulder. "*You* can help Crystal put away the stinking snacks. I've got homework."

"Lizzie, you get back here!" Emerald shouted, then sighed and shook her head.

Brianna, looking disgusted, headed in and Emerald turned to go, too, but I caught her arm. "Em, is everything okay? Maybe we can have a cup of tea back at your place and talk. I haven't even seen your new home yet."

Crystal came to the door and opened it, gazing out silently.

"Lizzie went home, Crystal," Emerald said, pulling her arm from my grasp. "I'll come and help in a sec." She turned to me and opened her mouth to speak.

Crystal called out, "Deety pee, Emerald, dear . . . deety pee."

"What does that mean?" I asked, wondering if it was some weird signal that she needed a bathroom break.

"Nothing. I have to go." She turned and trotted up the steps into her shop.

And then I got it: not deety pee, DTP. In Crystal-speak I was clearly a downward-trending person. I walked away in a funk, feeling like I had a communicable disease.

It was almost dark. Despite there being a murderer in our midst I still felt safe in Autumn Vale; maybe I was delusional. I strode down the sidewalk into the gloom, and turned the corner. Were those footsteps behind me? I paused; silence. Maybe it *wasn't* such a good idea to walk off alone. My heartbeat thudded in my ears, and chills raced down my back.

Perhaps I should have stayed with the others for a while. I turned and waited, but no one came around the corner. I got my keys out, splaying them between my fingers like I always did in the city, clutched my bag to my chest, and walked on.

Who had so brutally murdered Minnie Urquhart? Someone who knew her, I assumed, because she had apparently let them into her postal station. How, though, did the killer get the letter opener? I needed to confront Roma and ask her. Footsteps behind me echoed again as I trotted down the shadowy side street where the Caddy was parked. I turned, but there was still no one there. "Hello?" I called out.

A garbage can clattered nearby, a dog barked, and a cat screeched, the trifecta of woman-in-peril scenes in movies. Maybe it was normal to be unnerved when someone I knew had been murdered. I took a deep breath and relaxed, though I did not let down my guard. I got to my car, looked around, checked the backseat, then got in, started the Caddy, and cruised out of town, heaving a sigh of relief.

Safe at last!

I opened the window. As night fell the air got noticeably cooler, now that we were past the halfway mark in September. I hadn't forgotten about the one-year anniversary party I wanted to throw. I started to compile guest lists in my mind, and plan the food; maybe I could rope in Binny for baked treats and Patricia for a cake. Pish could do some show tunes on the piano. If Roma was still at the castle, she could sing. She'd love that, and it would be both good practice and advertisement for their opera.

I could see the headlights of a car bobbing in my rearview mirror. Well, that happened on occasion, even on my way down the lonely road back to the castle. We had come to a stretch that was enclosed by forest and had a sharp decline on the right, though if you weren't familiar with that section of the road you wouldn't know that because in the dark it was masked by the tall trees. I didn't see the headlights behind me anymore, and relaxed.

Then I felt a jolt and experienced that shock, the sick feeling in the core of your stomach when you know that your vehicle is no longer in your control. I shrieked as the car moved seemingly on its own, as if sliding on ice, even though I gripped the steering wheel so tight my fingers spasmed, freezing in place, pain shooting through them. Weirdly out of body, I caught a glimpse in the rearview mirror. There were no headlights, but a vehicle nudged me ever closer to that sharp drop-off, even though I wrenched the steering wheel with all my might in the direction I wanted to go.

But I knew the road after a year of driving it, and I knew the Caddy. I jerked the wheel the other way, using the full power of the '67 V8 engine and rear-wheel drive to get me off my assailant's front bumper. My heavy, lumbering, wonderfully sturdy American-made tank lurched to the left. Gravel skidded out from under me, pinging on the underbody, and the Caddy settled up on the opposite shoulder as the other vehicle roared past and down the road.

Silence settled with the dust. I started shaking and whimpering, quivering like a kicked puppy, my shoulders aching and my hands cramped on the wheel. I had to consciously flex my fingers to release the steering wheel. I was off-kilter, the seat belt digging into my shoulder.

Who had done this? And *why*? As I calmed I realized why I felt pressure and was on a slant; in wrenching the car so far away from the edge of the slope, I had gotten myself away from the jerk who was trying to wreck me, but had ended up on the opposite side with the car stuck up on something.

It was a moonless night. Just sitting there all evening wasn't an option. I took some deep yoga breaths, letting my heart rate decline. First step, I had to ascertain the damage. The car started but did not want to move, even though the rear wheels seemed to be in contact with the road or shoulder surface. I undid the seat belt and awkwardly climbed out of the car, rolled my aching shoulders, and peered into the dark, but couldn't see a bloody thing. I picked my way around the car to the trunk, where I kept a tool kit with a flashlight. Using my cell phone flashlight app—barely bright enough to find the keyhole and wrench open the trunk—I got it out. My car flashlight was big, the beam nice and wide. Hoping the car or truck that had run me off the road wasn't coming back, I checked out the bumper damage. It was crumpled, and my taillight was broken. Good old Detroit sturdiness had prevented more damage. Then I circled to the front.

"Well, that sucks!" I said. The Caddy was jammed up on a thick log from a tree that had fallen in the spring. County workers had shoved it off to the side of the road. It had saved me, I supposed, from hitting the rocky outcropping, which would have done a lot more damage to the car, and perhaps me.

A heavy motor rumbled, and I saw headlights coming down the road. My stomach lurched. I scrambled to get into the car, probably the best protection I could get, but awkward because of the angle it was on. The vehicle slowed as it got closer, and then stopped, facing the Caddy. The driver cut the headlights. Someone big emerged, and I saw the beam of a flashlight bob around, slicing through the darkness, circling the car. I whimpered and started, with shaking fingers, to dial Virgil's number.

When someone tapped on the window I jumped and screamed.

"Merry, are you okay?"

It was Dewayne Lester. He shone the flashlight away, angling it so there was enough light that I could see his face, his dark, intelligent eyes, his stubbly round chin. I nodded and took a deep breath, trying to calm my shaking. "I'm okay!" I asserted. What was he doing here? I had last seen him in the CC meeting, and he was still there, I thought, when I left. If he was my assailant, he would have zoomed past me, and if he circled back . . . I quivered, my nerves making me shudder. He would have come from that exact direction. "I'm fine. Really."

"No, you're not. You're in trouble here," he said, his voice muffled through the glass. He motioned to the front of the car. "Can I give you a hand?"

I paused. If I called Virgil he might not even get the message right away. "What are you doing along here?" I asked, rolling down the window an inch. "Last I saw you were at the meeting."

"I left right after you, but somehow I got turned around on my way out to Turner Construction, so I was backtracking," he said, watching my eyes. His expression was mild as he said, "Look, if you're freaked out I'll leave you alone. Pete drives a tow truck; I can call him. He'd be here in ten minutes. What can I do that will make you comfortable?"

That's exactly what a helpful man would and should say. I took a deep shaky breath and looked out at him, rolling the window down farther. "Someone tried to run me off the road— I don't know who. I managed to wrench the car in the other direction, but now I'm kind of wedged on that tree."

"Is your car still working?"

"It seems to be fine."

"They don't make 'em like this anymore," he said, nodding. "My dad worked in the plant that built them. Probably worked on this very car. My truck's a Ford F-150 and I have towing straps in the back, so I can pull you free, if you like. I don't think there'll be any damage." He shone his flashlight toward the front of the Caddy and squatted, looking under it. "You're not up on there far enough to have punctured anything, so if I can free you, you can at least get home. You don't have far to go now. Take the car to your mechanic tomorrow for a look-see."

"I'd appreciate the help," I said and took another deep breath. His matter-of-fact manner and helpfulness were restoring my nerves to their normally calm state. If I trusted my instincts, he was not my attacker.

It would take too long to describe how we managed it, but we did. He checked underneath the car again, and said I didn't appear to be leaking anything. I thanked him. In the city I would have offered a good Samaritan money, but we don't do that in the country. We're all in this together, and someday he might need a lift or some help. I clutched his strong, warm hand through the car window and he smiled.

He followed me back to the castle to make sure the car worked, then tooted his horn and turned in the driveway, heading back wherever he came from. I did have a fleeting thought; he seemed to know *exactly* where the castle was, despite never having been to it . . . to my knowledge.

Pish's car was in its spot, so Roma must be back from wherever she went. I didn't want to talk to anyone, I was so drained and unnerved. After locking up securely I retreated to my room, flung my clothes off, and climbed into bed naked, something I hadn't done in a long time. Becket seemed to sense my mood. He leaped up on the bed, butted my chin, then turned once on the cover, tucked his tail in over his eyes, and drifted to sleep, purring. Despite the fear I had felt—or maybe because of it and the consequent adrenaline rush depleting me—I, too, fell fast asleep, my hand resting on the purring cat.

THE NEXT MORNING I MADE A CUP OF COFFEE AND headed out, dressed in my silk robe over shortie pajamas hastily thrown on, to sit on the terrace. I had just settled when a sheriff's department car screamed up the lane and screeched to a halt, spraying gravel. Virgil, his face red, erupted from the car, tore up to the terrace and grabbed me up from my chair, kissing me so hard my coffee spilled everywhere and I would have fallen if he hadn't had a *very* firm hold on me.

I spluttered and wrenched myself away from him, shocked by his vehemence when I wasn't even awake all the way. "Steady, Sheriff!" I spluttered.

He pulled me back into his arms and held me against him; his heart was thudding like a jackhammer. "What the *hell* were you thinking, not calling me last night after you were run off the road by some lunatic?"

I pulled away again, looking up into his worried brown eyes. "I should have called the police, but I was so tired when I got home that I never thought of it. I'm sorry." Of course, he was right: if someone that crazy was out on the roads, they were a danger to others.

"*Screw* the sheriff's office," he said, his voice gruff. "You should have called *me*, your . . . your boyfriend. Or whatever you want to call me."

I was taken aback, thrilled, and then puzzled. "Wait, how did you even hear about it?"

"Dewayne Lester. He stopped by the station this morning on his way to work and asked if we'd found the guy who ran you off the road."

"That probably eliminates him as a suspect," I said with relief. "Being Johnny-on-the-spot as he was, I thought he might be the one who . . ." His gaze had become shifty, and I cocked my head to one side, watching him. "Virgil, what aren't you telling me?"

"You don't need to worry about Dewayne." He crossed his arms over his chest and glared over my head. "I know him."

Trying to keep from being distracted by bulging biceps in a short-sleeved sheriff's department shirt, I said, "You *know* him? I thought he was new in town."

"He is."

"Then how do you know him?" I righted my spilled coffee mug but didn't take my gaze from Virgil.

He didn't answer, his jaw flexing as it does when he's agitated. He rolled his shoulders. I put my hands on those shoulders and kneaded, feeling the tension knotted there. He'd called himself my boyfriend; *that* was an interesting development, since we'd never yet had that discussion. Adult dating is awkward sometimes.

A throaty growl murmured though his body, and he took

me in his arms, kissing me again, more gently. It was nice—very, *very* nice. Our relationship seemed to be leaping around in all directions, and I was confused.

However . . . "Virgil, I won't be distracted," I murmured as he nuzzled my neck. I sighed. His hand wandered down, cupping my bottom, pulling me to him. Oh dear. I moved his hand back up to the small of my back. "Virgil, how do you know Dewayne Lester?"

"He's a PI."

I jumped back like a scalded cat. "A *what*?"

He grimaced at my reaction. "A private detective from Buffalo."

I digested that. "But why . . . who . . . ? I don't get it. Who is he working for?"

"Me, indirectly. The county, actually."

"You've got some explaining to do, mister," I said, hands on my hips.

"I'm at your command."

I felt at a distinct disadvantage with him in his uniform and me in a shortie robe. "Wait here." I went in, got dressed, and made us both coffee and him some breakfast, bringing it out on a tray.

It was a secret for now. Gogi knew, but no one else, he told me between bites of leftover quiche and crisp bacon. About a month ago he'd decided that if the postal service wasn't going to send anyone to investigate Minnie, he'd try to get a line on what she was up to. It was his jurisdiction since it involved his citizens, he figured, and there may be crimes apart from those involving the post office that he could nab her on. Because of his thrifty management there was money in the department budget, so he allocated some to pay a private detective. It's not a common route to take, he admitted, but well within the law.

He had met Dewayne years before, when the man was a part-time firearms instructor at the police academy Virgil went to, as well as being a cop. In the years since then Dewayne had retired from police work and set up as a private investigator. When Virgil heard through the grapevine that Minnie was on one of the online dating sites, he had Dewayne contact her. His intent was to get information on what she was up to so Virgil knew what direction to pursue. On the strength of their "relationship"—which consisted of chatting online and talking on the phone—Dewayne thought there was enough justification to move temporarily to Autumn Vale to gather evidence.

The sweetheart ruse worked; Minnie had bragged about petty thefts, trying, in some absurd way, to impress her new beau. The woman was sly, Virgil told me. She had left very little actual evidence except for a string of complaints from citizens to the post office about missing mail. So far there hadn't been any evidence of check theft; it was mostly magazines, small packages, and cash. She never stole anything with a tracking number. Dewayne had discovered enough that the U.S. Postal Inspectors were *about* to raid her postal station and home.

But her murder got in the way. Her death *seemed* terribly coincidental, but coincidence is a part of life. Dewayne had given what information he had to the FBI, trying to help them in the murder case.

We then discussed whomever had run me off the road. It could have been reckless kids joyriding, some other random and possibly drunken jerk, or someone targeting me for something, who knew what? I had my fans, locally, and I had my haters.

"Dewayne is coming out to have a look at your car," Virgil said. "Can you stay put for the day?"

"Part of it. Hannah is coming out to visit this morning."

"I want to know if Dewayne can find any bits of paint from the other car. It's a specialty of his. Do you have any idea who it was?"

I thought, but shook my head. "If I think of anyone, I'll tell you."

"I'll be checking out every car with front-end damage; you can bet on that," he said, his tone grim.

"In Autumn Vale, that could well be every other car."

Virgil was finishing his breakfast when Roma came out dressed in only a red silk–and-lace peignoir set, stretching in an unconvincingly casual way. She practically purred when she saw Virgil, though her expression of delight faded when he got up, took my arm, and led me over to his sheriff's department car. He leaned me back against the car, kissed me thoroughly until my cheeks and chin were slightly sore from his constant stubble—the man could shave and an hour later he'd have stubble—and declared his intention to find the bastard who'd run me off the road if it took all his time and that of his department. He then departed on a call, promising to follow up with Dewayne.

I was smiling as I swayed past Roma, picked up my man's dishes, and sashayed into my castle, of which I was the queen. Then, being the adult I am, I washed the dishes, put them away, and considered that Virgil and I were going to have to have a talk, since we had apparently started "going steady" when I wasn't looking. Or something.

Patricia arrived with a box of assorted goodies from the bakery. She was there to lend moral support to Roma, who was nervous about the final recording of "O Mio Babbino Caro" she was doing that day. I was in a charitable mood, despite the frightening episode the previous night, so as Roma warmed up in the library, I sat down for a cup of tea and a Napoleon with Patricia. I told her that I had attended a CC introductory class the previous night, and asked if she had, too, and if so what she thought of Consciousness Calling and Crystal Rouse.

"I'm not one much for organized anything," she said. "But I was curious, so I went."

"Did you have one of those . . . what does she call them? A Calling Inner Consciousness session?"

"I did at one of the group sessions."

"What did you think of the Chanting the Contexts part? And what happened with the calling?"

"The chanting bit was interesting; I found myself relaxed, even sleepy. I thought it might be good for me." She frowned, her double chins tripling as she stared down into her tea mug. "But then, the Calling . . . well, I was lying on that massage table with the group feeling self-conscious."

She didn't need to say why. Big girls usually do feel self-conscious in a social setting, and Patricia is a good deal larger than I. Lying on a table with a bunch of other folks around? Not for me, not on your life.

"There were three other folks, and we each had a thirty-minute session. They put their hands on me while Crystal talked a bit and felt my head. She was touching what she called 'Consciousness Centers.' I'm not sure what I was supposed to get out of it. She *said* it would trigger memories, associations, and let my mind float. I can confidently tell you that nothing of mine floated."

"You didn't get anything out of it?"

"Nothing. She said I could talk, say whatever I wanted, sing, moan, whatever. All I could think was that my stomach probably looked even bigger lying on my back. And I worried about rolling off the table, which was not meant for a gal of my proportions. When we did the others, two of them swore they had the sensation of floating, and felt freer at the end of it."

"Did *they* say or do anything?"

She colored faintly. "The . . . uh . . . the one fellow got an erection." She giggled with a girlish smirk. Her smile died. "And one woman said some personal, painful stuff, things I don't think she should have shared with strangers."

I was curious about who that was, but knew Patricia well enough to not ask. She is a thoroughly nice person, and doesn't gossip. As the overweight daughter of a once-wealthy family, she had put up with a lot of mean-girl behavior in social circles and at private school.

"It almost sounds like hypnosis," I mused.

She sipped her tea and put down the china mug on the trestle table. She gazed out the window over the sink, which looks out on the woods. "I don't understand what the others got out of it that I didn't. *They* felt better afterward, lighter, freer. Crystal booked them for private sessions. I felt like I'd missed out on something."

"Don't think there's something wrong with you. If it was a form of hypnosis, some people are easier to hypnotize than others, and I've heard that some report what they think the hypnotist wants or expects to hear. It's not you, it's them. Did you go again?"

She met my gaze and rolled her eyes. "No *way*. She wanted three hundred dollars for a private session."

Three hundred dollars, and she said she could do four a day. That would be twelve hundred in one day, potentially. I chewed on my lip. "I'm worried about Emerald. She has shut me out, and I think I'm being shunned at Crystal's command."

"Emerald is a tough nut," Patricia said. "She'll be just fine."

I shook my head, not sure she was right. Em had been through a lot in the last year, and perhaps it was all crowding in on her now. Besides, I was more concerned with the effects of it all on Lizzie.

Patricia was called into the taping session. She was, it seemed, a calming presence to Roma. In truth, many singers do better with a live audience, and I didn't fault Roma for that.

I was finishing up some muffins for Patricia to take back to the bakery when I heard a vehicle outside. I went out to greet Hannah and her parents at the door off the butler's pantry, the only one we could get the motorized wheelchair through. Her parents saw her settled in the kitchen, and Mrs.

Moore was kind enough to ask if there was anything I needed. I overwhelmed her with a lengthy list and a fistful of cash. She laughed when I demurred, realizing what an imposition it could be, and said she loved grocery shopping. She bid a fond farewell to her daughter, the light of her life and headed off to shop at the Aldi and Hobby Lobby in Batavia.

We sat at the table and I made more tea, poured some, and told Hannah about my experience the previous evening. She was horrified and frightened for me, but then said, "See, I told you that you live an exciting life!"

"That kind of excitement I can do without. Anyway, Watson, what have we discovered?"

"Some interesting stuff."

Becket wandered downstairs, wound around my legs, then leaped up on Hannah, trying to find room to sit on her tiny lap. They managed to find a way to be comfortable, and she stroked his fur, picking at mats with her slim fingers, while indicating her laptop, on the table. "Fire it up, Sherlock, and I'll *show* you what I've discovered. I've made some notes, too, in a document file."

First there was information on Consciousness Calling. Hannah had bookmarked their website for me. It was indeed a franchise listed as a therapeutic health-care business. While emphasizing the spiritual nature of their company, they claimed that what they actually did was holistic healing, motivational training, and "teaching people to be happy." I didn't know you could teach folks that.

All the photos on the website showed shops with a teal banner that proudly proclaimed them to be Consciousness Calling businesses. There was nothing like that on Emerald and Crystal's shop, not even a sign in the window. I shared what I was thinking with Hannah. "I wonder if Crystal even has a legitimate franchise, without that branding."

"Maybe you can take that up with Aimee Jollenbeck."

"Do you happen to have an address?"

"I do," Hannah replied. "And I also know where she works. She's a cleaner at the Methodist church, *and* she's Helen Johnson's stepsister."

"Wow, *that's* a surprise. Helen was at the meeting last night."

Hannah ruffled Becket's fur and he took exception, jumping down. "Maybe she was gathering intel, spying for Aimee."

I smiled at my Watson's vivid imagination. However, she had been right more than once about things, and perhaps she was now, too. "I'll pay a visit to Ms. Jollenbeck," I said, and wrote down her address, which was in an unfamiliar section of town.

The huge knocker on the front door banged, and I excused myself and scooted out to answer it. There was my knight in shining armor. "Dewayne! Virgil said you'd be stopping by." I looked over my shoulder, closed the door behind me, grabbed his wrist, and led him to the edge of the terrace. "He told me who you are, too," I said, searching his dark brown eyes. "I'm sorry if I seemed hesitant last night."

He touched my shoulder with a sympathetic smile. "You had just been run off the road, and I charged up in a big old truck. You were right to be wary."

His round face was split by a ready grin, teeth slightly yellow, eyes a bit bloodshot; it was the face of an honest man. "Thank you. I did appreciate the help last night, and you were so calm. It made everything easier." I paused a beat, then asked, "What was Virgil like when you first met him?"

He smiled and shook his head. "Aw, no. No *way*. You'll have to discover Virgil Grace for yourself. I have the four-one-one on you two; he's nuts over you. Never seen him like this, not even when he first got engaged to Kelly."

I stayed silent; any mention of Virgil's ex-wife was dangerous ground for me. I never mentioned her by name, and tried not to criticize her. That was between them.

He eyed me with a slight smile and a nod. "Some folks

in town are a little afraid of you, you know. You're a strong, smart woman; lots of folks can't handle that. And you are a stone-cold fox, if you don't mind my saying."

Coming from some men I'd bristle at the last comment; women are too often considered primarily on physical appearance. But his first comment had been about my strength, intelligence, and ability to intimidate, so I didn't mind. "Your friend the sheriff is not always the easiest guy to talk to."

"He's like a classic novel: tough to get into, but once you start, you realize how worth the effort it is."

"Dewayne, were you following me last night? Is that how you came across me?" I thought maybe he'd seen who ran me off the road. He must have driven past the car or truck, since he was coming from that direction.

"No, Merry. If I were following you because I suspected someone, or had seen who did this, the driver would already be in lockup. I really did get lost on a back road. No one came past me, either; I think he or she must have turned down a side road."

"Darn. Thought it might be an easy solution. Anyway, I know you're here to look at the car, and I want to be here when you do, but I have a friend in the kitchen. I'd better go and tell her I'll be a minute."

"Why doesn't she come out and join us?"

"She's in a motorized wheelchair. It might be a little tough."

He examined the castle. "She came out in a vehicle equipped for her wheelchair and was dropped off at that door, right?" He pointed toward the far end of the castle wall where the door to the butler's pantry hall was. "I'd bet if she came out that way, her wheelchair could make it over the ground. If not I can always help her. Would she be interested, though, in me looking your car over?"

"Hannah is the town librarian," I said over my shoulder as I headed to the front door. "She's interested in *everything*!"

Hannah's wheelchair made it across the grassy area all right, but I decided then and there to work on making the front door wheelchair accessible. It actually wouldn't be that difficult. Since Turner Construction was back up and running, maybe they could do it.

Dewayne was not, however, at my car. "Dewayne?" I called out.

He looked up from what he was studying and said, "Whose car is this?"

"That's my friend Pish's," I said.

"Come here," he said, crooking his finger.

I circled the car. The front right bumper was crumpled and the headlight was busted. I looked up at the castle in shock. Roma had been out in Pish's car last evening, but got home before me. Was she my assailant?

Chapter Thirteen

�֍ ✖ ✖

HANNAH WAS INTENSELY interested in everything Dewayne had to say and show us. I was distracted and troubled by Pish's crumpled bumper, but for all I knew, as I pointed out to Dewayne, it may have happened before I even got home from Spain. We'd have to find out from Pish and Roma.

He examined my car and took pictures. For good measure (and without comment) he photographed Pish's bumper. As the sun rose, the day began to heat up. Virgil was busy with Esposito and his agents, so he sent Deputy Urquhart, Minnie's nephew, to collect the evidence from my close call. He and Dewayne gathered minute flakes of paint from the bumper, and the deputy took an official statement from me about the incident. He was thoroughly professional through the whole episode, despite past conflict between us.

As Dewayne explained his investigation kit to Hannah, I took the opportunity to speak with the tall young deputy.

"I'm so sorry about Minnie. It was a horrid thing, and I hope we find who did it."

He nodded, his jaw tightening.

I took a deep breath and faced him. "I know she didn't like me, Deputy. We had our differences, but I'm being sincere. I'm so *very* sorry this happened. Were you close?"

He took off his mirrored sunglasses. "Not lately. But when I was a kid, things were kind of crazy in my house. My parents . . ." He paused and glanced over at me. "You don't want to hear about this."

"Yes, Deputy, I do," I said, and touched his arm. Words sometimes fail us; sincerity can often be more effectively transmitted with a touch.

He took a deep breath. "My parents fought all the time. Aunt Minnie used to take me and my brother out for a drive when it got bad. The only normal things I remember from being a kid, I did with her. She took us to the county fair. We went camping, even though she hated it, and fishing, too. She made sure we had scouts' uniforms and sports equipment."

She had done all that? And yet she would gossip and name call and be petty with the worst of them. How mixed and flawed we all are, I thought. If only I could start over again with Minnie. But death robs us of any opportunity for a second chance. He looked like he was going to ugly-cry for a split second, but he regained his composure.

"It's got to be hard, then, to be shunted aside in the investigation," I said. "You must wish Virgil was in charge and you could help."

"Yeah."

He must know that the sheriff had been investigating his aunt for postal improprieties. But Virgil would have kept him out of the investigation; no matter how much he liked and trusted the younger man it would have been a conflict of interest, as well as putting the deputy in an untenable position.

"Was she still close to anyone in your family?"

He shook his head. "My brother moved overseas to teach, and she kinda thought I was a traitor; she thought the police were suspect."

"So there was no one she'd confide in?"

He shook his head again. "She'd broken off with most of us in the last few years."

"Do you know the kids she had boarding with her?"

He met my gaze. His eyes were light gray, and set deep in the sockets, with shadows under them. He was not handsome like Virgil, but there was an openness in his expression that I hadn't noticed before. I thought that had more to do with his changing perception of me than my perception of him.

"They don't seem to be bad kids, but . . ." He shrugged.

"I heard Karl Mencken had a fight with her and stormed off. *Or* they had a fight and Minnie threw him out. I've heard it both ways."

"I can't comment on an ongoing investigation."

I sighed. My curiosity had met a stone wall named Deputy Urquhart. "I drove by her house," I said, keeping my tone casual. "I wonder who inherits it now?"

He cleared his throat. "As a matter of fact, I do. Partly, anyway. My brother and I are her heirs."

I had questions but no opportunity to ask them. Urquhart walked away, spoke to Dewayne for a few minutes, then got in his sheriff's department car and took off down the lane, the heavy motor throbbing in the increasingly humid air. I invited the PI back into the kitchen to have a cup of coffee and some of the baked goods Binny had sent. As I made coffee, Hannah plied him with questions. Her curiosity knows no bounds, and though she has the mind of a librarian, I think she has the heart and soul of a writer.

Pish, Roma, and Patricia took a break and joined us. As I introduced them all to Dewayne, I wondered how to raise the topic of the damage to Pish's car. Roma flitted about as Pish sat down with Dewayne, Hannah, and me to drink coffee; she sang snatches of the song, her voice breaking in the same spot until she was almost in tears. I actually felt sorry for her.

"How is it going?" I asked Pish.

He shook his head. But all he said was, "I wish Zeke were here. His technical skills are so much better than mine for the sound recording. We may have to wait until I can get him out here for a short time."

"I have the boys coming tomorrow to do some grounds-keeping," I said. "If you need Zeke for the sound recording, maybe . . ." I had a sudden brilliant idea. "Maybe I can get them to bring another guy to work with Gordy, so Zeke can help you."

"That would be a relief." He passed one slim-fingered hand over his thinning hair. I swear he had aged five years since the morning. "It's not coming out how we want it."

I watched him for a moment as Dewayne eyed us both, probably getting the tension, but not sure of the source. Patricia had not yet sat down. She seemed flighty and distracted; I wasn't sure why.

Dewayne cleared his throat and said to Pish, "I have a rather direct question. How long has the front end of your car been bashed in?"

The room stilled. Roma had paused in midtwirl. I watched her; she looked guilty, a rare thing for the self-involved diva.

"I don't know what you mean," Pish said. He looked to me. "Merry, what is he talking about?"

"Your car's front end is crunched, Pish. The front right bumper. Your headlight is smashed. When did it happen?"

I was hoping he'd say it happened last week in Autumn

Vale, or the week before while negotiating a tricky spot in the Walgreens parking lot in Buffalo. But he looked mystified. Patricia was eyeing us all, her brow wrinkled in puzzlement.

"Roma, you're the only other person who has driven his car. Maybe you know something about this?" I asked.

"Oh, Pishie, darling, I'm so sorry!" she said, throwing her arms around his neck from behind and crooning in his ear. "I so didn't want to bother you about it! I had a teensy accident and wrinkled the bumper."

"When?" I asked.

"You don't need to badger me. It's not *your* car," she said with a pout, her full lips pursed.

"Roma, when did it happen?" I insisted.

She sighed and huffed, straightening when Pish didn't leap in to defend her from my questioning. "Last night. I was out for a drive and I kind of . . . dented it a little."

"Where? On what?"

"Why does it matter? Why is everyone *picking* on me?" she exclaimed, her voice rising in volume.

Pish's gaze had not moved from my face. "Merry, what's this about?"

"Last night someone ran me off the road. Dewayne, fortunately, came to my rescue."

"And you think Roma had something to do with it?" My friend's voice held a chill I didn't like.

"I didn't say that, Pish. I—"

"Mr. Lincoln, I'm the one who discovered the dent on your bumper and told Merry that it's exactly the kind of damage whoever shoved her off the road would have sustained," Dewayne said, his voice inflectionless.

"I've heard enough," Pish said. He was angry, his lightly lined face sporting deep grooves from his mouth being pinched in fury. A nerve twitched in his temple, the blue vein standing out in relief, blood pulsing through it. He stood, and took Roma's arm. "Merry, I know you and Roma don't get along, but I never thought you'd stoop to accusing her of trying to kill you."

Roma screeched. "No, oh! Pishie, is that what she's saying? Oh!" She "swooned" and Pish caught her, guiding her out of the room with murmurs of support.

They returned to my library as I cradled my head in my hands. Tears welled up and spilled over, dripping down my cheeks. It was too much in twenty-four hours, to be run off the road, and then to have my best friend angry at me. Patricia crouched down by me and touched my hair as Dewayne looked on. Hannah approached, the faint buzz of her motorized wheelchair loud in the now-silent room.

"Merry, it's okay," Patricia said gently, searching my face.

"No, it's not," I said, choking back a sob. "Pish is my dearest friend. If he's angry at me, I don't think I can stand it!"

"Merry, give him time," Hannah crooned. "It's a shock to him. He's trying to help Roma, and yet you've told him such a shocking thing. And maybe all that, about the damage to the car, didn't come across quite how you meant it. He's torn as to where his loyalties lie."

"His loyalties should lie with me, not *her*!"

Dewayne stood, setting down his empty coffee cup with a clatter. "I don't give a damn about some diva's hurt feelings. I'm going to take paint flakes off Mr. Lincoln's car. If we can eliminate it, *then* you can worry about apologizing for damaging her fragile ego."

Patricia straightened. "Let's everyone be calm," she said. "Mr. Lester, you should indeed check the paint flecks. I'm sure it won't be the car, but you need to eliminate it. I haven't known Roma long, but though she's self-centered, I don't believe she holds any ill will toward Merry. And as for Pish . . . I believe Hannah is right. I bet if you asked him, he's feeling doubt, too, and he's not sure how to process that. He wants to support Roma, but he loves you, Merry," she said, a serious look in her mild eyes. "To hear about what happened this way has shaken him. It's easier to be angry than scared."

Dewayne touched Patricia's shoulder, and they looked into each other's eyes. As I watched there seemed to be a spark between them. He smiled and she blushed, her full cheeks going a bright rosy red.

Pish poked his head into the kitchen. "Patricia, Roma would like to see you." She exited past him, heading to the library. "Merry, can we talk?"

I followed him out to the great hall near the dining room door. I could hear Roma in a storm of weeping, babbling to Patricia about something.

He pulled me into the shadows near the wall of tapestries and hugged me, his whole body trembling. "Merry, my darling, what happened? Why didn't you tell me you had been run off the road? I'm . . . I'm *shattered*. Are you all right?"

I sighed as he held me in his arms. "I was so tired last night when I came in, I went right to sleep. I didn't even call the police, which Virgil yelled at me for. And then this morning there was no time because you were busy with Roma." I sounded faintly aggrieved, but it was all the truth. "I didn't have a chance, truly, Pish. And I wasn't planning on accusing Roma of anything. It was Dewayne who noticed your car bumper."

"I'm sorry, Merry. I was shocked and I snapped at you." We kissed and made up nicely, then he looked over his shoulder toward the dining room doors. "Roma is having a meltdown."

"I'm sorry we contributed."

"That's just her latest excuse. There's something going on with her voice, but I'm not sure what. She's blaming everything else, but she's scared. If she can't sing, she doesn't know who she is. I'd better go back. Can't leave poor Patricia to bear the whole weight of Roma's emotional breakdown."

He scurried back in and closed the door behind him.

None of this explained where Roma was the evening before *and* the morning Minnie was murdered. I went out the front door, approaching Pish's car, which Dewayne knelt by. I watched as he used a box cutter–style knife to cut a section of paint from the damaged area, being very careful, as he told me, to get right down to the metal. He had a glassine envelope, and he dropped the paint chip in, folded the flap, wrote a label, and affixed it over the flap. "For comparison," he said. "In case that woman did try to kill you."

I didn't comment. "So the work you're doing at Shilo's and Jack's, that's a cover for why you're in town, right?"

"Sure, but I've done construction in my day. And I fixed up a couple of old houses in downtown Detroit, trying to improve the neighborhood I grew up in. I love old houses. They have soul."

I sat down on the edge of the terrace and watched him pack his identification kit away. "I appreciate all the trouble you're going through for me. If I can do anything for you, let me know."

"We'll work out a trade," he said, and winked. "Maybe you can set me and your friend up."

"My friend?"

"Patricia. My kind of woman. She married?"

"She's not." I had a feeling he was the hunky fellow she was describing when she told me Rusty had hired a couple of new guys. "I don't think you need me to set you up," I said. "She works at the bakeshop most days starting mid-morning and bakes the best cakes and cupcakes I've ever eaten. And I've eaten a lot of cupcakes in my day."

"Thanks for the intel." He strode back to his car whistling a cheery tune, tossed his tool kit in, and took off.

I returned to the kitchen and washed up the mugs and plates. Hannah dried as we chatted about the mystery surrounding Minnie's murder, Shilo's behavior of late, and everything else.

"You'll be at the library tomorrow morning, right?" I said. "What day does Brianna usually come in?"

The thing I love about Hannah is I never need to explain anything to the girl. She's so quick on the uptake, it's frightening sometimes.

"She'll come any time I tell her I've got a new batch of entertainment magazines. Mom is getting me some in Batavia today. I could text Brianna to come on in tomorrow morning. What do you want me to find out?"

I chuckled. "I'm going to have to find a new nickname for you. You're far too clever to be a Watson or Hastings." I sobered and took the dried dishes, stowing them in the cupboards, then sat down at the table. "I need as much as I can get about Brianna, Logan, and Karl. It seems to me that Karl is as likely a suspect as anyone, but I'm getting conflicting stories. The boys told me that Karl said he walked out after a quarrel with Minnie the night before she was murdered, but though I didn't have time to follow up with Brianna last night, she told me that Minnie kicked the guy out. It can't be both. I would like to know what was said, what they argued about, that kind of thing. Do you feel comfortable finding out? I don't want to put you in an awkward position."

"I'll see what I can find out without tipping her off."

"Perfect."

Hannah's parents arrived. We unloaded all the groceries they bought me, then settled up financially, since I owed them a bit more than I had given her. I insisted on giving them gas money, too; it only seemed fair given the huge favor they had done. I hugged Hannah good-bye and they drove away.

This had all gone on long enough, this multidirectional turmoil in my life. Shilo was upset and no one knew why. I was going to get to the bottom of that. Emerald was angry at me, and the rift between Lizzie and her had reappeared, and all because of some fake wannabe swami. Someone had killed Minnie for whatever reason, and *someone* appeared to be trying to kill me, too; they might—or might not—be the same person.

I had enough. If I was a catalyst, as Doc claimed, I was darn well going to be a catalyst in all directions.

Chapter Fourteen

❈ ❈ ❈

I T WAS AS good a time as any to take my banged-up car
to the fellow who looks after it for me, a lackadaisical and
oddball mechanic named Ford (short for Rutherford) Hayes.
He considers cars the greatest invention of mankind, behind
only the wheel and fire. On the way I would drop in on
Aimee Jollenbeck, who could tell me more about Crystal
Rouse, and why she had brought Consciousness Calling to
little old Autumn Vale, rather than a larger city.

I sat outside Aimee Jollenbeck's home, a slightly ragged-
looking bungalow on a street of other ragged-looking bungalows on the outskirts of town, and wondered how to
approach her. I had no right to bother the woman. She might
be ill, she might be sleeping, she might wish she'd never
heard of Crystal Rouse, or she might in secret be her best
friend and behind what felt like a scam, to me: the whole
three-hundred-dollar consciousness-clearing exercise.

But I'd never know if I didn't ask.

Feeling like a hapless vacuum cleaner saleslady, I hoisted

my purse like a shield, locked the car, and marched up the weedy walk to the house. I tapped on the aluminum door and waited. I was about to tap again when the inside door creaked open and a woman peeked out.

"Aimee Jollenbeck?" I said, staring through the screen.

"Yeah." She yawned, scratching her stomach and tugging down her top, a striped multicolored T-shirt she had paired with pajama pants that were patterned with images of hot air balloons. "Can I help you?"

"You don't know me, but we have mutual acquaintances. I believe you're friends with Crystal Rouse?"

She stilled in midscratch. "Who are you? Did Crystal send you?"

Gauging her alarmed reaction, I swiftly said, "Not at all. I barely know the woman, though I *am* friends with Emerald."

"So what do you want? I don't have anything to say about Crystal."

"May I come in for a moment?"

"Who *are* you?"

"I'm so sorry; I didn't even introduce myself. I'm Merry Wynter."

"I've heard about you. You inherited Wynter Castle, right?"

"Yes, I did. I know your stepsister Helen Johnson. She's been out to the castle for tea a few times."

"Okay. Yeah, Helen." She yawned. "I don't sleep well, so I was napping, and you woke me up." She retreated from the door.

Taking that as all the invitation I was going to get, I stepped into the dim interior, dust motes dancing in the sunlight that streamed through the front door. I closed it behind me and turned the lock, then followed her past closed doors down a dark hall to a sunny back kitchen in what was probably an addition to the tiny bungalow. The cooking area was U-shaped, with a breakfast bar on one end near a tiny dining area.

She entered the cooking space and plugged in an electric kettle. "You drink tea?"

"I do." I looked up and noticed teapots lining the top of her eighties-style cupboards. My own collection was more elegant, but hers was whimsical. She had a Mother Goose, a mama cat in an apron, a Noah's Ark, an old-style stove, and many more figural teapots. I chatted her up about them, pointing out the ones I liked as the kettle came to a boil and she threw two teabags in a big old Brown Betty, probably the best teapot ever made for actually brewing tea.

She seemed more relaxed. Bonding over teapots will do that to a gal. I examined her as she fixed our mugs, hers a chipped one that said, There's a Chance This Is Vodka. I got a plain pink one. She perched on the other bar stool, grabbed a pack of cigarettes from under an ashtray, and lit one, letting out a long puff of smoke with a satisfied sigh. She glanced over at me as she tapped some ash off her cigarette into the ashtray with a practiced move. "So, what do you want from me?"

"I understand you're involved in the Consciousness Calling, uh . . . group?"

"Was," she said taking a long drag, and then a big gulp of hot tea.

"I'm not sure I understand anything about it, but I'm concerned about Emerald's involvement, and I'm looking for information. Their website didn't tell me a whole lot."

"You think she's making a mistake?"

I watched her eyes. She had settled into amused detachment.

"What business is it of yours anyway?" she asked, when I didn't answer.

I thought about that. What business was it of mine to interfere if Emerald was happy with what she was doing?

None, maybe. But of all the regrets I had lately, the most poignant were for the things I had *not* said or done. I couldn't explain that without explaining a hundred other things about me, my life, and coming to Autumn Vale. "Emerald and her daughter are my friends. I've met Crystal and I'm not sure how I feel about her. I'm worried about Em and Lizzie, *especially* since Crystal is living in their house."

She nodded, pursed her lips, and blew out a stream of smoke as she stubbed her cigarette out. "Let's go and sit in the garden. I want to see if my cats are around."

The garden turned out to be a weedy patch of grass surrounding by tall cedars that blocked the view of every other yard, though I could hear things: a Weed eater somewhere, a dog barking, a baby crying, someone hammering on something metal. We sat in PVC chairs on a patio stone square at the back of the yard, our tea mugs on a glass-topped table stained with mug rings.

A big tabby male wandered in and sat at the edge of the patio licking himself, one foot pointing up to the sky, as a dainty calico stepped toward him, rubbed her body along him, then headed straight for Aimee and jumped on her lap with no warning.

"So, you and Helen are stepsisters?" I eyed Aimee, who had frizzy blonde dyed hair pulled back in a ragged ponytail and wore outlandish color combinations. Helen was always obsessively neat, her short gray hair groomed, clad in tweed and pearls. Probably slept in a skirt suit. "You don't seem to have much in common."

"She's my half sister, actually, the result of my dad marrying after my mom died, and having a second family. I don't have a lot in common with them, but Helen and I get along all right. She got me a job at the church, and I appreciate that. It's nice and quiet. I clean, do repairs, and help in the office. When my ex took off, he left everything a mess financially, and the ratfink doesn't pay me a cent. So . . ." She shrugged.

"From what I understand, Consciousness Calling is a franchise business. Did you go to San Diego to look into that?"

"You *have* done your homework, haven't you? Busy little nosy bee." She had carried her smokes and ashtray out and fired up another from a psychedelic-patterned Bic lighter. The calico took offense, wrinkling her little nose and jumping down, running off into the cedars, from which she glared out at us. "I heard about it from a friend online, so we met at the conference, but I knew damn well I couldn't afford a franchise."

I thought about my next question. Her expression seemed wary and watchful. "So you met Crystal there, at the conference, and she came back here with you?"

"Not quite. My friend flaked off early—said it sounded like a bunch of hooey, so she went home. I spent the money to go, so I decided I may as well see it through. I met Crystal the first day, and we hit it off; she can be a real hoot when she's had a couple of margaritas. I came home thinking we'd stay in touch on Facebook, through e-mail, you know. A week later she showed up on my doorstep."

"Why didn't you tell her to take off? Didn't that seem kind of pushy to show up uninvited?"

Her expression was shuttered as she drained her tea mug and set it down with a bang. "Hey, she was fun in San Diego, so I figured why not?" She stubbed out her cigarette, crushing it until it shredded and the filter wrinkled into a wad of stuffing.

I wasn't buying it; there seemed to be an undercurrent of anger in what she said and did. I thought about what she'd said so far. "I went to the information meeting last night. Helen was there. I thought maybe she was checking it out for you."

Aimee nodded. "I wondered what was going down. Crystal's making a pretty penny off of it, from what Helen tells me."

"She is. But what happens when she's made everything she can?" Aimee just looked blank. "I don't like how she's treating my friend," I said. "And I *don't* like what I've heard about how she is laughing behind people's backs about the information she gets from them while they're experiencing her . . . one of those sessions. Sounds like a form of hypnosis to me. Does she actually have a franchise? If she's using Consciousness Calling materials and their name and techniques, she must, right?"

Her plain pale face betrayed some internal struggle. Her gaze flicked away, and she took out another cigarette, lighting it with slightly shaky hands. "Okay, you did *not* hear this from me, but no, she doesn't have a franchise. They wanted ten thousand before you could set up and use the techniques we learned during the conference."

"Techniques?"

She blinked, took a long drag, and got up, saying, "I need another cup of tea."

"Aimee, please . . . Can you tell me anything about these techniques? I don't understand why Emerald has turned against me. There's something called a DTP, a downwardtrending person, and Crystal called me that. What makes a Consciousness Calling devotee label someone that? Can you tell me *anything*?"

She stood, holding her mug and looking down into it, for a long minute. Finally, she said, "Wait here. I'll come back out in a few minutes, and I'll tell you *some* stuff if you promise to keep me out of everything."

She was true to her word. When I left a half hour later, my brain was buzzing like I'd had five espressos and a shot of adrenaline. I now had an idea of what Crystal was up to, but I wasn't sure how to stop it. Aimee hedged and hemmed and hawed her way through much of her story, but she told me enough that I could guess there was worse she wasn't talking about. If I was right, Emerald would be dragged down in something so nasty that when it was exposed, she'd be lucky if she wasn't forced to leave town, hauling Lizzie away again just as the kid was getting settled into her new life.

I took my car to my genius, Ford Hayes, a funny old dude in overalls who loved cars like some men love the ladies. He was horrified by what had happened to my back end . . . the car's back end, rather. He spent a few minutes crooning over her, stroking her bumper, and telling her it would be all right, then said he could do some of what the car needed right away. Some people would call his place a junkyard, but he called it home, and had the lot neatly laid out, with dirt lanes between areas of junk separated by car manufacturer. He could fix the taillight from his vast array of car parts if I wanted to wait.

Where else was I going to go? When you find a mechanic as good as Mr. Hayes, you let him do whatever he wants, whenever he wants.

I sat cross-legged in the scrubby dry grass under a spreading chestnut tree (I'm not making that up, though there was no village smithy) and checked my phone. I had missed a few calls and texts, one from Hannah, so I leaned back against the tree trunk, stretched my legs out, and called her.

After salutations, she said, "I talked to Zeke and passed on your message. I guess they were supposed to kick Karl out of their apartment, right?"

"That's what Binny told them; she said she'd take the blame, if they wanted, as their landlady."

"Well, neither he nor Gordy seem to like him much, but they're too sweet to do it. He said he'd bring Karl out tomorrow to work with Gordy on the grass, if you want."

"Yes, please. I'll pay them and give the boys supper."

"I'll let him know. He's coming over to my house later, after work, to help me with my computer."

I suspect that Zeke has a thing for Hannah. He treated her with reverent solicitude that seemed beyond friendship, but she had been in love with Tom, Lizzie's father, and even a year after his death I didn't think she'd recovered wholly.

"Have you spoken with Brianna yet?"

"She's at work right now, but she's coming to the library tomorrow morning. Do you want me to handle this end of the investigation?"

I smiled at her eagerness. "That's probably wise. She didn't react well when I asked about Minnie and Karl. I think Crystal's hostility toward me is probably one of the reasons." I gave her a list of questions to ask, a tangle of ones about Brianna herself, her apparent love interest, Logan, Crystal, and Minnie. "But please, Hannah . . . be careful. There is a killer out there, and there's no guarantee it's not Brianna!"

I then texted Lizzie a quick question: where were they all the morning Minnie was killed? Given that she must have been in class, I was surprised by how quickly the answer came back. She said they were all at the house having breakfast that morning. Cereal and skim milk, if I needed to know, with fruit, thanks to Emerald's new health kick because of Crystal, she added. I jokingly texted back, poor kid!, but got a text back immediately that said, why u want to know?

Just wondering, I texted back. Gotta go. Getting my car fixed after some jerk tried to run me off the road last night . . . poor Caddy! I sent a smiley face emoji. She'd probably hear about the incident at some point, I figured, and I didn't want her to worry. There was text silence after that. I hoped she hadn't gotten in trouble for texting during class.

Mr. Hayes came toward me wiping his perpetually grease-stained hands on an orange rag and smiling a gap-toothed grin. "She's settled down some and is happier now," he said. "But I'll need to have her for a day or two to get the dings out. Or I can replace it—the bumper, I mean." He nodded and whipped the rag over his shoulder. "Tell ya what: I'll check around for a new bumper—an *old* new bumper—and maybe it'll be even cheaper than fixing this one. Meantime I checked out the oil pan and gas line, brake fluid, tranny, carb, everything. She's okay, but don't go getting run off the road again," he said, waggling an admonitory finger at me. "She don't like it!"

"I'll take that into consideration next time a homicidal maniac comes gunning for me."

He paused and knit his shaggy brows. They were interesting brows, with stray hairs that stuck out at random angles, like a bird's nest. "How about I call your sheriff honey? I can give him a good heads-up on the kind of car it might be. Seen a lot of wrecks in my day."

I wrote down Virgil's office number and Dewayne's contact information on the back of a receipt and handed it to him, telling him who Dewayne was. "I'd appreciate anything you can tell them."

I drove back through town and parked on main street. The post office was still closed and crime scene tape circled it. There was a grim-faced fellow in an FBI shirt at the front, and I thought I could see a car at the back, as well as the command center vehicle.

Janice was outside of her shop, fussing with a display of wrought iron patio furniture. A couple went into the Vale Variety and Lunch. Otherwise, on this hot September afternoon, there were few folks on the street. I needed to talk to Emerald alone, and there was no time like the present. She was in her shop—I could see her moving about—and Crystal was nowhere in sight. I locked the car and climbed the steps into Emerald Illusions. "Hi, Em. How are you today?"

She turned from her task, dusting the shelves that lined the wall, and eyed me warily. "I'm fine."

"How is Lizzie? She wasn't too happy last night."

"She's fine." Emerald checked her watch and glanced out the window.

"You waiting for someone?"

"A delivery. It was supposed to be here this morning."

I plucked one of the Consciousness Calling pamphlets off the table near the window and perused it, then looked at my friend. "I have to admit, I didn't understand Consciousness Calling from last evening's presentation. Maybe you could explain it to me?"

"Crystal says some people aren't ready to receive the message. It takes a certain kind of person to get it."

"Patricia didn't get it, either, she told me."

She shrugged.

I sighed and stared. How could I break through to Emerald? "How is your mother doing lately?"

"I haven't seen her in a while. She doesn't understand all of this," she said, waving her hand around the shop. "She doesn't approve."

"I'm sorry to hear that. You were mending your fences nicely, I thought."

"Crystal says we need to cut out of our lives the people who cause us grief or try to pull us down."

So the CC way of dealing with life was that at the first sign of difficulty in a relationship you cut and run? You'd be left with no one, eventually. I strode to her and grabbed her hand, staring into her eyes. "Em, is that what she's telling you about *me*? That you need to cut me out of your life? I'm your friend and want what's best for you, but I won't stand by and see you going the wrong way." I knew I had put my foot in my mouth the moment I said it. "I didn't mean that Consciousness Calling—"

"Yes, you *did*," she said, snatching her hands away and putting them behind her back. "You're like my mother, thinking I can't manage my life and Lizzie's. Crystal understands. All she wants is for me to be happy."

"Then why is she trying to pull you away from those of us who care?"

"She's *not*!"

"Em, she's got you working back at that sleazy bar, and you're not even seeing your mother. Lizzie's having trouble in school again."

"And that's all my fault?"

"I didn't *say* that!"

"You *are* saying it. Crystal is right; you interfere everywhere, stick your nose in everyone's business." She glared at me. "Consciousness Calling and Crystal are the best things that have happened to me in a long time. I finally own a business!"

For which she was working in a bar to pay.

"I'm on my way up, and none of you can see it." She was quivering with rage. "You're trying to pull me back down. Crystal's right; you're a DTP, Mom, too. You're all *bitter* and want me to stay suppressed so you all can feel better about yourselves."

I was stunned and angry, but kept a tight rein on my emotions. I found Crystal and the whole Consciousness Calling thing irritating, but it was unfair to take that out on Emerald, who was more impressionable than I had thought. Crystal was manipulating her. At this point I couldn't hit my friend with the full weight of what I suspected, but I *could* take another tack. "Let's not argue. But about the business . . . I notice you're using photocopied Consciousness Calling materials with their logo. Em, I'm concerned. If Crystal is not a proper franchisee, this could all be illegal."

"Shows how much *you* know," she said, crossing her arms over her chest. "I've *seen* the contract; it's all legal. She's paying off the franchise fee monthly."

I was sure I was right, but if I trod too heavily I risked losing Emerald completely.

My pause and silence must have given her some hope. She uncrossed her arms and clasped her hands together as if pleading. "Merry, I know you can't see it, but Crystal is wonderful! She's given me direction for the first time in my life. With her help I'm going to be rich! I mean, *super* rich, like helicopters-and-private-jets rich. This is just the beginning," she said, waving a hand around at the shop. "Crystal is going to help me get there. She's misunderstood. You can see that, can't you?"

The dream every con artist sells: easy wealth, riches beyond imagining. "I'm a little curious; what has she said to you about me?"

Emerald's eager expression died. "She doesn't know you. She thinks you're trying to destroy everything she's building here in Autumn Vale."

"She's labeled me a DTP, isn't that right? Are you supposed to even be talking to me?" I saw the truth in her eyes; Crystal had told her to shun me. "Emerald, you have to know this: my only hope is that you and Lizzie find peace and happiness. If you're truly happy, tell me now."

She blinked. If this was a hostage situation I'd think she was signaling me—blink once for *Help me.*

"Happiness isn't something handed to you, Merry. You should know that," she said, in a tight voice. "It's something you work for, hard. Something you *suffer* for. Something that you need to go through tests to get to."

"Em, no," I said softly, taking her hand and squeezing it. "Happiness isn't a prize at the end of some gauntlet, where you're battered senseless in the name of getting to a magical goal."

She had pulled her hand from my grasp but was silent, fiddling with the hem of her pale blue tunic top; the garment was unusual for her, making her look like an acolyte.

"I've thought about this a lot lately," I continued, watching her eyes. "Happiness is being surrounded by people who love you. Bad things will still happen. People will get sick. You may lose loved ones. But when that happens, the love of your friends and family will keep you sane. I know. That's what

Pish and Shilo did for me when I lost Miguel. Don't let anyone separate you from those people. Lizzie. Your mother. Me."

She was still silent.

I longed to reach out to her, but I was afraid of scaring her off. At least she was listening. "Em, I've had a lot on my plate in the last year. I worry about money all the time. There have been the awful murders. I don't know what to do with the castle, and if I can't figure it out, I don't know how I'm going to pay the taxes. But what I've found here in Autumn Vale . . ."

I shook my head. *Start again, Merry.*

"What I'm trying to say is, life in Spain was easy. I spent over two months in the lap of luxury with decent people. But what I found instead of happiness was numbness. It was all very nice, but I didn't feel *anything.* Happiness ebbs and flows. Sadness invades. Pain happens. Happiness is being with the people you care about and who love you, even amidst the worry, tension, and pain we all live through."

Crystal entered and eyed us. "Merry. Are you here for a session?"

"No, I was talking to my friend."

We had an awkward conversation about the town and the weather as I examined her, trying to decide if what I suspected was true. I thought of how Aimee had stiffened up, how she had seemed so wary and had refused to criticize Crystal or confirm much of what I suspected. She had hinted, alluded, and skirted around interesting accusations, though.

Aimee was scared, and it occurred to me why. I already knew Crystal's semihypnosis, likely learned at the CC seminar in San Diego, caused some people to tell things they wouldn't otherwise. Patricia had confirmed that. I was willing to bet that Aimee had told Crystal things she shouldn't have. The other possibility was that she had done something in San Diego at the conference that only Crystal knew about, and of which Aimee was ashamed.

It was all I could do not to tell the woman off, but I had plans. At the end of it all Emerald may not be speaking to me, but if I got rid of Crystal and saved Emerald from eventual humiliation or worse, it would be worth it.

I headed back to Wynter Castle. As I pulled up to my usual spot in the parking area, Esposito came out of the castle hauling Roma with him, her arm tightly clasped in his hand. I got out of my car as Pish rocketed out of the castle after them, phone up to his ear.

"What's going on?" I asked, racing to Pish's side.

Pish put the phone against his chest. "They're taking Roma in for more questioning."

"But they questioned her already."

"They've found something, but they won't tell me what."

"*Found* something?"

"In her clothes that they took away, or *something*. I don't know; they're not saying. I'm on the phone with Stoddart, and then I'm calling a lawyer friend in New York."

Roma looked over to me, her beautiful eyes filled with tears. "I didn't do anything. Merry, please, believe me!"

Esposito, his expression dead, said, "We're taking her to the command center for further questioning."

"So she's not under arrest?"

There was warning in his dead eyes. "Not at this time."

We could tell him to release her immediately. She didn't *have* to answer more questions. But without knowing what they had on her, I hesitated; to protest could force Esposito's hand and make him place her under arrest. I didn't say a word as he put her in a car and drove away.

Chapter Fifteen

❈ ❈ ❈

I DON'T LIKE Stoddart, Pish's last boyfriend and a regional something or other in the financial crimes investigation division of the FBI. They had met almost a year before during the federal investigation of the Autumn Vale bank, and hit it off. He was snarky, superior, smug, and a bunch of other stuff, but Pish liked him a lot, so the guy must have had some redeeming qualities. And he must have had some lingering feelings for Pish; even as Roma's high-powered attorney, renowned for getting clearly guilty people off the hook, was ensuring her silence and release from questioning, Stoddart found out what it was they had on her.

It was almost midnight by the time we got everything sorted out. Roma was asleep after taking a sedative with a glass of merlot. I wouldn't suggest that, but nobody asked me. Pish and I were in his sitting room, since he was e-mailing and messaging and who knew what else. I'd made tea and brought up two mugs with a wedge of double cream

Brie, cranberry preserves, and some water biscuits. When Pish is anxious he forgets to eat.

"I still don't know what to think, Pish," I said about the shocking news of what the FBI had uncovered that made them detain Roma for questioning. "How *did* Minnie Urquhart's blood get on an article of Roma's clothing?"

He shook his head. "Do you think they're telling the truth?"

I put one hand over my heart and fluttered my lashes. "I'm shocked you would suggest that the FBI would lie to anyone about evidence they may—or may *not*—have uncovered!"

He didn't even crack a smile at my jest. "You don't really believe Roma murdered Minnie, do you?" he asked, his expression troubled, frown marks etching deep lines under his eyes.

I thought about it. Roma was vain, needy, emotional, high-strung, borderline hysterical at times. She was also talented; I'd heard her sing beautifully. Though she had apparently threatened the music director at her opera company, she was the dramatic type who often said things she didn't mean. Long ago I'd heard her threaten to poison a rival and take a dagger to her own breast; her threats were operatic in their fervor and were *not* followed by violent actions.

Similar was her dramatic scene when she flew down the stairs, letter opener in hand, threatening to kill Minnie. It was reckless and stupid, but still, I didn't believe she intended to hurt Minnie, nor did I think she'd killed her. Reluctantly I shook my head; I say *reluctantly* because I didn't have another single idea of who had done it, using, apparently, Roma's letter opener. Plenty of folks were angry with Minnie, but to kill her using the letter opener? "No, Pish, I don't believe Roma did it. But if not her, then who? And Minnie's blood . . ." I shook my head in puzzlement.

"Esposito is too careful an agent to lie about something like that." Even though the police can and will lie to you to get a confession or for other reasons. They just can't lie in court.

"Stoddart got some more information for me," Pish said, turning in his chair away from his laptop. "He says that the medical examiner who did the autopsy doesn't believe the letter opener made the wound that killed her. He thinks there was another weapon." He took some Brie on a water biscuit, carefully dressed it with cranberry preserves, and ate.

"That's important." I pondered the possibility of two weapons, and perhaps two assailants.

He nodded, brushing crumbs from his linen shirt. "And if there was another weapon that killed her, why use the letter opener at all?"

"To implicate Roma. It was someone who had either witnessed the event here, or heard about it."

"Which doesn't narrow things down at all," he said. "Everyone in Autumn Vale has heard about it."

We sat gloomily sipping our tea and sharing the Brie. "Are you canceling the recording tomorrow with Zeke?"

"Roma begged me not to. She's terrified, but she needs this as a distraction."

"I've been listening in. Her voice is shaky. What's up with that?"

"I don't know, but it's been plaguing her for a while. She's okay, and then suddenly her voice gets this quaver and she can't control it. I had vocal doctors assess her before we left New York, and there's nothing physically wrong with her voice."

"She's fortunate to have a friend like you." I thought about it for a long minute. "Maybe 'O Mio Babbino Caro' isn't the right song. Is there anything you can use that shakiness in?"

"Anything worth singing must be sung with clarity and steadiness." His look became thoughtful. "But you *have* given me something to think about. Perhaps another song. I'll consider it." He reached across his desk and took my hand, gazing into my eyes. "Do you know how much I missed you while you were gone? I hope you do. You are my muse, my darling, and I'm overjoyed you came home."

BECKET HAD BOUNCED BACK TO HIS FULL VIGOR, AND at three in the morning he decided to start whining about going out. I pointed to the litter pan and threatened to shut him out of my room, which I finally had to do, shoving the litter box out my door into the hallway and him with it. There was enough room for him to roam in the castle without going out in the middle of the night.

But as I made my way to the kitchen in the morning, yawning and stretching, he paced back and forth, walking down the butler's pantry hall and back to me as his yowling got increasingly urgent and distracting. Finally, I'd had enough. There comes a point when a cat's gotta do what a cat's gotta do.

I followed him to the back door, picked him up for a long hug, and set him down. "Now, you be back before sunset, buddy, please," I said, wagging my finger at him while he stared up at me, waiting. "I know you're a big boy and can take care of yourself, but I worry." I opened the door and he scooted through, running by leaps and bounds toward the forest as if he had an urgent appointment.

The men in my life: always running for the woods. If Virgil was chosen and headed to Quantico and then to wherever he was stationed—I had no doubt he'd be chosen, nor did I doubt he'd make it through the course—we would have a long-distance relationship. We should talk about that. I sighed, returned to the kitchen, and put the coffee on.

I made breakfast, which featured, of course, muffins— chocolate walnut ones this time because I felt the oncoming need for chocolate. It was good to get back to baking and cooking after being gone so long, but I still didn't feel entirely like I was at home; maybe there was too much up in the air. Roma appeared fragile and weary, but Pish was bubbling with excitement, leafing through some notes and sheet music. He had his laptop and had e-mailed a friend, who sent him some music to use for the day's recording.

"So what piece are you going to do?" I asked looking from my friend to Roma, who picked at her food and sighed a lot. I felt for her. It could not be easy to be a suspect *and* know that you had brought it on yourself.

Pish shook his head. "It's going to be a surprise. As soon as Zeke gets here we'll close ourselves in the library, and I do *not* want to be disturbed. If the boys are going to mow today, could they start with the far field?"

"I'll make sure." Since my primary goal of the day was to talk to Karl Mencken, I was not worried about that in the slightest, even if they got no mowing done at all.

When Pish left the table to make a phone call in solitude, I watched Roma for a moment, then said, "I'm sorry this is happening to you, Roma."

She turned her tragic gaze to me. "I don't know what I ever did to deserve all this trouble."

Well, you threatened to kill a woman with a letter opener and then she died . . . after being stabbed with your letter opener. I didn't say it, but I sure thought it. "I still can't figure out how the killer got the letter opener. What exactly happened the day you threatened her?"

"I'd had enough. After Minnie's insults I went upstairs and fumed, then just . . . I saw red. I had been humiliated, and I was *not* going to take it. I picked up the closest thing, which was the letter opener—it sat on a little stand on my desk—and when I heard them all talking in the hall I came down the steps, and I guess . . . I *guess* I said I wanted to kill her. I don't remember that. I flew at her in a fury."

"And what happened to the letter opener?"

"That's what Agent Esposito asked me. I don't know."

"What did you do with it right then and there?"

She shrugged with a hopeless look. "I don't remember."

"*Think*, Roma, think back. Put yourself there, in that moment. What were you wearing that day?"

"I had on a red sleeveless silk blouse with a pair of white palazzo pants."

"Did the police take those clothes away?"

She nodded, her expression aggrieved. "And they're my favorite pants. Irreplaceable!"

Pish had described what happened. "So you tore down the stairs and flew at Minnie," I said. "What happened then?"

"I guess I slashed at her with the letter opener."

This was very important. "Roma, did you make contact with her at all? Do you remember?"

"I don't think so. I cut myself on something."

"Are you sure?"

"There was blood on my hand. I must have!"

It was safe to assume, I thought, that she actually did manage to pierce Minnie's skin with the letter opener; the blood on Roma's hand was Minnie's, not her own, and would have gotten on her clothes that way. In fact, the scab I saw Minnie picking at in the post office when I first got back could have been that healing cut. I would bet the FBI knew that was possible, which explained why they had not charged Roma, nor did they insist on holding her in the face of protestation.

But now the letter opener . . . "You've had the scuffle with Minnie and there is much excitement. Then you're separated. Everyone mills around for a moment, then goes home. Did you take the letter opener back upstairs? Drop it? Throw it? Give it to someone?"

Pish came back in and clapped, rubbing his hands together. "Zeke and the boys have arrived. Time to get down to business."

I put my hand up, not breaking my gaze from the opera singer. "Roma, concentrate!"

She stared off into space, wrinkling her nose. "I *think* I set it down, maybe on that round table in the middle of the great hall. There was a lot of commotion."

And that was all I got, but it was enough. Roma and Pish scurried off to the library and I let Zeke in so he could join them to see to the recording.

Roma's misty recollection made one theory possible. Doc told me about Minnie and her penchant for collecting "trophies" from her spats. I would bet dollars to doughnuts that Minnie Urquhart, pleased with the response she had elicited from the emotional soprano, grabbed the decorative letter opener and took it with her. She likely kept it somewhere, her home or the post office, where *anyone* could have seen it. She may even have bragged about it.

I called and left a lengthy message for Agent Esposito about what I had learned, my theory for Minnie's blood on Roma's clothes, and what I had heard from Doc about Minnie's "trophies." Then I headed outside, where Gordy was already backing the riding mower I had purchased second-hand out of the garage. The other guy was standing with his hands in his cargo shorts pockets, looking sulky.

"You must be Karl!" I said, approaching and holding out my hand. "I'm Merry Wynter. Thanks for helping us out today. Normally Zeke would be doing this with Gordy, but he's tied up with the sound engineering."

He didn't shake my hand.

"Huh. I could do that, no problem," he said, scruffing his weedy beard, then tugging at his earlobe, stretching the flesh tunnels. "I know everything there is to know about sound equipment. I'm in a band, you know," he continued. "I'm probably better than Zeke."

I was taken aback and examined him. I was offering paid

work, and he was sulking about it? "I rather thought, since you're staying with Zeke and Gordy, that you'd want to help."

He shrugged, watching Gordy fill the tank from a gas can kept in the garage, and picked at his acne. "Whatever."

"You must have been shocked when you heard about Minnie being murdered."

"Crazy!"

"Too bad you had such a nasty fight with her the night before."

His stance changed, and he stilled for a long moment, casting a glance my way. Then he cracked his knuckles, starting with his pinkie fingers and working through each one.

"I'm sure the FBI agent has asked you about that. What was the fight about, anyway?"

He grimaced, his mouth twisted. "Nothin' much. I used her car without her permission."

"That doesn't seem to be a huge deal," I said, to encourage him.

"I know, right?" He turned to me, his narrow face holding an eager expression. "So I used some gas, took off for a while, right? But you'd think I'd, like, killed someone or something."

He didn't seem to consider his words in light of Minnie's death, which meant he didn't consider much of anything he said, probably.

"It turned into a pretty big argument?"

His eyes widened. Did he see the danger? "Nah, not so big."

Big enough that he left or got kicked out. I didn't want to push too hard yet, so I didn't say it. "How do you get along with Brianna and Logan? I understand Minnie treated you all like family."

"Yeah, I guess." He looked glum, shoved his hands back in his pockets and watched as Gordy finished filling the machine and returned the gas can to the garage. Gordy came back out with a wheelbarrow full of tools. "Brianna was her favorite, probably because she's a girl. I liked Brianna at first, but she didn't help me much when Minnie and I got into it. She should keep her effin' nose out of stuff that doesn't concern her." His tone was dark, his expression furious.

"So you got kicked out after the argument that night. Or did you leave on your own? I've heard both versions."

He flicked an uncertain glance my way, his blue eyes narrowed. "Whatever. The effin' FBI have been breathing down my neck, and now you?" He shouted to Gordy, "Hey, we getting this done, or what?" He strode toward the other guy, suddenly eager to work. They had a brief discussion.

I approached, picking my way though the weeds. "Gordy, can you fellows start at the far end while Zeke and Pish are recording Roma? He's worried the heavy machinery sound will vibrate through the castle walls."

"Sure, no problem, Merry," Gordy said.

"Karl and I were discussing the night he arrived at your place. You told me he said he had stormed out of Minnie's place after an argument, right?"

"That's right," Gordy said, sweeping his thin hair out of his eyes. "That's what he said."

I turned to Karl. He looked trapped. "So did you storm out? Or were you kicked out? Brianna said you were kicked out."

He shrugged again, his favorite answer. "I don't know," he said finally. "I don't, honest. We were both mad. Maybe I said, *I'm leaving*, and she said, *Get out*, at the same moment."

That was actually quite possibly the answer to the conflicting stories. The two fellows headed off to the far field, where they would mow and trim the worst of the brush at the edge, working their way back toward the castle. I was definitely going to find out if the car he had used that had started the argument, Minnie's vehicle, was intact or damaged, and if it had been moved from behind the post office, where I'd last seen it. If he'd killed her and heard I was snooping around, and if he had an extra set of keys, perhaps he'd taken the car, followed me, and tried to run me off the road. It seemed unlikely, but it was possible.

I returned to the kitchen and was doing the breakfast dishes when I got a call from Hannah, who had spoken with Brianna. "How did it go?" I asked. "Did you find anything out?"

"I guess," she said, sounding uncertain. "She's really broken up about Minnie dying. She lost her mom years ago, and Minnie treated her like a daughter."

I didn't have the impression she was broken up about it when we spoke, but I was a stranger. She was more likely to show her true feelings to Hannah, a friend. "Did she say what it was like living with Minnie and the two guys?"

"She told me Karl was nice to her at first, but he got bent out of shape when she started dating Logan. And he got worse when Minnie showed a preference for Brianna and Logan."

"Did she tell you what happened the night Karl was kicked out?" I wondered if her story would stay consistent.

"She said Minnie was angry with Karl and they had a big fight. She said she and Logan stayed out of it."

"Were you able to work in a question about what she and Logan were doing the morning Minnie was murdered?" Brianna said that she was getting ready for work when she heard, but I wondered what she would tell Hannah.

"Well, uh . . ."

"Hannah?"

"I can't say," she whispered. "There are other people here!"

"I'm assuming she didn't say they were out killing Minnie."

"Of course not."

What would two twenty-something young people be doing once their landlady was out of the house and they

were alone that Hannah didn't feel she could say aloud in . . .
Oh! I bit my lip, fighting a grin. "Did she tell you that she
and Logan were, uh, fooling around? Getting frisky?"

She giggled. "She said it was so rare they were alone, so
they did that, and then she jumped in the shower, and that's
when the police came." Her tone sobered. "She said she felt
awful when she figured what she was doing while Minnie
was being killed."

That shone a new light on her alibi. When Brianna told
me she was in the shower when the police came the first
thing I thought of was, the killer would need to clean up
after the bloodbath that poor Minnie had suffered. But her
explanation to Hannah sounded legit, though who would
know other than her and Logan? "You went to school with
the young woman who works for Andrew Silvio, right?"

"Chrissie, his secretary," she said. "She's one of my best
friends. She comes in to the library all the time for those
lives-of-the-rich-and-famous novels, like Jackie Collins and
even old ones, like Judith Krantz and Harold Robbins."

Chrissie had helped us with information once, last year,
but it was minor stuff. "Is she up for a little skulduggery?"

Hannah paused a beat, then softly said, "Merry, I don't
think I can ask her to do any digging in Mr. Silvio's files. I
wouldn't want to get her in trouble. It's a good job, and
they're hard to find."

"Fair enough. Actually, I have one question, something
that will be a matter of public record soon anyway. How
about, if she's up for it, fine, but if she's the slightest bit uncomfortable, drop it?"

"I'm guessing it's something to do with Minnie's will,
since you said it will be public record soon."

"Exactly. Who inherits her house and any money? I actually may already know the answer. Deputy Urquhart says he
and his brother do. He ought to know, but I heard she was in

to talk to the lawyer about her will before she died. There is something else, though: I don't know if Chrissie can help us, but Minnie was having her house evaluated lately, and said she wanted to fix it up to make it worth something. Why?"

"You know, Minnie wasn't well liked," Hannah said. "But she did have a couple of friends, and I happen to know one who comes into the library all the time. She's kind of mean, and she talks about everyone behind their backs, but she probably knows more about what Minnie was up to than anyone else. I *could* call her."

I had qualms. "Hannah, maybe that's not a good idea."

"Tell you what," she murmured softly. "If I can think of a reason, I'll call her. If not, I won't. Either way, I'll talk to you later. I have to go."

I threw the ingredients for a hearty stew into the slow cooker, hoping it wasn't too hot outside for that. I longed for cooler weather, for fall to truly arrive. At dinner I was going to feed, besides Pish, Roma, and myself, the three young men, and their appetites were sure to be heartier than ours.

While I did that I made some notes, then made a call to San Diego, worldwide headquarters for Consciousness Calling. I had a fascinating conversation with a peppy West Coast type, and gave her information that was appreciated. I was set to be the spoiler in Emerald's big plans for wealth, which I would feel bad about if her plan had any shot in hell of coming true. Sometimes being a good friend means making difficult decisions, or at least that's what we tell ourselves for comfort when we do something of which we're not quite sure.

I also made platters of sandwiches and pickles, and a couple of big pitchers of iced tea, sticking it all in the huge commercial fridge. I left a note telling them all to help themselves. I could no longer wait to find out what was wrong with Shilo. She would, one way or another, tell me what was up. Garbed in town-worthy shorts and a sleeveless tunic top, I grabbed my keys and purse and left the castle. I shaded my eyes and looked off into the distance; Gordy and Karl were working, making slow but steady progress. It was going to take more than one day to whip the property back into shape.

The Caddy purred to a start, and I drove into town. Since being run off the road I had been a little tight-gripped on the wheel and excessively watchful, but it was likely, as I had conjectured, that my mishap was the result of some drunken jerk or joyriding kid.

I paused at Binny's to pick up fresh bread to go with the stew, though I'd probably make biscuits, too. Patricia was all atwitter; Dewayne had called and they were going to a movie in Batavia the next night. She slyly asked me about Virgil, but I wasn't biting. I strolled back to where I had parked my car, outside of Emerald's shop. She looked up from what she was doing, saw me, and stormed out, slamming the door behind her. She stood on the sidewalk and glared at me. "So now because of you Lizzie has gone to live with my mother."

"Because of *me*?" I took it in. "When did this happen?"

Emerald folded her arms across her chest, her eyes glittering with tears. "Yesterday morning. I was here to meet a delivery, as you well know. It was supposed to come early, and I waited all freakin' day. I guess she had a fight at home with Crystal and left. I thought she was at school, but they called yesterday afternoon about something. I said to ask Lizzie, and they told me she wasn't at school. She was listed as off sick."

"So where is she?"

"Like I said, my mom's place. She won't even come to the phone."

"So how is this *my* fault?"

She shook her head, her mouth trembling. "I don't know what to do."

"I'll text her and go talk to her," I said, digging my phone out of my purse. "She'll listen to reason."

She waved her hand, then knuckled her nose, sniffing. "She doesn't have her phone with her."

"Since when?"

"That's what they argued about yesterday morning. Crystal was trying to get Lizzie to pay attention, so she took away her phone. Lizzie got all bent out of shape and stormed off to my mother's place, and didn't go to school."

I stood very still, staring down at the sidewalk, examining the cracked concrete. I looked up. "Em, the morning that Minnie died, where were you?"

"At home," she said with a frown. "Why?"

"So, to clarify: you, Crystal, and Lizzie were home having breakfast?"

"No, I mean, me and Lizzie were. Crystal was meditating."

"In her room?"

"No, she does sunrise meditations somewhere," Emerald said, her expression puzzled.

"Where is that?"

"I don't know," she said with an impatient tone. "Crystal has to live with a noisy, nosy teenager; the woman needs privacy sometimes."

A prickling sensation down my back that started at the nape of my neck made me shiver. Crystal had Lizzie's phone and was the one who answered my text, saying they were all together that morning. If I hadn't asked Emerald I would never have figured that out. Why would Crystal lie about it?

I could think of one very good reason.

"Em, the other night when I left, and Lizzie stormed off, you and Crystal stayed at the shop, right?"

"Sure . . . well, kind of. I mean, with a homicidal maniac on the loose Crystal was worried; she kindly offered to follow Lizzie to make sure she got home all right."

"Crystal spoke to her?"

"No, she knew that would cause a giant fight. She followed Lizzie home, then came back."

"How long was she gone?"

"I don't know; awhile." Emerald looked watchful, alert. "Merry, where are you going with this?"

I couldn't say anything yet. "Nowhere. Em, why are you blaming me for Lizzie going to your mom's? Isn't that Crystal's fault?"

She looked sulky, an expression reminiscent of Lizzie at her worst. Arms crossed over her chest, hugging herself, she looked off down the street. "Crystal says the phone is a symbol. *You* gave it to her, after all. She says you're trying to usurp my parental authority. Lizzie listens to you more than me. She's always mad at me lately, and then you come waltzing back into her life from exotic Spain—"

"Em, it's not like that!" I hesitated, wanting to do more convincing, but I had an urgency about other things—Shilo in particular—and this conversation deserved more than simply bickering on the sidewalk. Folks were coming along, more than one lingering and listening in. In Autumn Vale if you talk about it at ten AM, by ten thirty everyone in the town will know what you said. I reached out and touched her arm, smiling at people who were passing, trying not to appear as if we were in the middle of an urgent talk. "Emerald, can we talk about this another day? I miss our friendship. I *hate* this feeling that I'm somehow on the wrong side of things, and you know how I feel about Lizzie. Can we get together and talk? Soon?"

"Maybe," Emerald said. Crystal was approaching down the sidewalk, and I saw Em's eyes flick to her. "I . . . I have to go. I have to get a ride out to work later today."

"Why? What's wrong with your car?"

"In the shop. It's acting up. Crystal offered to have it fixed, so we're hoofing it for now."

I was stunned into silence. Crystal motioned to Emerald, and they went into the shop together. What exactly was wrong with the car, I wondered, and since when? Many, *many* things were coming to a head and would explode—or implode—in the next few days. I had a lot to figure out if I wanted to manage the explosion so it wouldn't hurt anyone I cared about.

Chapter Sixteen

IT WAS TIME to figure things out—no more lollygagging, as my grandmother used to call it. If Crystal had murdered Minnie and run me off the road, she needed to be arrested before she hurt Em or Lizzie. If she hadn't, then I needed to take her down some other way, or Emerald was going to suffer for, at the very least, being a part of the woman's scam. I'd put things in motion by ratting Crystal out to Consciousness Calling, but who knew how long they would take to bring the hammer down on her and enforce their copyright?

Who'd murdered Minnie Urquhart? The FBI agents were working diligently, I had no doubt, but this was my town now, and I'd help if I could. I was reminded that Minnie had reportedly talked to a drug dealer in Ridley Ridge in the weeks before she was murdered. That was a possible lead, but not one that I could likely follow. Unless . . . I did have one friend in that sad town: Susan, a waitress at the café, who had, a year ago, roused herself out of her Ridley Ridge stupor and called the police, saving my life. I'd pay her a visit and see what she could tell me about the local dealers.

Karl's tale concerned me. He wasn't averse to taking Minnie's car whenever he felt like it, and who knew whether he'd had extra keys made? Though when I thought about it, he probably had access to Gordy's car. Something else to follow up.

Pete, the laconic Turner Construction newbie, was taking down the last of the scaffolding around the porch, which was newly built and sturdy-looking. There was another guy there, one I didn't recognize, and he had canvas drop cloths below one section of the porch, ready to paint the spindles and railing. He knelt on the ground, stirring a can of white exterior latex. Dewayne was nowhere in sight; perhaps he had given up the pretense of being a handyman now that the reason for it was done. The new guy was skinny and dark-haired, and bent to his work with zeal. One incongruity was his flashy boots: yellow snakeskin.

I caught a glimpse of Shilo through the window; she was staring out at the new guy with an odd look, speculative and worried. The conversation a few days before with Doc came back to me, about seeing Shilo talking to a skinny dark fellow wearing city clothes and flashy boots. Was this the mystery man? And what was he to Shilo? I wasn't leaving the house until I found out. I nodded to Pete as I passed, and examined the other fellow.

He looked up and smiled. "Ma'am," he said, in a soft Southern voice, and nodded a greeting.

"You're new in town," I said.

"Sure am."

"What brings you to Autumn Vale?"

"Family, ma'am."

"Let's get working, Lido!" Pete yelped, eyeing me with disfavor.

The fellow hustled to do his bidding. Pete must have

loved that Dewayne was no longer his partner. It would be easier to push around this soft-spoken stranger than brawny, self-assured Dewayne.

I just reached the door when Shilo, dressed in her boho best, a billowy patchwork skirt and tank top, her dark hair in waves over her shoulders, opened it and tugged me in by the arm. She wrapped me in a hug in the dim hallway. I let her cling for a long minute then held her away from me. "How are you, honey? I miss seeing you all the time, even though I know you're happy with Jack."

"He's the best," she said, taking my arm and leading me back to the sunny kitchen.

She had begun her redecorating, and I was stunned. The walls had been a plain canvas of white, but now Shilo was meticulously painting a brilliant tapestry of vines and flowers. "This is beautiful!" Every color of the rainbow and many more were used in her work, which flowed out from anchor points along window and door frames. "I knew you drew, but I have never seen *anything* like this!"

"I'm painting a big mandala on the living room wall, right where the sunlight will hit it," she said.

For a while I let her talk about the house, and Jack, and Jack's mother, who was recovering from a nasty summer cold. Jack's mother had taken to Shilo as if she were her own daughter, something I was thrilled to see. But even as we talked I was struck by how wistful Shilo seemed, underneath it all.

I reached across the table and took her hand. "Shilo, I know I keep hammering away at it, but I'm not the only one who thinks there's something wrong, something you're not telling us. Please, honey, you've got us all worried."

To my horror and surprise, she burst into tears. I circled the table and held her against my body, rocking her and stroking her hair. It took a while to calm her down, but finally she was able to talk. I moved my chair around the table and sat facing her while she sipped herbal tea.

"You know how I never talk about my family," she said, eyeing me from under her lashes. It was a shy yet captivating expression she had used to good effect in her modeling career.

"I never wanted to intrude because it seemed like something you felt uncomfortable with. But I'm your oldest friend, honey; you can tell me *anything*."

She sniffed, wiped her nose on a tissue I had retrieved from the half bath off the kitchen, then started her tale with running away from home at sixteen and living on the streets in New York, begging and shoplifting. As does happen on occasion—not often, but often enough—a modeling scout spotted her and saw something special. He gave her his card and fortunately he was legit, not a scam artist or lothario. She got an agency, and they put her up in an apartment with a half dozen other girls.

I remembered it well, the ratty, crappy apartment where she was crammed in with six other half-starved teenage waifs. I picked her up for a shoot I was styling and was appalled at the living conditions, but she chattered happily all the way about how awesome it was, and how nice the girls were.

But that was all so far in the past. How was it connected to her current unhappiness? "Why did you run away from your family?" I asked.

She shredded the tissue and cast me another covert look. "I've always told you I'm half-gypsy, half-Traveler."

I nodded.

"That's true, you know, at least that my family is Traveler. It's a group, kind of like gypsies. My ancestors came over here from Ireland a long time ago. Travelers stick together no matter what; you marry another Traveler or not at all.

Anyway, I grew up in West Virginia. When my momma died, I lived with my granny for a while, but when I was sixteen my daddy decided it was time for me to get married, and he set it up with my cousin Nattie Dinnegan."

"At sixteen? Why didn't you say no?"

She cast me a haunted look. "Only time I said no to my daddy I ended up with a broken shoulder that never did set quite right."

Horrified, I bolted out of my seat and took her in my arms again, bending over her as she sat. "Shi, why didn't you ever tell me any of this? Oh, honey, I didn't know. I mean, I knew there must be something, but I never knew what."

She nodded and sniffed, clinging to my arms. "I wanted to forget it all for a long time," she said, her voice muffled. "I hated Nattie. He was pure evil; used to peep at me while I undressed and try to get me alone. He hit the little kids and told me I was so skinny and ugly he was the only one who would ever marry me."

I gasped and sat back down opposite her. "How could anyone want you to marry someone like that? Especially your father!"

"Granny agreed that I shouldn't marry him; he's my first cousin. That's not even legal in West Virginia, Granny told him. But Daddy insisted. Said he'd take us to Virginia, where it's legal. Anyway, he took me to Welch to get my dress, and I slipped away, hitched to New York, and . . ." She shrugged. "That was it."

"And you've never seen any of your family since then?" I asked.

She shook her head, tears springing up in her eyes. "I got a message to my granny that I was okay, but nothing after that. I was that afraid Daddy would find me and take me back."

"But it's been so long! Surely you could . . ." I trailed off. The fear in her was so ingrained she was shaking even now.

It was not up to me, who had never been abused in my whole life, to decide how she should feel or how she should handle it. My mind was reeling, but as I settled, I realized it still didn't explain what was wrong. "Shi, what's up now, though? Why are you upset?"

"My b-brother told me Granny is sick and wants to see me, but I'm scared!"

My heart caught in my chest, and I felt like I was choking. "Oh, baby, darling, Shilo!" I scooted my chair closer to her and pulled her to me, hugging her tight again. She needed it to still her trembling. My face muffled in her hair, I said, "Don't be afraid. *Never* be afraid! You have people who love you and will protect you from anything and anyone." I let her go. "You say you've seen your brother?"

She nodded.

"Oh!" I exclaimed as it dawned on me who she was talking about. "That's the skinny dark fellow Doc saw you talking to. The fellow who is outside now, working on your house!"

She nodded. "That's Lido. I don't know what to do. Lido swears Daddy don't care that I run off," she said, her language reverting to the youthful twang she had when I first met her. "He wants me to go see Granny. And she sent me a letter, now that Lido told her where I am, begging me to come see her. What am I gonna do?" She broke down then, sobbing, face in her hands, her long dark hair hanging in a curtain over her shoulder.

That explained the letter she had received and wouldn't explain or let Jack see. "The first thing you're going to do is tell Jack. He's so worried, Shi."

She looked up, eyes wide with alarm. "Nuh-uh, I can't tell him what a screwed-up life I've had. I can't let him meet my family! He grew up nice and normal. His mama is so sweet, calls me her daughter."

I didn't answer. The fear emanating from her was

palpable, and I wasn't sure how to reassure her. After a year I knew Jack well. He was a wonderful man who loved Shilo so much he'd walk through fire for her. But I couldn't be sure how her revelations would affect him. Some guys don't deal well with crazy, and her family sounded crazy.

"Lido says he won't let Daddy hurt me, but I don't know if I believe him."

"Shilo, we need to resolve this. Either you'll go to your granny or say no, but you can't continue to be so worried and upset. We've all been concerned."

She took my hand and pressed it to my cheek. "I don't know what to do."

I made a snap decision. "Let me talk to Lido; I'll put up my bull-crap radar and see what I think. But this truly isn't something you can keep from Jack. He either loves you, warts and all, or he doesn't love you enough."

She nodded slowly. "I never thought of it like that. Is this a test, then?"

"No, honey, love doesn't set tests. But he's your husband and he adores you. He's going to be hurt you didn't tell him this before, but make sure he knows how scared you are of losing him. He needs to *know*."

She fetched her cell phone and texted Jack, then looked up at me with shining eyes, more the Shilo I've always known and loved. "You're right. If I can't tell him, what do I have?" Taking a shaky breath, she watched me for a moment. "Will you really talk to Lido? I want to believe him, but . . ." She shrugged. "Will you figure out if he's telling the truth?"

"I'll try." I felt some trepidation, but no wavering in my intention.

I heated up some soup and she ate quickly, hungrily, while finally, at long last, telling me about her family. And, wow, it's a big one. She has two brothers, Lido and Galveston, and six sisters, starting with Shenandoah, who is older, and Brandy, Aubrey, Candida, Cecilia, and Celeste, all younger, the last three fraternal triplets. Lido had filled her in on much that had happened: marriages, babies, sicknesses, and deaths. After an absence of so many years, Shilo was pining for them all. She had shut that part of her heart down over the ten or so years I had known her, but now it was full, flooded with familial longing.

Jack texted back that he was on his way home, and I knew I needed to give them privacy. But I was certainly going to talk to Lido before I left. I hugged Shilo hard, and she let me out the front door, retreating to give me time to talk to her brother. He was sitting in the shade of one of the big trees on the property eating a bag lunch while Pete sat in the pickup parked by the curb with the radio on and his feet up on the dash.

I approached and plunked down on the grass nearby. "So you're Lido Dinnegan," I said. "I'm Merry Wynter. Shilo and I have been friends for over ten years."

He nodded, watchful. "She's told me. Said you've been right good to her, ma'am, taking care of her from the moment y'all met."

"Is it true that your grandmother is ill?"

He nodded, never taking his gaze from mine. "She's got the cancer. Lady parts. She's old, but tough as nails. Sent me to find Shilo."

"And your father?"

Lido became introspective, gazing down at the sandwich in his hands. "Shilo remembers this big, blustery fellow, but he's been knocked down by life. I think it scared the crap outta him when Nattie kilt a guy and got sent to prison. He seen that he shouldn't ought've tried to make Shilo marry him."

"She's afraid of your father still."

He nodded. "I understand. He hurt her bad. I wasn't there, but Shenan was and said it scared *her* something awful; that's why she run off and married her first husband, so

Daddy wouldn't choose someone for her, too. I missed Shi, growing up. I was only twelve when she took off, but she was my favorite sister."

I thought about it for a long minute. He seemed on the level. "She is scared, but she wants to see your grandmother."

"I want her to meet my wife and kids. I'm missing my youngest's first birthday to be here, but this is important to Granny, so it's important to me. Shilo's a missing piece of the family."

He seemed so young to me, probably only twenty-three or so if he was twelve when Shilo left, but it appeared they all married young.

Jack screeched his little Smart car to a halt in front of the house and unfolded his lanky frame from it, his expression panicked. "Is everything okay, Merry?" he asked as he came through the gate. "What's going on? Shi's text was weird."

"Everything's going to be fine—she just needs to talk to you." I got up, dusted off my shorts, and gave him a hard hug. I grabbed his upper arms and looked up into his earnest, honest eyes. "Shi loves you deeply; always know that. *So* deeply that she's scared to death of losing you."

He looked even more alarmed, but I wasn't the one to soothe his worries. Shilo was inside, and she could do it better than I.

"Tell her I said Lido's okay, I believe him," I said. "She'll know what I mean. Just tell her that *exactly*. I'll call later, when you two have sorted everything out."

"Okay, sure, yeah," he said, even as he darted up the walk and leaped up the steps. "Talk to you later!" he said and bolted inside.

"He sure does love her," Lido said. "Homeliest fella I ever seen, but he surely does love Shilo."

I looked down, watching him. "Lido, why now? I know your grandmother is ill, but why not try to reconnect years ago?"

He thought about it and met my gaze. "God says for everything there is a season. It was time. And Papa is so worried about his mama—our granny—that he's a changed man."

"I don't know if I believe in that complete a change."

Lido nodded. "I understand that, ma'am, but I'm grown-up now. I won't let him hurt Shi, even if he was of a mind to." He looked up to the house. "And she's got a husband now. I don't think he'd let anyone hurt her neither."

I stopped at my car and looked back before getting in; framed in the big picture window I could see Jack holding Shilo close. Lido saw it, too, and he clasped his hands together in a prayerful expression of hope. I drove away.

One problem down; one to go. Who killed Minnie Urquhart? I pointed the Caddy toward Ridley Ridge and headed out of the valley. I had the suspects boiled down to just a few now: Crystal Rouse, Karl Mencken, or Brianna and Logan. Or Roma—though I didn't think she did it, it was still possible. She was hiding something.

Ridley Ridge: no matter how long I'm away from it, it never seems long enough. I pulled to a stop, parked, and got out of the car. Ridley Ridge is like the upstate New York version of those towns in old Western movies that look deserted, but you know there are peeping eyes behind every pair of curtains. I crossed the street to the café and entered. Where was Susan, my favorite laconic waitress, who was usually pouring sludgy coffee or texting friends? I strolled through the café, where a few patrons whispered, heads bent together, eyeing me with mistrust. The waitress today was a thin, dark-haired girl with a stained uniform.

"Where's Susan?"

"Susan?" The girl had a reedy voice, and she was blank of expression, her pale gray eyes soulless.

"Susan. The waitress who works here."

"She left."

"Left. The café? Town? The country?"

"She got accepted to college over the summer and left."

I was staggered, stunned, *amazed*. Susan had never seemed to have ambition. She wasn't stupid, but she felt stuck where she was, doing what she did. But she broke free! I was proud of her. It wasn't that I thought life in a small town was bad in any way, but it should be a choice, not a sentence.

Especially when it's Ridley Ridge.

"College . . . good for her! I'm Merry Wynter. I supply the café with muffins, but I've been away for a couple of months, and I'm wondering if I should resume. Can I leave a message for Joe, the owner?"

"Okay."

I dug a notebook out of my purse and wrote a brief note, handing it over to the girl. "What's your name?"

"Lisa."

"Hi, Lisa. Susan used to give me information when I needed it, too."

She nodded, and some faint color bloomed on her thin cheeks. "I know. We heard all about it, and how she saved your life."

I watched the hopeful look on her face; perhaps I had found another ally. I leaned on the counter and murmured, "I was told that Minnie Urquhart, the woman who was murdered in the post office in Autumn Vale, was in contact with a drug dealer in Ridley Ridge and had been seen talking to him. Do you know who I'm talking about?"

Her eyes widened and she nodded.

"Do you know where I could find him?"

She nodded again, only this time I got that she was subtly pointing to someone. I looked over my shoulder to where a long-haired man in jeans sat in a booth alone with a newspaper spread out in front of him. "Name?" I whispered.

"Cash," she said. "Just . . . Cash."

I strolled through the café until I reached his booth and slid in across from him. He rattled his paper, much like a gentleman in a Victorian club might when disturbed, and folded it, eying me with mild, bloodshot eyes.

"Can I help you?" he asked, his voice gruff but polite enough.

"You're Cash, correct?"

"Some call me that."

Others in the coffee shop were trying to listen in, so I kept my tone low. "I've been told that you may recently have been in contact with a woman named Minnie Urquhart."

He nodded. "She's related to Les Urquhart."

"My name is Merry Wynter. You likely know who I am." I'd had my dealings with Les, a nasty character, and our little conflict had been local gossip fodder for months.

He nodded. "Les is a crud. Glad he's not around now."

Good to know. If he'd loved the man like a brother I might be in trouble, since I helped put him away. "And you know what happened to Minnie?"

He nodded. "For the people of a town that considers itself superior to Ridley Ridge, you Autumn Vale folk sure have trouble keeping citizens alive."

I let that go, but he did have a point. "Why did Minnie come to you, if you don't mind me asking?"

He frowned down at his newspaper. "You want what she said to me or what I think was going on?"

"Both."

"Well she came to me 'bout a month ago the first time, then again a week or so later. She tracked me down and asked if I could sell her some . . . let's call it medicinal herbs. Said she had a condition and needed it for pain. I don't do that kind of thing anymore, I told her. Then she says, *Well, what about something stronger?*" He shook his head. "She was bullheaded, wouldn't take no for an answer. Asked me if I sold meth, or if I knew someone who did!"

"*Meth?*" Whatever I was expecting, it wasn't that.

"I know, what the hell?" he said, his lean face drawn with

an offended look, like he'd smelled something putrid. "I don't deal in that crap. No way was she a meth head, so I figured she was looking to bust whoever sells. *It ain't me*, I said. And that was that."

I sat for a moment tapping the tabletop. I felt my phone vibrate in my purse but ignored it. "Was she worried about someone she knew, a friend or relative, perhaps?"

He nodded reluctantly. "Thought crossed my mind. Urquharts in this town are quite the bunch. Coulda been any one of her nieces or nephews she was worried about being an addict. More'n a little pot, I mean."

Or maybe not kin—maybe one of her boarders. Perhaps the fight she had with Karl wasn't about a misappropriated vehicle at all but about his drug use. I needed to ask Logan and Brianna about that fight, what they knew, what they'd seen or heard. I stood. "Thanks, Cash. I appreciate the talk." I didn't know if he'd been completely honest, but he *seemed* open enough.

"Anytime, pretty lady!" His gaze darted out the window and he stiffened. "I'll walk you out," he said.

I felt all eyes on me as we left the coffee shop, his hand cupping my elbow, behaving like the gentleman he seemed to be. What was going on?

When we got to the sidewalk, he said, "You might just have a look across the street at a fellow sitting on a doorstep. He's the only dude in town who sells the junk I don't touch, if you know what I mean."

I glanced across and experienced a shudder of recognition. It was the guy from whom Brianna had accepted a package in the parking lot of the seniors' home.

"Now, I can tell you've seen him before, but I would not advise you talking to him. If he sniffs trouble, he'll follow you home and beat you black and blue."

I nodded and tore my gaze away. "Thanks for the warning, Cash."

"Thanks for heeding it. Wouldn't want that lovely face busted open."

That certainly seemed like confirmation: Brianna must be a drug user of the hard stuff, and perhaps the reason Minnie was trying to track down the dealer. I returned to my car and leaned against it as I checked my phone. The shifty drug merchant heaved himself to his feet and shuffled off in the opposite direction.

Hannah had called and left a message. "Merry, Deputy Urquhart is going to be disappointed if he thinks he's the heir to Minnie's estate. Apparently the heir is someone named Casey Urquhart. Call me later!"

Chapter Seventeen

❋ ❋ ❋

I WAS TICKING things off a mental list, at the bottom of which was *Who killed Minnie Urquhart?* No answer to that yet, but at least I knew what was going on with Shilo and some progress had been made on that front. I had other things on my mind; one was Lizzie and her estrangement from her mom, the source of which was Crystal, who might be the murderer. I drove back through Autumn Vale to a little side street with modest bungalows where I'd first met Emerald at Lizzie's grandmother's home.

My young friend was mowing the front lawn; she had her wild hair restrained by a scrunchy and wore ragged cutoffs and a T-shirt from which the arms had been torn. She was happy to see me, like a puppy when the owner comes home unexpectedly, wriggling and yipping. It was gratifying and a little sad, especially since Lizzie normally takes teen dourness to all new depths. She fetched a bottle of water for us each and we sat on the sagging front step.

"I hear Crystal seized your phone yesterday when you

and she had a big fight, and that's why you're back here with your grandmother."

"I hate that witch," she said in a matter-of-fact tone. "I wish she'd die."

I thought of censuring her remarks, but sometimes that's how you feel when you're a teenager. "So what time did the cell phone incident happen?"

She shrugged. "Early. I was texting Alcina, and Crystal McBitchy thought I wasn't paying enough attention to every boring, stupid word she said, so she yanked it away from me. We had a huge fight and I left. I don't have to live like that, not when Grandma is happy to have me here. I think she needs me, you know?"

I looked around the property; she had a point. The garbage was piling up, and one bag had clearly been torn into by raccoons or some other critter. "I'm amazed that Alcina has a cell phone." The girl's family ekes out a living selling their vegetables, and Alcina is homeschooled, or rather, *un*schooled, and yes, *unschooling* really is a thing; I looked it up.

"They qualify for some free cell phone program so they have access to the outside world. Her mom doesn't know how to use it. Alcina does all their calling and texting."

"Crystal still has it?"

"My phone? Heck yeah. Can I charge her with theft?"

I smiled, though she sounded serious. So . . . Lizzie did *not* have her phone when I texted. Crystal had used the opportunity to mislead me, but why? "According to your mom, Crystal goes off to meditate every morning."

"Meditate? Hah." Lizzie snorted. "She goes to smoke pot and drink. I saw her sneaking something into her purse one morning when she was leaving to 'meditate.' When she came back I snooped. In her bag was a cigarette pack with a twisted ciggie in it and a flask with some kind of smelly booze. Who does she think she's fooling?"

"She's an adult. Why hide it?"

"Because she's full of crap, that's why. She tells Mom that booze and drugs are crutches, that ascending to a higher plane can be achieved with meditation. She's a freakin' fraud."

I was distracted by my thoughts; why had Crystal texted me that lie to make it seem like she was with Em and Lizzie? The only reason I could think of was, she was busily murdering Minnie. She had zoomed to the top of my suspect list, but I wasn't sure Esposito would see it that way. I needed to track down Emerald's car and see if it had damage to the front consistent with a driver cold-bloodedly trying to run me off the road. A shiver crawled down my spine. "I hear your mom's car is in the shop. Does she have a regular mechanic?"

"Why?"

"Just asking."

"Her cousin always fixes it when it breaks down."

But Crystal wouldn't likely have taken it to Em's cousin, so if what I suspected was true and the car had body damage rather than an engine problem, it would be someone else nearby who would do body work. I cast a glance over at Lizzie, who had her knees up and was resting her chin on her arms. "I'm sorry this is going on just when you and your mom seemed to have it together. She's pretty desperate to make a good life for you both, and I think she's lost track of things. Adults can get taken in, sometimes, you know. Emerald wants so badly to be a success for both of your sakes that she can't recognize the truth: that Crystal is a fraud."

"Why can't she see it when I do?"

I had no answer to that. "I'll do my best to take Crystal down and not involve your mom, okay?"

She nodded. I didn't want to say anything more because I didn't want the kid to worry about the hot water her mother could be in if we didn't manage to implicate Crystal only.

"Are you going to stay with your grandmother for a while?"

She nodded again.

"But you're going to go back to school on Monday, right? And you're going to stick with the plan, to get better grades so that you can get into a good college with a scholarship and get a diploma in fine arts photography?"

She sighed hugely and nodded.

"Good. I have to get going and see what Gordy and Karl Mencken are up to on my property. If you need anything, kiddo, or just want to talk, call me."

She snuck a look sideways at me. "I'm glad you're back, even if I *was* mad at you for staying away so long."

"I know. Be good."

She stood and I hugged her good-bye, then drove away, watching in my rearview mirror as she resumed mowing.

So it could well have been Crystal who tried to run me off the road. There were a few reasons why she might have, two that had nothing to do with Minnie's murder and one that did. Based on her conversation with Emerald about the cell phone, she resented my influence over Emerald and Lizzie in particular. Perhaps she didn't intend to kill me but to rattle me, in that case. Or did she want me out of Emerald and Lizzie's lives because of my suspicion about her Consciousness Calling enterprise? There is nothing a con artist hates more than a skeptic. In that case, maybe she *did* intend to kill me.

Or Crystal may have killed Minnie—why else would she lie about where she was that morning?—then become concerned when I appeared ready to investigate. I was infamous around Autumn Vale both for the murders that had happened in or near Wynter Castle, and for my success in helping capture the killers. She may have thought she was safe killing Minnie because of my own problems with the woman. Roma and Minnie's dramatic fight at the castle was gossip that had spread through the whole town, so using the letter opener was meant to point toward someone in my household as the guilty party. Otherwise, why use the letter opener at all when another weapon actually killed the poor woman?

But why would Crystal kill Minnie? Again, my overactive imagination was ready with several scenarios, any one of them possible.

One: she resented Minnie disrupting her meetings because she didn't approve of the hold Crystal was getting over Brianna and Logan. That was weak.

Two: Minnie either had already or was close to figuring out that Crystal was conning folks with her fake Consciousness Calling enterprise. That was more of a motive.

I pulled up the long lane and came around the curve, emerging from the wooded section. In the hours I had been gone Gordy and Karl had done a lot, and the property was beginning to lose the abandoned look. As good as Pish was at looking after the place, he was not always practical about organization, nor did he notice the exterior like I did.

I waved to the boys, who were working along the edge of the arboretum section of the woods. Becket emerged from the forest and bounded across the shorn grass, hightailing his way away from the nosy machinery. I held the big oak door open for him. He scooted past me and raced up the stairs as I entered, closing the door softly behind me. I heard voices only, no music, coming from the library; I could hear because they had the doors open for some reason.

There was an argument, then a storm of weeping. Funereal orchestral music with a solemn, rhythmic undertone started, and then . . . *"Sola, perduta, abbandonata . . . in landa desolata! Orror! Intorno a me s'oscura il ciel . . . Ahimè, son sola! E nel profondo deserto io cado, strazio crudel, ah! Sola abbandonata, io, la deserta donna!"*

Translated, this means, roughly, "Alone, lost, abandoned in this desolate plain, ah, the horror! Around me the day darkens. I am alone and in the depth of this desert I fall. What cruel torment! Alone, abandoned, a woman deserted!"

Roma's voice was strong and clean, deeply emotional yet controlled, with the perfect essence of weeping for such a forlorn piece. I had heard it done badly, the top notes wriggly and wavering, quavering, uncontrolled, everything people hate about soprano opera singers' arias. Roma's version was sublime. Pish had figured out the right selection for Roma's state of mind, the final soprano aria from Puccini's *Manon Lescaut*, "Sola, Perdutta, Abandonatta." When she sings this, Manon is dying, reflecting on her life. Whatever mojo had helped Roma climb from the chorus to principal soprano, she had it back. With Pish's help, she might regain her position someday. She was, indeed, brilliantly talented.

I left them to it and went to clean up the kitchen.

And there, at my kitchen table, was Virgil, in uniform, wolfing down a sandwich while reading the local newspaper. He was a good antidote for the melancholy and confusion I felt, and when he looked up, smiling, I smiled back. "Sheriff, what are you doing here eating my food with no sheriff's car in the lane?"

He watched as I crossed to the counter and covered the almost-empty platter of sandwiches, putting it back in the fridge. I lifted the kettle to be sure there was water in it, then turned on the burner.

"I had Urquhart drop me off. I wanted to talk to you. Gordy said you would be back anytime."

His voice and expression were serious. "What's up?"

"Come here," he said.

I crossed to him, my stomach twisting as it always does when he looks at me like that, his brown eyes warm. He pulled me down on his lap and tugged my hair out of the clip that held it piled on the top of my head. It tumbled down until it fell like a curtain around our faces. He threaded his fingers through my hair and kissed me. At first I could taste the ham sandwich and coffee, and felt the stubble scraping my chin and cheeks, but then I was lost in the kiss, and felt how much he wanted me. It was luscious and delirious.

What a man! And I mean that in the best way, completely and utterly. I am so grateful that he's not controlling or withholding like some men, who pull back if you don't do exactly what they want or expect. The teakettle shrieked and awoke me from bliss. I jumped off his lap, breathless, and he smothered a grin as I turned it off, filled the teapot, and returned, sitting demurely across from him, heat flooding my face. "So, you want to talk to me—what about?"

His grin died and he looked down at his hands, laced together in front of him on the table. I reached across and he grasped mine and squeezed.

"Virgil, what's up?"

"Kelly is visiting her parents until tomorrow. I'm going there to talk to them all together. I need to force the issue, or she's never going to come clean. I can't have this shadow hanging over me. Over us."

Kelly was his ex-wife, and she had done him a terrible disservice in lying about him to her father, who happened to be the sheriff of Ridley Ridge. "Virgil, is that wise? If you show up, won't it seem like you're bullying or threatening her?"

"I talked to her yesterday. She agrees that she needs to come clean to her dad, and she's okay with my being there. I'll stay out of it unless she needs my support."

His *support*? After what she did to him? I kept my temper under control. I admired him for his tactic and hoped it would work, but Sheriff Ben Baxter was a hard man and would not take kindly to finding out that he had been wrong about Virgil for years. I didn't know him well enough to understand him, but I do know that some people, once their opinion has solidified about a person or event, cannot be swayed. Kelly had let things go too far for too long, and I wasn't sure that it would work.

But I could be wrong this time. Virgil did need to do something, and I trusted his judgment. I would cross my fingers, hold my breath, and hope for the best. I was thinking about returning to his lap to kiss him a whole lot more, but Pish, Roma, and Zeke came into the kitchen just then, the two fellows chatting about some technical problem they were having. Roma looked drained and exhausted. Virgil had gotten up to leave, but Roma sighed, didn't flirt, and said she was going up for a nap.

Urquhart called Virgil and said he was pulling into the lane. Virgil was ready to go, so I walked him out, kissed him, and *didn't* tell him I loved him. I wanted to, but I wanted to do it when we were together alone, not in a hurried, rushed way. I wasn't afraid to say it first.

I returned to the kitchen. Zeke was alone, drinking a coffee and reading the paper Virgil had left open. He ran his finger along the line of print, muttering the lines aloud as he read, sometimes repeating words or phrases. Despite a brilliant mind and great technical prowess with computers and electronics, Zeke has reading difficulties. But Hannah had been helping him for some time, and he now had the tools and awareness to solve reading problems himself as they cropped up. He looked up when I approached.

"Where's Pish?" I asked.

"He's running the tape through and listening alone to Miss Roma's song. She's good, isn't she?"

"Now that Pish has found the right piece, she's brilliant. So you're putting together a video of her singing to upload online?"

He nodded. "I've got a lot of it worked out, but now we need some photos of Miss Roma out in the woods. Pish thought of asking Lizzie's help. She's such a good photographer."

"I think she would be positively thrilled, and it would be

good experience for her. Tomorrow's Sunday; why don't I call her and ask if she'll come out? She's staying at her grandmother's right now."

He nodded.

"Zeke, I understand Karl is still staying with you. Did Binny's advice not work out? Or did you change your mind?"

"He worked on Gordy while I wasn't around. He got Gordy to say it was okay if he stayed for a while."

I sat down opposite him and watched his face. Something was wrong. "Did you and Gordy fight about it?"

He nodded.

"So Karl's bunking on your couch, still?"

He nodded, and his expression became more clouded.

"Zeke, something's wrong. Please tell me what it is?"

He looked furtively toward the door, then craned his head to look down the hall, where the back door was. He hunkered down and muttered, "I don't know if I ought to tell the police something. It's about Ms. Urquhart's murder. Maybe, or maybe not. I don't know!"

"Tell me, and I'll help you decide."

His expression cleared some. "That morning, the morning Ms. Urquhart was murdered, Karl was sleeping on our couch, right?"

I nodded.

"I came out of my room earlier to go to the bathroom, and he wasn't there. I mean, he wasn't on the couch. I don't know *where* he was."

"Did you ask him about it?"

He shook his head. "What if he did it? We're just across from the post office; it would be easy. I mean, he had a big fight with Ms. Urquhart just the night before and left, right?"

"Or was kicked out. That's what Brianna and Logan say—that Minnie kicked him out. He was probably pretty mad about that."

"He was. He came to our place and went on and on. We

were chilling, eating pizza and watching *Dr. Who*. I was like, *Dude, we're not interested*, but he wouldn't shut up. I don't like the guy, but Gordy does."

"Did he say what they fought about?"

Zeke frowned. "It was kind of a jumble, but I think she said he stole something or took something. I don't know."

That was interesting. "And he said he walked out?"

Zeke nodded.

I thought about it for a long minute. "You're all staying for dinner; why don't we talk about it then? I'll see if I can bring the topic up."

He looked uneasy.

"Are you afraid he's dangerous?"

"Maybe. I mean, the stuff he says is weird! Like, he talks about how he beat kids up back in school. Says they deserved it because they were wusses."

"Where is he from?"

"Ridley Ridge."

"Did he get along with Brianna and Logan?"

He shrugged.

I had a sudden thought when I remembered Gordy's car from the morning of the murder. "Zeke, where does Gordy keep his car keys?"

"I don't know, maybe his room somewhere?"

"Would Karl have access to them?"

"Not Gordy's, but there's a spare set on a peg by the door in case I need the car anytime."

I saw the vehicle once again in my mind's eye, a beat-up beige sedan, with lots of damage on the front bumper badly held together with duct tape and Bondo. Would Gordy even notice if it received more front-end damage?

Pish called Zeke away to work on something technical. I got my phone and called Dewayne, leaving a message on his voice mail briefly asking about the paint chip tests, urging him to let me know as soon as possible. Then I called

Hannah. I got her voice mail and left a message, but she called me back immediately. I wandered out to the terrace and watched Karl and Gordy work as we talked first about her day, what she was up to, and then what info she had discovered for me.

"I have so much to tell you!" she said, breathless with excitement. I could practically see her big gray eyes gleaming. "First, what Chrissie told me: Deputy Urquhart and his brother *were* Minnie's heirs, but that changed a couple of months ago. The deputy wouldn't know about the change unless she told him."

"And the new heir is named Casey Urquhart," I said. "You told me that in your message. Who is he or she to Minnie? A niece or nephew? She was close to a lot of her nieces and nephews."

"That's the thing; I've talked to friends in Ridley Ridge and no one knows a Casey Urquhart. Even the *Urquharts* I've talked to don't know a Casey Urquhart!"

I was silent, not sure what to make of this information.

"So I found a reason to call Minnie's friend," Hannah went on. "I told her I was computerizing cardholders' information—which is true—and needed to ask her a few questions. We went through that, and then I said how sorry I was, that I knew she and Minnie were good friends. Well, *that* opened the floodgates!"

"I'll bet."

She told Hannah a lot about Minnie's parents, both dead, and her brothers, who sired a whole bunch of the Urquharts in Ridley Ridge, and how many were alive, dead, or in jail. "I guess when they were young they hung out together, too, Minnie and this friend," Hannah continued. "They'd known each other a *long* time. But here's where it gets interesting— Merry, this is huge! Minnie *did* have a baby, back when they were in their teens. She gave it up, and no one has heard about the child ever since." She paused, then said, "Guess what the baby's name was?"

I felt my heart drop. There was only one answer. "Casey." I tried to wrap my mind around what I had heard. If it was true, that explained the Casey Urquhart who'd inherited. But it probably meant nothing, then, to the investigation, nor had anything to do with Minnie's death. "So do we know where this child is? He or she would be . . . what, mid-forties at least, maybe almost fifty?"

"That's just it. As far as I can tell, no one has ever heard of *anyone* by that name, male or female."

"Maybe Minnie traced her child through the adoption agency and has been in contact with him or her recently. She wouldn't tell anyone about that, not even her best friend. She liked to gossip about other people, but I don't think she liked being gossiped about. It seems like it doesn't have anything to do with her murder, though we can't rule it out."

"I'll see if I can find out any more and talk to you tomorrow."

"I'll be in town," I said. "Bringing muffins to the coffee shop. I'm back in the muffin business, after all. Are you going to be around?"

"I'll be at Golden Acres with my mom and dad for a special memorial service for one of the folks who passed away, a lady who enjoyed my visits a lot."

I said I'd drop in and talk to her there. Pish and Zeke finished up in the library, which I looked forward to getting back after they were done. Gordy and Karl, tired, dirty, and hungry, were done, too. I got them some towels and had them clean up in one of the spare bedrooms.

We gathered in the breakfast room, my second-favorite place to eat after the kitchen. It's a turret room, lovely and hexagonal, and centered with a beautiful old rosewood table. I have a huge antique Eastlake sideboard that holds the more elegant pieces of my teapot collection, Limoges, Spode, Crown Derby, and a few others.

I had the fresh bread from Binny's, had baked cheddar biscuits to go with the stew, and had thrown together a tarte tatin for dessert. Roma decided not to come down for dinner, which was just as well. She does tend to dominate any gathering, and with men there, would be in full-on flirt mode. I needed Karl's focus. I let everyone eat for a few minutes. Zeke and Pish chatted quietly about their technical problems while I quizzed Gordy and Karl about the work they had done, lavishing praise on them for their labor.

"Where are you from, Karl?"

"Here and there."

"You must have been born somewhere."

He chewed and watched me, then grabbed another biscuit, breaking it open and slathering it with herbed butter. "My folks live in Henrietta."

That wasn't exactly what I asked, and I had been told by Zeke that he came from Ridley Ridge. Hmm. "You were born in Henrietta?"

He nodded.

Not the chattiest of fellows. "Have you spoken to Brianna and Logan lately?" I asked, after a few minutes of quiet.

"No."

"They're still living in Minnie's house."

"Good for them."

"So the night you fought with Minnie, the night before she died, did you also fight with them?"

Zeke kept his head down, but looked up under his flopping hair while Gordy blithely continued eating, taking his third biscuit and a second helping of stew from the covered tureen.

"No. They kept giving each other these weird looks, and I didn't appreciate it that they didn't stick up for me."

"Weird looks?"

He shrugged and chewed.

"So the argument with Minnie . . . it truly was about you borrowing her car?"

He got that watchful look again. "That's what I said, right?"

"Nothing else, not that she accused you of stealing?"

He stilled. "Maybe she said something like that. But I didn't! I never took *nothing* from her!"

"You also said that you stormed out, while Brianna and Logan say you were *kicked* out. Which was it?"

"What's it to you?" he asked, standing suddenly, his knee catching on the table and making it jump. Gordy's cup tipped over, spilling milk all over the tablecloth.

"Hey, man, cool it!" Gordy said. "What's up with you?" He blinked and looked from me to Karl and then at Pish and Zeke, who watched.

"I'm just curious," I said as Pish trotted off to get paper towels. I was not going to be distracted from my questions. "Where were you the morning Minnie was murdered?"

"I was asleep on the frickin' couch at these guys' place," he bellowed, waving toward Gordy and Zeke, his face getting red.

"But you weren't," Zeke said, his voice shaking slightly. "I came through the living room to go to the can, and you weren't in the apartment."

"You didn't say that before," Gordy, his eyes goggling, said to his best friend. "Why didn't you tell me that?"

Zeke shrugged. "I didn't know what to say. You guys seem so close."

Karl had become watchful and withdrawn.

"Where were you, Karl?" I asked.

"I was probably out on the fire escape having a smoke."

"We don't like smoking in the apartment," Gordy said helpfully. "Karl's been real good about it."

"Where were you Thursday evening?" I asked, not letting my attention waver.

"How am I supposed to remember?"

"It wasn't that long ago," I replied, watching him, trying to figure out what was going on behind those eyes. I turned to Gordy. "You remember that night, don't you? Did you guys go anywhere?"

He shook his head. "I think we watched a movie or something. I was beat. It's harvest, and I've been working extra hours for my uncle."

Zeke nodded. "We watched an old movie and Gordy fell asleep on the sofa. I had to wake him up and make him go to bed, because I knew I couldn't leave him there, since Karl would need it." He looked over at Karl, who still stood, watchful. "You went out that night and came back late."

"Where did you go, Karl?" I asked. "Did you use Gordy's car that night?"

"Merry, what is this about?" Pish asked. "Is it to do with—"

I held up my hand, and he stopped abruptly. "Karl?"

"I've heard all about your reputation, lady," Karl said with a sneer. "You think you're some kind of detective."

Gordy looked uneasy; I assumed that information came from him. "No, I'm no detective, Karl. But you can't deflect the question by attacking."

"I don't remember what I was doing that night, and I've never driven Gordy's car. Why are you asking?"

"What's going on, Merry?" Gordy bleated plaintively.

Hopefully Dewayne would have his paint chip results back and would answer my message. I'd definitely ask him the color, and if there was any Bondo in the mix. But until then, I'd shut my mouth. It was enough to know Karl was out of the apartment and wouldn't explain where he'd been. "It's nothing."

Chapter Eighteen

�֎ ✖ ✖

ONCE GORDY, KARL, and Zeke left, I washed dishes with Pish, and we talked. I told him all I had learned and discovered. He was so happy for Shilo, and felt guilty for not noticing and helping. I asked him his thoughts on Crystal, whether he figured a con artist—which was what I thought her—would be capable of killing someone they feared was onto them.

"It's possible. Most scammers aren't violent; they rely on their wits to get out of tight situations. But many violent folks are con artists, if you know what I mean."

"I get you. There are a lot of loose ends, I suppose." I told him briefly what Hannah had learned about Minnie having a child. "It doesn't seem to have anything to do with the murder, even though Casey is the heir. Nobody's heard of him or her." I paused. "I've heard that Minnie was romancing some other guy online, though I don't know who. Online romances sometimes end badly." I sighed. "I have to think the most logical suspects are Crystal, Karl, Brianna, and/or Logan."

"But I'm sure the FBI are looking further afield, and most fiercely at Roma."

"We know she didn't do it, Pish. It'll be okay." I gave him a side hug, keeping my soapy hands off his lovely jacket. To distract him, I said, "I can't believe the difference in Roma's voice. What made you think of 'Sola, Perdutta, Abandonatta' for her to sing?"

"You did, indirectly, when you asked if there was another piece that would make use of the break in her voice." He dried a bowl and set it on the counter, staring absently out the window, where the autumn sunset blazed. "It was the *feeling* of *Sola* that called to me, the sense of desperate woe; Roma is unhappy, and she's an emotional singer."

I was taken aback; unhappy? I hadn't seen that. Upset, yes, scared, maybe, but *unhappy*? "I guess you'd know better than I. What makes you say she's unhappy?"

"She misses her life in New York City. I thought being here would be good for her, but she feels isolated."

"I guess I can understand that. I may have felt the same if you and Shilo hadn't followed and stayed here with me." I glanced at him, then grabbed another bowl out of the soapy water and scrubbed. "Have I told you lately how much I appreciate you?"

He smiled, his eyes crinkling in the corners. "You don't even need to say it, my darling. I know how you feel."

"Still . . . thank you."

"Even despite bringing Roma here?"

"I've been a jerk about that. I'm sorry. She needed you, and you were there for her. That's what you do."

He smiled and took the dripping bowl from my hand, getting to work drying it. "You'd be horrified if you knew my thoughts completely . . . how the castle would be a wonderful summer home for the Lexington Opera Company, and their orchestra. Kind of like the Tanglewood estate is to the Boston Symphony Orchestra."

I shuddered. "Good lord, Pish, don't even mention that. We don't have adequate facilities, anyway."

"I suppose," he said, eyeing me speculatively. "Though a philanthropist might chip in."

I didn't like when he got that look. But his next words were innocuous enough.

"So what about the party you want to have, the one-year celebration?" he asked.

"I thought of a musical open house rather than a big party. In fact, I thought maybe you could play the piano, and Roma could sing."

He set the dry bowl down and took the next one from my dripping hands. "Would you consider leaving some planning to me?"

"Pish, you always go overboard," I said, a little alarmed at the thought of my friend planning things. We'd end up with flame swallowers and jugglers, Renaissance dancers, and that darn opera company to boot, if I didn't keep a tight rein on him.

"I'll put ideas together and present them to you before I do anything. I know I tend to be a little extravagant, but my darling, I'd be paying for it."

"No. Pish, just . . . no. I want this local and homegrown, not New York or Broadway. I don't mind Roma, since she's staying here, but we're not flying in an opera company or ordering food or décor from the city."

"I am shocked—*shocked*, I say—that you think so poorly of me," he said, with a chuckle. "And . . . you caught me. Okay, local and homegrown. And on another topic . . . have you figured out how you're going to afford to keep the castle?"

I sighed and thrust my hands into the hot, soapy water. "Not really. I'll put the word out to the film companies again, use any old contacts I can scare up." A production company had used Wynter Castle last winter to film externals for a historical movie, and maybe other people would be interested. Even our interiors would be suitable, and the pay was good, though it was a lot of trouble and turmoil having a film crew around.

We finished the dishes, Pish took some food up to Roma—another wedge from the huge Brie wheel I had in the fridge, and some water crackers—then we took our tea into the parlor. It's a cozy room tucked between the dining room and kitchen, furnished with antiques from the castle's own collection, with the addition of some pieces I had bought from Janice. Wine-colored Victorian curtains drape the windows, and a faded Persian rug warms the floor; an antique settee and two slipper chairs surround a low rose-wood table, which holds my silver tea set, a wedding gift from Maria Paradiso. I no longer looked upon it with chagrin, since we had made our peace.

We talked about other schemes for making enough money to keep the castle going, but they mostly involved turning it into a hotel, an inn, or a conference center. I am not, by nature, a hotelier, something reaffirmed for me when I hosted a group of elderly ladies last spring.

"Have you ever thought of asking the locals their opinion?"

"What I should do to keep the castle? I'd be *afraid* to ask."

He shrugged. "You're thick-skinned; you can take some insults. You may be surprised by what they come up with."

I sipped tea and pondered it. "What about running a What Shall We Do Next? contest?"

He loved the idea, and we discussed prizes, like a stay in the castle during Halloween, or a dinner for two in the dining room. But my mind kept racing around my other entanglements. I had never divulged to Pish what Virgil told me about his ex-wife and his problems with Kelly's father, and I wasn't about to. That was private. Pish and Shilo are my best friends, but there are some lines we don't cross, mostly to do with our personal affairs, love and otherwise.

Minnie's murder was still on my mind, though, and so was his darling diva. "Pish, you know I don't think Roma is capable of Minnie's murder, but nonetheless, we are left with some troubling facts." I watched his eyes, and noticed how he withdrew the moment I said her name. "She won't tell us where she was the morning of Minnie's death, nor the evening I was run off the road. Both times she had your car. And now your car has a dinged front end."

He nodded, slid a glance over at me, and sipped his tea. But didn't answer.

I sighed. "Doc tells me that you've been kept busy stomping out the fires Roma sets with her behavior toward people. She offends people so easily, it's second nature to her, and I know sometimes she doesn't even realize it. But sometimes she *does* know what she's doing. She's a pure narcissist—you have to admit that. She could have angered any number of people that we don't even know of."

"True. But none of that says why she'd kill Minnie. She doesn't have that violence in her."

"Okay, we'll leave that for now. I don't think she did it; maybe whoever killed Minnie intended Roma to take the blame. I think the likeliest motives for Minnie's murder are money or revenge, given that she doesn't seem the type to inspire love or lust."

He cast me a censorious look.

"Pish, I'm not saying that because she was old or heavy, I'm saying it because she was a thoroughly unpleasant woman to almost everyone."

"But we know for a fact that she had begun dating. She hooked up with Dewayne—"

"—who was only dating her to investigate her activity at the post office," I interjected.

"—and by your own words supposedly had another gentlemen on the hook."

I shook my head, unable to fathom it. I know how people

can behave differently when they want to impress someone, but Minnie . . . It was too bizarre for me to imagine because she was so unpleasant to almost everyone. "Be reasonable, Pish; her murder had the hallmarks of something personal, yes, but something motivated by hate. She had enemies and seemed to enjoy taunting them. Take Crystal Rouse: Minnie was peeved that Crystal was taking over Brianna. Brianna and Logan are at every Consciousness Calling meeting, from what I understand, and thus were moving away from Minnie's sphere of influence. Minnie treated Brianna, Logan, and Karl as kind of a pseudo-family, so I assume she was angry that Brianna was having the wool pulled over her eyes. I'm kind of with Minnie on that; Crystal is a fraud. One of the possibilities I've been thinking about is, if Crystal wanted Minnie dead, maybe she wouldn't do it herself, but she'd talk someone else into doing it."

"Like one of those three kids."

I shared what Zeke had told me. "That's why at dinner I was asking Karl where he was that morning, and wondering about Gordy's car."

"Charismatic leadership can have its dark side. Consider Charles Manson and what he got his followers to do. Not that I'm saying Crystal is like Manson, but you get what I mean."

"I do."

"A charismatic leader has a hold over his or her followers and could, potentially, convince a follower that it's in their best interest to get rid of someone threatening them in some way. You've met Crystal; do you think she has that kind of charisma?"

I pondered that. "Not to me. At least, not for long."

"The magnetism of a charismatic leader doesn't affect everyone. Some are immune."

"Emerald seems wholly taken with her, and Brianna, too. Why does she leave me cold, and yet others are taken in?"

"A charismatic leader—and I'm lumping suave salesmen and con artists into that group—is one who can swiftly identify what people want and need to hear. They use it to motivate that person or group to do whatever they want, or to buy what they want them to buy. Those vulnerable want something badly, and the leader has to be able to figure out what that is, and sell it to them, whether that's leadership, money, confidence . . . or snake oil."

"Crystal focused on her listeners getting what they want out of life in the way of wealth and personal satisfaction." I was more worried about what else I suspected Crystal was up to, but I didn't want to get into it. "Well, I ain't buying what she's selling. I'm worried that if Crystal is conning people as I believe she is, how that may impact Emerald in the long run. It's funny, you know—Lizzie is just fifteen, but she sees through Crystal as if the woman is glass."

He smiled. "I like her sturdy irascibility; it will take her far. Be careful, Merry. Crystal is positioning you as the adversary. She's gained a foothold with our friend, and that's hard to break. If you let her sideline you as the enemy, Emerald will be lost."

I nodded and yawned. "I have a phone call to make, and then it's sleep for me." I stood.

He did, too, and hugged me. "I'm so glad you're back, my dear, despite all this turmoil. I missed you."

I went up to my room and called Lizzie's grandmother's home. Fortunately, I got Lizzie. "How are you doing, kiddo?"

"All right, I guess. I get under Grandma's skin and on her last nerve, she says."

"Hang tight and we'll see what we can do about getting your mom back for you." I told her that we needed some photos of Roma in the woods, in costume. "Could you do a photo shoot for Pish and Zeke tomorrow?"

"That would be *awesome*," she said, her voice rising in excitement. "Ms. Toscano is amazing; it's like watching a character from a movie, you know, like the snotty girl you hope gets taken down, but you kinda admire her balls."

I laughed and agreed. "Most of us call that confidence, and sometimes people fake it, even when they don't feel it."

"Fake it 'til you make it," she said.

"Exactly. I'll come out and pick you up tomorrow."

THE NEXT MORNING WAS ONE OF THOSE FALL DAYS that start out misty. Lizzie called me at the crack of dawn and said to pick her up right away because she wanted shots of the forest in the mist, to use for a photography contest she had found in a photo magazine. I stumbled out to the car in my pajamas and sleepily drove, yawning and complaining, even though in truth, I was happy to oblige. For a kid like Lizzie, who hadn't had it easy, encouraging her passion for photography was the best thing I could do. I had known a lot of artists over the years, and every single one of them was sustained through times of trouble by their art; tormented, tortured occasionally, but sustained and carried, buoyed by their love of it. I saw that in Lizzie.

I barely pulled up to the castle when she darted from the Caddy and set out for the woods accompanied by Becket, who thought it was a grand game to leap ahead of her, wait, and then pounce into her path. I returned to the castle and baked muffins, the usual bran, apple, and cheddar, to take to Golden Acres and the coffee shop. I let them cool and went up to shower and change. When I descended, Karl, Zeke, and Gordy had just arrived. The boys were working already. Zeke was helping outdoors, since Roma was dressing for her photography session. Apparently Zeke was virtually done with the video for YouTube; all he had to do was slot in the photos Lizzie would be taking, and since he had a computer set up in the library, they were going to spend the rest of the day finishing it.

I packed up my muffins, leaving some out with a full urn of coffee for the folks, and left them all to it. It was mid-morning. I drove into town at a sedate pace, noticing the changing colors of the leaves. Autumn would always be a special time for me at Wynter Castle and in Autumn Vale, and my conversation with Pish the night before had grounded me about my intentions. This was my home now, and I had to find a way both to keep it, *and* to ingratiate myself with the majority of Autumn Vale folks. I accepted that I would always have my detractors, and have learned the hard way that you can't please everyone. I'd settle for making those I care about happy.

I drove along the familiar route, but saw a crew ahead with the crossroad blocked. And then I saw the reason! Something Binny had said came back to me, about Turner Construction moving a house for the county sheriff's department. Sunday was probably chosen as a light traffic day. As another car pulled up behind me, I saw one of Virgil's deputies, directing traffic. She approached and told me that yes, Turner Construction was moving the house to an empty plot of land, where it was going to be renovated for a young family who had bought it for one dollar. It would take ten minutes or so before the building was clear from the intersection.

By the end of the ten minutes I was bored and ready to start eating muffins as a way to pass the time, but finally I was allowed to move on. I dropped off muffins at the coffee shop, leaving them with the weekend manager. I told her I'd be back on a regular schedule, then drove to Golden Acres. I parked in back and came through the kitchen, carrying my muffins in, making sure they had what they needed, and then chatting with the kitchen manager, a woman who I'd befriended when I started supplying them with muffins.

"Is Brianna working today?" I asked, glancing around.

Her expression darkened, and for the next ten minutes I listened to her diatribe on why Brianna was about to get fired and how late she was. At the end of it the back door opened and Brianna sauntered in.

"You," the kitchen manager yelled, her face red. "You're a half hour late. I want to see you in the office, right *now!*"

Sullenly, she headed toward the office. I took the kitchen manager aside and asked if I could speak to the girl for a moment. She was hesitant, but said yes, so I followed Brianna into the office, a tiny windowless box about eight feet square, with just a metal desk and a couple of chairs. Boxed goods were stacked along the wall.

The girl was perched on a folding chair opposite the manager's desk. "What do *you* want?" she asked, rifling through her purse and taking out a stick of gum, popping it in her mouth and chewing loudly.

I leaned on the desk and looked down at her. She was so young, just a few years older than Lizzie, despite her world-weary expression. "I want a word with you on Karl Mencken's behalf."

She looked startled, but masked it quickly and lounged back in the office chair. It screeched and groaned. "What about him?"

"Well, it's more about Zeke and Gordy."

"What do those two losers have to do with me?"

"Karl is crashing on their couch. They haven't said so, but I know they'd like their apartment back. Can Karl go back and live with you guys? What's the situation there, with Minnie gone?"

She shifted and sat up straight, shaking her head. "I don't think . . . I mean . . . it's up to the lawyer right now, I guess."

I sat down on the edge of the only other chair nearby, a plastic patio chair. "Brianna, I get the feeling you don't want Karl around. Is there a reason?" I searched her face, the vivid blue eyes and reddish freckles of a girl with natural auburn hair, though hers was dyed a patchy black. "He had that raging argument with Minnie the night before she died. What was that about?"

"I don't remember." She didn't meet my eyes.

"And you said he was kicked out, but *he* says he left on his own." Actually, he said it was possible that both were true, that they had been talking over each other, but I wanted to see what she would say.

"Whatever. Look, what do you want?" she asked, glaring up at me. "Why are you asking *me*?"

"I thought you might be able to say if he could move back in."

"Like I said, *ask the freakin' lawyer.*"

"You moved here from out of town, right?"

"Sure."

"Where are you from?"

"A little town . . . Houghton. Even smaller than Autumn Vale."

"Why did you come here?"

She shrugged. "Seemed like a good idea."

I watched her as I asked, "Is Minnie's car still parked behind the post office, or has it been moved?"

Startled, she frowned at me. "You're asking *me*? I don't know. Geez, first the freakin' FBI and now you!"

"The FBI asked the same question?"

"Not *that*, but they've asked a million other questions, and sometimes the same ones over and over. That guy, the FBI agent, he's been, like, following me." She shivered. "He scares the crap out of me. I mean, I've heard of them pinning stuff on people. What if they decide to do that with me? I didn't *do* anything!"

I processed that. Did it indicate they were unduly interested in Brianna, or were they dogging everyone involved in the same way? "I understand the argument between Karl and Minnie was about that—him using her car without permission."

She just stared defiantly, done with questions, it appeared.

"You seem pretty tight with Crystal," I said. "She paying you to shill for her?" I was being deliberately provocative, and it fired her up.

Her blue eyes blazed, and she said, "I don't know what you're talking about. She's helped me. A *lot*! She showed me I *deserve* stuff out of life, not the crap that's been handed to me. She's been real—"

The kitchen manager came in and gave me a look. Brianna shut up and shut down. She hunched her shoulders, staring into her purse like it held the secrets of the universe. There was nothing more I could do, so I reluctantly departed wondering what, if anything, I had learned.

I headed to the front rooms, where the memorial service was being held, and took a seat, listening to the service. Afterward, most departed, but Hannah stayed in the living area while her parents went to Gogi's office to talk to her about an elderly aunt who was thinking about moving into Golden Acres.

"I don't suppose you have any more news for me," I said. "Given that we just talked last night."

"I did a little more research after we hung up," she said, frowning down at her slim hands clasped together on her lap. "I have an idea."

"What is it?"

"No, let me look into it first," she said. "Actually, it's more than one idea, and I want to chase down what threads I can before telling you about it."

"Tease," I said affectionately. "At least you could tell me what it's about."

She smiled and shook her head. "I don't want to, and I can be very stubborn once I make up my mind. I don't want to tell you because it may amount to nothing."

"I'd still want to know."

"And so you shall, but not before I investigate. And to do

that, I need a Monday when all government offices are open."

"Government offices? You *are* a provocative imp and should be shaken until your teeth rattle," I said.

She chuckled and waggled her finger. "Now, now; don't threaten the invalid."

I laughed and took my leave as Hannah's parents came back. I drove home and spent the rest of the day providing Roma, Pish, Lizzie, Zeke, Gordy, and Karl with food and drink, while I worked on a business plan for an idea that had occurred to me while driving. It was a bit of a weird plan, could be totally impractical, would take some time, require a lot of work and planning, but I thought there might be others in the town and surrounding areas who would be able to help and make some money off the project. It could do so many things: endear me to Autumn Valers—which I longed for with the pathetic yearning of a teenage girl for a pop star—provide work, and make Wynter Castle a running enterprise.

At the end of a long day the video was uploaded, everyone was weary but happy, and all went home and to bed. But not to sleep, at least not for me. I knew Virgil had met Kelly at her parents' home that day to try to tell Ben Baxter that what his daughter had told him about Virgil was a lie. I sent up a silent prayer and hugged my pillow, hoping it all worked out.

Chapter Nineteen

✖ ✖ ✖

I SLEPT BADLY and rose late, so I was yawning in the kitchen at eight when Pish and Roma came in together. Pish was carrying his laptop and grinning ear to ear. Roma was almost vibrating, her eyes glittering strangely, two dark spots of color on her cheeks, like a doll's rouge.

"What's up?" I asked, arrested by their behavior.

"You're never going to guess!" Pish set the laptop down on the long table and tapped the built-in mouse pad. "Watch this."

It was the video that Zeke, Lizzie, Pish, and Roma had worked on and uploaded the night before. Lizzie's photos were remarkable; Roma was positively haunting, gazing directly at the viewer in the photos as her beautiful voice keened "Sola, Perdutta, Abbandonata." There was even a bit of film from Lizzie's camera, with Roma fleeing through the woods, slow motion, her curls bouncing and her Evanescence-like clothing drifting behind her as she looked back over her shoulder. As the music faded, she dropped to the forest floor, then looked over her shoulder directly into the camera's eye.

"Roma, Pish, that is *truly* remarkable," I said, my voice catching. I had taken it all so lightly, but Pish, Zeke, Lizzie, and Roma had come up with something extraordinary.

Roma sat down next to me and hugged my arm. "It makes me cry! I'm so marvelous, I almost can't believe it."

"But, Merry, even better . . ." Pish said. "Look at the number of views!"

I looked where he was pointing . . . more than three thousand overnight. "That's amazing! How did so many people find it?"

"I sent out an e-mail blast to everyone I know," Pish admitted.

He has hundreds of people on his e-mail list, but still, it was impressive. They must have passed the link on to others.

"And the comments," Roma said, pointing to comments below the video.

I scanned through them. Words like "radiant," "astonishing," "inspiring," and "haunting" were used with abandon.

"Look at this," Roma said, then read aloud one in particular. "'I had the untrammeled pleasure of witnessing Ms. Toscano's principle soprano debut at the LSO; she was brilliant, like a Maria Callas for the modern age. Brava, Ms. Toscano. So happy to see you back! The opera world awaits, breathless with anticipation.'"

I complimented her warmly, but it wasn't enough; of course, she must compliment herself even more vividly, and then demand more compliments from Pish, who was indulgent, smiling, and nodding, though he was gray with weariness. Once Roma had flitted from the room, I made my friend sit and got him a cup of coffee, plunking it down in front of him.

"And now *you* are going to rest and take care of yourself, my friend," I said firmly, hand on his shoulder. "You've done it; she's a big hit. Maybe now she'll go back to the city, I hope."

He smiled wryly. "My darling, I hesitate to say it, but I hope so, too."

Intermittently I worked on my business plan, doing Internet research to see if what I wanted to do was even possible. It had never been done, that I could see, but I didn't see why not. I'd need to discuss it with Pish, and maybe Gogi and others whose opinion I respected. Roma flitted about and dashed into my room every hour or so, telling me about the mounting views and comments. By late afternoon they were approaching a hundred thousand views and it had been shared on Facebook and Twitter, a viral success. The opera community seemed ready to welcome her back.

I called Lizzie after school and congratulated her on her work, certain Roma never would. My young friend was over the moon, happy to be back at school. Pish had e-mailed her the link, of course, and her media arts teacher was duly impressed. It would become part of her portfolio when she applied to arts college. I was relieved; no matter what happened between her and her mother, she would live her life and follow her muse.

Even as I did all that, I waited for a phone call or visit from Virgil. Surely if there was good news after his weekend visit with his ex he would have called me last night. Or this morning. I fretted nonstop but got through the day. I didn't have to worry about dinner; Pish, knowing he had to do *something* to celebrate the video victory, had called Roma's best Autumn Vale friend, Patricia, to ask her to come out to the castle for dinner. Since she was going out (again!) with Dewayne, Patricia instead invited them to go with the couple to dinner. That gave Roma a focus and she spent the next couple of hours bathing, doing her hair, and choosing her wardrobe.

As a former stylist you might think she would consult me, but Roma seemed to have forgotten that I was ever a professional and consulted only Pish, who mildly vetted everything and agreed to her choices. Therefore she descended the stairs one costume change away from a ball gown, I was convinced. She wore a cocktail dress that was very fetching, a red number with an impressive décolletage, and long gloves. It would have worked for the opera, or a cocktail party at the Lincoln Center. Knowing the restaurant they were going to, I thought a sleek pencil skirt or trousers and silk blouse would have been more suitable, but I am no longer a stylist, I reminded myself, and that was okay.

Roma and Pish drove off into the early autumn twilight to meet Patricia and Dewayne. I carried a steaming cup of chai tea and walked through the castle wishing Virgil were with me. What we could do all alone in the place! I shivered to think about it, but he had finally texted me that he was coaching another team, girls' hockey, this evening. Absolutely no mention of Kelly or what had happened at the Baxter residence in Ridley Ridge. He said he'd talk to me tomorrow.

The people of Autumn Vale would miss Virgil so much when he made it into the FBI training program and headed off to Quantico. The whole county would miss him as sheriff; they wouldn't know how much until he was gone. But he gave even more as an individual, not in his official capacity. Who would take over his multitude of coaching duties? I was mildly curious as to which of his deputies he had in mind to run for sheriff, but he'd tell me in his own time.

I paused in the great hall to examine by the dim illumination of the sconce light the huge tapestries that lined the walls, turning in a complete circle. I stopped and eyed the staircase; all I could think of was making love with Virgil, like the couple in some insanely romantic movie, too delirious with desire to even wait until we were upstairs. It had

not eluded me that I was completely and utterly head over
heels in love with the man now that I had let go of my long-
lasting grief. I was mind, body, and soul committed to Virgil, just when he had decided to go do something dashing
with his life.

Would things have been different if I had come back
when Maria died? I sighed, the sound like a ghostly echo in
the upper reaches of the great hall as I climbed the stairs.
Becket brushed past me and trotted toward my room; I was
happy he had decided he was an indoor-at-night cat again.

I drifted down the gallery toward my room, sipping my
spicy chai, inhaling the fragrance. It suddenly occurred to
me that not only was I alone, Roma would not be back for
hours. A devilish plan crept into my mind. I tried to resist,
but I had never wholly escaped suspicion of her. She would
tell neither Pish nor I where she was the morning Minnie
was murdered, nor even the night I was run off the road.
She loathed Minnie, and I suspected she disliked me
intensely for many reasons, not the least of which being that
Pish was devoted to me. There was something going on with
that woman. I couldn't see her murdering Minnie, but if not
that, then what was she hiding?

I quickened my pace to my room where Becket sat, waiting, in the middle of my bed, the only male who had done
so in quite a while. I set down my tea and retrieved from
my bedside table the ring of skeleton keys that opened almost everything. I wasn't sure what I was looking for, but I
was going to search Roma's room.

Becket leaped down from the bed and followed me, loving the new game of dash around the castle. I sped down
the gallery to Roma's room, bending and fitting the key in
the lock with trembling hands. Maybe it was idiotic, especially since the FBI had already searched. I didn't know
what I was looking for, but if there was anything that pointed
to a secret life, I'd see it when they, perhaps, focused on the

murder and looking for blood, would not. I'm a woman, and I know how other women think and behave. We are an odd lot, at times, saving things that have no meaning except to ourselves. Receipts, tickets, news clippings . . . I didn't know what I might find, or what it would indicate, but my curiosity would be soothed.

Her room smelled of Roma, a mixture of her fragrance—Dior's Hypnotic Poison, redolent of sandalwood—and the peppermint Thayers Dry Mouth Spray she used before performing. Becket prowled, snooping everywhere; as Roma did not like cats and wouldn't allow him anywhere near her, he had never explored her stuff. Despite my determination, it still felt crappy to be searching her belongings. But a woman had died, and I had come too close; this was for the greater good, and yes, I'm aware that is how the authorities in a police state think when they trample people's rights to privacy.

She was messy, her clothes flung all around, and her attached washroom adrift in lingerie, makeup, powder, and pills. She took sedatives, sleep aids, and birth control pills. She also took fiber diet capsules guaranteed to make you feel full with just a glass of water. I was familiar with all of that, having dealt with models for so long. Even plus-size models fall prey to it, since plus-size in the modeling industry is about a size eight or ten.

Once upon a time opera singers, at least, were celebrated no matter their size; it was their talent that was important. But lately it seems that they, too, need to be model thin and gorgeous to get the parts, and more than one celebrated (female) singer has been fired for being too fat. That doesn't apply so much to male singers, of course.

I was losing heart, sad at what Roma's stuff said about her state of mind: sleepless, obsessed with her weight, having trouble with her voice. The room was like her life: chaotic, messy, with no order or method. Becket sniffed all her

stuff but headed out of the room, tail high in the air flicking
back and forth, likely sent away by that pervasive peppermint smell.

I certainly wasn't finding anything incriminating. There
was one last place to search: her closet. I opened it and
checked through her clothes, the sensible stuff she wore
most days—slacks and skirts, sweaters, light blouses—and
even went through the clothing bags protecting her fancier
dresses and gowns. On the floor was a zippered bag shoved
back behind her shoes and suitcases, something moderately
heavy for its size. I pulled it out and sat on the floor, angling
myself so the room light shone on the plain canvas tote,
totally unlike her other luggage. I unzipped it and pulled
out a portable tape recorder. Maybe she used it to practice
and listen back, I thought. She wouldn't be the first, though
most singers now use a laptop or other device to rehearse,
recording and listening back so they can correct mistakes.
There was a tape inside; I pressed Play.

It was not singing, but a muffled conversation. A man
was talking, and his tone was intimate, sexy. I was riveted,
while feeling faintly dirty. Was this a boyfriend of Roma's?
It sounded like a recorded phone conversation.

". . . you have a sexy voice. Real sexy. Makes me wonder
what it would be like whispering in my ear."

I felt a shiver down my back, and not in a good way. He
sounded like the kind of creep who would call a phone sex
line, or the guy who blind dials you to ask what you're
wearing.

A woman's giggle filled the next section, then her voice
saying, "You're so bad! Don't misbehave or I'll have to cut
you off!"

I yelped out loud in surprise and hit the Pause button.
This required serious contemplation; it was not at all what
I expected . . . not *who* I expected. I released the pause and
listened on as he spouted some more nonsense and so did

she. I was half listening, half reeling and processing who the woman was, and wondering why Roma had this tape. They had gone from sex talk to some more serious conversation, and she said, "Yeah, I had a kid a long time ago, but gave it up for adoption. My biggest regret."

Again, I was stunned and began to do rapid calculations. What did this mean? I clicked the machine off, clambered to my feet, put Roma's room back together as best I could, but took the machine and tape back to my room. I was going to wait up and confront Roma, ask her why she had a taped recording of a phone conversation between some strange man and Minnie Urquhart. Did this have anything to do with the postmistress's murder?

I spent the rest of the evening doing online research and taking notes. I was planning for the future, but with so many things up in the air (Lookin' at you, Virgil, I thought) I was unsettled and kept peering out windows, waiting, pacing to the door downstairs and looking out. Finally, at about eleven thirty, I was rewarded when I spotted headlights blinking through the trees that lined my lane.

They were coming back.

I had intended to confront Roma in front of Pish the moment they came home, but recalled my dear friend's gray, weary face. After dinner out—as much as he likely loved it—he would only be more tired. He needed to rest, and this was between me and her. I also didn't want him defending her; not this time. I raced upstairs, closing my door and waiting by it. I heard the downstairs door swing shut—it's so big that the sound when it closes echoes through the whole castle—and then they both ascended to the gallery, talking loud at first, then whispering.

Finally, after a few minutes, I trusted that Pish was in his room and showering, as he always does, before slipping into his pajamas. He habitually wears what are called kurta pajamas, an Indian style of long top over pajama pants, very elegant in linen or more often silk, Pish's preference. I slipped from my room and down the hall, tapping on Roma's door.

"En-ter," she sang, likely thinking it would be Pish.

I heeded her offer. She had thrown off her dress and wore a silk dressing gown, pale pink, and pom-pom mule slippers, satin, the very image of a 1950s star, which was how she saw herself in her better moments. She sat at her dressing table and efficiently wiped makeup from her face using makeup remover cream and cosmetic pads.

"I was thinking, Pishie darling, that if we are to go on with *Much Ado About Nothing* we should film it and upload it to YouTube, given how many views *Sola* is getting."

"I'm sure he'll agree with you when you tell him that in the morning, Roma."

She jumped and shrieked, tipping over her bottle of makeup remover and hastily wiping up the spill with a tissue. "Merry, you startled me," she finally said, tossing the tissue at the garbage can under the dressing table but missing. "What do you want?"

"To ask you again where you were the morning Minnie was murdered. Did you go to the post office to discuss her love life? Blackmail her? Minnie was never easy to get along with—I know that from experience. Did it break out into an argument and you lost your temper, saw the letter opener, and went for it?" That wasn't quite how it must have gone, given that I knew the letter opener was not the only weapon, but I had to ask.

Her face in the dim light from the sconce was deathly white, a bit of the makeup remover still visible in a line along her jaw, her visage bizarre, with one eye still made-up and the other bare. "What do you mean?" she whispered.

I crossed the room and sat on the end of her bed, staring at her, my gaze never leaving her face. "I know you were plotting, Roma, but plotting *what*?"

She shook her head and opened her mouth, but no sound came out.

"I've heard it, you know; you taped a phone conversation between Minnie and her new love interest. I don't know how. I don't know why. But you did it."

Her dark eyes widened. She leaped to her feet, dashed to her closet, and fell to her knees, pushing aside her luggage and pulling the canvas bag out, rooting around in it. She whirled and sat down with a thump, glaring across the room at me. "You searched my room! How *could* you? You're so self-righteous, but you're a nasty piece of . . . I'll tell Pishie right this minute unless you give it back. I'll let him know how despicable—"

"Don't even *try* to destroy my relationship with Pish," I said, my tone frosty. "I could have done this in front of Pish. Instead I decided to give you a chance to explain yourself."

"I never explain. *Ever.*"

"Then we have a problem."

We bantered like that for a few minutes more: threats and wheedling on her side, demands and ultimatums on mine. She returned to her dressing table and took off the rest of her makeup. She was trying to figure out what to do, given my refusal to go away or be silent.

"Fine. I'll tell you what happened, since you're being such a witch about it," she finally said, turning and facing me, all the blotches and blemishes of a normal woman's skin now evident.

"That's all I want. How did you get a tape of Minnie talking to a lover?"

She bit her lip and smothered a smile. "That is *not* a lover," she trilled, her voice musical with suppressed laughter. "That's an actor friend of mine who is doing a cabaret show in Rochester right now."

Stunned at her smirk, I was silent for a moment. An actor.

It took me a minutc, but I got there. "You hired an actor to romance her on the phone. But why?"

She gave me a withering look. "She was planning on making my life miserable if I stayed. I thought I'd beat her to the punch."

I recognized that given the circumstances, it would have seemed completely reasonable to Roma. Minnie had attacked the only thing she cared about, her identity as an opera singer, so she would attack back. Women can be vicious when their children are threatened; Roma's singing career was her child. Making Minnie a laughingstock in Autumn Vale would have been a return ten times for the damage Roma had suffered. I spared a thought for the dead woman; poor Minnie, two lovers, and neither one genuine.

The explanation was not satisfactory, though, in so many ways. "Roma, where were you the morning Minnie was murdered?"

"I was getting that tape from my actor friend. Think about it, for heaven's sake. I didn't know she was *dead*. I had planned to confront her with the tape and all the ridiculous things she said, or . . . or play it in the coffee shop, or something! If I knew how to use the Internet I'd have loaded it up there, or whatever you call it, with a photo of her so everyone in the world could hear that *pathetic* woman spout love poetry." She had the grace to look slightly guilty at that, clasping her hands between her knees. "Once she was dead, of course, I had no use for it."

"What about the night I was run off the road?"

"Merry, dear, you *do* need to stop being so dramatic," she said, casting me a snide glance. "Why would I do something so dreary to you? I simply went for a drive and met my friend for drinks, that's all."

"So your actor friend is actually a *lover*!"

"On occasion. I don't have any money, but Bertram is easygoing. It amused him to play Minnie's 'phonamour,' and the price was merely my company. He finds me entertaining. We had some wine and went to a motel; I *may* have had a wee tipple too much and ran into a parking lot barricade. The motel will tell you everything. As a matter of fact, they'll be contacting Pish about it." She glanced at herself in the mirror, pinched some color into her cheeks, and smiled. The smile faded. "I suppose I need to tell him what happened." Her gaze switched to me, in the mirror. "I wanted to wait until after . . ."

She didn't need to finish. She wasn't going to tell him until after they'd finished the video, in case it put him off and he refused to do it. How little faith she had in Pish. She bit her lip and smiled at me. "I don't suppose *you'd*—"

"No, Roma. It's up to you to tell Pish what you did to his car and everything else, even about Minnie. Have fun." I stood. "I'll be checking this all out, you know."

Now that I had refused to help her, she was back to being snotty. "Go ahead, you suspicion little peon. He'll be amused. I have told him *so* much about you."

I headed to the door, but turned and eyed her with dislike. "Tell Pish why his car is dinged the moment you're up tomorrow. If you don't, I will, and I won't sugarcoat the whole sick little plan, like you will." I would be talking to him anyway, to make sure he confirmed her story, but I'd let her tell him her own way first.

"All right, *okay*."

She muttered to herself and flung some clothes around as I left. In my room my cell phone had a voice message on it from Hannah, telling me to call her right away. I did, and found her breathless with excitement.

"What's going on? Is everything all right?"

"Merry, I couldn't wait, and I didn't think you'd want to, either. I have news."

"What is it?"

"I started with Minnie's child."

"Yes . . ."

"We figured out that the kid would be late forties by now if Minnie had the baby as a teenager."

I sighed with exaggerated impatience. "Are you going to make me go through every step of your investigation?"

"I am," she said, with a laugh. "You know me by now, Merry. I want you to hear it all, so you know how clever I am."

I laughed. "I already know that, but go ahead. We'll get there." I lay on the bed and put my hand on Becket, feeling him purr.

"So, I started from the information we had. I had a name, and an approximate date of birth, from Minnie's friend."

"Right. But no one around here seemed to know about the baby except her friend."

"Yes, but everything we do in life is tracked and recorded."

I remembered her mysterious need to wait until government offices were open. "You didn't go all the way to . . . *wherever* for birth records, did you?"

"Not exactly. I used the power of the Internet."

"How did that help you?"

"It took a lot of cross-referencing, but I started with Minnie, and children in the area born around then, and the name we know she gave the child."

"Casey Urquhart," I supplied.

"Uh-huh. For a price you can search databases that hold all of our information, and I mean *everything*: date of birth, marriages, licenses. Adoption. Change of name." She paused, then said, "Death."

"Oh. *Oh!* Is Casey Urquhart dead?"

"She died a long time ago, when she was just nineteen."

"That's so sad. Did Minnie know?"

"I think so."

"I can't believe you found all this out in one day." Hannah is an extraordinary researcher, like many librarians: part researcher, part human resources, part Internet goddess, and part rat terrier fixated on one task until it is mastered and defeated. I would never have figured out all she did, nor stuck with it as long. There had to be something more, judging by the excitement in Hannah's voice at first. "So what's got you jumping?"

"Merry, the poor girl died in childbirth, but the baby *survived*."

I was silent for a moment, stunned. "Minnie had a grandchild?"

"She did."

"Did she know that?"

"Oh yes, she certainly did. *And* changed her will accordingly. The baby was adopted at birth and given a different last name from Urquhart. Not a name anyone around here would know, you see."

"Oh. *Oh!* Do we . . . no, that's too much to ask." I paused. "Or maybe not. Do we have a name?"

"We do."

"Do I know the individual?"

"You do."

And then she told me who it was, and everything fell into place.

Chapter Twenty

❋ ❋ ❋

THE FBI HAD caused quite a stir in town, with exhaustive interviews and searches. The gossip mill was grinding exceedingly fine, with every bit of minutiae available from every person who had been questioned, every neighbor who had been canvassed, every single little bit discussed and microdiscussed down to the finest grain of detail. I heard it all as I did the rounds of muffin deliveries. I had purposely left early, giving Roma enough time to fess up to Pish what she had planned to do to Minnie, but I knew darn well she'd sugarcoat it, and that Pish was a pushover.

I didn't expect any major blowouts, but my friend is a kind man, and I thought he'd be disappointed with the diva. The way she'd planned on humiliating Minnie was particularly female and vicious. Though in life I had disliked Minnie intensely, in death I felt nothing but pity for her, especially after hearing the latest news from Hannah. The least we could do was find her murderer because she had been slaughtered, if I was right, by someone for whom she cared. It must have been awful.

I visited the library, got the information that Hannah had printed for me, and insisted on reimbursing her for the services for which she had paid. Perhaps there was some way I could charge it to my taxes under medical, as a treatment for SD, snooping disorder.

Then I stopped at the FBI trailer and spoke to Esposito. As I climbed up into the vehicle I asked about Minnie's car and he confirmed that it had been impounded the day of her death. That was the answer to my question, then, about Karl's access to it after Minnie's death: he didn't have any. The inside of the command center was dull gray and lined with computer terminals, mostly dead, with one fellow doing something official-looking. Or maybe playing Candy Crush. Esposito had me sit in the passenger seat while I told him everything I knew. He nodded. A lot.

"Did you know any of this? All of it?"

He smiled. "You know I can't divulge what I did or didn't know, Ms. Wynter."

I restrained the urge to roll my eyes like Lizzie talking to her mother. "Have you, perchance, been to one of Crystal Rouse's Consciousness Calling introductory meetings?"

"That's beyond the scope of our murder investigation, though we have looked into both Emerald Proctor and Crystal Rouse, of course, as two suspects who Minnie Urquhart had run-ins with."

I squinted and eyed him. "I don't suppose you'll tell me what you've found out about Crystal."

"Of course not. However, I will say we've been contacted by a young woman at Consciousness Calling in San Diego. She said she had spoken with you, and was very concerned about Crystal Rouse's misappropriation of the CC brand and methodology, as she called it."

That was good. "They've advertised another introductory meeting tonight, and I'm going. Maybe you should have someone there. I think interesting things are going to happen."

He watched me for a moment, perhaps digesting the subtext of what I was saying. "I don't have a single agent in this town who would not be recognized instantly."

"Well, that's a problem, isn't it?" I said, opening the vehicle door, slipping from the seat, and looking back at him. "I would imagine you have lots of other agents within an hour's drive."

"I'll take that under advisement, Ms. Wynter. We greatly appreciate your intimate involvement in our investigation."

He might have been joking, but I'll confess I wasn't sure. I went on my merry way. Every way is my Merry way; that was a joke my grandmother used to make.

I hadn't forgotten my dear friend, Shilo. I had called the evening before but got their machine, a jaunty new message with Shilo singing off tune "We Are Family." I drove to their new house with the last of the muffins to find Jezebel haphazardly backed into the drive and the trunk open. The front door of the house was open, too. *Everything* was open.

I hesitantly climbed up the steps and poked my head in the front door, inhaling the odor of paint and sawdust. "Hello?" I called.

I heard something fall and a laugh, followed by a slightly lower laugh that was very similar. I followed the sound. Shilo was in the kitchen doing dishes with Lido. "Hi!" I said.

"Merry!" She raced at me and hit me with the full force of her slender frame. Luckily I am sturdy and not easily sent flying.

Lido smiled and nodded, softly saying, "Howdy, Merry."

"Hi, Lido. What's going on?" I asked, my gaze returning to Shilo, who had returned to the dishes. "Jezebel's sitting out in the lane with her trunk wide-open." I heard a noise in the other part of the house like someone clattering down stairs.

"Jack is loading up the old girl," Shilo replied. "Can you give him a hand, Lido?" Her brother nodded and raced through the house, joining Jack, who I could hear shout a welcome to his brother-in-law. "Oh, Merry, it's so wonderful!" Shilo said, taking my arm and clutching it against her. "Jack and Lido had a long talk. We're going to go see my granny!"

I was relieved, if a bit miffed that no one had bothered to tell me. However, Shilo was free-spirited Shilo. "I'm so happy, honey. I told you Jack would be okay with it."

"And his mama was even better! She hugged me and told me she was worried about me, and happy now that I was okay. She was afraid I was sick or something. I said that other than being a little ralphie, I was fine."

"Ralphie?" That was a new one. "What does that mean?"

"Ralphie . . . like I want to ralph all the time. The girls I knew in New York always said they were going to visit Uncle Ralph when they were getting rid of a meal. I can't keep food down the last few days."

My mind immediately went *there*, and I stared at her, the glitter in her eyes, her pearly skin, and her pink cheeks. "Shilo, honey, have you taken a pregnancy test lately?"

She stilled and her eyes widened. "Do you think . . . Is that why I'm sick?"

"I'd check it out if I were you."

She promised she would. I told her to call me the moment she knew one way or the other. In the meantime, we decided not to say a word to Jack or Lido. Jack, happier than I had ever seen him, was jovial and scattered and erratic with love. He and Shilo would celebrate their first anniversary in December; I hoped by then I'd be well on my way to being an honorary aunt. I helped them pack Magic, her bunny, in his cage in the backseat with Lido, got a spare set of keys, promised to water Shilo's plants, and waved good-bye to them.

It happened that quickly. I checked that the doors were

locked securely and drove back to Wynter Castle to find out
if Roma had done what she promised to do. The place was
silent and chilly. Becket, who had gone out at dawn, followed me in, went to his food bowl, then climbed the stairs
and disappeared into my room. I found Pish in his study,
where he was listening to Bartok and reading Shakespeare.
I closed the door behind me and sat in the other club chair,
watching him.

He met my gaze and smiled, then reached out and took
my hand. "Yes, to your unspoken question, my darling;
Roma told me what she was about to do to Minnie, though
with much railing about how you forced her into telling me,
and that she hated to hurt me, but had decided it was for the
best. But that you *forced* her into telling me."

I nodded. "And what exactly did she say?"

"That she intended to pull a harmless little prank on
Minnie by setting up a lover, recording the conversations,
and then playing them in a public and embarrassing way."

"And what did you think when she told you that?"

He looked down at the Shakespeare volume he held, a
beautifully gilt-bound edition, and was silent for a long
moment. He closed it, set it aside, and took my hand. "I
thought that I will forever be grateful that you are my best
girl and always will be."

Emotion welled up in me. I had been jealous of Roma's
hold on Pish, true, but what I felt now was not triumph but
gratitude. He was so important to me, and I feared that I had
changed our relationship by my months of self-absorption
in Spain. "I've been searching my heart to try to figure out
if some part of me wanted her to tell you about it so I'd gain
some edge, appear superior, but I think I can honestly say
that was not my intent. I wanted you to hear it from her,
because it may come out in some other way. I didn't want
you to be blindsided by the revelation."

He squeezed and released my hand. "I know that.

Fortunately, I was never blind to her faults. I want to help her get back to where she needs to be: the stage."

"And you've done that beautifully." I changed the subject and told him what I had planned for that evening. "I told the FBI what's going on; now it's up to them if they set something up and have a presence."

"Is it wise, my dear?"

"I think there's safety in numbers. That's why I'm going to make sure I have backup. I can't ask Virgil; the FBI could give him grief, and I don't want to jeopardize his future career. But Dewayne may help me out."

"I'll be relieved if you have stalwart Dewayne there." He paused and watched me for a moment. "And now, what *about* Virgil? Have you sorted out your problems?"

"I don't know. He was taking care of something this weekend, but he hasn't talked to me about it yet."

"I'm assuming it had to do with his ex-wife?"

I nodded. "It's something that's private to Virgil, so I can't talk about it. I think it's a bad sign that he hasn't called or visited yet. Or maybe it's taking longer to resolve."

Pish took up my hand and squeezed. "One thing I can say for sure: that man loves you."

"I hope so, because I love him, too."

"Do you love him enough to wait while he does the FBI thing?"

"I do. I'll be here for him. I can't say I'll move where he goes, but we'll work it out somehow."

The rest of the afternoon flew by as I prepared to unmask a killer. Or killer*s*. Dewayne agreed to be there, and he thought Patricia might want to come, too. She would be good cover for him; he had attended just the once, but hadn't stayed, nor had he talked to Crystal that evening. She might think it odd, him returning, but not if he attended with Patricia. I spoke to Zeke, and he agreed to have Gordy and Karl there. I saw Roma briefly, but she ignored me and crept around the castle avoiding Pish. If she understood him at all, she'd know that the best way to get back in his good graces would be to fully accept responsibility for her wrongdoing and move forward, like an adult. I didn't have high hopes of that.

I made a light dinner, we all ate separately, and I drove off into the twilight toward town. I got a half mile and saw the flashing lights of a cruiser in my rearview mirror. I slowed, pulling off to the edge of the road.

Deputy Urquhart came to my window and shone his flashlight in at me. "License and registration, ma'am," he said.

"Oh, come on, Urquhart," I said, shielding my eyes against the light. "You know who I am and you know this vehicle is mine."

"Sheriff Grace told me to stop you and bring you in, ma'am."

I was stunned. "I beg your pardon?"

He repeated his command.

"That's ridiculous. Who does Virgil think he is? What's the charge?"

"No charge, ma'am. Protective custody, he says."

Aha! Dewayne—the traitor—must have spoken to him. Of *course* he would; they were buddies. Bro code, and all that. What an *idiot* I was for not foreseeing this. I looked out my window and examined the deputy by the dome light in my car. "You tell Virgil that if he wants something, he has to come to me directly. If you want to take me in, you'll have to get me out of this car and carry me. I wouldn't advise trying. Good evening, Officer."

I rolled up my window and drove away at a sedate pace, smiling as I imagined Urquhart's frustration, and how he was going to have to confess to Virgil his failure. What I *didn't* count on, as I pulled down a side street and parked, was Virgil also being parked there. He got out of his cruiser and approached.

"Sheriff, how are you? Long time, no hear," I said, hoisting my purse over my shoulder and crossing my arms over my chest. He crossed his arms over his chest, too. We both have impressive chests in different ways.

"Come on, Merry, don't be like that."

Of course, *that* lit my fuse. *Don't be like that*? "How *dare* you send your lackey to try to stop me from doing what I need to do?" I said, my hands going to my hips and my purse sliding down. "And how *dare* Dewayne call you and inform on me!"

He got that alert, hesitant look men get when they unexpectedly infuriate their lady friends. "Dewayne thought I should know. And he's right."

"Virgil, this isn't your case. There's nothing you can do. Did Dewayne tell you that I *did* let the FBI in on my plans?"

"You did?"

"Yes, Virgil, I did." I realized I was talking too loud, glanced down the street, and lowered my tone. "I'm not an idiot. I spoke to Esposito and recommended that they have someone there tonight."

"So there's going to be an agent there tonight?"

"You've met Esposito; does he seem particularly forthcoming to you? I don't know."

He sighed, uncrossed his arms, and tried to pull me to him, but I pulled back. "Wait a minute, mister, not so fast. You haven't told me one thing about what went down this weekend. How did it go?"

He looked off into the distance. "I'd prefer to talk about this when we have more time," he said.

"Certainly. And I'd prefer to *kiss* you when I have more time. Right now I have to go."

Not a man to be put off lightly, he pulled me to him and moved me into the shadows and kissed me until all rational thought had fled.

"Nice job, Sheriff," I said, breathless, squashed against

his chest, his hand firmly on my butt. "Now I won't be able to think logically for half an hour."

"We could solve that by taking you home right now," he said in my ear, with a growl in his voice.

I pulled away and settled my clothes, hoisting my heavy shoulder bag more securely. "I'd rather wait until you can tell me what went down with Kelly," I said, my voice tremulous. "I need to know before we get . . . before anything else."

"Okay."

"And I *am* doing this," I said, waving my hand toward the street. "I protected myself by having Dewayne there. You trust him, don't you?"

"With my life."

"And with mine?"

He was quiet for a minute. I could hardly see him in the shadows, but his jaw was working. "I guess," he said reluctantly.

That told me that my life was more important to him than his own. "I'll be careful, Virgil, and I promise I'll rely on Dewayne. We've talked this through, and he knows what to expect."

"I know. He told me everything after he spoke to you."

I sighed. "I suppose I should have assumed he would. I'll talk to you later, Virgil. I promise."

"I won't be far."

I walked away from him aware of his gaze on me. Once I got to the main street, where there was more light, I turned the corner and stopped, catching my breath. That man! He sure did know how to rattle me. Taking a deep breath, I sauntered down the street to Emerald's shop, ablaze with light that spilled out of the naked window to the walk below. A chilly wind swept down the sidewalk, and with it a few early leaves.

It was time.

I entered, the bells jingling merrily over the door. Crystal looked up from her clipboard of attendees, her expression darkening as she gazed at me. She wasn't quick enough to hide it, and Emerald saw the look, glanced toward me, and half smiled. She waved, then caught Crystal's disapproving look and stopped.

The room was full. Dewayne and Patricia had already signed in, it seemed. Patricia waved at me cheerily, but Dewayne didn't indicate by any sign that he recognized me. Gordy and Zeke were huddled in a corner, chatting with Karl and Logan, while Crystal and Emerald examined the clipboard. Brianna, her eyes bright, was bouncing around setting up the table with snacks and coffee at the back, her energy effervescent. Occasionally she would race to the front of the room and whisper to Crystal and Emerald, then dash away again.

A young couple entered, a slim blonde woman and crew-cut man, neither of whom I had ever seen before. FBI? I hoped so. A couple of others folks wandered in, but certainly *not* FBI. One was a scruffy-looking motorcycle-type dude, and the other was a woman in mom jeans and a stained T-shirt. She was clearly exhausted, rings under her eyes, her hair in a messy ponytail that looked like it had been tugged at by children with sticky fingers. More suckers for Crystal's you-can-have-it-all message.

I sat down in the middle of the middle row, the best place for my purposes. Crystal whispered something to Emerald; my friend nodded and approached, perching on the edge of chair next to me.

"So, Merry, why are you here tonight?" she asked, with a searching gaze.

I turned and looked her right in the eyes, crossed my fingers, and lied, though it hurt to do it. "I don't think I gave this whole thing a proper chance last time, Em."

"Good," she said, with a nod. "Crystal was worried you were here to disrupt things, but I told her you would never do anything to hurt me!"

I felt a pang in my heart. "I hope you know that I truly . . . I *truly* have only your best interests at heart always," I said, even as I was hoping Crystal would be in police custody by the end of the evening, if all went according to plan. Emerald gave me a hug and scooted back up to the front, whispering reassurances to her business partner. My swiftly approaching betrayal stung in my eyes.

Crystal started the meeting by welcoming newcomers. She then gave a stern warning that those who were skeptics were welcome to stay, but *not* welcome to disrupt the experience for the others. I suppose that was aimed at me. We did those "contexts" again, though why they were called that, I'll never know. We chanted, "I deserve love, I deserve wealth, I deserve happiness."

Then Crystal beckoned Brianna to the front and put her arm over the girls' shoulders. "Everyone, in case you didn't know, this is Brianna, and she's new to Autumn Vale." The girl waved and gave a little hop of excitement, her eyes glittering. "Brianna has some news for us. It has something to do with Consciousness Calling, so pay attention!" She put her hand on the girl's shoulder, looking like she was holding down a balloon about to float away. "Brianna, what happened to you this week?"

The girl skipped forward. "Well, I got the surprise of my life, is what happened," she said, her voice vibrating with excitement. "I've been coming to these meetings a few weeks now, and chanting the contexts, making it a part of my daily life, you know? And all of a sudden I got called in by a lawyer to come see him in his office. I was scared. I've never met a lawyer before."

She glanced over her shoulder to Crystal, who nodded. "So anyway, I go to see him, and he up and tells me that I've inherited money, and a house, and life insurance. Just out of the blue like that! I got wealth, so I've got happiness, and that's from chanting the contexts for a few weeks!"

Crystal stepped forward. "Now, *here* is proof that when
you stay positive and practice chanting the contexts, which
align your energy and your intent toward positivity, you get
what you *need* in life, as well as what you want."

Emerald was watching Crystal with a tiny frown, as if she
couldn't quite believe what her leader and business partner
was spouting. At least Em didn't appear to be in on the con.

I hadn't intended to, but I spoke up. "Are you saying,
Crystal, that positive thinking and chanting killed Minnie
Urquhart?" Someone snorted in a half laugh, but I ignored
it, watching Crystal, who paused and eyed me with disfavor.
"I kind of thought there was a human at work, considering
that Minnie was murdered. That's where the inheritance
came from, Brianna, right? Minnie Urquhart's *murder*?"

"I wasn't saying that, Merry, as you well know," Crystal
snapped. "I was simply referring to Brianna's little bit of
good luck."

Good luck, she called it. Emerald's expression now was
one of *extreme* disbelief. She tugged at Crystal's sleeve, and
whispered, "Crys, that's not exactly . . . maybe we ought—"

Crystal yanked her sleeve away from Emerald. "Brianna,
why don't you tell us how it happened?" she said, putting
her arm over the girl's shoulders again. "I know you've had
a tough life. Tell us your story, and how Consciousness Calling has turned things around."

"I never had family," she began, and spoke of the foster
care system, out of which she was ejected at eighteen. "I was
living in a shelter and got a message to call this lady Minnie
Urquhart, who said she could get me a job and had a place
for me to live. I didn't have anything else to do, so I agreed."

"And then?" Crystal asked. "You found *us*, didn't you?"

Brianna looked faintly startled at her story being chan-
neled like that. "Uh, yeah."

"Go on."

"Minnie was really, uh, kind to me, and to Logan."

Karl snorted and muttered something under his breath.

"And she, like, started to take an interest in what I was doing, and got me a job at the old-age home, and was like the mom I never had. Anyway, turns out, I didn't know it, but all along, she was my birth grandmother!"

There was a chorus of surprised exclamations and an outburst of applause. I waited for that to die down.

"And you didn't know until you were told about the inheritance?" I asked.

Brianna nodded, but regarded me suspiciously through narrowed eyes.

I reached in my purse, clicked the tape recorder on. I had the sound set as high as it would go, so out of my purse came Minnie's scratchy voice, from beyond the grave it seemed. "I was trying to keep it a secret, but there were all these fights, and then the kid was threatening to leave. Straight back into the drug world? I didn't see as I had a choice. I said, *Don't go, I'm your grandma.*" Deep sigh. "But now the twerp figures I'm going to hand over money, and whatever. I'm not so sure now about the changes I made to my will. I might need to change it back so my meth-head grandkid doesn't snort or shoot whatever I leave."

Stunned silence followed. Crystal looked as bewildered as the rest. I clicked the tape off. "So I'm thinking your tale of the inheritance coming as a big fat surprise doesn't hold much water now, from Minnie's own lips. You knew, Brianna; you knew *exactly* what you were getting. But she threatened that she was going to go back and rewrite the will to strike you out if you didn't give up drugs."

Brianna had stiffened and looked poised to flee. "I . . . It doesn't matter. So what if I knew? It doesn't change anything. I didn't do *nothing* to her."

"You didn't?" I turned my head and looked over at her boyfriend. "Maybe Logan did something, then? Since you two were each other's alibi for the time of the murder?"

Brianna had gone still, her lips pressed together. I had blown my chance, I thought, unless the FBI had physical evidence. But Logan erupted from his seat and headed toward me. He reached out and grabbed my purse, hollering, "It's a trick! You're lying."

Dewayne, of course, launched himself across the space, knocking over a chair in his way as he grabbed the kid in a half nelson hold.

"Logan, shut up!" Brianna said. "She's trying to get you to admit something. Just shut the f—"

"It was all *her* idea," Logan yelped, struggling against Dewayne's firm grasp, his long-fingered hands clawing at my friend's beefy arms. "Brianna set it up," he squawked, his voice choked from Dewayne's hold. He beat at the man with his fists. "Let me go, you . . ." He let loose a string of filth toward Dewayne I won't repeat.

The young couple I assumed were FBI cowered together in horror, while the motorcycle dude and woman in mom jeans moved forward in sync. As the place descended into chaos the male agent removed Logan from Dewayne's grasp and the female FBI agent caught up to Brianna, who had pushed Crystal out of the way and was headed toward the back of the shop.

The fuss was all over in minutes, quite the anticlimax compared to my expectations. As the two culprits were ushered out together, Karl Mencken, shaking, clenched his fists and muttered, his face turning red.

"It's over, man; it's okay," Gordy said to him, hand on his shoulder.

"Now I get it! *That's* why she made that fight happen! *That's* why Brianna egged me on!"

I turned and saw Emerald in a heated conversation with Crystal.

"How could you *say* something like that?" Emerald asked, hands on her hips, looking very much like Lizzie in that moment. "How could *positive* energy lead to someone getting murdered so Brianna could inherit? That's just *awful*, Crystal."

"It's not like that," Crystal muttered, flicking a glance toward me. "Merry is trying to get me in trouble. Can't you see that?"

"It has nothing to do with Merry; it's what you said," Emerald declared. "I've been ignoring a lot of crap, Crystal, but I'm going to have to think things over."

I stepped forward. "Em, I think you need to know some stuff about Crystal and her true connection—or lack of connection—to Consciousness Calling. Have you been giving her money to put toward her franchise?"

Emerald nodded.

"Well, she hasn't been paying anything to them. Nothing. She has absolutely no connection to CC; I know, because I've talked to them. So she's been pocketing every cent you gave her. Come out to the castle and we'll talk. Will you do that for me?" She looked uncertain, but as she glanced over at Crystal then back to me, she nodded.

Chapter Twenty-one

❊ ❊ ❊

I INVITED MY favorite people to come out to the castle the next day for kind of a postmortem on the fallout from Minnie's murder and Brianna and Logan's arrest. *And* Crystal's arrest. Apparently, federal prosecutors, who had been reviewing information submitted by me, with supporting documentation from Aimee and the CC connection in San Diego, and through more digging of their own, had enough dirt to charge Crystal with all kinds of fraud.

She had been accepting fees from trusting locals, which wasn't a crime. If people are willing to hand you money because you made them believe they should, I suppose it's on them. But there was much more; besides using the Consciousness Calling brand without a franchise or permission, Crystal had also developed a number of online personas and was running both a fortune-telling enterprise *and* some mail frauds, using a post office box that was cleared when everything was moved out of the post office in the wake of Minnie's murder. That's where she was sneaking out to most mornings, including the morning of Minnie's murder; she was making some calls to do with her separate enterprises and using Emerald's car to go to Ridley Ridge, to her more recent post office box there.

And then there was the little matter of attempted murder. Dewayne and Virgil had tracked down, with Ford Hayes's help, the guy who was doing body work on Emerald's car. Crystal had indeed used it to try to run me off the road. I didn't think it was a serious murder attempt, just something to keep me off balance and preoccupied enough that I wouldn't interfere in her little scheme until she had milked Emerald and Autumn Vale dry. But if Virgil, who was coldly furious at her crime against me, wanted to charge her with attempted murder, I wouldn't protest.

So Crystal was under arrest, but Lizzie, the morning after the drama, was *still* not willing to move home. Determined to reunite her with Emerald and see if they could resolve their differences, I had Lizzie take the day off school. Gogi was picking her up and bringing her to the castle.

As I baked scones and muffins in the kitchen in advance of my guests arriving, the phone rang. It was Shilo. They were in South Carolina, and she was delirious at seeing her grandmother, sisters, nieces, and nephews, getting to know the little ones. She hadn't seen her father yet, and didn't know if she would. I caught her up to date with everything that had happened in Autumn Vale.

"I can't believe I missed the fun!" she said. "Why didn't that Crystal woman try to reel *me* in? I'm the perfect mark."

I laughed. "Shilo, honey, you would have seen through her in two seconds. She has a fake kind of pretend charisma used on the unwary, but you have more spirituality in your little fingernail than she has or ever will have." I waited a beat. "So have you taken a pregnancy test yet?"

"Nuh-uh. I'm scared. What if I'm not?"

"Then you won't have lost anything by finding out for sure."

"I'm . . . Oh, this will sound *silly*! Merry, I'm afraid of so much happiness. I'm gonna talk to Granny about it today."

"She'll sort you out, Shi. Just don't wait too long. And start taking the right vitamins—folic acid!"

Pish, carrying a sheaf of papers and looking elegant in a smoking jacket—honestly, he can carry it off!—entered the kitchen as I hung up. I told him about Shilo. He then took a seat at the table and donned his reading glasses as I finished my baked goods.

"So, the party."

"Yes, the party," I said.

"October first, a fall celebration, everyone invited. Janice tells me that the Brotherhood of the Falcon has what they call a hillbilly band? And they play a washboard, a jug, and a bass made out of a washtub." He looked up over his glasses. "Is that even *possible*?"

I hugged him, being careful not to get my floury hands on his elegant satin, then went back to work. "What a sheltered life you lead, Pish," I said over my shoulder. "While you're relaxing with Bartok and Dvorak, many others are enjoying country music and bluegrass. Not that that has anything to do with a hillbilly band, but it *is* all part of American folk music tradition."

"If you say so."

"There's more to American music than Copland. Aren't you going a bit far with this harvest theme, though? A hillbilly band? Really?"

Doubt heavy in his voice, he said, "Janice seems to think it will endear us to the people of Autumn Vale to include the Brotherhood."

I let him go on, and saw a theme emerge that went beyond his harvest idea. It was all about Autumn Vale, the people, the groups, the interests of those we knew, and those we didn't know. But he wasn't shying away from his interests, either.

"I've decided not to make the others do *Much Ado About*

Nothing, the opera," he said, with a regretful sigh. "Roma and I will do the duet from it at the open house, and I'll have her sing '*Sola, Perdutta, Abandonatta.*' But she is actually a very good vocalist for jazz as well, so I'm brushing up on some Sarah Vaughan." He was silent for a moment, and then said, "She's afraid to come down and speak to you, you know. She thinks you hate her."

Emotional manipulation—the woman couldn't help herself. "I don't *hate* her, Pish, though I don't like her much. But she's got nothing to be afraid of from me."

"Her agent called. She has received some offers from the video being online and will be heading back to New York after the party."

"Excellent."

I heard the heavy thud of the knocker on the oak door, and soon the kitchen was full of my friends, chattering, laughing, and talking. Gogi had brought Lizzie along, as I'd asked. Binny, Emerald, Gordy, and Zeke (both took the morning off) rode together—leaving Patricia to take care of the bakery—Janice, as a kindness, had insisted Isadore come on her only day free from the coffee shop, and Hannah's parents dropped her off, though they didn't want to stay. Instead they headed off to visit Mrs. Moore's mother, who was in a nursing home in Ridley Ridge. They were going to stay there and have lunch, then come and pick Hannah up midafternoon.

Dewayne arrived and was greeted with enthusiastic claps on the back and hugs from the ladies. Everyone had heard of his swift action in grabbing Logan at the meeting, related with breathless inaccuracy by Zeke and Gordy. Virgil, extremely handsome in his uniform, arrived, but there was so much bustle I couldn't do much but get a hasty kiss, which was watched and whooped over by the less mature members of our group. Lizzie. And Hannah, too. I could feel my cheeks blaze with color, and I don't normally blush.

"Come into the breakfast room, everyone," I said. "I thought it would be easier to dissect the outcome with everyone, rather than using the gossip chain, which, in Autumn Vale, is notoriously unreliable."

Lizzie and Hannah both wanted to sit with Dewayne, intent on quizzing him about being a private detective, so I placed him between them at the big, round table and served coffee, tea, and all kinds of goodies, kind of a midmorning brunch. I had made individual quiches, because real men do eat quiche. Isadore silently filled a plate and listened in, but many of the others peppered me with questions and comments.

"Hold on!" I said, hands up. "Listen to Gogi for a minute."

Gogi related a spare accounting of Minnie's murder. My thoughts organized, I then said, "Worried that this was going to affect my household, I knew we needed the murder solved quickly."

Virgil chuckled, and I shot him a look. "It's not that I didn't trust the FBI, but I know this town: they don't. We actually covered much of the same ground. I considered several people as suspects." Glancing over at Emerald, I said, "I had to consider Crystal as a possibility. She was absent at the right times, and there was real animosity between her and Minnie. Also, Em, she had taken your car the evening I was run off the road, and it then disappeared afterward for suspiciously timed engine troubles."

Lizzie snorted, spraying quiche crust crumbs across the table. Emerald censured her with a look, and Lizzie rolled her eyes. Pretty normal teenager-parent exchange—an encouraging sign. Better than frigid silence.

I looked over to Pish. "I seriously considered Roma as a suspect." Roma was still up in her room, consulting with her agent on the phone. "She, too, had an open hostility toward Minnie, and had even publicly attacked her. She also had access to a car, which was then dinged in the right spot, and was absent at the correct times."

"My darling, I don't mean to interrupt," Pish said. "But I can assure you, Roma is not a good enough driver to make the maneuvers you described happening to you. I have been in a car with her driving and it is a terrifying experience. Not because of anything she purposely does, simply because she seems to have no awareness of where her car ends and others begin."

"We know now what she was up to," I said, without elaborating. Enough said on that topic. I was not going to expose her to the censure of Autumn Vale folks by revealing her plot to discredit Minnie. I gathered the others in my gaze. "One of the mistakes I made was tying in being run off the road with my investigation into who killed Minnie. I mistook correlation for causation. They weren't the same person."

"Who did do it, then?" Hannah asked.

I turned to Dewayne. "Your turn to explain."

"When I was asked to look into it I took lots of samples. I even snuck around town a bit taking samples from any car with a dinged-in front bumper. Like yours, Gordy."

Gordy looked wide-eyed and fearful. "I'd never . . . I mean, I didn't—"

"We knew that," I assured Gordy. "But I established that Karl had access to your keys, and when I was thinking of suspects, Karl was definitely in the mix, from what Zeke told me."

Zeke hunched one shoulder. "I told Gordy about Karl not being on the couch the morning Minnie was killed. I guess he really was out on the fire escape smoking."

"I eliminated all those cars," Dewayne continued. "Then Merry told me about Emerald's car being in the shop. We discovered it was not with her normal mechanic. That was certainly suspicious."

Emerald was red-faced and her eyes watery. I reached over and patted her arm. "You couldn't know what she was up to, Em."

"I should have."

"Ford Hayes knows every single person who works on car for a five-county surround. With his help I tracked Emerald's car to a back-road body shop guy, one who does work under the table. He was cooperative enough," Dewayne said, one corner of his mouth quirking up in a tight smile. "And I took paint samples. It was a match."

"So the person who ran me off the road was, indeed, Crystal."

"I *knew* she was a crook from the beginning!" Lizzie said.

"But she wasn't a murderer," I said. "I *think* she was trying to distract and rattle me. She wanted me to forget about her and worry about some crazy killer on the loose, trying to get me."

"But she wasn't home that morning Ms. Urquhart was killed," Lizzie said. "And she *lied* about it, pretending to be me in a text message!"

Pish said, "Good con artists know to stick to the truth as often as possible; less to remember, fewer things to trip you up."

"She *isn't* a good one," I said. "Crystal's instinct is to lie at the slightest hint of suspicion. She'll lie even when the truth won't hurt her. The FBI had already established that the morning of the murder she was seen in Ridley Ridge, clearing her post office box. She had begun diverting her mail to it, since Minnie was getting snoopy and suspicious. It was just a matter of time before Minnie, who was angry at Crystal for 'brainwashing' Brianna, as she thought of it, looked into it and figured out the fraud Crystal was perpetrating."

"What is it with this town and fraud?" Binny asked plaintively. Her father had become accidentally entangled the year before, and the repercussions were still affecting the bank and Isadore.

"But one thing I kept coming back to was the fight that got Karl kicked out of the house. It seemed so convenient that only Brianna and Logan were in the house, and then Minnie was murdered the very next morning." I went over, briefly, the clues that led me to the pair, and then said, "Ultimately, what tripped Brianna up was her senseless lies about what went on with Minnie in private, her claim that Minnie had never told her she was her grandmother. Logan didn't know much but that Brianna was going to inherit what they thought of as a lot of money. I have a feeling Brianna intended, in the end, to cut him out of her windfall. We had that tape, though, the one I played at the meeting." I explained briefly, about Minnie being on the phone with a man who she thought was a new love interest, but who was actually an actor (hired by Roma, though I didn't exactly say that) catfishing her. "You all heard; Minnie said her grandchild was trying to milk her for money for drugs. We were able to prove Brianna lied."

"I'm sorry for Minnie," Dewayne said. "I can't speak to the other fake romance, but she would have been hurt if she'd discovered my deception."

"However, you were hired by a police force to investigate a possible crime, which you did uncover," I said to Dewayne. "Thanks to your information, and the further investigation of the FBI and the Postal Inspection Service, we now know that Minnie was using the post office as her own personal shopping mall while blaming losses on thieves further back in the system. Her postal outlet had more complaints than average, and would have been busted sooner or later. I don't know how she thought she'd get away with it."

"I've been agitating for change for some time, and Virgil was helping move ahead with proof," Gogi said.

"She didn't deserve to die," Dewayne said softly. "I feel bad for her. And to die at the hands of someone she wanted to help, too!"

"It's like she arranged it herself, in a sense," I mused. "She offered Brianna a vision of life with some money, or at least a house and life insurance, and then threatened to take it all away if the girl couldn't kick her addictions."

"I don't think Brianna was a serious addict," Gogi said. "I know how to spot them. She was a casual user, and I'll say that in court if she tries to use addiction in an insanity defense."

"I overheard her making fun of Minnie once," Janice said, dusting brownie crumbs from her jutting bosom. "I told her she was a crappy little ingrate. She called me something I won't repeat. That girl was trouble."

"Minnie created a toxic environment, a recipe for disaster," I said. "Based on what I've learned about how good she was to her nieces and nephews, I believe Minnie truly cared about her granddaughter and wanted to make up for the tough knocks the kid had in life. But you can't assume that because you care for someone, they care for you the same way."

Virgil spoke up for the first time. "Don't waste any sympathy on Brianna, Merry. Tough knocks? Hah! The girl's birth mother *did* die, but the rest of her tale of woe is a lie. She was adopted almost immediately and grew up with three *also* adoptive siblings who are all just fine. Despite everything, her adoptive parents are sticking by her, claiming that she must have been duped by Logan Katsaros, who doesn't have any protective parents to help him out. He'll probably end up taking the fall for the whole thing."

That was a surprise, and changed the complexion of the case for me. I hoped Brianna got what was coming to her. When she and Logan showed up at the back of the postal station that morning Minnie had probably let them in, thinking nothing of it. The young woman and man cold-bloodedly murdered her with a butcher knife they'd brought from Minnie's own kitchen, and then proceeded to stage the scene with the letter opener that the postal employee had taken from Wynter Castle after her confrontation with our resident opera singer. They were hoping to pin the killing on Roma, since Minnie had raved and complained about the opera diva to her boarders.

We all talked of other things, and eventually discussed the party for my one-year anniversary at Wynter Castle. Pish told Hannah and Janice that they would not be forced to sing *Much Ado About Nothing: The Opera*. Hannah, Lizzie, and Alcina, her friend, would reprise their piece from *Die Zauberflöte*. "Look East" was the high point of that evening.

Janice trilled a bit of her favorite pieces from *The King and I*, and Pish told her he would be happy to accompany her on piano, if she would like to perform. She was thrilled, and forgave him for his bringing that disruptive force Roma Toscano into their midst.

Finally, everyone began to drift away to resume their lives after the drama of the last couple of weeks. Binny was going to take the boys back to town, and then Gordy was driving Zeke to Ridley Ridge to work at the police station, while he headed to his uncle's farm. Janice took Isadore away; she was paying her to help with some organization of stuff at her junk warehouse, I understood. Dewayne was heading out to visit Ford Hayes; something about an old Charger Dewayne was buying to fix up.

Virgil whispered a request to come back later, and I nodded, smiling up at him. His expression was intense, something Hannah and Lizzie both caught as they waited together for Hannah's parents to back up the van in the sparkling, chilly sunlight. Virgil drove away, and I turned back to find both girls staring at me.

"You look so beautiful when you look at him," Hannah said.

I didn't know how to respond.

"That was intense," Lizzie said, eyeing me with a frown. "Do you honestly like the big galoot? He's such a dark, gloomy—"

"He's *not* gloomy, Lizzie!" Hannah protested. "He's just . . . brooding. Kind of passionate. I think it's romantic."

"Isn't *brooding* another word for *gloomy*?" Lizzie said, trudging off to talk to her mother, who stood uncertainly watching her daughter with longing on her face.

As Hannah's parents backed into the drive and opened the back doors for the wheelchair lift, Zeke crouched down to talk to her. I once again noted his absorption with her, and the tenderness of his expression. Maybe I was just in the mood for love, but I had always suspected he had loving feelings for the young lady, and I was fairly certain I was right, based on how he treated her. I wished him well. But then he headed off to an impatiently waiting Binny. Emerald caught a lift with them, while Lizzie hitched a ride with Hannah's parents in the van.

I returned to the castle through the front door, after waving good-bye to everyone.

Pish was talking to Roma, who had crept down the stairs and clung to the banister. They looked up from a whispered conference. "Roma has to be back to the city by October seventh to start rehearsal for a charity function her agent has booked her for. I'm going to drive her there and stay for a week to visit my mother and Auntie Lush. You're welcome to join us."

I stood listening to his voice echo.

"Or you could stay here alone. Maybe Virgil could keep you company," he said with a sly smile.

Heat suffused my cheeks, and I nodded.

"Anyway, we're going out with Dewayne and Patricia again tonight," he said. "I understand Virgil is coming over to talk to you."

I nodded again.

The rest of the day I tried to relax and take stock of my new life, now that I had made the decision to stay at my inherited castle and make a go of it. I had to find out if my plans, just a tiny seed right now, could sprout into something bigger. *If* it was even legal to do what I wanted, it would require some help from the new zoning commissioner, who was the former zoning commissioner, Elwood Fitzhugh. I had just had a bath and was sitting at my dressing table setting my hair in hot rollers when I heard a tap at my door. "Come in!" I called.

Pish strolled in, natty in a dark suit jacket over a polo-necked pullover and casual slacks. That is his equivalent of jeans and a sweatshirt, as casual as he ever gets. He sat down on the end of my bed and I turned to face him.

"We're heading out in half an hour. What time is Virgil coming over?"

"Eight. It's his birthday tomorrow. I offered dinner, but he said no. I've got some Brie, though, and a fresh baguette that Binny brought for lunch, and some merlot."

"'A loaf of bread, a jug of wine, and thou,'" he quoted, with a smile.

"I'm a little nervous. He seemed . . . oh, I don't know. Mysterious. He still hasn't told me what went down between him and his ex."

"He's a very deliberate man, not hasty, not ill-judged."

"He's so mature he makes me feel like a teenager sometimes."

"That's good. You *should* feel like a teenager when you're in love." He hesitated, but then continued, "May I say something about Miguel?"

I sighed. "I don't know if I'm in the mood to talk about my late husband."

"Honey, it's something good." He looked down at his loafers and polished the toe of one against his pant leg. "You know how much I adored Miguel. But with you he was . . . a trifle controlling. He took care of you."

"I needed it. He made me feel secure."

"But in the normal course of life you would have grown up and become more mature, as you have, and more able and willing to make your own decisions. I've thought about this often, how, had he lived, you would have clashed, inevitably. Oh, I think you would have worked it out," he said, his hand up, before I could interject. "But not without some fighting. Virgil, on the other hand, is so unlike that. He's ready-made for you."

"Maybe you're right. I'm not in a rush, though." I paused, then said, "Do you remember, Pish, how when Miguel first died and I got the inheritance and life insurance, I thought I could handle it?"

He sighed, with a rueful expression. "Still one of my biggest regrets that I didn't make you listen to me, but I didn't want to be as controlling with you as Miguel was."

"I don't think you could have stopped me, my darling Pish. I was both asserting my new independence and throwing the money away. I think . . . I felt like I didn't *deserve* it. I didn't want a . . . a reward for Miguel's death, as silly as that sounds."

"How very wise you have become, my darling," he said, standing before me. He kissed my forehead. "I'll say good night now." He cradled my face in his graceful, long-fingered hands, tilting my chin up to him. "Be young. Be in love. Don't worry about anything for tonight."

THE PARLOR WAS SET UP WITH THE FIRE GOING—I have become quite good at starting a fire—and the wine, bread, and Brie in a warming dish. The door knocker echoed, and I scuttled to the door, my stomach fluttering. When I opened it, Virgil took me in his arms and gave me a long, passionate kiss that would have melted my socks, if I was wearing any. We walked together to the parlor, and settled on the floor in front of the fire. I had intended to wear something sexy, a cleavage-displaying dress, but had opted instead for something less distracting.

We chatted for a moment about the afternoon's revelations. I summoned my courage, finally, and spoke of my time in Spain with the Paradiso family. "I came away from it with a better understanding of the strengths and weaknesses of my marriage to Miguel. I took a long look at it. It wasn't a perfect marriage, and there would have been some stormy seas ahead if he had lived." I told him what Pish had said to me earlier. "I think I was afraid to let go of the idealized version of Miguel in my head. It felt like a betrayal."

He was silent, and there was more I wanted to say, so I continued. "Virgil, while I was there Tony proposed to me."

His eyes narrowed.

"I refused, of course," I said, not adding that I even considered it. "I have never felt anything for him but friendship, and he doesn't love me. But being there reminded me that my marriage, as good as it was, was not perfect. *Miguel* was not perfect. He liked that I was unsure of myself, I think, and he saw himself as my mentor as well as husband. I loved him, and the young girl I was will *always* love him. But I'm all grown up now."

He smirked. "You certainly are."

I laughed.

He drank some of the wine, but I knew he really wanted a beer, so I got him one and he rested back against a pillow, examining me with serious eyes. "Talking to Kelly this weekend did much the same for me. Not that our marriage ever had a chance—it didn't. But I think we understand it better. We went into marriage for all the wrong reasons. I was so worried about Mom that I wanted to show her I'd be okay, no matter what. And Kelly . . . She was trying to work out issues she couldn't address with her father. She's been in therapy the last two years. I think she's getting herself together."

I watched him, feeling that there was more, even as he hesitated. He sat up and took my hand.

"Merry, she told her father the truth, that I never hit her, that we broke up because we weren't right for each other. And she told him why she'd lied to him, that she was afraid he wouldn't love her if she told him the truth, that he would blame her for the marriage breaking up. It didn't go well, at least at first."

"I can imagine." Sheriff Baxter was hard-nosed and found it easy to place blame . . . on anyone else.

"But I think they have some basis to work things out now. Anyway, she went back to Ohio and Ben actually apologized to me and shook my hand."

I sighed. "That's wonderful! I'm happy, Virgil. I know that dealing with him as sheriff of the next county has been a nightmare for you."

"Not a nightmare, but not a picnic, either."

"Has it changed anything?" I wondered if he might decide to stay sheriff instead of joining the FBI.

"Not about being sheriff. I've already removed myself from the ballot, and Urquhart has added his name."

Urquhart? Oh, joy. Still, the name didn't fill me with as much dismay as it would have before this investigation. "Isn't it too late for that? Aren't there filing deadlines?"

"This is an exceptional circumstance, because I've eliminated myself and the county can't go without a sheriff."

"Oh."

He pulled me close and we kissed. I sighed against his lips and curled against his body, feeling the warmth radiate from him. We kissed a little more, then I pulled away from him, intent on getting one last thing out. "Virgil, I just want to say, I'm here for good. I know you'll be going to Quantico, and I know you may be stationed anywhere in the U.S., but I'll always be here for you. We'll work something out." I paused, and was about to say *I love you*, when he put his finger against my lips. I searched his eyes, so dark, but warm.

"Merry, I've made a decision," he said, his voice husky. "The FBI was my dream when I was twenty-five, but going through the application . . . I realized it's not me now. I'm not applying."

"*What?* Are you *sure*?"

"I am."

"But if you're not doing that, and you're not the sheriff, what *will* you do?"

He smiled. "I've already got a job. You're looking at the newest detective for the Two Cops Detective Agency, owned and operated by Dewayne Lester and Virgil Grace."

"Detective? You mean . . ."

"I'm a private dick now," he said, with an unusually mischievous grin. "Dewayne has more work than he can handle, and I've got skill sets and connections he can use. Plus, we know, like, and trust each other, and he's got his office in Buffalo. I can center mine wherever I want."

"In Autumn Vale?"

"In Autumn Vale," he said with a laugh, lying back and pulling me on top of him. He kissed me senseless, then rolled me onto my back, staring down into my eyes. "I know what I want from life, and it's all here: my family, work I believe in and am excited about, and . . . you." He kissed me. "Most of all, you."

He kissed me again, his mouth hungry and demanding, but then abruptly stopped and rolled off of me, much to my chagrin. He dug in his jeans pocket then knelt beside me as I awkwardly scrambled to sit. "Merry, I've never met anyone like you. I love how I feel when I'm with you, and I love your spirit, your heart." He paused and stared at me intensely, his face taut with anxious desire. "I love *you*. Will you marry me?"

Gasping, I stared at up him, the firelight flickering on his handsome face, his dark eyes shadowed by thick, dark brows, his perfect lips firmly together. It took me a moment to understand. I had gone from hoping he'd still want to be together, even when he was at Quantico, to knowing he was staying in Autumn Vale, to being asked to spend the rest of my life with him.

"Merry? Am I too . . . Is *this* too much? Too fast?" he asked, pushing the ring box toward me.

I jumped up and knelt in front of him. "No! I mean, no, it's not too much. Not too fast. But yes, *yes*, I'll marry you!" I threw my arms around him and we kissed for several delirious minutes. Belatedly I looked at the ring. It was gorgeous, a deep blue stone rimmed in diamonds, with a filigree bridge and gallery, vines, and curls. "Oh, Virgil, it's extraordinary!" I whispered.

He took the ring out of the box, which he flung aside. He slipped it on my finger. It fit perfectly, and sent sparkles flashing in the firelight. "It's the blue of your eyes. Extraordinary? *Nothing* is as extraordinary as you."

I met his gaze and held it; I thought I'd be first to say it, but realized he'd beaten me to it. Never too late, though. "Virgil Grace, you are an amazing man, and I *love* you."

"I *am* an amazing man," he growled, pulling me to him and kissing me deeply. "Now, may I escort you to your boudoir, or shall I ravish you right here?"

"*Oh!*" I exclaimed, as he kissed my neck, his breath warm, his lips moist. "Here. Right . . . here."

Recipes

Apple Crisp Muffins

Makes 10–12 muffins

¼ cup butter, softened to room temperature
¼ cup vegetable or canola oil
⅓ cup white sugar
⅓ cup brown sugar
¼ cup unsweetened applesauce
1 egg
1 teaspoon vanilla
1-½ cups all-purpose flour
½ teaspoon cinnamon
½ teaspoon baking soda
½ teaspoon baking powder
¼ teaspoon salt
1-½–2 cups finely chopped apple (I recommend Honeycrisp)

Topping:

½ cup brown sugar
½ cup old-fashioned oats

¼ cup all-purpose flour
¼ cup butter, softened to room temperature
¼ teaspoon cinnamon

Preheat oven to 350°F. Line a 12-unit muffin tin with paper liners and set aside.

In a large bowl, mix together butter, oil, sugars, and applesauce until combined, about 1 minute (mixture will look curdled). Add egg and vanilla, then mix to combine.

In a separate bowl, stir together flour, cinnamon, baking soda, baking powder, and salt. Remove two tablespoons of the flour mixture and toss with the chopped apples in a separate bowl to coat.

Add remaining flour mixture to wet ingredients in two batches, mixing until just combined after the first before adding the next batch. Gently fold in the apples.

Scoop batter into prepared muffin cups, filling them ¾ of the way full.

Mix the topping ingredients together in a small bowl until well combined, then sprinkle a heaping tablespoon—or more—on top of each muffin.

Bake for 23–28 minutes, or until a toothpick inserted into the center comes out clean.

Let cool in muffin tins for 10 minutes then remove to a cooling rack to cool completely.

These muffins are so good—all the flavor of an apple crisp, but in an individual delight. Great with coffee or tea as an afternoon treat!

Double Chocolate Walnut Muffins

Makes 12 muffins

1 cup all-purpose flour
½ teaspoon baking soda
¼ teaspoon salt
3–4 tablespoons cocoa powder (4 if you like it *very* dark
    chocolaty)
1 cup chocolate chips (whatever kind you like best—I use
    milk chocolate)
½ cup chopped walnuts (more if you like it nutty!)
1 large egg
½ cup Greek yogurt (I use plain, but vanilla would be okay.)
¼ cup canola oil
½ cup brown sugar, packed
1 teaspoon vanilla extract
1 cup *overripe* bananas (about 2 large)

Preheat oven to 350°F.

Spray muffin tin with spray oil, then dust with cocoa powder. Muffin liners are NOT recommended, as the muffins tend to stick to them.

In a small bowl, mix the flour, baking soda, salt, cocoa powder, then toss in the chocolate chips and chopped nuts and stir.

Mash the bananas well and measure. Set aside.

In a larger bowl, whisk together the egg and Greek yogurt first, then stir in the oil, brown sugar, vanilla extract, and mashed bananas, blending well.

Add half the dry ingredients to the wet, stir well, then add the rest of the dry ingredients and stir until mixture is smooth, but don't beat or overmix!

Ladle the batter into the muffin cups.

Bake for 18–23 minutes, or until a toothpick inserted into the center comes out clean.

Allow to cool on a rack, then remove muffins; you may need to loosen them with a butter knife around the edges to help pull them out.

Store in an airtight container, or freeze.

These are great when you need a hit of chocolaty sweetness, but don't want something too decadent!

FROM NATIONAL BESTSELLING AUTHOR
VICTORIA HAMILTON

Muffin but Murder

A Merry Muffin Mystery

For muffin maker Merry Wynter, the high cost of maintaining her upstate castle has left her with crumbs. To entice some prospective buyers, she hosts a soiree. But when the party ends in murder, Merry must unmask the killer before her plans turn into a recipe for disaster.

**"[Has all] the ingredients for a
wonderful cozy mystery series."**
—Paige Shelton, national bestselling author

victoriahamiltonmysteries.com
facebook.com/TheCrimeSceneBooks
penguin.com

M1508T0614

Murder is best served cold...

FROM NATIONAL BESTSELLING AUTHOR
VICTORIA HAMILTON

FREEZER
I'LL SHOOT

❧ A Vintage Kitchen Mystery ❧

Vintage kitchenware enthusiast and soon-to-be columnist Jaymie Leighton retreats to her family's cottage on Heartbreak Island, where she hopes to write an article about the Ice House restaurant, owned by siblings Ruby and Garnet Redmond. Once an actual icehouse, the restaurant is charmingly decorated with antique tools of the trade, including a collection of ice picks.

But when Jaymie stumbles upon a dead body, her blood runs cold: it's Urban Dobrinskie, whose feud with the Redmonds is no secret—and he's got an ice pick through his heart. Now Jaymie's got to sharpen her sleuthing skills to prove the siblings' innocence—before someone else gets picked off...

INCLUDES A RECIPE!

"Charming."

—Sheila Connolly,
New York Times bestselling author

victoriahamiltonmysteries.com
facebook.com/AuthorVictoriaHamilton
facebook.com/TheCrimeSceneBooks
penguin.com